RaeAnne Thayne

The Holiday Gift
and A Cold Creek Noel

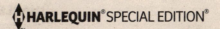

HARLEQUIN® SPECIAL EDITION®

ISBN-13: 978-0-373-83796-0

The Holiday Gift and A Cold Creek Noel

Copyright © 2016 by Harlequin Books S.A.

The publisher acknowledges the copyright holder of the individual works as follows:

The Holiday Gift
Copyright © 2016 by RaeAnne Thayne

A Cold Creek Noel
Copyright © 2012 by RaeAnne Thayne

PLEASE RECYCLE THIS PRODUCT IS RECYCLABLE

Recycling programs for this product may not exist in your area.

HARLEQUIN®
www.Harlequin.com

Printed in U.S.A.

CONTENTS

THE HOLIDAY GIFT   7

A COLD CREEK NOEL   205

To Lisa Townsend, trainer extraordinaire, who is gorgeous inside and out. And to Jennie, Trudy, Karen, Becky, Jill and everyone else in our group for your example, your encouragement, your friendship, your laughter—and especially for making me look forward to workouts (except the burpees—I'll never look forward to those!).

THE HOLIDAY GIFT

Chapter 1

Something was wrong, but Faith Dustin didn't have the first idea what.

She glanced at Chase Brannon again, behind the wheel of his pickup truck. Sunglasses shielded his eyes but his strong jaw was still flexed, his shoulders tense.

Since they had left the Idaho Falls livestock auction forty-five minutes earlier, heading back to Cold Creek Canyon, the big rancher hadn't smiled once and had answered most of her questions in monosyllables, his mind clearly a million miles away.

Faith frowned. He wasn't acting at all like himself. They were frequent travel companions, visiting various livestock auctions around the region at least once or twice a month for the last few years. They had even gone on a few buying trips to Denver together, an eight-hour drive from their little corner of eastern Idaho. He was her oldest friend—and had been since she and her sisters came to live with their aunt and uncle nearly two decades ago.

In many ways, she and Chase were really a team and comingled their ranch operations, since his ranch, Brannon Ridge, bordered the Star N on two sides.

Usually when they traveled, they never ran out of things to talk about. Her kids and their current dramas, real or imagined; his daughter, Addie, who lived with her mother in Boise; Faith's sisters and their growing families. Their ranches, the community, the price of beef, their future plans. It was all grist for their conversational mill. She valued his opinion—often she would run ideas past him—and she wanted to think he rated hers as highly.

The drive to Idaho Falls earlier that morning had seemed just like usual, filled with conversation and their usual banter. Everything had seemed normal during the auction. He had stayed right by her side, a quiet, steady support, while she engaged in—and eventually won—a fierce bidding war for a beautiful paint filly with excellent barrel racing bloodlines.

That horse, intended as a Christmas gift for her twelve-year-old daughter, Louisa, was the whole reason they had gone to the auction. Yes, she'd been a little carried away by winning the auction so that she'd hugged him hard and kissed him smack on the lips, but surely that wasn't what was bothering him. She'd kissed and hugged him tons of times.

Okay, maybe she had been careful not to be so casual with her affection for him the last six or seven months, for reasons she didn't want to explore, but she couldn't imagine he would go all cold and cranky over something as simple as a little kiss.

No. His mood had shifted after that, but all her subtle efforts to wiggle out what was wrong had been for nothing.

His mood certainly matched the afternoon. Faith glanced out at the uniformly gray sky and the few random, hard-edged snowflakes clicking against the windshield. The weather wasn't pleasant but it wasn't horrible either. The snowflakes weren't sticking to the road yet, anyway, though she expected they would see at least a few inches on the ground by morning.

Even the familiar festive streets of Pine Gulch— wreaths hanging on the streetlamps and each downtown business decorated with lights and window dressings— didn't seem to lift his dark mood.

When he hit the edge of town and turned into Cold Creek Canyon toward home, she decided to try one last time to figure out what might be bothering him.

"Did something happen at the auction?"

He glanced away from the road briefly, the expression in his silver-blue eyes shielded by the amber lenses of his sunglasses. "Why would you think that?"

She studied his dearly familiar profile, struck by his full mouth and his tanned, chiseled features—covered now with just a hint of dark afternoon shadow. Funny, how she saw him just about every single day but was sometimes taken by surprise all over again by how great-looking he was.

With his dark, wavy hair covered by the black Stetson he wore, that slow, sexy smile, and his broad shoulders and slim hips, he looked rugged and dangerous and completely male. It was no wonder the waitresses at the café next to the auction house always fought each other to serve their table.

She shifted her attention away from such ridiculous things and back to the conversation. "I don't know. Maybe because that's the longest sentence you've given me since we left Idaho Falls. You've replied to everything else with either a grunt or a monosyllable."

Beneath that afternoon shadow, a muscle clenched in his jaw. "That doesn't mean anything happened. Maybe I'm just not in a chatty mood."

She certainly had days like that. Heaven knew she'd had her share of blue days over the last two and a half years. Through every one of them, Chase had been her rock.

"Nothing wrong with that, I guess. Are you sure that's all? Was it something Beckett McKinley said? I saw him corner you at lunch."

He glanced over at her briefly and again she wished she could see the expression behind his sunglasses. "He wanted to know how I like the new baler I bought this year and he also wanted my opinion on a…personal matter. I told him I liked the baler fine but told him the other thing wasn't any of my damn business."

She blinked at both his clipped tone and the language. Chase didn't swear very often. When he did, there was usually a good reason.

"Now you've got my curiosity going. What kind of personal matter would Beck want your opinion about? The only thing I can think the man needs is a nanny for those hellion boys of his."

He didn't say anything for a long moment, just watched the road and those snowflakes spitting against windshield. When he finally spoke, his voice was clipped. "It was about you."

She stared. "Me?"

Chase's hands tightened on the steering wheel. "He wants to ask you out, specifically to go as his date to the stockgrowers association's Christmas party on Friday."

If he had just told her Beck wanted her to dress up like a Christmas angel and jump from his barn roof, she wouldn't have been more surprised—and likely would have been far less panicky.

"I… He…what?"

"Beck wants to take you to the Christmas party this weekend. I understand there's going to be dancing and a full dinner this year."

Beck McKinley. The idea of dating the man took her by complete surprise. Yes, he was a great guy, with a prosperous ranch on the other side of Pine Gulch. She considered him a good friend but she had never *once* thought of him in romantic terms.

The unexpected paradigm shift wasn't the only thing bothering her about what Chase had just said.

"Hold on. If he wanted to take me to the party, why wouldn't Beck just ask me himself instead of feeling like he has to go through you first?"

That muscle flexed in his jaw again. "You'll have to ask him that."

The things he wasn't saying in this conversation would fill a radio broadcast. She frowned as Chase pulled into the drive leading to his ranch. "You told him I'm already going with you, didn't you?"

He didn't answer for a long moment. "No," he finally said. "I didn't."

Unease twanged through her, the same vague sense

that had haunted her at stray moments for several months. Something was off between her and Chase and, for the life of her, she couldn't put a finger on it.

"Oh. Did you already make plans?" She forced a cheerful smile. "We've gone together the last few years so I just sort of assumed we would go together again this year but I guess we should have talked about it. If you already have something going, don't worry about me. Seriously. I don't mind going by myself. I'll have plenty of other friends there I can sit with. Or I could always skip it and stay home with the kids. Jenna McRaven does a fantastic job with the food and I always enjoy the company of other grown-ups, but if you've got a hot date lined up, I'm perfectly fine."

As she said the words, she tasted the lie in them. Was this weird ache in her stomach because she had been looking forward to the evening out—or because she didn't like the idea of him with a hot date?

"I don't have a date, hot or otherwise," he growled as he pulled the pickup and trailer to a stop next to a small paddock near the barn of the Brannon Ridge Ranch.

She eased back in the bench seat, a curious relief seeping through her. "Good. That's that. We can go together, just like always. It will be a fun night out for us."

Though she knew him well enough to know something was still on his mind, he said nothing as he pulled off his sunglasses and hooked them on the rearview mirror. What did his silence mean? Didn't he *want* to go with her?

"Faith," he began, but suddenly she didn't want to hear what he had to say.

"We'd better get the beautiful girl in your trailer unloaded before the kids get home."

She opened her door and jumped out before he could answer her. Yes, sometimes she was like her son, Barrett, who would rather hide out in his room all day and miss dinner than be scolded for something he'd done. She didn't like to face bad things. It was a normal reaction, she told herself. Hadn't she already had to face enough bad things in her life?

After a moment, Chase climbed out after her and came around to unhook the back of the trailer. The striking black-and-white paint yearling whinnied as he led her out into the patchy snow.

"She's a beauty, isn't she?" Faith said, struck all over again by the horse's elegant lines.

"Yeah," Chase said. Again with the monosyllables. She sighed.

"Thanks for letting me keep her here for a couple of weeks. Louisa will be so shocked on Christmas morning."

"Shouldn't be a problem."

He guided the horse into the pasture, where his own favorite horse, Tor, immediately trotted over as Faith closed the gate behind them. As soon as Chase unhooked the young horse from her lead line, she raced to the other side of the pasture, mane and tail flying out behind her.

She was fast. That was the truth. Grateful for her own cowboy hat that shielded her face from the worst of the frost-tipped snowflakes, Faith watched the horse race to the other corner of the pasture and back, obviously overflowing with energy after the stress of a day at the auction and then a trailer ride with strangers.

"Do you think she's too much horse for Lou?" she asked while Chase patted Tor beside her.

He looked at the paint and then down at Faith. "She comes from prime barrel racing stock. That's what Lou wants to do. For twelve, she's a strong rider. Yeah, the horse is only green broke but Seth Dalton can train a horse to do just about anything but recite its ABCs."

"I guess that's true. It was nice of him to agree to take her, with his crazy training schedule."

"He's a good friend."

"He is," she agreed. "Though I know he only agreed to do it as a favor to you."

"Maybe it was a favor to you," he commented as he pulled a bale of hay over and opened it inside the pasture for the horses.

"Maybe," she answered. All three Dalton brothers had been wonderful neighbors and good friends to her. They and others in the close-knit ranching community in Cold Creek Canyon and around Pine Gulch had stepped up in a hundred different ways over the last two and a half years since Travis died.

She would have been lost without any of them, but especially without Chase.

That vague unease slithered through her again. What was wrong between them? And how could she fix it?

She didn't have the first clue.

What was a guy supposed to do?

Ever since Beck McKinley cornered him at the diner to talk about taking Faith to the stockgrowers' holiday party, Chase hadn't been able to think straight. He felt like the other guy had grabbed his face and dunked it in an ice-cold water trough, then kicked him in the gut for good measure.

For a full ten seconds, he had stared at Beck as a host

of emotions galloped through him faster than a pack of wild horses spooked by a thunderstorm.

Beckett McKinley wanted to date Faith. *Chase's* Faith.

"She's great. That's all," Beck had said into the suddenly tense silence. "It's been more than two years since Travis died, right? I just thought maybe she'd be ready to start getting out there."

Chase had thought for a minute his whole face had turned numb, especially his tongue. It made it tough for him to get any words out at all—or maybe that was the ice-cold coating around his brain.

"Why are you asking me?" he had finally managed to say.

If possible, Beck had looked even more uncomfortable. "The two of you are always together. Here at the auction, at the feed store, at the diner in town. I know you're neighbors and you've been friends for a long time. But if there's something more than that, I don't want to be an ass and step on toes. You don't have to tell me what happens to bulls who wander into somebody else's pen."

It was all he could do not to haul off and deck the guy for the implied comparison that Faith was just some lonely heifer, waiting for some smooth-talking bull to wander by.

Instead, he had managed to grip his hands into fists, all while one thought kept echoing through his head.

Not again.

He thought he was giving her time to grieve, to make room in her heart for someone else besides Travis Dustin, the man she had loved since she was a traumatized girl trying to carve out a new home for her and her sisters.

Chase had been too slow once before. He had been a steady friend and confidant from the beginning. He figured he had all the time in the world as he waited for her to heal and to settle into life in Pine Gulch. She had been so young, barely sixteen. He wasn't much older, not yet nineteen, and had been busy with his own struggles. Even then, he had been running his family's ranch on his own while his father lay dying.

For six months, he offered friendship to Faith, fully expecting that one day when both of them were in a better place, he could start moving things to a different level.

And then Travis Dustin came home for the summer to help out Claude and Mary, the distant relatives who had raised him his last few years of high school.

Chase's father was in his last few agonizing weeks of life from lung cancer that summer. While he was busy coping with that and accepting his new responsibilities on the ranch, Travis had wasted no time sweeping in and stealing Faith's heart. By the time Chase woke up and realized what was happening, it was too late. His two closest friends were in love with each other and he couldn't do a damn thing about it.

He could have fought for her, he supposed, but it was clear from the beginning that Travis made her happy. After everything she and her sisters had been through, she deserved to find a little peace.

Instead, he had managed to put his feelings away and maintain his friendship with both of them. He had even tried to move on himself and date other women, with disastrous consequences.

Beck McKinley was a good guy. A solid rancher, a devoted father, a pillar of the community. Any woman would probably be very lucky to have him, as long as she could get past those hellion boys of his.

Maybe McKinley was exactly the kind of guy she wanted. The thought gnawed at him, but he took some small solace in remembering that she hadn't seemed all that enthusiastic at the idea of going out with him.

Didn't matter. He knew damn well it was only a matter of time before she found someone she *did* want to go out with. If not Beck, some other smooth-talking cowboy would sweep in.

He hadn't fought for her last time. Instead, he had stood by like a damn statue and watched her fall in love with his best friend.

He wouldn't go through that again. It was time he made a move—but what if he made the wrong one and ruined everything between them?

He felt like a man given a choice between a hangman's noose and a firing squad. He was damned either way.

He was still trying to figure out what to do when she shifted from watching the young horse dance around the pasture in the cold December air. Faith gazed up at the overcast sky, still dribbling out the occasional stray snowflake.

"I probably should get back. The kids will be out of school soon and I'm sure you have plenty of things of your own to do. You don't have to walk me back," she said when he started to head in that direction behind her. "Stay and unhitch the horse trailer if you need to."

"It can keep. I'll walk you back up to your truck. I've got to plug in my phone anyway."

A couple of his ranch dogs came out from the barn to say hello as they walked the short distance to his house. He reached down and petted them both, in total sympathy. He felt like a ranch dog to her: a constant, steady companion with a few useful skills that came in handy once in a while.

Would she ever be able to see him as anything more?

"Thanks again, Chase," Faith said when they reached her own pickup truck—the one she had insisted on driving over that morning, even though he told her he could easily pick her up and drop her back off at the Star N.

"You're welcome," he said.

"Seriously, I was out of my depth. Horses aren't exactly my area of expertise. Who knows, I might have brought home a nag. As always, I don't know what I would do without you."

He could feel tension clutch at his shoulders again. "Not true," he said, his voice more abrupt than he intended. "You didn't need me. Not really. You'd already done your research and knew what you wanted in a barrel racer. You just needed somebody to back you up."

She smiled as they reached her pickup truck and a pale shaft of sunlight somehow managed to pierce the cloud cover and land right on her delicate features, so soft and lovely it made his heart hurt.

"I'm so lucky that somebody is always you," she said.

He let out a breath, fighting the urge to pull her into his arms. He didn't have that right—nor could he let things go on as they were.

"About the stockgrowers' party," he began.

If he hadn't been looking, he might have missed the leap of something that looked suspiciously like fear in her green eyes before she shifted her gaze away from him.

"Really, it doesn't bother me to skip it this year if you want to make other plans."

"I don't want to skip it," he growled. "I want to go. With you. On a date."

He intended to stress the last word, to make it plain this wouldn't be two buddies just hanging out together, like they always did. As a result, the word took on unnatural proportions and he nearly snapped it out until it arced between them like an arrow twanged from a crossbow.

Eyes wide, she gazed at him for a long moment, clearly startled by his vehemence. After a moment, she nodded. "Okay. That's settled, then. We can figure out the details later."

Nothing was settled. He needed to tell her *date* was the operative word here, that he didn't want to take her to the party as her neighbor and friend who gave her random advice on a barrel racing horse for her daughter or helped her with the hay season.

He wanted the right to hold her—to dance with her and flirt and whisper soft, sexy words in her ear.

How the hell could he tell her that, after all this time, when he had so carefully cultivated a safe, casual relationship that was the exact opposite of what he really wanted? Before he could figure that out, an SUV he didn't recognize drove up the lane toward his house.

"Were you expecting company?" she asked.

"Don't think so." He frowned as the car pulled up beside them—and his frown intensified when the passenger door opened and a girl jumped out, then raced toward him. "Daddy!"

Chapter 2

He stared at his eleven-year-old daughter, dressed to the nines in an outfit more suited to a photo shoot for a children's clothing store than for a working cattle ranch.

"Adaline! What are you doing here? I didn't expect to see you until next weekend."

"I know, Dad! Isn't it great? We get extra time together—maybe even two whole weeks! Mom pulled me out of school until after Christmas. Isn't that awesome? My teachers are going to email me all my homework so I don't miss too much—not that they ever do anything the last few weeks before Christmas vacation anyway but waste time showing movies and doing busywork and stuff."

That sounded like a direct quote from her mother, who had little respect for the educational system, even the expensive private school she insisted on sending their daughter to.

As if on cue, his ex-wife climbed out of the driver's side of what must be a new vehicle, judging by the temporary license plates in the window.

She looked uncharacteristically disordered, with her sweater askew and her hair a little messy in back where she must have been leaning against the headrest as she drove.

"I'm so glad you're home," she said. "We took a chance. I've been trying to call you all afternoon. Why didn't you answer?"

"My phone ran out of juice and I forgot to take the charger to the auction with us. What's going on?"

He knew it had to be something dramatic for her to bring Addie all this way on an unscheduled mid-week visit.

Cindy frowned. "My mother had a stroke early this morning and she's in the hospital in Idaho Falls."

"Oh, no! I hadn't heard. I'm so sorry."

He had tried very hard to earn the approval of his in-laws but the president of the Pine Gulch bank and his wife had been very slow to warm up to him. He didn't know if they had disliked him because Cindy had been pregnant when they married or because they didn't think a cattle rancher with cow manure on his boots was good enough for their precious only child.

They had reached a peace accord of sorts after Addie came along. Still, he almost thought his and Cindy's divorce had been a relief to them—and he had no doubt they had been thrilled at her second marriage to an eminently successful oral surgeon in Boise.

"The doctors say it appears to be a mini stroke. They

suspect it's not the first one so they want to keep her for observation for a few days. My dad said I didn't have to come down but it seemed like the right thing to do," Cindy said. "Considering I was coming this way anyway, I didn't think you would mind having extra visitation with Addie, especially since she won't be here over the holidays."

He was aware of a familiar pang in his chest, probably no different from what most part-time divorced fathers felt at not being able to live with their children all the time. Holidays were the worst.

"Sure. Extra time is always great."

Cindy turned to Faith with that hard look she always wore when she saw the two of them together. His ex-wife had never said anything but he suspected she had long guessed the feelings he had tried to bury after Faith and Travis got married.

"We're interrupting," she said. "I'm sorry."

"Not at all," Faith assured her. "Please don't be sorry. I'm the one who's sorry about your mother."

"Thanks," Cindy said, her voice cool. "We spent an hour at the hospital before we came out here and she seems in good spirits. Doctors just want to keep her for observation to see if they can figure out what's going on. Dad is kind of a mess right now, which is why I thought it would be a good idea for me to stay with him, at least for the first few days."

"That sounds like a good idea."

"Thanks for taking Addie. Sorry to drop her off without calling first. I did try."

"It's no problem at all. I'm thrilled to have her."

The sad truth was, they got along and seemed to parent together better now that they were divorced than during the difficult five years of their marriage, though things still weren't perfect.

"I packed enough for a week. To be honest, I don't know what I grabbed, since I was kind of a mess this morning. Keith was worried about me driving alone but he had three surgeries scheduled today and couldn't come with me. His patients needed him."

"He's a busy man," Chase said. What else *could* he say? It would have been terribly hypocritical to lambast another man in the husband department when Chase had been so very lousy at it.

"I should get back to the hospital. Thanks, Chase. You're a lifesaver."

"No problem."

"I'm so sorry about your mother," Faith said.

"Thank you. I appreciate that."

Cindy opened the hatchback of the SUV and pulled out Addie's familiar pink suitcase. He hated the tangible reminder that his daughter had to live out of a suitcase half her life.

After setting the suitcase on the sidewalk, Cindy went through her usual drawn-out farewell routine with Addie that ended in a big hug and a sloppy kiss, then climbed into her SUV and drove away.

"My feet are cold," Addie announced calmly, apparently not fazed at all to watch her mother leave, despite the requisite drama. "I'm going to take my suitcase to my room and change my clothes."

She headed to the house without waiting for him to answer, leaving him alone with Faith.

"That was a curveball I wasn't expecting this afternoon."

"Strokes can be scary," Faith said. "It sounds like

Carol's was a mild one, though, which I'm sure is a relief to everyone. At least you'll get to spend a little extra time with Addie."

"True. Always a bonus."

He had plenty of regrets about his life but his wise, funny, kind daughter was the one amazing thing his lousy marriage had produced.

"I know this was a busy week for you," Faith said. "If you need help with her, she's welcome to spend time at the Star N. Louisa would be completely thrilled."

He had appointments all week with suppliers, the vet and his accountant, but he could take her with him. She was a remarkably adaptable child.

"The only time I might need help is Friday night. Think Aunt Mary would mind if she stayed at your place with Lou and Barrett while we're at the party?"

Her forehead briefly furrowed in confusion. "Oh. I almost forgot about that. Look, the situation has changed. If you'd rather stay home with Addie, I completely understand. I can tag along with Wade and Caroline Dalton or Justin and Ashley Hartford. Or, again, I can always just skip it."

Was she looking for excuses not to go with him? He didn't want to believe that. "I asked you out. I want to go, as long as Mary doesn't mind one more at your place."

"Addie's never any trouble. I'm sure Mary will be fine with it. I'll talk to her," she promised. "If she can't do it, I'm sure all the kids could hang out with Hope or Celeste for the evening."

Her sisters and their husbands lived close to the Star N and often helped with Barrett and Louisa, just as Faith helped out with their respective children.

"I'll be in touch later in the week to work out the details."

"Sounds good." She glanced at her watch. "I really do need to go. Thanks again for your help with the horse."

"You're welcome."

As she climbed into the Star N king-cab pickup, he was struck by how small and delicate she looked compared to the big truck.

Physically, she might be slight—barely five-four and slender—but she was tough as nails. Over the last two and a half years, she had worked tirelessly to drag the ranch from the brink. He had tried to take some of the burden from her but there was only so much she would let him do.

He stepped forward so she couldn't close the door yet.

"One last thing."

"What's that?"

Heart pounding, he leaned in to face her. He wanted her to see his expression. He wanted no ambiguity about his intentions.

"You need to be clear on one thing before Friday. I said it earlier but in all the confusion with Addie showing up, I'm not sure it registered completely. As far as I'm concerned, this is a date."

"Sure. We're going together. What else would it be?"

"I mean a date-date. I want to go out with you where we're not only good friends hanging out on a Friday night or two neighboring ranchers carpooling to the same event. I want you to be my date, with everything that goes along with that."

There. She couldn't mistake *that*.

He saw a host of emotions quickly cross her features—shock, uncertainty and a wild flare of panic. "Chase, I—"

He could see she wasn't even going to give him a chance. She was ready to throw up barriers to the idea before he even had a chance. Frustration coiled through him, sharp as barbed wire fencing.

"It's been two and a half years since Travis died."

Her hands clamped tight onto the steering wheel as if it were a bull rider's strap and she had to hang on or she would fall off and be trampled. "Yes. I believe I'm fully aware of that."

"You're going to have to enter the dating scene at some point. You've already got cowboys clamoring to ask you out. McKinley is just the first one to step up, but he won't be the last. Why not ease into it by going out with somebody you already know?"

"You."

"Why not?"

Instead of answering, she turned the tables on him. "You and Cindy have been divorced for years. Why are you suddenly interested in dating again?"

"Maybe I'm tired of being alone." That, at least, was the truth, just not the whole truth.

"So this would be like a...trial run for both of us? A way to dip our toes into the water without jumping in headfirst?"

No. He had jumped in a long, long time ago and had just been treading water, waiting for her.

He couldn't tell her that. Not yet.

"Sure, if you want to look at it that way," he said instead.

He knew her well enough that he could almost watch

her brain whir as she tried to think through all the ramifications. She overthought everything. It was by turns endearing and endlessly frustrating.

Finally she seemed to have sifted through the possibilities and come up with a scenario she could live with. "You're such a good friend, Chase. You've always got my back. You want to help make this easier for me, just like you helped me buy the horse for Louisa. Thank you."

He opened his mouth to say that wasn't at all his intention but he could see by the stubborn set of her jaw that she wasn't ready to hear that yet.

"I'll talk to Aunt Mary about keeping an eye on the kids on Friday. We can work out the details later. I really do have to go. Thanks again."

Her tone was clearly dismissive. Left with no real choice, he stepped back so she could close the vehicle door.

She was deliberately misunderstanding him and he didn't know how to argue with her. After all these years of being her friend and so carefully hiding his feelings, how did he convince her he wanted to be more than that?

He had no idea. He only knew he had to try.

Faith refused to let herself panic.

I want you to be my date, with everything that goes along with that.

Despite her best efforts, fear seemed to curl around her insides, coating everything with a thin layer of ice.

She couldn't let things change. End of story. Chase had been her rock for two years, her best friend, the one constant in her crazy, tumultuous life. He had been the first one she had called when she had gone looking for Travis after he didn't answer his cell and found him unconscious and near death, with severe internal injuries and a shattered spine, next to his overturned ATV.

Chase had been there within five minutes and had taken charge of the scene, had called the medics and the helicopter, had been there at the hospital and had held her after the doctors came out with their solemn faces and their sad eyes.

While she had been numb and broken, Chase had stepped in, organizing all the neighbors to bring in the fall harvest. He had helped her clean up and streamline the Star N operation and sell off all the unnecessary stock to keep their head above water those first few months.

Now the ranch was in the black again—thanks in large part to the crash course in smart ranch practices Chase had given her. She knew perfectly well that without him, there wouldn't *be* a Star N right now or The Christmas Ranch. She and her sisters would have had to sell off the land, the cattle, *everything* to pay their debts.

Travis hadn't been a very good businessman. At his death, she'd found the ranch was seriously overextended with creditors and had been operating under a system of gross inefficiencies for years.

She winced with the guilt the disloyal thought always stirred in her, but it was nothing less than the truth. If her husband hadn't died and things had continued on the same course, the ranch would have gone bankrupt within a few years. Through Chase's extensive help, she had been able to turn things around.

The ranch was doing so much better. The Christmas Ranch—the seasonal attraction started by her uncle and aunt after she and her sisters came to live with them—was finally in the black, too. Hope and her husband, Rafe, had done an amazing job revitalizing it and making it a powerful draw. That success had only been augmented by the wild viral popularity of the charming children's book Celeste had written and Hope had illustrated featuring the ranch's starring attraction, Sparkle the Reindeer.

She couldn't be more proud of her sisters—though she did find it funny that, of the three of them, *Faith* seemed the one most excited that Celeste and Hope had signed an agreement to allow a production company to make an animated movie out of the first Sparkle book.

Despite a few preproduction problems, the process was currently under way, though the animated movie wouldn't come out for another year. The buzz around it only heightened interest in The Christmas Ranch and led to increased revenue.

The book had helped push The Christmas Ranch to self-sufficiency. Without that steady drain on the Star N side of the family operation, Faith had been able to plow profits back into the cattle ranch operation.

As she drove past the Saint Nicholas Lodge on the way to the ranch house, she spotted both of her sisters' vehicles in the parking lot.

After taking up most of the day at the auction, she had a hundred things to do. As she had told Chase, Barrett and Louisa would be home from school soon. When she could swing it, she liked being there to greet them, to ask about their day and help manage their homework and chore responsibilities.

On a whim, though, she pulled into the parking lot and hurriedly texted both of her children as well as Aunt

Mary to tell them she was stopping at the lodge for a moment and would be home soon.

The urge to talk to her sisters was suddenly overwhelming. Hope and Celeste weren't just her sisters, they were her best friends.

She had to park three rows back, which she considered a great sign for a Tuesday afternoon in mid-December.

Tourists from as far away as Boise and Salt Lake City were making the trek here to visit their quaint little Christmas attraction, with its sleigh rides, the reindeer herd, the village—and especially because this was the home of Sparkle.

As far as she was concerned, this was just home.

The familiar scents inside the lodge encircled her the moment she walked inside—cinnamon and vanilla and pine, mixed with old logs and the musty smell of a building that stood empty most of the year.

She heard her younger sisters bickering in the office before she saw them.

"Cry your sad song to someone else," Celeste was saying. "I told you I wasn't going to do it again this year and I won't let you guilt me into it."

"But you did such a great job last year," Hope protested.

"Yes I did," their youngest sister said. "And I swore I wouldn't ever do it again."

Faith poked her head into the office in time to see Hope pout. She was nearly three months pregnant and only just beginning to show.

"It didn't turn out so badly," Hope pointed out. "You ended up with a fabulous husband and a new stepdaughter out of the deal, didn't you?"

"Seriously? You're giving the children's show credit for my marriage to Flynn?"

"Think about it. Would you be married to your hunky contractor right now and deliriously happy if you hadn't directed the show for me last year—and if his daughter hadn't begged to participate?"

It was an excellent point, Faith thought with inward amusement that Celeste didn't appear to share.

"Why can't you do it?" Celeste demanded.

"We are booked solid with tour groups at the ranch until Christmas Eve. I won't have a minute to breathe from now until the New Year—and that's with Rafe making me cut down my hours."

"You knew you were going to be slammed," Celeste said, not at all persuaded. "Talk about procrastination. I can't believe you didn't find somebody to organize the variety show weeks ago!"

"I *had* somebody. Linda Keller told me clear back in September she would do it. I thought we were set, but she fell this morning and broke her arm, which leaves me back at square one. The kids are going to be coming to practice a week from today and I've got absolutely no one to lead them."

Hope shifted her attention to Faith with a considering look that struck fear in her heart.

"Oh, no," she exclaimed. "You can forget that idea right now."

"Why?" Hope pouted. "You love kids and senior citizens both, plus you sing like a dream. You even used to direct the choir at church, which I say makes you the perfect one to run the Christmas show."

She rolled her eyes. Hope knew better than to seriously consider that idea. "Right. Because you know I've got absolutely nothing else going on right now."

"Everyone is busy. That's the problem. Whose idea was it to put on a show at Christmas, the busiest time of the year?"

"Yours," Faith and Celeste answered simultaneously.

Hope sighed. "I know. It just seemed natural for The Christmas Ranch to throw a holiday celebration for the senior citizens. Maybe next year we'll do a Christmas in July kind of thing."

"Except you'll be having a baby in July," Faith pointed out. "And I'll be even more busy during the summer."

"You're right." She looked glum. "Do you have any suggestions for someone else who might be interested in directing it? I would hate to see the pageant fade out, especially after last year was such a smash success, thanks to CeCe. You wouldn't believe how many people have stopped me in town during the past year to tell me how much they enjoyed it and hoped we were doing another one."

"I believe it," Celeste said. "I've had my share of people telling me the same thing. That still doesn't mean I want to run it again."

"I wasn't even involved with the show and I still have people stop me in town to tell me they hope we're doing it again," Faith offered.

"That's because you're a Nichols," Hope said.

"Right. Which to some people automatically means I burp tinsel and have eggnog running through my veins."

Celeste laughed. "You don't?"

"Nope. Hope inherited all the Christmas spirit from Uncle Claude and Aunt Mary."

The sister in question made a face. "That may be true, but it still doesn't give me someone to run the show this year. But never fear. I've got a few ideas up my sleeves."

"I can help," Celeste said. "I just don't want to be the one in charge."

Faith couldn't let her younger sister be the only generous one in the family. She sighed. "Okay. I'll help again, too. But only behind the scenes—and only because you're pregnant and I don't want you to overdo."

Hope's eyes glittered and her smile wobbled. "Oh. You're both going to make me cry and Rafe tells me I've already hit my tear quota for the day. Quick, talk about something else. How did the auction go today?"

At the question, all her angst about Chase flooded back.

She suddenly desperately wanted to confide in her sisters. That was the whole reason she'd stopped at the lodge, she realized, because she yearned to share this startling development with them and obtain their advice.

I want you to be my date, with everything that goes along with that.

What was she going to do?

She wanted to ask them but they both adored Chase and it suddenly seemed wrong to talk about him with Hope and Celeste. If she had to guess, she expected they would probably take his side. They wouldn't understand how he had just upended everything safe and secure she had come to depend upon.

When she didn't answer right away, both of her sisters looked at her with concern. "Did something go wrong with the horse you wanted to buy?" Celeste asked. "You weren't outbid, were you? If you were, I'm sure you'll be able to find another one."

She shook her head. "No. We bought the horse for about five percent under what I was expecting to pay and she's beautiful. Mostly white with black spots and lovely black boot markings on her legs. I can't wait for Louisa to see her."

"I want to see her!" Hope said. "You took her to Chase's pasture?"

"Yes, and a few moments after we unloaded her, Cindy pulled up with Addie. Apparently Carol Johnson had a small stroke this morning and she's in the hospital in Idaho Falls so Cindy came home to be with her and help her father."

At the mention of Chase's ex-wife, both of her sisters' mouths tightened in almost exactly the same way. There had been no love lost between any of them, especially after Cindy's affair with the oral surgeon who eventually became her husband.

"So Cindy just dropped off Addie like UPS delivering a surprise package?" Hope asked, disgust clear in her voice.

"What about school?" ever-practical Celeste asked. "Surely she's not out for Christmas break yet."

"No. She's going to do her homework from here." She paused, remembering the one other complication. "I haven't asked Mary yet if she's available but in case she's not, would either of you like a couple of extra kids on Friday night? Three, actually—my two and Addie. Chase and I have a…a thing and it might run late."

"Oh, I wish I could," Hope exclaimed. "Rafe and I promised Joey we would take him to Boise to see his mom. We're staying overnight and doing some shopping while we're there."

"How is Cami doing?" Faith asked. "She's been out of prison, what, three months now?"

"Ten weeks. She's doing so well. Much better than Rafe expected, really. The court-ordered drug rehab she had in prison worked in her case and the halfway house is really helping her get back on her feet. Another six months and she's hoping she can have her own place and be ready to take Joey back. Maybe even by the time the baby comes."

Hope tried to smile but it didn't quite reach her eyes and Faith couldn't resist giving her sister's hand a squeeze. Celeste did the same to the other hand. Hope and her husband had cared for Rafe's nephew Joey since before their marriage after his sister's conviction on drug and robbery charges. They loved him and would both be sad to see him go.

Joey seemed like a different kid than he'd been when he first showed up at The Christmas Ranch with Rafe, two years earlier, sullen and confused and angry...

"We're trying to convince her to come back to Pine Gulch," Hope said, trying to smile. "It might help her stay out of trouble, and that way we can remain part of Joey's life. So far it's an uphill battle, as she feels like this is where all her troubles started."

Her sister's turmoil was a sharp reminder to Faith. Hope might be losing the boy she considered a son, and Celeste's stepdaughter, Olivia, still struggled to recover from both physical injuries and the emotional trauma of witnessing her mother's murder at the hands of her mentally ill and suicidal boyfriend.

In contrast, the problem of trying to figure out what to do with Chase seemed much more manageable.

"Anyway," Hope said, "that's why I won't be around Friday to help you with the kids. Sorry again."

"Don't give it another thought. That's exactly where you need to be."

"The kids are more than welcome at our place," Celeste said. "Flynn and Olivia are having a movie marathon and watching *Miracle on 34th Street* and *White Christmas*. I'll be writing during most of it, but hope to sneak in and watch the dancing in *White Christmas*."

She used to love those movies, Faith remembered. When she was young, her parents had a handful of very old, very worn VCR tapes of several holiday classics and would drag them from place to place, sometimes even showing them at social events for people in whatever small village they had set their latest medical clinic in at the time.

She probably had been just as baffled as the villagers at the world shown in the movies, which seemed so completely foreign to her own life experience, with the handsomely dressed people and the luxurious train rides and the children surrounded by toys she could only imagine.

"That sounds like the perfect evening," she said now. "Maybe I'll join the movie night instead of going to a boring Christmas party with Chase. I can bring the popcorn."

"You can't skip the stockgrowers' party," Celeste said. "It's the big social event of the year, isn't it? Jenna McRaven always caters that gala so you know the food will be fantastic, plus you'll be going with Chase. How can any party be boring with him around?"

Again, she wanted to blurt out to her sisters how strangely he was acting. She even opened her mouth to do it but before she could force the words out, she heard familiar young voices outside in the hallway just an instant before Barrett and Louisa poked their heads in, followed in short order by Celeste's stepdaughter, Olivia, and Joey. Liv went straight to Celeste while Joey practically jumped into Hope's outstretched arms.

It warmed her heart so much to see her sisters being such loving mother figures to children who needed them desperately.

"Joey and Olivia were coming to the house to hang out when I got your text," Louisa said. "We saw all your cars so decided to stop here to say hi before we walk up to the house from the bus stop."

"I'm so glad you did," Faith said.

She hugged them both, her heart aching with love. "Good day?" she asked.

Louisa nodded. "Pretty good. I had a substitute for science and she was way nicer than Mr. Lewis."

"Guess who got a hundred-ten percent on his math test?" Barrett said with a huge grin "Go on. Guess."

She made a big show of looking confused and glancing in the other boy's direction. "You did, Joey? Good job, kid!"

Rafe's nephew giggled. "I only got a hundred percent. I missed the extra credit but Barrett didn't."

Her son preened. "I was the only one in the class who got it right."

"I'm proud of both of you. What a smart family we have!"

Except for her, the one who couldn't figure out how to protect the friendship that meant the world to her.

Chapter 3

As he drove up to the Star N ranch house four days after the auction, Chase couldn't remember the last time he'd been so on edge. He wasn't nervous—or at least he would never admit to it. He was just unsettled.

So many things seemed to hinge on this night. How was he supposed to make Faith ever view him as more than just her neighbor and best friend? She had to see him for himself, a man who had spent nearly half his life waiting for her.

He didn't like the way that made him sound weak, like some kind of mongrel hanging on the fringes of her life, content for whatever scraps she threw out the kitchen door at him. It hadn't been like that. He had genuinely tried to put his unrequited feelings behind him after she and Travis got married. For the most part, he had succeeded.

He had dated a great deal and had genuinely liked several of the women he dated. In the beginning, he had liked Cindy, too. She had been funny and smart and beautiful. He was a man and had been flattered— and susceptible—when she aggressively pursued him.

When she told him she was pregnant, he decided marrying her and making a home for their child was the right thing to do. He really had tried to make their marriage work but he and Cindy were a horrible mismatch from the beginning. He could see now that they would never have suited each other, even if that little dusty corner of his heart hadn't belonged to the wife of another man.

"This is going to be so fun," Addie declared beside him. She was just about dancing out of her seat belt with excitement. "Seems like it's been forever since I've had a chance to hang out with Louisa and Olivia. It's going to be awesome."

The plan for the evening had changed at the last minute, Faith had told him in a quick, rather awkward conversation earlier that day. Celeste and Flynn decided to move their movie party to the Star N ranch house and the three girls were going to stay overnight after the movie.

If Lou and Olivia were as excited as Addie, Celeste and Mary were in for a night full of giggling girls.

His daughter let out a little shriek when he pulled up and turned off the engine.

"This is going to be *so fun*!" she repeated.

He had to smile as he climbed out and walked around to open the door. He never got tired of seeing the joy his daughter found in the simple things in life.

"Hand me your suitcase."

"Here. You don't have to carry everything, though. I can take the rest."

After pulling her suitcase from behind the seat, she hopped out with her pillow and sleeping bag.

"Careful. It's icy," he said as they headed up the sidewalk to the sprawling ranch house.

She sent him an appraising look as they reached the front door. "You look really good, Dad," she declared. "Like, Nick Jonas good."

"That's quite a compliment." Or it would be if he had more than the vaguest idea who Nick Jonas was.

"It's true. I bet you'll be the hottest guy at the party, especially since everyone else will be a bunch of married old dudes, right?"

He wasn't sure about that. Justin Hartford was a famous—though retired—movie star and Seth Dalton had once been quite a lady's man in these parts.

"You're sweet, kiddo," he said, kissing the top of her head that smelled like grape-scented shampoo.

Man, he loved this kid and missed her like crazy when she was staying with her mother.

"Doesn't their house look pretty?" she said cheerfully as she rang the doorbell.

The Star N ranch house was ablaze with multicolored Christmas lights around the windows and along the roofline, and their Christmas tree glowed merrily in the front bay window.

It was warm and welcoming against the cold, starry night.

The first year after Travis died, Faith had refused to hang any outside Christmas lights on the house and had only had a Christmas tree because Chase had decorated her Christmas tree with the kids and Aunt Mary.

Faith hadn't been up to it and had claimed ranch business elsewhere while they did it.

Last year, he and Rafe had hung the outside Christmas lights.

This year, Faith herself had hung the lights, with Barrett and Lou helping her.

He wanted to think there was some symbolism in that, one more example that she was moving forward with her life.

Addie was about to ring the doorbell again when it suddenly opened. Faith's aunt stood on the other side and at the sight of him, Mary gave a low, appreciative whistle that made him feel extremely self-conscious.

"I should yell at you for ringing the doorbell when I've told you a hundred times you're family, but you look so good, I was about to ask Miss Addie what handsome stranger brought her to our door."

His daughter giggled and kissed the wrinkled cheek Mary offered. "Hi, Aunt Mary. It's just my dad. But I told him on the way that he looked super hot. For an old guy, anyway."

He *felt* hot in his suit and tie, but probably not the way she meant. Mary grinned. "You're absolutely right," she said. "Nice to see you dressed up for once."

"Thanks," he answered.

Before he could say more, Louisa burst into the room and started dancing around Addie. "You're here! You're here! I've been dying to see you and do more than just talk on the phone and text and stuff. It feels like *forever* since you've been here."

The girls hugged as if they had been separated for months.

"Need me to carry your stuff to your room?" he asked.

"It's just a suitcase and sleeping bag, Dad. I think we can handle it."

"Let's hurry, before Barrett finds out you're here and starts bugging us," Louisa said.

Poor Barrett, who until recently had been completely outnumbered by all the women in his life. At least now he had a couple of uncles and an honorary cousin in Rafe's nephew, Joey.

"Faith only came in from the barn about half an hour ago so she's still getting ready," Mary said, her plump features tight with disapproval for a moment before she wiped the expression away and gave him a smile instead. "I heard the shower turn off a few minutes ago so it shouldn't be long now."

He tried not to picture Faith climbing out of the shower, all creamy skin with her tight, slender body covered in water droplets. Once the image bloomed there, it was tough to get it out of his head again to focus on anything else.

"It's fine," he answered. "We've got plenty of time."

"You're too patient," Mary said. Her voice had an unusually barbed tone to it that made him think she wasn't necessarily talking about him waiting for Faith to get dressed for their night out.

"Maybe I just don't want to make anybody feel rushed," he answered carefully—also talking about more than just that evening.

Mary sniffed. "That's all well and good, but sometimes time can be your worst enemy, son. People get set in their ways and can't see the world is still brimming over with possibilities. Sometimes they need a sharp boot in the keister to point them in the right direction."

Well, that was clear enough. Mary *definitely* wasn't talking about the time Faith was taking to get ready. He gave her a searching look. Maybe he hadn't been as careful as he thought about not wearing his heart on his sleeve.

He loved Faith's aunt, who had opened her home and her heart to Faith and her sisters after the horrible events before they came to Pine Gulch. She and Claude had offered a safe haven for three grieving girls but they had provided much more than that. Through steady love and care, the couple had helped the girls begin to heal.

Mary had truly been a lifesaver after Travis's death, as well. She had moved back into the ranch house and stepped up to help with the children while Faith struggled to juggle widowhood and single motherhood while suddenly saddled with the responsibilities of running a big cattle ranch on her own.

"I'm just saying," Mary went on, "maybe it's time to get off your duff and make a move."

He could feel tension spread out from his head to his shoulders. "That's the plan. What do you think tonight is about?"

"I was hoping."

She frowned, blue eyes troubled. "Just between me and you and that Christmas tree, I've got a feeling that might be the reason why a certain person just came in from the barn only a half hour ago, even though she knew all day you were on the way and exactly what time she would need to start getting ready."

Did that mean Mary thought Faith was avoiding the idea of going on a real date with him? He couldn't tell and before he had the chance to ask for clarification, Flynn Delaney came into the living room.

The other man did a double take when he spotted Chase talking to Mary. "Wow. A tie and everything."

Chase shrugged, though he could feel his skin prickle. "A Christmas party for the local stockgrowers association might not be a red-carpet Hollywood affair, but it's still a pretty big deal around here."

"Take it from me—it will be much more enjoyable for everyone involved."

He wasn't so sure about that, especially if Faith was showing reluctance about the evening.

"Sometime this week, Rafe and I are planning to spruce up the set we used last year for the Christmas show. If you want to lend a hand, we'll pay you in beer."

He had come to truly enjoy the company of both of Faith's brothers-in-law. They were both decent men who, as far as he was concerned, were almost good enough for her sisters.

"Addie's in town right now and I feel bad enough about leaving her tonight when our time together is limited. I'll have to see what she wants to do but I'm sure she wouldn't mind coming out again and riding horses with Lou."

"I get it. Believe me."

Flynn had been a divorced father, too. He and his famous actress wife had been divorced several years before she was eventually killed so tragically.

The other man looked down the hallway, apparently to make sure none of the kids were in earshot. "I hear a certain *H-O-R-S-E* is safely ensconced at your place now."

"Lou is twelve years old and can spell, you know," Mary said with a snort.

Flynn grinned at the older woman. "Yeah. But will she slow down long enough to bother taking time to do it? That's the question."

Chase had to laugh. The horse and Louisa would be perfect for each other. "Yeah. She's a beauty. Louisa is going to be thrilled, I think. You all are in for a fun Christmas morning."

"You'll come over for breakfast like you usually do, won't you?" Mary asked.

He wasn't so sure about that. Maybe he would have to see how that evening went first. He hoped like hell that he wasn't about to ruin all his most important relationships with Faith's family by muddying the water with her.

"I hope so," he started to say, but the words died when he heard a commotion on the stairs and a moment later, Faith hurried down them wearing a silver-and-blue dress that made her look like a snow princess.

"Sorry. I'm so sorry I'm late," Faith exclaimed as she fastened a dangly silver earring.

He couldn't have responded, since his brain seemed to have shut down.

She looked absolutely stunning, with her hair piled on top of her head in a messy, sexy bun, strands artfully escaping in delectable ways. She wore a rosy lipstick and more eye makeup than usual, with mascara and eyeliner that made her eyes look huge and exotically slanted.

The dress hugged her shape, with a neckline that revealed just a hint of cleavage. She wore strappy sandals that made him wonder if he was going to have to scoop her up and carry her through the snow.

He was so used to seeing her in jeans and a T-shirt and boots, wearing a ponytail and little makeup except lip balm.

She was beautiful either way.

He swallowed, realizing he had to say something and not just stand there like an idiot.

"You're worth the wait," he said.

His voice came out rough and she flashed him a startled look before he saw color climb her cheeks.

"I don't know about that. It's been a crazy day and I feel like I've been running since five a.m. I'll probably fall asleep the moment I get into your truck."

He would love to have her curl up beside him and sleep. It certainly wouldn't be the first time.

"I'll have to see what I can do to keep you awake," he murmured.

"Driving with the windows down and the music cranked always helps me," Flynn offered.

"I spent too long fixing that hair for you to mess it up with a wind tunnel," Celeste Nichols Delaney said as she followed her sister down the stairs.

Her words brought Chase to his senses and he realized he had been standing in the entryway, gaping at her like he'd never seen a beautiful woman before.

He cleared his throat and forced himself to smile at Celeste. "We can't have that. You did a great job."

"I did, especially with Faith trying to send three emails, put on her makeup and help Barrett with his English homework at the same time."

"I appreciate your hard work," Faith said. "I think I'm finally ready. I just need my coat."

She made it the rest of the way down the stairs on the high heels and reached inside the closet in the entryway, but before she could pull off the serviceable ranch coat she always wore, Celeste slapped her hand away. "Oh, no you don't."

Faith frowned at her sister. "Why not? This is a stockgrowers' dinner. You think they've never seen a ranch coat before?"

"Not with that dress, they haven't. That's why I brought over this."

She pulled a soft fawn coat reverently from the arm of the sofa. "I bought this last month in New York when Hope and I were there meeting with our publisher."

"I don't want to wear your fancy coat."

"Too bad. You're going to."

Celeste could be as stubborn as the other sisters. "Fine," Faith finally sighed, reaching for the coat that looked cashmere and expensive. With a subtle wink, Celeste ignored her sister's outstretched hand and gave it to Chase instead. It was soft as a newborn kitten. He felt inordinately breathless as he moved behind Faith and helped her into it.

She smelled…different. Usually she smelled of vanilla and oranges from her favorite soap but this was a little more intense, with a low, flowery note that made him want to bury his face in her neck and inhale.

"There you go," he said gruffly.

"Thanks." It was obvious she wasn't comfortable dressing up, perhaps because so much of her childhood was spent with parents who gave away most of their material possessions to the people they worked with in impoverished countries.

"Are you happy now?" Faith said to her sister.

"Yes. You're beautiful." Celeste's eyes were soft and a little teary. "Sometimes you look so much like Mom."

"She must have been stunning," Flynn said, kissing his sister-in-law on the cheek.

Chase cleared away the little catch in his throat. "Breathtaking," he agreed.

Her cheeks turned pink at the attention. "I still think we'd have much more fun staying home and watching Christmas movies with the kids," she said. She smiled at the three of them but he was almost certain he saw a flicker of nervousness in her eyes again.

"Now, there's absolutely no reason for the two of you to rush back," Celeste assured them. "The three of us have got this covered. The kids will all be fine. Go and have a great time."

"That's right," Mary said. She gave Chase a pointed look, as if to remind him of their conversation earlier. "You ask me, these parties end way too soon. I suppose that's what you get when you hang out with people who have to wake up early to feed their livestock. So don't feel like you have to come straight home when it's over. You could even go catch a movie in town if you wanted or grab drinks at that fancy new bar that opened up on the outskirts of town."

"The only trouble is we both *also* have to wake up early to take care of our livestock," Faith said with a laugh that sounded slightly strained.

"Louisa. Barrett," she called. "I'm leaving. Come give me a hug."

All the children, not only her two, hurried down the stairs to join them.

"You look beautiful, Faith," Addie exclaimed. "What

a cute couple you guys are. Wait. Let me get a picture so I can show my friends."

She pulled out the smartphone he didn't think she needed yet and snapped a picture.

"Oh! What a good idea," Celeste said. "I want a picture, too."

"We're just going to a Christmas party. It's not the prom," Faith said. Her color ratcheted up a notch, especially when Aunt Mary pulled out her phone as well and started clicking away taking pictures.

"I'm posting this one," her aunt declared. "You both look so good. In fact, you better watch it, Chase, or you'll have about a hundred marriage proposals before the night is over. My friends on social media can be a wild bunch."

Faith's cheeks by now were as red as the ornaments on the tree. This was distressing her, and though he didn't quite understand why, it didn't matter. His job was to protect her—even from loving relatives with cell phone cameras.

"Okay, that's enough paparazzi for tonight. We'll really be late if this keeps up."

"You don't want that. You'll miss all of Jenna McRaven's good food," Mary said.

"Exactly." He hugged his daughter. "Be good, Ads. I imagine you'll still be up when I bring Faith back but if you're not, I'll see you in the morning."

"Bye, Dad. Have fun."

He waited for Faith to hug and kiss her kids and admonish them to behave for Aunt Mary and the Delaneys, then he held the door open for her and they headed out into the cold air that felt refreshing on his overheated skin.

Neither of them said anything as he led her to his pickup and helped her inside. He wished he had some kind of luxury sedan to take her to the party but that kind of vehicle wasn't very practical on an eastern Idaho ranch. At least he'd taken the truck for a wash and had vacuumed up any dried mud and straw bits out of the inside.

It took a little effort to tuck the soft length of her coat inside. "Better make sure I don't shut the door on Celeste's coat," he joked. "She would probably never forgive me."

He went around and climbed inside, then turned his pickup truck around and started heading toward the canyon road that would take them to Pine Gulch and the party.

"My family. Ugh. You'd think I never went to a Christmas party before, the way they carry on." Faith didn't look at him as she fiddled with the air vent. "I don't know what's gotten into them all. I mean, we went together last year to the exact same party and nobody gave it a second thought."

A wise man would probably keep his mouth shut, just go with the flow.

Maybe he was tired of keeping his mouth shut.

"If I had to guess," he said, after giving her a long look, "they're making a fuss because they know this is different, that we're finally going out on a real date."

Chapter 4

At his words, tension seemed to clamp around her spine with icy fingers.

We're finally going out on a real date.

She had really been hoping he had forgotten all that nonsense by now and they could go to the party as they always had done things, as dear friends.

She didn't know what to say. She couldn't stop thinking about that moment when she had started down the stairs and had seen him standing there, looking tall and rugged and gorgeous, freshly shaved and wearing a dark Western-cut suit and tie.

He had looked like he should be going to a country music awards show with a beautiful starlet on his arm or something, not the silly local stockgrowers association party with *her*.

She had barely been able to think straight and literally had felt so weak-kneed she considered it a minor miracle that she hadn't stumbled down the stairs right at his feet.

Then he had spotted her and the heat in his eyes had sent an entire flock of butterflies swarming through her insides.

"Every time I bring up that this is a date, you go silent as dirt," he murmured. "Why is that?"

She drew in a breath. "I don't know what to say."

He shot her a quick look across the bench seat of his truck. "Is the idea of dating me so incomprehensible?"

"Not incomprehensible. Just…disconcerting," she answered honestly.

"Why?" he pressed.

How was she supposed to answer that? He was her best friend and knew all her weaknesses and faults. Surely he knew she was a giant coward at heart, that she didn't *want* these new and terrifying feelings.

She had no idea how to answer him so she opted to change the subject. "I haven't had a chance to ask you. How's Louisa's new horse?"

He shifted his gaze from the road, this time to give her a long look. She thought for a moment he would call her on it and press for an answer. To her relief, he turned back to the road and, after a long pause, finally answered her.

"Settling in, I guess. She seems to have really taken to Tor—and vice versa."

"I hope they won't be too upset at being separated when we send the new horse to Seth Dalton's after Christmas."

"I'm sure they'll survive. If not, we can always arrange visitation."

That word inevitably reminded her of his ex-wife.

"How is Cindy's mother doing?" she asked.

He shrugged. "Fine, from what I hear. She's probably going to be in the hospital another week."

"Does that mean the cruise is off?"

"Cindy insists they don't want to cancel the cruise unless it's absolutely necessary. I'm still planning my Christmas celebration with Addie on December 20."

"It's just another day on the calendar," she said.

"Don't let Hope hear you say that or she might ban you from The Christmas Ranch," he joked.

They spoke of the upcoming children's Christmas show and the crowds at the ranch and the progress of her sisters' movie for the remainder of the short drive to the reception hall where the annual dinner and party was always held.

He found a parking space not far from the building and climbed out to walk around the vehicle to her side. While she waited for him to open her door, Faith took a deep breath.

She could do this. Tonight was no different from dozens of other social events they had attended together. Weddings, birthday parties, Fourth of July barbecues. Things had never been awkward between them until now.

We're finally going out on a real date.

When she thought of those words, little starbursts of panic flared inside her.

She couldn't give in. Chase was her dear friend and she cared about him deeply. As long as she kept that in mind, everything would be just fine.

She wasn't certain she completely believed that but she refused to consider the alternative right now.

The party was in full swing when they arrived. The reception hall had been decorated with an abundance of twinkling fairy lights strung end to end and Christmas trees stood in each corner. Delectable smells wafted out of the kitchen and her stomach growled, almost in time to the band playing a bluegrass version of "Good King Wenceslas." A few couples were even dancing and she watched them with no small amount of envy. She missed dancing.

"You'd better give me Celeste's New York City coat so I can hang it up," Chase said from beside her.

She gave him a rueful smile. "I'm a little afraid to let it out of my sight but I guess I can't wear it all night."

"No, you can't. Go on inside. I'll hang this and be there in a moment."

She nodded and stepped into the reception room. Her good friend Jennie Dalton—Seth Dalton's wife and principal of the elementary school—stood just inside. Jennie was talking with Ashley Hartford, who taught kindergarten at the elementary school.

While their husbands were lost in conversation, the two women were speaking with a young, lovely woman she didn't recognize—which was odd, since she knew just about everyone who came to these events.

Jennie held out a hand when she spotted her. "Hello, my dear. You look gorgeous, as always."

Faith made a face, wishing she didn't feel like a frazzled, overburdened rancher and single mother.

She held a hand out to the woman she didn't know. "Hi. I'm Faith Dustin."

The woman had pretty features and a sweet smile. "Hello. I'm Ella Baker. You may know my father, Curt."

"Yes, of course. Hello. Lovely to meet you."

Curt Baker had a ranch on the other side of town. She didn't know him well but she had heard he had a daughter he didn't know well who had spent most of her life living with her mother back East somewhere. From what she understood, his daughter had returned to help him through a health scare.

"Your dad is looking well."

Ella glanced at her father with a troubled look, then forced a smile. "He's doing better, I suppose."

"Ella is a music therapist and she just agreed to take the job of music teacher at the school for the rest of the school year," Jennie said, looking thrilled at the prospect.

"That's a long time coming."

"Right. We've had the funding for it but haven't been able to find someone suitable since Linda Keller retired two years ago. We've been relying on parent volunteers, who have been wonderful, but can only take the program so far. I'm a firm believer that children learn better when we can incorporate the arts in the classroom."

"I completely agree," Faith said, then was suddenly struck by a small moment of brilliance. "Hey, I've got a terrific way for you to get to know some of the young people in the community."

"Oh?"

"My family runs The Christmas Ranch. You may have seen signs for it around town."

"Absolutely. I haven't had time to stop yet but it looks utterly delightful."

"It is." She didn't bother telling the woman she had very little to do with the actual operations of The Christmas Ranch. It was always too complicated explaining that she ran the cattle side of things—hence her presence at this particular holiday party.

"Last year we started a new tradition of offering a children's Christmas variety show and dinner for the senior citizens in town. It's nothing grand, more for fun than anything else. The children only practice for the week leading up to the show, since everyone is so busy this time of year. Linda Keller, the woman who retired a few years ago from the school district, had offered to help us this year but apparently she just broke her arm."

"That's as good an excuse as any," Ashley said.

"I suppose. The point is my sisters are desperate for someone to help them organize the show. I don't suppose there's any chance you might be interested."

It seemed a nervy thing to ask a woman she had only met five minutes earlier. To Faith's relief, Ella Baker didn't seem offended.

"That sounds like a blast," Ella exclaimed. "I've been looking for something to keep me busy until the New Year when I start at the school part-time."

Hope was going to owe her *big-time*—so much that Faith might even claim naming rights over the new baby.

"Great! You'll have fun, I promise. The kids are so cute and we've got some real talent."

"This is true," Ashley said. "Especially Faith's niece, Olivia. She sings like an angel. Last year the show was so wonderful."

"The senior citizens in the area really ate it up," Jennie affirmed. "My dad couldn't stop talking about it. The Nichols family has started a wonderful thing for the community."

"This sounds like a great thing. I'm excited you asked me."

"If you give me your contact info, I can forward it to my sister Hope. She's really the one in charge."

"Your name is Faith and you have a sister named Hope. Let me guess, do you have another one named Charity?"

"That would be logical, wouldn't it? But my parents never did what was expected. They named our youngest sister Celeste."

"Celeste is the children's librarian in town and she's also an author," Ashley said. "And Hope is an illustrator."

"Oh! Of course! Celeste and Hope Nichols. They wrote 'Sparkle and the Magic Snowball'! The kids at the developmental skills center where I used to work loved that story. They even wrote a song about Sparkle."

Faith smiled. "You'll have to share it with Celeste and Hope. They'll be thrilled."

She and Ella were sending contact information to each other's phones when she felt a subtle ripple in the air and a moment later Chase joined them.

Speaking with the women had begun to push out some of the butterflies inside her but they suddenly returned in full force.

"Sorry I was gone so long. I got cornered by Pete Jeppeson at the coatrack and just barely managed to get away."

"No worries. I've been meeting someone who is about to make my sisters very, very happy. Chase Brannon, this is Ella Baker. She's Curt's daughter and she's a music therapist who has just agreed to help out with the second annual Christmas Ranch holiday show."

Chase gave Ella a warm smile. "That's very kind of you—not to mention extremely brave."

The woman returned his smile and Faith didn't miss the sudden appreciative light in her eyes, along with a slightly regretful look, the sort a woman might wear while shopping when someone else in line at the checkout just ahead of her picks out the exact one-of-a-kind piece of jewelry she would have chosen for herself.

"Brave or crazy," Ella said. "I'm not sure which yet."

"You said it. I didn't," Chase said.

Both of them laughed and as she saw them together, a strange thought lodged in her brain.

The two of them could be perfect for each other.

She didn't want to admit it but Ella Baker seemed on the surface just the sort of woman Chase needed. She had only just met the woman but she trusted her instincts. Ella seemed smart and pretty, funny and kind.

Exactly the sort of woman Chase deserved.

He said he was ready to date again and here was a perfect candidate. Wouldn't a truehearted friend do everything in her power to push the two of them together—at least give Chase the chance to get to know the other woman?

She hated the very idea of it, but she wanted Chase to be happy. "Will you both excuse me for a moment? I just spotted Jenna McRaven and remembered I need to talk to her about a slight change in the menu for the dinner next week."

She aimed a bright smile at them. "You two should dance or something. Go ahead! I won't be long."

She caught a glimpse of Ella's startled features and the beginnings of a thundercloud forming on Chase's but she hurried away before he could respond.

He would thank her later, she told herself, especially if Ella turned out to be absolutely perfect for him.

He only needed to spend a little time with her to realize the lovely young woman who had put her life on hold to help her ailing father was a much better option than a prickly widow who didn't have anything left in her heart to give him.

She found Jenna in the kitchen, up to her eyeballs in appetizers.

This was the absolute worst time to bug her about a catering job, when she was busy at a different one. Faith couldn't bother her with a small change in salad dressing—especially when she was only using this as an excuse to leave Chase alone with Ella Baker. She would call Jenna later and tell her about the change at a better time.

"Hi, Faith! Don't you look beautiful tonight!"

She almost gave an inelegant snort. Jenna's blond curls were piled on her head in an adorable messy bun and her cheeks looked rosy from the heat of the kitchen and probably from the exertion of preparing a meal for so many people, while Faith had split ends and hands desperately in need of a manicure.

"I was just going to say the same to you," she said. "Seriously, you're the only person I know who can be neck-deep in making canapés and still manage to look like a model."

Jenna rolled her eyes as she continued setting out appetizers on the tray. "You're sweet but delusional. Did you need something?"

Faith glanced through the open doorway, where she could see Chase bending down to listen more closely to something Ella was saying. The sight made her stomach hurt—but maybe that was just hunger.

"Not at all. I was just wondering if you need any help back here."

Jenna looked startled at her question but not ungrateful. "That's very sweet but I'm being paid to hang out here in the kitchen. You're not. You should be out there enjoying the party."

"I can hear the music from here, plus helping you out in the kitchen would give me the chance to talk to a dear friend I don't see often enough. Need me to carry out a tray or two?"

Jenna blew out a breath. "I should say no. You're a guest at the party. I hate to admit it, but I could really use some help for a minute. It's a two-person job but my assistant has the flu so I'm a little frantic here. Carson will be here to help me as soon as he can, but his flight from San Francisco was delayed because of weather so he's running about an hour behind."

Faith found it unbearably sweet that Jenna's billionaire husband—who commuted back and forth between Silicon Valley and Pine Gulch—was ready to help the wife he adored with a catering job. "I can help you until he gets here. No problem."

Jenna lifted her head from her task long enough to frown. "Didn't I see you come in with Chase when I was out replenishing the Parmesan smashed potatoes? I can't let you just ditch him."

She glanced at the door where he was now smiling at something Ella said.

"We drove here together, yes," she answered. "But I'm hoping he'll be dancing with Curt Baker's daughter in a moment."

"Oh. Ella. Jolie just started taking piano lessons from her. She's a delight."

"I think she would be great for Chase so I'm trying to give them a chance to get to know each other. Let nature take its course and all."

Jenna's busy hands paused in her work and she gave Faith a careful look. "You might want to ask Chase his opinion on that idea," she said mildly.

"I don't need to ask him. He's my best friend. I know what he needs probably better than he knows himself."

Jenna opened her mouth to answer, then appeared to think better of it.

She was right, Faith told herself. Chase would thank her later; she was almost certain of it.

Chapter 5

Faith was trying to ditch him.

He knew exactly what she was doing as she moved in and out of the kitchen carrying trays of food for Jenna McRaven's catering company. It wasn't completely unusual for her to help out behind the scenes, but he knew in this case she was just looking for an excuse to avoid him.

He curled his hands into fists, trying to decide if he was more annoyed or hurt. Either way, he still wanted to punch something.

The woman beside him hummed along with the bluegrass version of "Silver Bells." Ella Baker had a pretty voice and kind eyes. He felt like a jerk for ignoring her while he glowered after Faith, even though Ella wasn't the date he had walked in with.

"What were you doing before you came back to Pine Gulch to stay with your father?" he asked.

"I was the music instructor at a residential school for developmentally delayed children in Upstate New York, the same town where you can find the boarding school I attended myself from the age of eight, actually."

Boarding school? What was the story there? He wouldn't have taken Curt Baker as the sort of guy to send his kid to boarding school to be raised by someone else most of the year. He couldn't imagine it—it was hard enough packing Addie off to live with her mother half the time.

"Sounds like you were doing good work."

"I found it very rewarding. Some of my students have made remarkable progress. Music can be a comfort and a joy, as well as open doors to language and auditory processing skills I wouldn't have imagined before I started in this field."

"That sounds interesting."

She made a face. "To me, anyway. Sorry. I tend to get a little passionate when I talk about my job."

"I admire that in a person."

"It's not all I do, I promise. I did play piano and I sing in a jazz trio on the weekends."

"That's great! Maybe you ought to perform at the holiday show yourself."

She made a face. "I probably would be a little out of place, since it sounds like this is mostly a show featuring children. I'm happy enough behind the scenes."

The band changed to a slower song, a wistful holiday tune about regret and lost loves.

"Oh, I love this song," she exclaimed, swaying a little in time to the music.

What was the etiquette here? He had come to the party with a woman who was doing her best to stay away from him. Meanwhile another one was making it clear she wanted to dance.

He didn't know the social conventions but he figured simple politeness trumped the rules anyway.

"Would you like to dance?" he finally asked. If Faith would rather hide out in the kitchen than spend time in conversation with him, he probably wasn't committing some grave faux pas by asking another woman for a simple dance.

Ella's smile was soft with delight. "I would, actually. Thanks."

How weird was this night turning out? Chase wondered as he led the woman out to the dance floor with about a dozen other couples. He had come to the party hoping to end up with Faith in his arms. Instead, she was currently busy carrying out a pot of soup while he was dancing with a woman he had only just met.

Ella was a good conversationalist. She asked him about his ranch and Pine Gulch and the surroundings. He told her about Addie and the cruise she was going on with her mother and stepfather over the holidays and his plans to have their own Christmas celebration a few days before the twenty-fifth.

He actually enjoyed himself more than he might have expected, though beneath the enjoyment he was aware of a simmering frustration at Faith.

When the song ended, he spotted Ella's father on the edge of the dance floor speaking with a ranching couple he knew who lived up near Driggs. He led her there, visited with the group for a moment, then made his excuses and headed straight for the kitchen.

He found Faith plating pieces of apple pie. She was talking to Jenna McRaven but her words seemed to stall when she spotted him.

"Are you going to hide out in here all night?"

Her gaze shifted away from his but not before he saw the shadow of nervousness there. "I'm not hiding out," she protested. "I was just giving Jen a hand for a minute. Anyway, you've been busy dancing with Ella Baker."

Only because his real date was as slippery as a newborn calf.

"You've done more than enough," Jenna assured her. "I'm grateful for your help but I'm finally caught up in here. Carson's plane just landed and he's on his way here to help me with the rest of the night. You really need to go out and enjoy the party."

Faith opened her mouth to protest but Jenna gave her a stern look. "I'm serious, sweetie. Go out and enjoy all this delicious food I've been slaving over for a week. Now hand over the apron and back away slowly and nobody will get hurt."

"Fine. If you insist." Faith huffed out a little breath but untied her apron and set it on an empty space on the counter. Chase wasn't about to let her wriggle away again. He hooked his hand in the crook of her elbow and steered her out into the reception hall and over to the buffet line.

They grabbed their food, which all appeared delicious, then Faith scanned the room. "I see a couple of chairs over by Em and Ashley. Why don't we go sit with them?"

He enjoyed hanging out with their neighbors but right now he would rather find a secluded corner and have this out. Barring that, he would rather just go home and get the hell out of this suit and tie.

Nothing was working out as he planned and he felt stupid and shortsighted for thinking it might.

"Sure. Sounds good," he lied.

She led the way and as soon as they were seated, she immediately launched into a long conversation with the other couples.

By the time dinner was over, he was more than ready to throw up his hands and declare the evening a disaster, convinced she was too stubborn to ever consider they could be anything but friends.

Sitting at this table with their neighbors and friends filled him with a deep-seated envy that left him feeling small. They were all long-married yet still obviously enamored with each other, with casual little touches and private smiles that left him feeling more lonely than ever.

The band had begun to move away from strictly playing holiday songs and began a cover of a popular upbeat pop song, adding a bluegrass flair, of course. Ashley Hartford lit up. "Oh! I love this song. Come dance with me, darling."

Though they had four children and had been married for years, Justin gave her the sort of smoldering look Chase guessed women enjoyed, since the man had made millions on the big screen, before he walked away from it all to come to Pine Gulch.

"Let's do it," he said.

"We can't let them show us up," Emery declared to her husband. "I know you hate to dance but will you, just this once?"

Nate Cavazos, former army Special Forces and tough

as nails, sighed but obediently rose to follow his petite wife out to the dance floor. Their departure left him alone at the table with Faith, along with an awkward silence.

He gestured to the floor. "Do you want to dance?"

Panic flickered in her eyes and his gut ached. She had been his friend for nearly two decades. They had laughed together, cried together, confided secrets to each other.

Why the hell couldn't she see they were perfect for each other?

"Forget it," he said. "You're not enjoying this. Why don't I just go get Celeste's fabulous coat and we can take off?"

Her lush mouth twisted into a frown. "That's not fair to you."

She looked at the dance floor for a moment, then back at him. "Actually, let's go dance. I would like it very much."

He wanted to call her out for the lie but it seemed stupid to argue. Instead, Chase scraped his chair back, then reached a hand out. She placed her slim, cool, working-rancher hand in his and he led her out to the dance floor.

Just as they reached it, the music shifted to a song he didn't know, something slow and dreamy, jazzy and soft. He pulled her into his arms—finally!—and they began to move in time to the music.

"This is nice," she murmured, and he took that as encouragement to pull her a little closer. She smelled delicious, that subtle scent he had picked up earlier, and he closed his eyes and tried to burn the moment into his memory.

She stumbled a little and when he glanced down, she was blushing. "Sorry. I'm not very good at this. I never learned to dance, unless you count some of the native dances we did in South America and Papua New Guinea."

"I'd like to see some of those."

She laughed. "I doubt I could remember a single one. Hope probably can. She was always more into them than I was. You're a very good dancer. Why didn't I know that?"

"I guess we haven't had much call to dance together."

His mother had taught him, he remembered, when he was about fourteen or fifteen, before his father's diagnosis and his family fell apart.

His mother had told him he needed to learn so he wouldn't be embarrassed at school dances. Turns out, he hadn't needed the lessons. His father's cancer and the toll the treatment had taken on him had left Chase little time for frivolous things like proms. It was all he could do to keep the ranch running while his mother ran his dad back and forth to the cancer center in Salt Lake City.

Despite the long, difficult fight, his father had lost the battle. After he died, things had been worse. His mother had completely fallen apart that first year and had slipped into a deep, soul-crushing depression that lasted for a tough four years, until she finally went to visit a sister in Seattle, fell in love with a restaurant owner she met there and moved there permanently.

Sometimes he wondered what might have happened if his father hadn't died, if Chase hadn't been forced to put his own plans for college on the back burner.

If he had been in a better place to pursue Faith first.

If.

It was a word he really hated.

A few more turns around the dance floor and she appeared to relax and seemed to be enjoying the music and the moment. He even made her laugh a few times. The music shifted into another slow dance and she didn't seem in a hurry to stop dancing so he decided to just go with it.

If he had his choice, he would have frozen that moment forever in time, just savoring the scent of her hair and the way her curves brushed against him and the way she fit so perfectly in his arms.

Too quickly, the music ended and she pulled away.

"That was nice," she said. "Thanks."

Dancing with him had been a big step for her, he knew.

"They're about to serve dessert," he said on impulse. "What do you say we grab a couple slices of that apple pie in a couple of to-go boxes and take off somewhere to enjoy it where we can look at Christmas lights?"

"We don't have to leave if you're enjoying yourself."

"I just want to be with you. I really don't care where."

He probably shouldn't have been that blunt. She nibbled on her lip, clearly mulling her options, then smiled.

"Let's go."

She hated being a coward.

Her sister Hope plowed through life, exploring the world as their parents had, experiencing life and collecting friends everywhere she went. Celeste, the youngest, was shy and timid and could be socially awkward. That seemed to have changed significantly since her marriage to Flynn and since her literary career took off, requiring more public appearances and radio interviews. Celeste seemed to be far more comfortable in her own skin these days.

Now Faith was the timid one.

Losing her husband and becoming a widow at thirty-two had changed her in substantial ways. Sometimes she wasn't even sure who she was anymore.

She had never considered herself particularly brave, though she had tried to put on a strong front for Hope and Celeste after their parents died. They had needed her and while she wanted to curl up into herself, she had tried to set an example of courage for her sisters.

After Travis died, she had wanted to do the same. That time, her children had needed her. She had to show them that even in the midst of overwhelming grief they could survive and even thrive.

Right now, that facade of strength seemed about to crumble to dust. In her heart, she was terrified and it seemed to be growing worse. She was so afraid of shaking up the status quo, setting herself up for more pain.

More than that, she was afraid of hurting Chase.

She wouldn't worry about that now. Once they were alone, just the two of them, they could forget all this date nonsense and just be Chase and Faith again, like always.

Jenna McRaven didn't ask questions when they asked if she had any to-go boxes. She pulled out a cardboard container that she loaded with two pieces of caramel-topped apple pie.

A moment later, without giving explanations to anyone, they grabbed Celeste's luxurious coat and hurried outside into the December night.

Her breath puffed out as they made their way to his

pickup but she wasn't cold. She wanted to give credit to the fine cashmere wool but in truth she was still overheated from the warm dance floor and her own ridiculous nerves.

"Where should we go for dessert?" he asked. "What do you think about Orchard Park? It offers a nice view of town."

She would rather go back to the Star N and change into jeans and a T-shirt. Barring that, Orchard Park would have to do. "Sounds good," she answered.

He turned on a Christmas station and soft, jazzy music filled the interior of his pickup truck as he drove the short distance from the reception hall to an area of new development in Pine Gulch.

A small subdivision of single-family homes was being built here on land that had once been filled with fruit trees. The streets had names like Apple Blossom Drive, Jubilee Lane and McIntosh Court and only about half the lots had new houses.

Chase pulled above the last row of houses to a clearing at the end of the road, probably where the developer planned to add more houses eventually.

He put the vehicle in Park but left the engine running. Warm air poured out of the vents from the heater, wrapping them in a cozy embrace.

"I'm sorry I didn't think to get a bottle of wine but I should have some water in my emergency stash."

He climbed out and rummaged in a cargo box in the backseat before emerging with a couple of water bottles.

Given the harsh winters in the region, most people she knew kept kits in their vehicles with water bottles, granola bars and foil emergency blankets in case they were stranded in a blizzard.

"Don't forget to replenish your supply," she said when he slid back in the front seat.

"I won't. Nothing worse than being stuck in four-foot-high drifts somewhere with nothing to drink but melted snow."

That had never happened to her, thankfully. She unscrewed the cap and took a drink of the water, which was remarkably cold and refreshing, then handed him the to-go carton of pie Jenna had given them along with the fork her friend had provided.

"I guess it's fitting we should eat an apple pie here," she said.

His teeth gleamed in the darkness as he smiled. "Anything else wouldn't seem as appropriate, would it?"

With the glittery stars above them and the colorful lights of town below, she took a bite of her pie and nearly swooned from the sheer sensory overload.

"Wow. That's fantastic," she breathed. It was flaky and crusty and buttery, with just the right hint of caramel. "Jenna is a master of the simple apple pie. I've got her recipe but I can never make it just like this. I don't know what she does differently from me or Aunt Mary or my sisters but it's so fantastic."

"Even without ice cream."

She laughed. "I was thinking that but didn't want to say it."

It seemed a perfect moment, so much better away from the public social pressure of the party. She took a deep breath and realized she hadn't fully filled her lungs all evening. Stupid nerves.

"I love the view from this area," she said. "Pine Gulch seems so peaceful and quiet."

"I suppose it looks so peaceful because you can't

see from up here how old Doris Packer is such a bitter old hag or how Ben Tillman has a habit of shortchanging his customers at the tavern or how Wilma Rivera is probably talking trash about her sister-in-law."

He was so right. "It's easy to simply look at the surface and think you know a place, isn't it?"

"Right." He sent her a sidelong look. "People are much the same. You have to dig beneath the nice clothes and the polite polish to find the essence of a person."

She knew the essence of Chase Brannon. He was a kind, decent, *good* man who so deserved to be happy.

She sighed and could feel the heat of his gaze.

"That sounded heavy. What's on your mind?"

She had a million things racing through her thoughts and didn't know how to talk to him about any of it. She couldn't tell him that she felt like she stood on the edge of a precipice, toes tingling from the vast, unknown chasm below her, and she just didn't know how much courage she had left inside her to jump.

"I'm feeling bad about taking you away from the party," she lied.

"You didn't take me away. Leaving was my idea, remember?"

He reached up to loosen his tie. Funny how that simple act seemed to help her remember this was Chase, her best friend. She wanted him to be happy, no matter what.

"It was a good idea. Still, if we had stayed, maybe you could have danced with Ella Baker again."

He said nothing but annoyance suddenly seemed to radiate out of him in pointed rays.

"She seems very nice," Faith pressed.

"Yes."

"And she's musical, too."

"Yes."

"Not to mention beautiful, don't you think?"

"She's lovely."

"You should ask her out, since you suddenly want to start dating again."

He made a low sound in the back of his throat, the kind of noise he made when his tractor broke down or one of his ranch hands called in sick too many times.

"Who said I wanted to start dating again?" he said, his voice clipped.

"You did. You're the one who insisted this was a *date-date*. You made a big deal that it wasn't just two friends carpooling to the stockgrowers' party together, remember?"

"That doesn't mean I'm ready to start dating again, at least not in general terms. It only means I'm ready to start dating *you*."

There it was.

Out in the open.

The reality she had been trying so desperately to avoid. He wanted more from her than friendship and she was scared out of her ever-loving mind at the possibility.

The air in the vehicle suddenly seemed charged, crackling with tension. She had to say something but had no idea what.

"I… Chase—"

"Don't. Don't say it."

His voice was low, intense, with an edge to it she rarely heard. She had so hoped they could return to the easy friendship they had always known. Was that gone forever, replaced by this jagged uneasiness?

"Say…what?"

"Whatever the hell you were gearing up for in that tone of voice like you were knocking on the door to tell me you just ran over my favorite dog."

"What do you want me to say?" she whispered.

"I sure as hell don't want you trying to set me up with another woman when you're the only one I want."

She stared at him, the heat in his voice rippling down her spine. She swallowed hard, not knowing what to say as awareness seemed to spread out to her fingertips, her shoulder blades, the muscles of her thighs.

He was so gorgeous and she couldn't help wondering what it would be like to taste that mouth that was only a few feet away.

He gazed down at her for a long, charged moment, then with a muffled curse, he leaned forward on the bench seat and lowered his mouth to hers.

Given the heat of his voice and the hunger she thought she glimpsed in his eyes, she might have expected the kiss to be intense, fierce.

She might have been able to resist that.

Instead, it was much, much worse.

It was soft and unbearably sweet, with a tenderness that completely overwhelmed her. His mouth tasted of caramel and apples and the wine he'd had at dinner—delectable and enticing—and she was astonished by the urge she had to throw her arms around him and never let go.

Chapter 6

For nearly fifteen years, he had been trying *not* to imagine this moment.

When she was married to one of his closest friends, he had no idea she tasted of apples and cinnamon, that she smelled like oranges and vanilla sprinkled across a meadow of wildflowers.

He hadn't wanted to know she made tiny little sounds of arousal, little breathy sighs he wanted to capture inside his mouth and hold there forever.

It was easier *not* knowing those things. He could see that now.

He had hugged her many times and already knew how perfectly she fit against him. Sometimes when they would come back from traveling out of town together—Idaho Falls for the livestock auction or points farther away to pick up ranch equipment or parts—she would fall asleep, lulled by the motion of the vehicle and the rare chance to sit in one place for longer than five minutes.

He loved those times. Invariably, she would end up curled against him, her head on his shoulder. It would always take every ounce of strength he possessed not to pull her close, tuck her against him and drive off into the sunset.

He had always tried to remember his place as her friend, her support system.

Aching and wistful, he would spend those drives wishing he could keep driving a little extra or that when they arrived at their destination, he could gently turn her face to his and wake her with a kiss.

It was a damn good thing he hadn't ever risked something so stupid. If he had, he would never have been able to let her go.

He had her now, though, and he wasn't about to let this moment go to waste. She needed to see that she was still a lovely, sensual woman who couldn't spend the rest of her life hidden away at the Star N, afraid to let anybody else inside.

If he couldn't talk her into giving him a chance, perhaps he could seduce her into it.

It wasn't the most honorable thought he'd ever had, but right now, with her mouth warm and open against his and her silky hair under his fingertips, he didn't care.

He deepened the kiss and she froze for a second, and then her lips parted and she welcomed him inside, her tongue tangling with his and her hands clutching his shirt.

She might never be able to love him as he wanted but

at least she should know she was a beautiful, desirable woman who had an entire life ahead of her.

He wasn't sure how long they spent wrapped around each other. What guy could possibly pay attention to insignificant little details like that when the woman he loved was kissing him with abandon?

He only knew he had never been so grateful for his decision to get a bench seat in his pickup instead of two buckets. Without a console in the way, she was nearly in his lap, exactly where he wanted her...

This was the dumbest thing he had ever done.

Even as he tried to lose himself in the kiss, the thought seemed to slither across his mind like a rattlesnake across his boot.

He was only setting himself up for more heartache. He should have thought this through, looked ahead past the moment and what he wanted right now.

How could he ever go back to being friends with her, trying like hell to be respectful of the subtle distance she so carefully maintained between them? He couldn't scrub these moments from his mind. Every time he looked at her now, he would remember this cold, star-filled night with the glittering holiday lights of Pine Gulch spread out below them and her warm, delicious mouth tangling with his.

Some small but powerful instinct for self-preservation clamored at him that maybe he better stop this while he still could, before all these years of pent-up desire burst through his control like irrigation water through a busted wheel line. He couldn't completely lose his head here.

He drew in a sharp breath and eased away from her. Her features were a pale blur in the moonlight but her lips were swollen from his kiss, her eyes half-closed. Her hair was tousled from his hands and she looked completely luscious.

He nearly groaned aloud at the effort it took to slide away from her when his entire body was yelling at him to pull her closer.

She opened her eyes and gazed at him, pupils dilated and her ragged breathing just about the most erotic sound he'd ever heard.

He saw the instant awareness returned to her eyes. They widened with shock and something else, then color soaked her cheeks.

She untangled her hands from around his neck and eased away from him.

"It's been a long time since I made out with a pretty girl in a pickup truck," he said into the suddenly heavy silence. "I forgot how awkward it could be."

She swallowed hard. "Right," she said slowly. "It's the pickup truck making things awkward."

They both knew it was much more than that. It was the years of history between them and the weight of a friendship that was important to both of them.

"I so wish you hadn't done that," she said in a small voice.

Her words carved out another little slice of his heart.

"Which? Kissed you? Or stopped?"

She shifted farther away from him and turned her face to look out at the town below them.

Instead of answering him directly, she offered up what seemed to him like a completely random change of topic.

"Do you remember the first time we met?"

Of course he remembered. Most guys remembered

the days that left them feeling as if they had been run over by a tractor.

"Yes. You and your sisters had only been here with Mary and Claude a day or two."

"It was February 18, a week after our mother's funeral. We had been in Idaho exactly forty-eight hours."

She remembered it so exactly? He wasn't sure what to think about that. He only remembered that he had been sent by his mother to drop off a meal for "Mary's poor nieces."

The whole community knew what had happened to her and her sisters—that their parents had been providing medical care in a poor jungle town in Colombia when the entire family had been kidnapped by rebels looking for a healthy ransom.

After all these years, he still didn't know everything that had happened to her in that rebel camp. She didn't talk about it and he didn't ask. He did know her father had been shot and killed by rebels during a daring rescue mission orchestrated by US Navy SEALs, including a very young Rafe Santiago, now Hope's husband.

He didn't know much more now than he had that first time he met her. When the news broke a few months earlier and her family returned to the US, it had been big news in town. How could it be otherwise, given that her father had grown up in Pine Gulch and everyone knew the family's connection to Claude and Mary?

Unfortunately, the family's tragedy hadn't ended with her father's death. After their rescue, her mother had been diagnosed with an aggressive cancer that might have been treatable if she hadn't been living in primitive conditions for years—and if she hadn't spent the last month as a hostage in a rebel camp.

That had been Chase's mother's opinion, anyway. She had been on her way out of town to his own father's cancer treatment but had told him to drop off a chicken rice casserole and a plate of brownies to the Nichols family.

He remembered being frustrated at the order. Why couldn't she have dropped it off on her way out of town? Didn't he have enough to do on the ranch, since he was basically running things single-handedly?

Claude had answered the door, with the phone held to his ear, and told him Mary was in the kitchen and to go on back. He had complied, not knowing the next few moments would change his life.

He vividly remembered that moment when he had seen Faith standing at the sink with Mary, peeling potatoes.

She had been slim and pretty and fragile, with huge green eyes, that sweet, soft mouth and short, choppy blond hair—which she later told him she had cut herself with a butter knife sharpened on a brick, because of lice in the rebel camp.

He also suspected it had been an effort to avoid unwanted attention from the rebels, though she had never told him that. He couldn't imagine they couldn't see past her choppy hair to the rare beauty beneath.

Yeah, a guy tended to remember the moment he lost his heart.

"I gave you a ride into town," he said now. "Mary needed a gallon of milk or something."

"That's what she said, anyway," Faith said, her mouth tilted up a little. "I think she only wanted me to get out of the house and have a look at our new community and also give me a chance to talk to someone around my own age."

Not *that* close in age. He had been eighteen and had felt a million years older.

She had been so serious, he remembered, her eyes solemn and watchful and filled with a pain that had touched his heart.

"Whatever the reason, I was happy to help out."

"Everyone else treated us like we were going to crack apart at any moment. You were simply kind. You weren't overly solicitous and you didn't treat me like I had some kind of contagious disease."

She turned to face him, still smiling softly at the memories. "That was the best afternoon I'd had in *forever*. You told me jokes and you showed me the bus stop and the high school and the places where the kids in Pine Gulch liked to hang out. At the grocery store, you introduced me to everyone we met and made sure cranky Mr. Gibbons didn't cheat me, since I didn't have a lot of experience with American money."

She had been an instant object of attention everywhere they went, partly because she was new to town and partly because she looked so exotic, with a half-dozen woven bracelets on each wrist, the choppy hair, her wide, interested eyes.

"A few days later, you came back and said you were heading into town and asked if Aunt Mary needed you to come with me to pick anything else up."

That had basically been a transparent ploy to spend more time with her, which everyone else had figured out but Faith.

"That meant so much to me," she said. "Your own father was dying but that didn't stop you from reaching out and trying to help me acclimatize. I've never forgotten how kind you were to me."

Was it truly kindness, when he was the one who had benefited most? "It couldn't have been easy to find yourself settled in a small Idaho town, after spending most of your childhood wandering around the world."

"It was easier for me than it was for Hope and Celeste, I think. All I ever wanted was to stay in one place for a while, to have the chance to make friends finally. Friends like you."

She gave him a long, steady look. "You are my oldest and dearest friend, Chase. Our friendship is one of the most important things in my life."

He wanted to squeeze her hand, to tell her he agreed with her sentiments completely, but he didn't dare touch her again right now.

"Ditto," he said gruffly.

She drew in a breath that seemed to hitch a little. She looked out the windshield, where a few clouds had begun to gather, spitting out stray snowflakes that spiraled down and caught the light of the stars.

"That's why I have to ask you not to kiss me again."

Chapter 7

The hough she didn't raise her voice, her hard-edged words seemed to echo through his pickup truck.

I have to ask you not to kiss me again.

She meant what she said. He knew that tone of voice. It was the same one she used with the kids when meting out punishment for behavioral infractions or with cattle buyers when they tried to negotiate and offered a price below market value.

Her mind was made up and she wouldn't be swayed by anything he had to say.

Tension gripped his shoulders and he didn't know what the hell to say.

"That's blunt enough, I guess," he finally answered. "Funny, but you seemed to be into it at the moment. I guess I misread the signs."

Her mouth tightened. "It's a strange night. Neither

of us is acting like ourselves. Can we just…leave it at that?"

That was the last thing he wanted to do. He wanted to kiss her again until she couldn't think straight.

He hadn't misread *any* signs and they both knew it. After that first moment of shock, she returned the kiss with an enthusiasm and eagerness that had left him stunned and hungry.

"Can you just take me home?" she asked in a low voice.

"If that's what you want," he said.

"It is," she answered tersely.

A few moments ago she had wanted *him*.

She was attracted to him. Lately he had been almost sure of it but some part of him had worried his own feelings for her were clouding his judgment. That kiss and her response told him the sexual spark hadn't been one-sided.

Nice to know he was right about that, at least.

She was attracted to him but she didn't want to be. How did a guy work past that conundrum?

The task suddenly seemed insurmountable.

He put the pickup in gear and focused on driving instead of on the growing realization that she might never be willing to accept him as anything more than her oldest and dearest friend.

Maybe, just maybe, it was time he accepted that and moved on with his life.

Though his features remained set and hard as he drove her back to the Star N, Chase carried on a casual conversation with her about the new horse, about a bit of gossip he heard about cattle futures at the stockgrowers' party, about Addie's Christmas presents that still needed to be wrapped.

Under other circumstances, she might have been quite proud of her halfway intelligent responses—especially when she really wanted to collapse into a boneless, quivering heap on the truck seat.

She couldn't stop remembering that kiss—the heat and the magic and the wild intensity of it.

Her heartbeat still seemed unnaturally loud in her ears and she hadn't quite managed to catch her breath, though she could almost manage to string two thoughts together now.

She felt very much like a tiny island in the middle of a vast arctic river just beginning the spring thaw, with chunks of ice and fast-flowing water buffeting against it in equal parts, bringing life back to the frozen landscape.

She didn't *want* to come to life again. She wanted that river of need to stay submerged under a hard layer of impenetrable ice forever.

Knowing that hollow ache was still there, that her sexuality hadn't shriveled up and died with Travis, completely terrified her.

She was a little angry about it, too, if she were honest. Why couldn't she just resume the state of affairs of the last thirty months, that sense of suspended animation?

This was *Chase*. Her best friend. The man she relied on for a hundred different things. How could she possibly laugh and joke with him like always when she would now be remembering just how his mouth had slid across hers, the glide of his tongue, the heat of his muscles against her chest.

She didn't want that river of need to come to churning, seething life again.

Yes, her world had been cold and sterile since Travis died, but it was *safe*.

She felt like she was suffocating suddenly, as if that wild flare of heat between them had consumed all the oxygen.

She rolled her window down a crack and closed her eyes at the welcome blast of cold air.

"Too warm?" he asked.

Oh, yes. He didn't know the half of it. "A little," she answered in a grave understatement.

He turned the fan down on the heating system just as her phone buzzed. She pulled it from the small beaded handbag Celeste had offered for the occasion.

It was a text from her sister: Girls are asleep. Don't rush home. Have fun.

She glanced at the message, then slid her phone back into the totally impractical bag.

"Problem?" he asked.

"Not really. I think Celeste was just checking in. She said the girls are asleep."

"I hope Addie was good."

"She's never any trouble. Really, we love having her around. She always seems to set a good example for my kids."

"Even Barrett?"

She relaxed a little. Talking about their children was much easier than discussing everything else.

"He can be such a rascal when Addie's there. I don't get it. He teases both of them mercilessly. I try to tell him to cut it out but the truth is I think he has a little crush on her."

"Older women. They're nothing but trouble. I had the worst crush on Maggie Cruz but she never paid me the slightest bit of attention. Why would she? I was in fifth grade and she was in eighth and we were on totally different planets."

The only crush she could remember having was the son of the butcher in the last village where they'd lived in Colombia. He had dark, soulful eyes and curly dark hair and always gave her all the best cuts when she went to the market for her family.

That seemed another lifetime ago. She couldn't even remember being that girl who once smiled at a cute boy.

By the time Chase pulled up to the Star N a few moments later, her hormones had almost stopped zinging around.

He put the truck in Park and opened his door.

"Since Addie's asleep, you don't have to come in," she said quickly, before he could climb out. "You don't really have to walk me to the door like this was a real date."

Why did she have to say that? The words seemed to slip out from nowhere and she wanted to wince. She didn't need to remind him of the awkwardness of the evening.

He said nothing, though she didn't miss the way his mouth tightened and his eyes cooled a fraction before he completely ignored what she said and climbed out anyway.

Everything between them had changed and it made her chest ache with regret.

"Thanks, Chase," she said as they walked side by side through the cold night. "I had a really great time."

"You don't have to lie. It was a disaster from start to finish."

The grim note in his voice made her sad all over again. She sighed. "None of that was your fault. Only mine."

"The old, *it's not you, it's me* line?" he asked as they reached the door. "Really, Faith? You can't be more original than that?"

"It *is* me," she whispered, knowing he deserved the truth no matter how painful. "I'm such a coward and I always have been."

He made a low sound of disbelief. "A coward. You."

"I am!"

"This is the same woman who woke up the day after her husband's funeral, put on her boots and went to work—and who hasn't stopped since?"

"What choice did I have? The ranch was our livelihood. Someone had to run it."

"Right. Just like somebody jumped into a river to save a villager in Guatemala while everybody else was standing on the shore wringing their hands."

She stared at him. "How did you… Where did you hear that?"

"Hope told me once. I think it was after Travis died. She also told me how you took more than one beating while you were all being held hostage because you stepped up to take responsibility for something she or Celeste had done."

She was the oldest. It had been her job to protect her sisters. What else could she do especially since it was her fault they had all been taken hostage to begin with?

She had told that cute boy she had a crush on the day they were supposed to go to Bogota so her mother could see a doctor and that they would probably be leaving for good in a few weeks.

She had hoped maybe he might want to write to her. Instead, he must have told the psychotic rebel leader their plans. The next time she saw that boy, he had been proudly wearing ragged army fatigues and carrying a Russian-made submachine gun.

"You're not a coward, Faith," Chase said now. "No matter how much you might try to convince yourself of that."

A stray snowflake landed on her cheek and she brushed it away. "You are my best friend, Chase. I'm so afraid of destroying that friendship, like I've screwed up everything else."

He gave her a careful look that made her wish she hadn't said anything, had just told him good-night and slipped into the house.

"Can we... More than anything, I would like to go back to the way things were a few weeks ago. Without all this...awkwardness. When we were just Faith and Chase."

He raised an eyebrow. "You really think we can do that, after that kiss?"

She shivered a little, from more than simply the cold night. "I would like to try. Please, Chase."

"How do two people take a step backward? Something is always lost."

"Can't we at least give it a shot? At least until after the holidays?"

She hoped he couldn't hear the begging tone of her voice that seemed so loud to her.

"I won't wait forever, Faith."

"I know," she whispered.

"Fine. We can talk again after the New Year."

Her relief was so fierce that she wanted to weep. At least she would have his friendship through the holidays. Maybe in a few more weeks, she would be able to find the courage to face a future without his constant presence.

"Thank you. That's the best gift anyone could give me this year."

She reached up to give him a casual kiss on the cheek, the kind she had given him dozens of times before. At the last minute, he turned his head, surprise in his eyes, and her kiss landed on the corner of his mouth.

Instantly, the mood shifted between them and once more she was aware of the heat of him and the coiled muscles and the ache deep within her for him and only him.

He kissed her fully, his mouth a warm, delicious refuge against the cold night. His scent surrounded her— leather and pine and sexy, masculine cowboy—and she desperately wanted to lean into his strength and surrender to the delicious heat that stirred instantly to life again.

Too soon, he stepped away.

"Good night," he said, his eyes dark in the glow from the porch light. He opened the door for her and waited until she managed to force her wobbly knees to carry her inside, then he turned around and walked to his pickup truck.

She really wanted nothing more than to shrug out of Celeste's luxurious coat, kick off her high heels, slip away to her room and climb into bed for the next week or two.

Unfortunately, a welcoming party waited for her inside. Celeste, Flynn and Aunt Mary were at the table with mugs of hot chocolate steaming into the air and what looked like a fierce game of Scrabble scattered around the table—which hardly seemed a fair battle since Celeste was a librarian and an author with a freaky-vast vocabulary.

All three looked up when she walked into the kitchen.

"Chase didn't come in?" Mary asked, clear disappointment on her wrinkled face.

Sometimes Faith thought her great-aunt had a little crush on Chase herself. What other reason did she have for always inviting him over?

"No," she said abruptly.

How on earth was she going to face him, again, now that they had kissed twice?

"How was your date?" Celeste asked. Though the question was casual enough, her sister gave her a searching look and she suddenly wanted desperately to confide in her.

She couldn't do it, at least not with Flynn and Mary listening in. "Fine," she answered.

"Only fine?" Mary asked, clearly surprised.

"Fun," she amended quickly. "Dinner was delicious, of course, and we danced a bit."

"Chase is a great dancer," Mary said, her eyes lighting up. "I could have danced with him all night at Celeste's wedding, except Agatha Lindley kept trying to cut in. I don't think he wanted to dance with her at all but he was just too nice."

"She was there tonight, though she didn't cut in. Unless she tried it when he was busy dancing with Ella Baker."

"Ella Baker?" Celeste frowned. "I don't think I know her."

"She's Curt Baker's daughter. She's moved to Pine Gulch to look after her father."

"The girls at the salon were talking about her when I went for my color this week," Mary said. "She teaches music or something, doesn't she?"

With a jolt, Faith suddenly remembered her conversation with the woman at the beginning of the party, which seemed like a dozen lifetimes ago. "Oh! I have news. Big news! I can't believe I almost forgot."

"You probably had other things on your mind," Flynn murmured, his voice so dry that she shot him a quick look.

Did her lips look as swollen as they felt, tight and achy and full? She really hoped not.

"You owe me so big," she said. "I begged Ella Baker to help out with the Christmas program. I told her my sisters were desperate and she totally agreed to do it!"

Celeste's eyes widened. "Are you kidding? What's wrong with the woman?"

"Nothing. She was very gracious about it and even said it sounded like fun."

"Right. Fun," Celeste said with a shake of her head.

"You had fun, don't deny it," Mary said. "Look how it ended up for you. Married to a hot contractor, tool belt and all."

"Thanks, my dear." Flynn gave a slow grin and picked up Mary's hand and kissed the back of it in a totally un-Flynn-like gesture that made Celeste laugh and Mary blush and pull her hand away.

"That was a definite side benefit," Celeste murmured, and Flynn gave her a private smile that made the temperature in the room shoot up a dozen degrees or so.

"Well, I'm afraid we don't exactly have more hot contractors to go around for Ella Baker," Faith said. "Though I do think she would be absolutely perfect for Chase. I told him so, but for some reason, he didn't seem to want to hear it."

All three of them stared at Faith as if she had just unleashed a rabid squirrel in the kitchen.

"You told Chase you think this Ella Baker would be perfect for him," Celeste repeated, with such disbelief in her voice that Faith squirmed.

"Yes. She seems like a lovely person," she said, more than a little defensive.

"I'm sure she is," Celeste said. "That doesn't mean you should have tried to set Chase up with her while the two of you were out together on a date. I'll admit I didn't have a lot of experience before I met Flynn but even I know most guys in general probably wouldn't appreciate that kind of thing. Chase in particular probably didn't want to hear you suggest other women you think he ought to date."

Why Chase in particular? She frowned, though she was aware she had botched the entire evening from the get-go. How was she possibly going to fix things between them?

"We're friends," she retorted. "That's the kind of things friends do for each other, pick out potential dating prospects."

None of them seemed particularly convinced and she was too exhausted to press the point. It was none of their business anyway.

She pulled off Celeste's coat and hung it over one of

the empty chairs and also pulled all her personal things out of the little evening bag.

"Thanks for letting me use your coat and bag."

"You're welcome. Anytime."

Right. She wasn't going to another stockgrowers' party. *Ever.*

"I'm going to go change into something comfortable."

"I'll come help you with the zipper. That one sticks, if I remember correctly."

"I don't need help," she said.

"That, my dear, is a matter of opinion."

Celeste rose and followed her up the stairs. As she helped Faith out of the dress, her sister talked of the children and what they had done that evening and about the latest controversy at the library.

Beneath the light conversation, she sensed Celeste had something more to say. She wasn't sure she wanted to hear it but she couldn't stand the charged subtext either.

After she changed into her favorite comfy pajamas, she sat on the edge of her bed and finally braced herself. "Okay. Out with it."

Celeste deliberately avoided her gaze, confirming Faith's suspicions. "Out with what?" she asked, her tone vague.

"Whatever is lurking there on your tongue, dying to spill out. I can tell you have something to say. You might as well get it over with, for both our sakes. What did I do wrong?"

After a pause, Celeste sat down next to her on the bed.

"I'm trying to figure out if you're being deliberately

obtuse or if you honestly don't know—all while I'm debating whether it's any of my business anyway."

"Remember what mom used to say? Better to keep your nose in a book than in someone else's business. Most of your life, you've had a pretty good track record in that department. Don't ruin it now."

Celeste sighed. "Fine. Deliberately obtuse it is, then."

She pulled her favorite sweatshirt over her head. This was more like it, in her favorite soft pajama bottoms and a comfortable hoodie. She felt much more at ease dressed like this than she ever would in the fancy clothes she had been wearing all evening.

"I don't know about *deliberate* but I'll admit I must be obtuse, since I have no idea what you're trying to dance around here."

"Really? No idea?"

The skepticism in her sister's voice burned. "None. What did I do wrong? I was careful with your coat, I promise."

"For heaven's sake, this isn't about the stupid coat."

"I'm not in the mood to play twenty questions with you. If you don't want to tell me, don't."

Celeste's mouth tightened. "Fine. I'll come out and say it, then. Can you honestly tell me you have no idea Chase is in love with you?"

At her sister's blunt words, all the blood seemed to rush away from her brain and she was very glad she was sitting down. Her skin felt hot for an instant and then icy, icy cold.

"Shut up. He is not."

Celeste made a disgusted sound. "Of course he is, Faith! Open your eyes! He's been in love with you *forever*. You had to have known!"

Whatever might be left of the apple pie and the small amount she had eaten at dinner seemed to congeal into a hard, greasy lump in her stomach.

She didn't know whether to laugh at the ridiculous joke that wasn't really funny at all or to tell her sister she was absolutely insane to make such an outrageous accusation. Underneath both those reactions was a tangled surge of emotion and the sudden burn of tears.

"He's not. He *can't* be," she whispered.

It couldn't be true. Could it?

Celeste squeezed her fingers gently, looking as if she regretted saying anything. "Use your head, honey. He's a good neighbor, yes, and a true friend. But can you really not see that his concern for you goes way beyond simple friendship?"

Chase was always there, a true and loyal friend. The one constant, unshakable force in her world.

"I don't want him to be." Her chest felt tight now and she could feel one of those tears slip free. "What am I going to do?"

Celeste squeezed her fingers. "You could try being honest with yourself and admit that you have feelings for him, too."

"As a friend. That's all," she insisted.

Celeste's eyes were full of compassion and exasperation in equal measures. "I love you dearly, Faith. You know I do. You've been my second mother since the day I was born, and from the time I was twelve years old you helped Aunt Mary and Uncle Claude raise me. You're kind and loving, a fantastic mom to Barrett and Lou, a ferociously hard worker. You've taught me so much about what it is to be a good person."

She tugged her hand away, sensing her sister had plenty more to say, and steeled herself to hear the rest.

"But?"

Celeste huffed out a breath. "But when it comes to Chase Brannon, you are being completely stupid and, as much as I hate to say it, more than a little cruel."

"That's a harsh word."

"The man is in love with you and when you sit there pretending you didn't know, you are lying to me, yourself and especially to Chase."

"He has never *once* said anything." She still couldn't make herself believe it.

"The last two years, he has shown you in a thousand different ways. You think he comes over three or four times a week to help Barrett with his homework because he loves fourth grade arithmetic? Can anyone really be naive enough to think he adores cleaning out the rain gutters in the spring and autumn because it's his favorite outdoor activity? Does he check the knock in your pickup's engine or help you figure out the ranch accounts or take a look at any sick cattle you might have because he wants to? No! He does all of those things because of *you*."

Faith could come up with a hundred other things he did for her or for the kids or Aunt Mary. That didn't necessary mean he was in *love* with her, only that he was a good, caring man trying to step up and help them after Travis's death.

The nausea inside her now had an element of panic. Had she been ignoring the truth all this time because she simply hadn't wanted to see it? What kind of horrible person was she? It made her feel like the worst kind of user.

"He's my best friend," she whispered. "What would I do without him?"

"I'm afraid you might have to figure that out sooner than you'd like, especially if you can't admit that you might have feelings for him, too."

With that, her sister rose, gave her a quick hug. "We all loved Travis. He was like the big brother I never had. He was a great guy and a good father. But he's gone, honey. You're not. I'll give you the benefit of the doubt and accept that maybe you didn't want to see that Chase is in love with you so you have avoided facing the truth. But now that you know, what are you going to do about it?"

Her sister slipped from the room before she could come up with a response—which was probably a good thing since Faith had no idea how to answer her.

Chapter 8

"Why couldn't Lou come with us to take me home?" Addie asked Faith as they pulled out of the Star N driveway to head toward Chase's place.

Faith tried to smile but it ended in a yawn. She was completely wrung out after a fragmented, tortured night spent mostly staring up at her ceiling, reliving the evening—those kisses!—and her conversation with Celeste and wondering what she should do.

She must have slept for a few hours, on and off. When she awoke at her five-thirty alarm, all she wanted to do was pull the covers over her head, curl up and block out the world for a week or two.

Faith blinked away the yawn and tried to smile at Chase's daughter again. "She had a few chores to do this morning and I decided it was better for her to finish them as soon as she could. Sorry about that."

Addie gave her a sudden grin. "Oh. I thought it was maybe because you didn't want her to see her Christmas present in the pasture."

She winced. She should have known Addie would figure it out. The girl was too smart for her own britches. She only hoped she could also keep a secret. "How did you know about that?"

"My dad didn't tell me, in case you're wondering. It wasn't that hard to figure it out, though, especially since Lou hasn't stopped talking about the new barrel racing horse she wants. It seemed like too much of a coincidence when I saw a new horse suddenly had shown up in my dad's pasture."

Faith didn't see any point in dissembling. Christmas was only a few weeks away and the secret would be out anyway. "It wasn't a coincidence," she confirmed. "Your dad helped me pick her out and offered to keep her at Brannon Ridge until after Christmas, when we take her to the Dalton ranch to be trained."

"Louisa is going to be so excited!"

"I think so." Her daughter was a smart, kind, *good* girl. Louisa worked hard in school, did her chores when asked and was generally kind to her brother. She had channeled her grief over losing her father at such a young age into a passion for horse riding and Faith wanted to encourage that.

"I won't tell. I promise," Addie said.

"Thank you, honey."

Addie was a good girl, as well. Some children of divorce became troubled and angry—sometimes even manipulative and sly, pitting one parent against the other for their own gain as they tried to navigate the difficult waters of living in two separate households. Addie was the sweetest girl—which seemed a minor miracle, considering her situation.

"Maybe once she's trained, Lou might let me ride her once in a while," the girl said.

Faith didn't miss the wistful note in Addie's voice. "You know, if you want a horse of your own, you could probably talk your dad into it."

Quite frankly, Faith was surprised Chase hadn't already bought a horse for his daughter.

"I know. Dad has offered to get me one since I was like five. It would be nice, but it doesn't seem very fair to have a horse of my own when I could only see it and ride it once or twice a month. My dad would have to take care of it the rest of the time without me."

"I'm sure he wouldn't mind. He already has Tor. It wouldn't be any trouble at all for him to take care of two horses instead of only one."

"Maybe if I lived here all the time," Addie said in a matter-of-fact tone. "It's hard enough, only seeing my dad a few times a month. I hate when I have to go back to Boise. It would be even harder if I had to leave a horse I loved, too."

Faith swallowed around the sudden lump in her throat. The girl's sad wisdom just about broke her heart. "I can understand that. But you do usually spend summers on the ranch," she pointed out. "That's the best time for riding horses anyway."

"I guess." Addie didn't seem convinced. "I just wish I could stay here longer. Maybe come for the whole school year sometime, even if I wouldn't be in the same grade with Louisa."

"Do you think you might come here to go to school at some point?"

"I wish," she said with a sigh. "My mom always says she would miss me too much. I guess she thinks it's okay for Dad to miss me the rest of the time, when I'm with her."

If she hadn't been driving, Faith would have hugged her hard at the forlorn note in her voice. Poor girl, torn between two parents who loved and wanted her. It was an impossible situation for all of them.

She and Addie talked about the girl's upcoming cruise over the holidays with her mother until they arrived at Chase's ranch. When she pulled up to the ranch, she spotted him throwing a bale of hay into the back of his pickup truck like it weighed no more than a basketball.

She shivered, remembering the heat of his mouth on hers, the solid strength of those muscles against her.

On the heels of that thought came the far more disconcerting one born out of her conversation with Celeste.

The man is in love with you and when you sit there pretending you didn't know, you are lying to me, yourself and especially to Chase.

Butterflies jumped around in her stomach and she realized her fingers on the steering wheel were trembling.

Oh. This would never do. This was *Chase*, her best friend. She *couldn't* let things get funky between them. That was exactly what she worried about most.

Celeste had to be wrong. Faith couldn't accept any other possibility.

The moment she turned off the vehicle, Addie opened the door and raced to hug her dad.

Could she just take off now? Faith wondered. She

was half-serious, until she remembered Addie's things were still in the back of the pickup truck.

In an effort to push away all the weirdness, she drew in a couple of cleansing breaths. It didn't work as well as she hoped but the extra oxygen made her realize she had probably been taking nervous, shallow breaths all morning, knowing she was going to have to face him again.

She pulled Addie's sleeping bag out from behind the seat and pasted on a casual smile, knowing even as she did it that he would be able to spot it instantly as fake.

When she turned around, she found him and Addie just a few feet away from her. His eyes were shaded by his black Stetson and she couldn't read the expression there but his features were still, his mouth unsmiling.

"Looks like we caught you going somewhere," she said.

"Just down to the horse pasture to check on, uh, things there."

If she hadn't been fighting against the weight of this terrible awkwardness, she might have managed a genuine smile at his attempt be vague.

"You don't need to use code. Your daughter is too smart for either of us."

"You don't have to tell me that." He smiled down at Addie and something seemed to unfurl inside Faith's chest. He was an excellent father—and not only to his daughter.

Since Travis died, he had become the de facto father figure for Louisa and Barrett. Oh, Rafe and Flynn did an admirable job as uncles and showed her children how good, decent men took care of their families. But Louisa and Barrett turned to Chase for guidance most. They saw him nearly every day. He was the one Louisa had invited when her class at school had a father-daughter dance and that Barrett had taken along to the Doughnuts with Dad reading hour at school.

They loved him—and he loved them in return. That had nothing to do with any of the nonsense Celeste had talked about the night before.

"Did you have fun last night?" Chase asked Addie now.

"Tons," she declared. "We popped popcorn and watched movies and played games. I beat everybody at UNO like three times in a row and Barrett said I was cheating only I wasn't. And then we all opened our sleeping bags under the Christmas tree and put on another movie and I fell asleep. This morning we had hot chocolate with marshmallows and pancakes shaped like snowmen. It was awesome."

"I'm so glad. Here, I can take that stuff."

He reached to grab the sleeping bag and backpack from Faith. As he did, his hand brushed her chest. It was a touch that barely connected through the multiple layers she wore—coat, a fleece pullover and her silk long underwear—but she could hardly hold back a shiver anyway.

"I'll just take it all into the house now," Addie said. "Thanks for the ride, Faith."

"You're very welcome," she said.

After she strapped the bag over her shoulder and Chase handed her the sleeping bag, she waved at Faith and skipped into the house, humming a Christmas carol.

What a sweet girl, Faith thought again. She didn't let her somewhat chaotic circumstances impact her enjoyment of the world around her. Faith could learn a great deal from the girl's example.

"I'll add my thanks to you for bringing her home," Chase said. "I appreciate it, though I could have driven over to get her."

"I really didn't mind. I've got to run into Pine Gulch for a few things anyway. Can I bring you back anything from the grocery store?"

They did this sort of thing all the time. He would call her on his way to the feed store and ask if she needed anything. She would bring back a part from the implement store in Idaho Falls if she had to go for any reason.

She really hoped the easy, casual give-and-take didn't change now that everything seemed so different.

"We could use paper towels, I guess," he said, after a pause. "Oh, and dishwasher detergent and dish soap."

"Sure. I can drop it off on my way home."

"No rush. I'll pick it up next time I come over."

"Sounds good," she answered. At his words, her smile turned more genuine. This seemed much like their normal interactions—and if he was talking about coming to the ranch again, at least he wasn't so upset at her that he was going to penalize the kids by staying away.

"Did you hear Jim Laird messed up his knee?" he asked. "Apparently he slipped on ice and wrenched things and Doc Dalton sent him over to Idaho Falls for surgery yesterday. I wondered why he wasn't at the party last night. I was hoping Mary Beth wasn't in the middle of a relapse or something."

She didn't like hearing when bad things happened to their neighbors. Jim was a sweet older man in his seventies whose wife had multiple sclerosis. They ran a small herd of about fifty head and he often bought alfalfa from her.

"As if he didn't have enough on his plate! What is

Mary Beth going to do? She can't possibly do the feedings in the winter by herself."

"Wade Dalton, Justin Hartford and I are going to split the load for a few weeks, until he can get around again."

He was always doing things like that for others in the community.

"I want into the rotation. I can take a turn."

"Not necessary. The three of us have it covered."

She narrowed her gaze. "For six months after Travis died, ranchers up and down the Cold Creek stepped up to help us at the Star N. I'm in a good place now, finally, and want to give back when I can."

The ranch wouldn't have survived without help from her neighbors and friends—especially Chase. She had been completely clueless about running a cattle ranch and would have been lost.

Now that she had stronger footing under her, she wanted to start doing her best to pay it forward.

Chase looked as if he wanted to argue but he must have seen the determination in her expression. After a moment, he gave an exasperated sigh.

"Fine. I'll have Wade give you a call to work out the details."

She smiled. "Thanks. I don't mind the early-morning feedings either."

"I'll let Wade know."

There. That was much more like normal. Celeste had to be wrong. Yes, Chase loved her—just as she loved him. They were dear friends. That was all.

"I better run to the store before the shelves are empty. You know how Saturdays get in town."

"I do."

"So paper towels, dish soap and dish detergent. You

can pick up everything tomorrow when you come for dinner," she said.

"That would work."

She felt a little more of the tension trickle away. At least he was still planning to come for dinner.

She loved their Sunday night tradition, when she and her sisters and Aunt Mary always fixed a big family meal and invited any neighbors or friends who would care to join them. Chase invariably made it, unless he was driving Addie back to Boise after a weekend visitation.

"Great. I'll see you tomorrow."

He looked as if he wanted to say something more but she didn't give him the chance. Instead, she jumped into her pickup and pulled away, trying her best not to look at him in the rearview mirror, standing lean-hipped and gorgeous and watching after her.

They had survived their first encounter post-kiss. Yes, it had been tense, but not unbearably so. After this, things between them would become more comfortable each time until they were back to the easy friendship they had always enjoyed.

She cared about him far too much to accept any other alternative.

He stood and watched her drive away, fighting the urge to rub the ache in his chest.

The entire time they talked about groceries and hot chocolate and Jim Laird's bum knee, his damn imagination had been back in a starlit wintry night, steaming up the windows of his pickup truck.

That kiss seemed to be all he could think about. No matter what else he might be trying to focus on, his brain kept going back to those moments when he had held her and she had kissed him back with an enthusiasm he had only dreamed about.

Hot on the heels of those delicious memories, though, came the cold, hard slap of reality.

I have to ask you not to kiss me again.

She was so stubborn, fighting her feelings with every bit of her. How was he supposed to win against that?

He pondered his dwindling options as he headed inside to find Addie so she could put on her winter clothes and help him feed the horses.

He found her just finishing a call on her cell phone with a look of resignation.

"Who was that?" he asked, though he was fairly sure he knew the answer. He and Cindy were just about the only ones Addie ever talked to on the phone.

"Mom," she said, confirming his suspicion. "She said Grandma is doing better and Grandpa says he doesn't really need her help anymore. She decided to take me back tomorrow so I can finish the last week of school."

Why didn't she call him first to work out the details?

He was surrounded by frustrating women.

"That's too bad. I know you were looking forward to practicing for the show with Louisa."

Her face fell further. "I forgot about that!" she wailed. "If I don't go to practice, I don't know if I can be in the show."

"I'm sure we can talk to Celeste and Hope and get special permission for you to practice at home. You'll be here next weekend and the first part of next week so you'll be able to be at the last few practices."

"I hope they'll let me. I really, really, *really* wanted to be in the Christmas show."

"We'll work something out," he assured her, hoping he wasn't giving her unrealistic expectations. "Meanwhile, why don't you grab your coat and boots. Since you're so smart and already figured out the new horse is for Lou, do you want to meet her for real so you can tell me what you think?"

"Yes!" she exclaimed.

"You'll have to work hard to keep it a secret."

"I know. I would never ruin the surprise."

With that promise, his daughter raced for the mudroom and her winter gear and Chase leaned a hip against the kitchen island to wait for her and tried not to let his mind wander back to those moments in his pickup that were now permanently imprinted on his brain.

Chase headed up the porch steps of the Star N ranch house with a bag of chips in one hand and a bottle of his own homemade salsa in the other, the same thing he brought along to dinner nearly every Sunday.

The lights of the house were blazing a warm welcome against the cold and snowy Sunday evening but his instincts were still urging him to forget the whole thing and head back home, where he could glower and stomp around in private.

He was in a sour mood and had been since Cindy showed up three hours earlier than planned to pick up Addie, right as they were on their way out the door to go to their favorite lunch place.

It was always tough saying goodbye to his daughter. This parting seemed especially poignant, probably because Addie so clearly hadn't wanted to go. She had dragged her feet about packing up her things, had asked if they could wait to leave until after she and Chase had lunch, had begged to say goodbye to the horses.

Cindy, annoyed at the delays, had turned sharp-tongued and hard, which in turn made Addie more pouty than normal. Addie had finally gone out to her mother's new SUV with tears in her eyes that broke his heart.

Being a divorced father seriously sucked sometimes.

In his crazier moments, he thought about selling the ranch and moving to Boise to be closer to her, though he didn't know what the hell he would do for a living. Ranching was all he knew, all he had ever known. But he would do whatever it took—work in a shoe factory if he had to—if his daughter needed him.

He wasn't sure that was the answer, though. She loved her time here and seemed to relish ranch life, in a way Cindy never had.

With a sigh, he rang the doorbell, grimly aware that much of his sour mood had roots that had nothing to do with Cindy or Addie.

He had been restless and edgy since the last time he rang this doorbell, when he had shown up at this same ranch to pick up Faith for that disaster of a date two nights earlier.

How many mistakes could one man make in a single evening? Part of him wished he could go back and start the whole stupid week over again and just let his relationship with Faith naturally evolve from friendship to something more.

How long would that take, though? He had a feeling he could have given her five years—ten—and she would still have the same arguments.

Despite all his mistakes, he had to hope he hadn't

completely screwed up their friendship for good, that things weren't completely wrecked between them now.

As she had a few nights earlier, Aunt Mary was the one who finally answered the doorbell.

"It's about time," she said, planting hands on her hips. "Faith needs a man in the worst way."

He blinked at that, his imagination suddenly on fire. "O-kay."

Mary looked amused and he guessed she could tell immediately what detour his brain had taken.

"She needs your grilling skills," she informed him.

He told himself that wasn't disappointment coursing through him. "Grilling skills. Ah. You're grilling tonight."

"We *would* be, but Faith is having trouble again with that stupid gas grill. I swear that thing has it out for us."

He gestured behind him to the elements just beyond the porch. "You do know it's starting to snow, right?"

Aunt Mary shrugged. "You hardly notice out there, with the patio heater and that cover Flynn built us for the deck. Steaks sounded like a great idea at the time, better than roast or chicken tonight, but now the grill is being troublesome. Rafe and Hope aren't back yet from visiting Joey's mom, and Flynn had to fly out to California to finish a project there. That leaves Celeste, Faith and me. We could really use somebody with a little more testosterone to figure out what we're doing wrong."

"I'm not an expert on gas grills but I'll see what I can do."

"Thanks, honey."

He followed Mary inside, where they were greeted by delectable smells of roasting potatoes and yeasty rolls. No place on earth smelled better than this old ranch house on Sunday evenings.

"I've got to finish the salad. Go on ahead," Mary said.

He walked through the kitchen to the door that led to the covered deck. Faith didn't see him at first; she was too busy swearing and fiddling with the controls of the huge, fancy silver grill Travis had splurged on a few months before his death.

She was dressed in a fleece jacket, jeans and boots, with her hair loose and curling around her shoulders. His chest ached at the sight of her, like it always did. He wished, more than anything, that he had the right to go up behind her, brush her hair out of the way and kiss the back of that slender neck.

Little multicolored twinkly Christmas lights covered all the shrubs around the deck and had been draped around the edges of the roof. He didn't remember seeing Christmas lights back here and wondered if Hope had done it to make the rear of the house look more festive. It did look over The Christmas Ranch, after all.

Faith wasn't the biggest fan of Christmas, which he found quite ironic, considering she was part owner of the largest seasonal attraction in these parts.

She fiddled with the knobs again, then smacked the front of the grill. "Why won't you light, you stupid thing?"

"Yelling at it probably won't help much."

She whirled around at his comment and he watched as delectable color soaked her cheeks. "Chase! Oh, I'm so glad to see you!"

He was aware of a fierce, deep-seated need to have

her say those words because she wanted to see *him*, not because she had a problem for him to solve.

"Mary said you're having grill trouble."

"The darn thing won't ignite, no matter what I do. It's not getting propane, for some reason. I've been out here for ten minutes trying to figure it out. It's a brand-new tank that Flynn got for us a few weeks ago and we haven't used it since. I checked the propane tank. I tried dropping a match in case it was the ignition. I tried all the knobs about a thousand times. I just think this grill hates me."

He found it more than a little amusing that she had learned to drive every piece of complicated farm machinery on the place over the last two years and could round up a hundred head of cattle on her own, with only the dogs for help, but she was intimidated by a barbecue grill.

"This one can be finicky, that's for sure."

She frowned at the thing. "Travis had to buy the biggest, most expensive grill he could order—forget that the controls on it are more confusing than the space shuttle."

She didn't say disparaging things about her late husband very often. In this case, he had to agree with her. He had loved the guy, but she was absolutely right. Travis Dustin always had to have the best, even when they couldn't afford it. His poor management and expensive tastes in equipment—and his gross negligence in not leaving her with proper life insurance—had all contributed to the big financial hole he had left his family when he died.

"I'll take a look," he said.

She stepped aside and he knelt down to peer at the

connection. It only took him a moment to figure out why the grill wouldn't work.

"Here's your trouble. Looks like the gas hose isn't connected tightly. It's come loose from the tank."

He made the necessary adjustment, then stood, turned on the propane and hit the ignition. The grill ignited with a whoosh of instant heat.

She made a face. "Now I feel like an idiot. I swear I checked that already."

"It's easy to overlook."

"I guess my mind must have been on something else."

He had to wonder what. Was she remembering that kiss, too? He cast her a sidelong look and found a pink tinge on her cheeks again that might have been a blush—or just as easily might have been from the cold.

"Thank you for figuring it out," she said.

"No problem. You'll need to let the grill heat up for about ten minutes, then I can come back and take care of the steaks."

"Thank you. No matter how well I think I know my way around all the appliances in my kitchen, apparently this finicky grill remains my bugaboo. Or maybe it's outdoor cookery in general."

"I can't agree with that. I seem to remember some mean Dutch oven meals where you acted as camp cook when Trav and I would combine forces for roundup in the fall."

"That seems like a long time ago."

"Not that long. I still dream about your peach cobbler." Usually his dreams involved her kissing him between thick, gooey spoonfuls, but he decided it would probably be wise not to add that part.

Still, something of his thoughts must have appeared on his face because she seemed to catch her breath and gazed wide-eyed at him in the multicolored glow from the Christmas lights.

"I didn't know you liked it that much," she said after a moment, her voice a little husky. "Dutch oven cooking is easy compared to working this complicated grill. I'll be happy to make you a peach cobbler this summer, when the fruit is in season."

"Sounds delicious," he answered, his own voice a little more gruff than usual, which he told himself was because of the cold—though right now he was much warmer than he might have expected.

She swallowed hard and he was almost positive her gaze drifted to his mouth and then quickly away again. He *was* sure the color on her cheeks intensified, which had to be from more than the cold.

Was she remembering that kiss, too? He wanted to ask her—or better yet, to step forward and steal another one, but the door from the house opened and Louisa popped her head out.

"Hey, Chase! Where's Addie? Didn't she come with you?"

He took a subtle step back. "No. She went back to Boise with her mom this afternoon. Didn't she tell you?"

Her face fell. "Oh, no! Does that mean she won't be able to do the show with us? She thought she could! She and I and Olivia were going to sing a song together!"

"She still wants to. She'll have to miss the first few rehearsals, but she should be here next week for the actual show. We'll do our best to get her back here for rehearsal by Thursday. I might have to run into Boise to make it happen."

"Isn't that your day to help out at Jim Laird's place?"

Rats. He had forgotten all about that. "Yes. I'll figure out a way to swing it."

"I'll help," she said promptly. "I can either run to Boise for you or take your day at Jim's house. Either way, we will get Addie here."

His heart twisted a little that with everything she had to do here at the Star N, she would even consider driving six hours round-trip to pick up his daughter.

"Thank you, but I think I can manage both. If I take off as soon as I finish feeding my stock and his, I should be able to have Addie back in time for practice. It's important to her so I'll figure out a way to make it happen."

Both Faith and her daughter gave him matching warm looks that made him forget all about the snow just beyond their little covered patio.

"Thanks, Chase. You're the *best*," Lou said. Despite the cold, she padded out to the deck in her stocking feet and threw her arms around his waist. He smiled a little and hugged her back, thinking how much he loved both Louisa and her brother. They were great kids, always thinking of others. They were like their mother in that respect.

"Better head back inside. It's cold out here and you don't have shoes or a coat."

"I do have to go back in. I have to finish dessert. I made it myself. Aunt Mary hardly helped at all."

"I can't wait," he assured her.

She grinned and skipped back into the house, leaving him alone again with Faith. When he turned away from the doorway, he found her watching him with an expression he couldn't read.

"What did I say?" he asked.

"I… Nothing," she mumbled. "I'll go get the steaks."

She hurried past him before he could press her, leaving him standing alone in the cold.

Chapter 9

Faith couldn't leave the intimacy of the covered deck quickly enough.

She felt rattled and unsettled and she hated it. With a deep sense of longing, she remembered dinner just the previous Sunday, when they had laughed and joked and teased like always. He had stayed to watch a movie and she had thrown popcorn into his mouth and teased him about not shaving for a few days.

There had been none of this tension, this awareness that seemed to hiss and flare between them like that stupid grill coming to life.

She had wanted him to kiss her. It was all she could seem to think about, that wondrous feeling of being alive, desired.

Another few moments and she would have been the one to kiss him.

She forced herself to move away from the door and into the kitchen, where Aunt Mary looked up from the rolls she was pulling apart.

"Tell me Chase saved the day again."

"We're in business. It was all about the gas connection. I feel stupid I didn't look there first."

"Sometimes it takes an outside set of eyes to identify the problem and find the solution."

Could someone outside her particular situation help her figure out how to go back in time and fix what felt so very wrong between her and Chase?

"Where are the steaks?" she asked her aunt.

"Over there, by the microwave."

"Whoa," she exclaimed when she spotted them. "That's a lot of steak for just us."

"I took out a few extras in case we had company or so we could use the leftovers for fajitas one day this week. Good thing, because Rafe and Hope said they're only about fifteen minutes out. I'm sure glad they'll beat the worst of the snow. I feel a big storm coming on."

"The weather forecast said most of the storm will clip us."

"Weather forecasts can be wrong. Don't be surprised if we get hit with heavy winds, too."

She had learned not to doubt her great-aunt's intuition when it came to winter storms. After a lifetime of living in this particular corner of Idaho, Mary could read the weather like some people read stock reports.

Sure enough, the wind had already picked up a little when she carried the tray of steaks out to the covered deck. Chase stood near the propane heater, frowning as he checked something on his phone.

"Trouble?" she asked, nodding at the phone.

"Just Cindy," he answered, his voice terse.

"I'm sorry."

He made a face as he took the tray from her and used the tongs to transfer the steaks onto the grill.

"Nothing new," he said as the air filled with sizzle and scent. "Apparently Addie sulked all the way to Boise about having to go back when she was expecting to stay through the week with me and practice for the show with Olivia and Lou. Of course Cindy blames me. I shouldn't have gotten her hopes up, etc. etc.—even though *she* was the one who changed her mind from her original plan."

Faith wanted to smack the woman. Why did she have to be so difficult?

"Maybe you should petition again for primary custody."

He sighed. "She would never agree. I don't know if that would be the best thing for Addie anyway. Her mom and stepfather have given her a good life in Boise. I just wish she could be closer."

She decided not to tell him about her conversation with Addie the previous morning. What a difficult situation for everyone involved. Her heart ached and she wished, more than anything, that she could give him more time with his daughter for Christmas.

He was such a good man, kind and generous. He deserved to be happy—which was yet another reason she needed to help him find someone like Ella Baker.

That was what a true friend would do, help him find someone whose heart was whole and undamaged, who could cherish all the wonderful things about him.

Some of her emotions must have appeared on her features because he gave her an apologetic look. "Sorry. I didn't mean to bring you down."

She mustered a smile. "You didn't. What are friends for, if you can't complain about your ex once in a while?"

"I shouldn't complain about her at all. She's my child's mother and overall she takes excellent care of her. She loves her, too. I have to keep reminding myself of that." He shrugged. "I'm not going to worry about it more tonight. For now, let's just enjoy dinner. And speaking of which, I can handle the steaks from here, if you want to go back inside. That wind is really picking up."

"I was planning on grilling," she protested. "You should be the one to go inside. I can take over, as long as you've got the grill working."

"I don't mind."

"If you go inside now, I bet you could nab a hot roll from Aunt Mary."

"Tempting. But no." He wiggled the utensil in his hand. "I've got the tongs, which gives me all the power."

She gave him a mock glare. "Hand them over."

"Come get them, if you think you're worthy."

He held them over his head, which was way over *her* head.

Despite the cold wind, relief wrapped around her like a warm blanket. He was teasing her, just like normal and for a ridiculous moment, she wanted to weep.

Perhaps they *could* find an even footing, return to their easy, dependable friendship.

"Come on. Give," she demanded. She stretched on tiptoe but the tongs were still completely out of reach.

He grinned. "Is that the best you can do?"

Never one to back down from a challenge, she hopped up and her fingers managed to brush the tongs. So close! She tried again but she forgot the wooden planks of the deck were a bit slippery with cold and condensation. This time when she came down, one boot slid and she stumbled a little.

She might have fallen but before she could, his arms instantly came around her, tongs and all.

They froze that way, with his arms around her and her curves pressed against his hard chest. Their smiles both seemed to freeze and crack apart. Her gaze met his and all the heat and tension she had been carefully shoving down seemed to burst to the surface all over again. His mouth was *right there*. She only had to stand on tiptoe again and press her lips to his.

Yearning, wild and sweet, gushed through her and she was aware of the thick churn of her blood, a low flutter in her stomach.

She hitched in a breath and coiled her muscles to do just that when she heard the creak of the door hinges.

She froze for half a second, then quickly stepped away an instant before Rafe tromped out to the deck.

Her brother-in-law paused and gave them a long, considering look, eyebrows raised nearly to his hairline. He hesitated briefly before he moved farther onto the deck.

"You people are crazy. Don't you know December in Idaho isn't the time to be firing up the grill?"

Something was definitely fired up out here. The grill was only part of it. Her face felt hot, her skin itchy, and she could only hope she had moved away before Rafe saw anything—*not* that there had been anything to see.

"Steaks just don't taste the same when you try to cook them under the broiler," Chase said. "Though the purist in me would prefer to be cooking them over hot coals instead of a gas flame."

"You ever tried any of that specialty charcoal?" Rafe asked. "When I was stationed out of Hawaii, I tried the Ono coals they use for luaus. Man, that's some good stuff. Burns hot and gives a nice crisp crust."

"I'll have to try it," Chase said.

"I came to see if you needed help but it looks like you don't need me. You two appear to have things well in hand," he said.

Was his phrasing deliberate? Faith wondered, feeling her face heat even more.

"Doing our best," Chase replied blandly.

She decided it would be wise to take the chance to leave while she could. "Thanks for offering, Rafe. I actually have a few things I just remembered I have to do before dinner. It would great if you two could finish up out here."

She rushed into the house and tried to tell herself she was grateful for the narrow escape.

Chase took another taste of Aunt Mary's delicious mashed potatoes dripping with creamy, rich gravy, and listened to the conversation ebb and flow around him.

He loved listening to the interactions of Faith and her family. With no siblings of his own, he had always envied the close relationships among them all. They never seemed to run out of things to talk about, from current events to Celeste's recent visit to New York to the progress of Hope's pregnancy.

The conversation was lively, at times intense and heated, and never boring. The sisters might disagree with each other or Mary about a particular topic but they always did so with respect and affection.

It was obvious this was a family that loved each other. The girls' itinerant childhood—and especially the tragedy that had followed—seemed to have forged deep, lasting bonds between Faith and her sisters.

Sometimes they opened their circle to include others. Rafe and his nephew Joey. Flynn and Olivia. Chase.

He could lose this.

If this gamble he was taking—trying to force Faith to let things move to the next level between them—didn't pay off, he highly doubted whether Mary would continue to welcome him to these Sunday dinners he treasured.

Things very well might become irreparably broken between them. His jaw tightened. Some part of him wondered if he might be better off backing down and keeping the status quo, this friendship he treasured.

But then he would see Rafe touch Hope's hand as he made a point or watch Celeste's features soften when she talked about Flynn and he knew he couldn't let it ride. He wanted to have that with Faith. It was possible; he knew it was. That evening on the deck had only reinforced that she was attracted to him but was fighting it with everything she had.

They could be as happy as Rafe and Hope, Celeste and Flynn. Couldn't she see that?

He had told her he would give her time but even though it had only been a few days, he could feel his patience trickling away. He had waited so long already.

"Who's ready for dessert?" Louisa asked eagerly, as the meal was drawing to a close.

Barrett rolled his eyes. "I haven't even finished my steak. You're just in a hurry because you made it."

"So? I never made a whole cheesecake by myself before. Mom or Aunt Mary always helped me, but I made this one all by myself. I even made the crust."

"I saw it in the kitchen and it looks delicious," Chase assured her. "I can't wait to dig in."

She beamed at him and his heart gave a sharp little ache. This was another reason he didn't want to remain on the edge of Faith's life forever. Louisa and Barrett were amazing kids, despite everything they had been through. He wanted so much to be able to help Faith raise them into the good, kind people they were becoming.

He had no idea what he would do next if she was so afraid to take a chance on a relationship with him that she ended up pushing him out of all of their lives.

He would be lost without them.

He set his fork down, the last piece of delicious steak he had been chewing suddenly losing all its flavor.

He had to keep trying to make her see how good they could all be together, even when the risks of this all-or-nothing roll of the dice scared the hell out of him.

"Okay, do you want chocolate sauce or raspberry?" Lou asked.

He managed a smile. "How about a little of both?"

"Great idea," Mary said. "Think I'll have both, too."

Louisa went around the table taking orders like a server in a fancy restaurant, then she and Olivia headed for the kitchen. When Faith rose to go with them to help, Louisa made her sit back down.

"We can do it," she insisted.

The girls left just as another gust of wind rattled

the windows and howled beneath the eaves of the old house. The electricity flickered but didn't go out and he couldn't help thinking how cozy it was in here.

They talked about the record-breaking crowd at The Christmas Ranch that weekend until the girls came back with a tray loaded with slices of cheesecake. They were cut a little crooked and the presentation was a bit messy but nobody seemed to mind.

"This is delicious. The best cheesecake I think I've ever had," Chase said after his first bite, which earned him a huge grin from Louisa.

"It is really excellent," Celeste said. "And I've had cheesecake in New York City, where they know cheesecake."

Louisa couldn't have looked happier. "Thanks. I'm going to try an apple pie next week."

He couldn't resist darting a glance at Faith and wondered if he would ever be able to eat apple pie again without remembering the cinnamon-sugar taste of her mouth.

She licked her lips, then caught his eyes and her cheeks turned an instant pink that made him suddenly certain she was thinking about the kiss, too.

"That wind is sure blowing up a storm," Rafe commented.

"The last update I heard on the weather said we're supposed to have another half foot of snow before morning," Hope said.

"Yay!" all of the children exclaimed together.

"Maybe we won't have school," Joey said with an unmistakably hopeful note in his voice.

"Yeah!" Barrett exclaimed. "That would be awesome!"

"I wouldn't plan on it," Mary said. "I hate to be a downer but I've lived here most of my life and can tell you they hardly ever close school on account of snow. As long as the buses can run, you'll have school."

"It really depends on the timing of the storm and the kind of snowdrifts it leaves behind," Chase said, not wanting the kids to completely give up hope. "If it's early in the morning before the plows can make it around, you might be in luck."

"We should probably head home before the worst of it hits," Rafe said.

"Same here," Celeste said. "I'm so glad Flynn put new storm windows in that old house this summer."

Flynn had spent six months renovating and adding on to his late grandmother's old house down the road, a project which had been done just days before their wedding in August.

Chase remembered that lovely ceremony on the banks of the Cold Creek, when the two of them—so very perfect for each other—had both glowed with happiness.

Watching them together had only reinforced his determination to forge his own happy ending with Faith, no matter what it took. He had spent the past few months touching her more in their regular interactions, teasing her, trying anything he could think of to convince her to think of him as more than just her friend and confidant.

Right now he felt further from that goal than ever.

Sometimes their Sunday evening dinners would stretch long into the night when they would watch a movie or play games at the kitchen table, but with the storm, everyone seemed in a hurry to leave. They stayed only long enough to clean up the kitchen and then only he, Mary, Faith and her children were left.

"How's the homework situation?" Faith asked from her spot at the kitchen sink drying dishes, a general question aimed at both of her children.

"I had a math work sheet but I finished it on the bus on the way home from school Friday," Louisa said. Chase wasn't really surprised. She was a conscientious student who rarely left schoolwork until Sunday evening.

"How about you, Barrett?"

"I'm almost done. I just had a few problems in math and they're *hard*. I can ask my teacher tomorrow. We might not even have school anyway so maybe I won't have to turn them in until Tuesday."

"Let's take a look at them," Chase said.

Barrett groaned a little but went to his room for his backpack.

"You don't have to do that," Faith said.

"I don't mind," he assured her.

They sat together at the desk in the great room while the Christmas lights glowed on the tree and a fire flickered in the fireplace. It wasn't a bad way to spend a Sunday night.

After only three or four problems, a lightbulb seemed to switch on in the boy's head—as it usually did.

"Oh! I get it now. That's easy."

"I told you it was."

"It wasn't easy the way my teacher explained it. Why can't you be my teacher?"

He tried not to shudder at the suggestion. "I'm afraid I've already got a job."

"And you're good at it," Mary offered from the chair where she sat knitting.

"Thanks, Mary. I do my best," he answered humbly. He loved being a rancher and wanted to think he was a responsible one.

Now that the boy seemed to be in the groove with his homework, Chase lifted his head from the book and suddenly spotted Faith in the mudroom, putting on her winter gear. He had been so busy helping Barrett, he hadn't noticed.

"Where are you off to? Not out into that wind, I hope."

"I just need to make sure the tarp over the outside haystack is secure. Oh, and check on Rosie," she said, referring to one of her border collies. "She was acting strangely this morning, which makes me think she might be close to having her puppies. I've been trying to keep her in the barn but she wanders off. Before the storm front moves in, I want to be sure she's warm and safe."

Chase scraped his chair back. "I'll come with you."

"You don't need to. You just spent a half hour working on Barrett's homework. I'm sure you've got things to worry about at your place."

He couldn't think of anything. He generally tried to keep things in good order, addressing problems when they came up. He always figured he couldn't go wrong following his father's favorite adage: an ounce of prevention was worth a pound of cure. Better to stop trouble before it could start.

"I'll help," he said. "I'll check the hay cover while you focus on Rosie."

Her mouth tightened for an instant but she finally

nodded and waited while he threw his coat on, then together they walked out into the storm.

Darkness came early this time of year near the winter solstice but a few high-wattage electric lights on poles lit their way. The wind howled viciously already and puffed out random snowflakes at them, hard as sharp pebbles.

Below the ranch house, he could see that the parking lot of The Christmas Ranch—which had been full when he pulled up—was mostly cleared out now, with a horse-drawn sleigh on what was probably its last go-round of the evening making its way back to the barn near the lodge.

He would really like to find time before Christmas to take Addie on a ride, along with Faith and her children.

The Saint Nicholas Lodge glowed cheerily against the cold night. Beyond it, the cluster of small structures that made up the life-size Christmas village—complete with indoor animatronic scenes of elves hammering and Santa eating from a plate of cookies—looked like something from a Christmas card.

Her family had created a celebration of the holidays here, unlike anything else in the region. People came from miles around, eager to enhance their holiday spirit.

"It's nice that Hope has hired enough staff now that she doesn't have to do everything on her own," he said.

"With the baby coming, Rafe insisted she cut back her hours. No more fourteen-hour days, seven days a week from Thanksgiving to New Year's."

Those hours were probably not unlike what Faith did year-round on the Star N—at least during calving and haying season and roundup. In other words, most of the year.

She worked so hard and never complained about the burden that had fallen onto her shoulders after Travis died.

When they reached the haystack, tucked beneath a huge open-sided structure with a metal roof, he heard the problem before he saw it, the thwack of a loose tarp cover flapping in the wind. Each time the wind dug underneath the tarp, it pulled it loose a little further. If they didn't tie it down, it would eventually pull the whole thing loose and she would not only lose an expensive tarp but potentially the whole haystack to the storm.

"That's gotten a lot worse, just in the last few hours," she said, pitching her voice louder to be heard over the wind. "I should have taken time to fix it earlier when I first spotted the problem, but I was doing about a hundred other things at the time. I was going to fix it in the morning, but I didn't take into account the storm."

"It's fine," he said. "We'll have it safe and secure in no time. It might take both of us, though—one to hold the flap down and hold the flashlight while the other ties it."

They went to work together, as they had done a hundred times before. He wrestled the tarp down, which wasn't easy amid the increasing wind, then held it while she tied multiple knots to keep it in place.

"That should do it," she said.

"While we're out here, let's tighten the other corners," he suggested.

When he was satisfied the tarp was secure—and when the bite of the wind was close to becoming uncomfortable—he tightened the last knot.

"Thanks, Chase," she said.

"No problem. Let's go see if Rosie is smart enough to stay in from the cold."

She clutched at her hat to keep the wind from tugging it away and they made their way into the relative warmth and safety of her large, clean barn.

The wind still howled outside but it was muted, more like a low, angry buzz, making the barn feel like a refuge.

"That wind has to be thirty or forty miles an hour," she said, shaking her head as she turned on the lights inside the barn.

"At least this storm isn't supposed to bring bitter cold along with it," he said. "Where's Rosie?"

"I set her up in the back stall but who knows if she decided to stay put? I really hope she's not out in that wind somewhere."

Apparently the dog knew this cozy spot was best for her and her pups. They found her lying on her side on an old horse blanket with five brand-new white-and-black puppies nuzzling at her.

"Oh. Will you look at that?" Faith breathed. Her eyes looked bright and happy in the fluorescent barn lights. "Hi there, Rosie. Look at you! What a good girl. Five babies. Good job, little mama!"

She leaned on the top railing of the stall and he joined her. "The kids will be excited," he observed.

"Are you kidding? *Excited* is an understatement. Puppies for Christmas. They'll be thrilled. If I let her, Louisa probably would be down here in a minute and want to spend the night right there in the straw with Rosie."

The dog flapped her tail at the sound of her name and they watched for a moment before he noticed her water bowl was getting low. He slipped inside the stall and picked up the food and the water bowls and filled them each before returning them to the cozy little pen.

For his trouble, he earned another tail wag from Rosie and a smile from Faith.

"Thank you. Do you think they'll be warm enough out here? I can take them into the house."

"They should be okay. She might not appreciate being moved now. They're warm enough in here and they're out of the wind. If you're really worried about it, I can bring over a warming lamp."

"That's a good idea, at least for the first few days. I've got one here. I should have thought of that."

She headed to another corner of the barn and returned a moment later with the large lamp and they spent a few moments hanging it from the top beam of the stall.

"Perfect. That should do the trick."

While the wind howled outside, they stood for a while watching the dog and her pups beneath the glow of the heat lamp. He wasn't in a big hurry to leave this quiet little scene and he sensed Faith wasn't either.

"Seems like just a minute ago that she was a pup herself," she said in a soft voice. "I guess it's been a while, though. Three years. She was in the last litter we had out of Lillybelle, so she would have been born just a few months before Travis…"

Her voice broke off and she gazed down at the puppies with her mouth trembling a little.

"Life rolls on," he said quietly.

"Like it or not, I guess," she answered after a moment. "Thanks for your help tonight, first with Barrett's homework and then with storm preparation. You're too good to us."

"You know I'm always happy to help."

"You shouldn't be," she whispered.

He frowned. "Shouldn't be what?"

She kept her attention fixed on the wriggling puppies. "Celeste gave me a lecture the other night. She told me I'm not being fair to you. She said I take you for granted."

"We're friends. Friends help each other. You feed me every Sunday and usually more often than that. Addie practically lives over here when I have visitation and also ranch work I can't avoid. And you bought my groceries the other day, right?"

"Don't forget to take them home when you go." She released a heavy sigh. "We both know the ledger will never be balanced, no matter how many groceries I buy for you. The Star N wouldn't have survived without you. I don't know why you are so generous with your time and energy on our behalf but I hope you know how very grateful we are. How very grateful *I* am. Thank you. And I hope you know how…how much we all love you."

He looked down at her, wondering at the murky subtext he couldn't quite read here.

"I'm happy to help out," he answered again.

She swallowed hard, avoiding his gaze. "I guess what I wanted to tell you is that things are better now. The Star N is back in the black, thanks in large part to you and to The Christmas Ranch finally being self-sustaining. I'll never been an expert at ranching but I kind of feel like I know a little more what I'm doing now. If you…want to ease away a bit so you can focus more on your own ranch, I would completely understand. Don't worry. We'll be fine."

It took about two seconds for him to go from confusion to being seriously annoyed.

"So you're basically telling me you don't want me hanging around anymore."

She looked instantly horrified. "No! That's not what I'm saying at all. I just…don't want you to feel obligated to do as much as you have for us. For me. I needed help and would have been lost without you the last two years but you can't prop us up forever. At some point, I have to stand on my own."

"Would you be saying this if I hadn't kissed you the other night?"

Her eyes widened and she looked startled that he had brought the kiss up when they both had been so carefully avoiding the subject.

Finally she sighed. "I don't know," she said, her voice low again and her gaze fixed on the five little border collie puppies. "It feels like everything has changed."

She sounded so miserable, he wanted to pull her into his arms and tell her he was sorry, that he would do his best to make sure things returned to the way they were a week ago.

"Life has a way of doing that, whether we always like it or not," he said, knowing full well he wouldn't go back, even if he could. "Nobody escapes it. The trick is figuring out how to roll with the changes."

She was silent for a long time and he would have given anything to know what she was thinking.

When she spoke, her voice was low. "I can't stop thinking about that kiss."

Chapter 10

At first he wasn't sure he heard her correctly or if his own subconscious had conjured the words out of nowhere.

But then he looked at her and her eyes were solemn, intense and more than a little nervous.

He swallowed hard. "Same here. It's all I could think about during dinner. I would like, more than anything, to kiss you again."

She opened her mouth as if she wanted to object. He waited for it, bracing himself for yet one more disappointment. To his utter shock, she took a step forward instead, placed her hands against his chest and lifted her face in clear invitation.

He didn't hesitate for an instant. How could he? He wasn't a stupid man. He framed her face with his hands, then lowered his mouth, brushing against hers once, twice. Her mouth was cool, her lips trembling, and she tasted of raspberry and chocolate from Louisa's cheesecake—rich, heady. Irresistible.

At first she seemed nervous, unsure, but after only a moment, her hands slid around his neck and she pressed against him, surrendering to the heat swirling between them.

He was awash in tenderness, completely enamored with the courageous woman in his arms.

Optimism bubbled up inside him, a tiny trickle at first, then growing stronger as she sighed against his mouth and returned his kiss with a renewed enthusiasm that took his breath away. For the first time in days, he began to think that maybe, just maybe, she was beginning to see that this was real, that they were perfect together.

They kissed for several delicious moments, until his breathing was ragged and he wanted nothing more than to find a soft pile of straw somewhere, lower her down and show her exactly how amazing things could be between them.

A particularly fierce gust of wind rattled the windows of the barn, distracting him enough to realize a cold, drafty barn that smelled of animals and hay might not be the most romantic of spots.

With supreme effort, he forced his mouth to slide away from hers, pressing his forehead to hers and giving them both a chance to collect their breath and their thoughts.

Her eyes were dazed, aroused. "I feel like I've been asleep for nearly three years and now… I'm not," she admitted.

He pressed a soft kiss on her mouth again. "Welcome back."

She smiled a little but it slid away too soon, replaced by an anxious expression, and she took another step away. He wanted to tug her back into his arms but he knew he couldn't kiss her into accepting the possibilities between them, as tempting as he found that idea.

"I'm afraid," she admitted.

His growing optimism cooled like the air that rushed between them. "Of what? I hope you know I would rather stab myself in the foot with a pitchfork than ever hurt you."

"Maybe I don't want to hurt *you*," she whispered, her features distressed. "You're the best man I know, Chase. When I think about…about not having you in my life, I feel like I'm going to throw up. But I'm not sure I'm ready for this again—or that I ever will be."

Well. That was honest enough. He had to respect it, even if he didn't like it. It took him a moment to grab his scrambled thoughts and formulate them into something he hoped came out coherently.

"That's a decision you'll have to make," he said, choosing his words with care. "But think about those puppies. We can keep them here under that heat lamp forever where it's safe and warm and dry. That's the best place for them right now, I agree, while they're tiny and vulnerable. But they won't always be the way they are right now, and what kind of existence would those puppies have if they could never really have the chance to experience the world? They're meant to run across fields and chase birds and lie stretched out in the summer sunshine. To live."

She let out a breath. "You're comparing me to those puppies."

"I'm only saying I understand you've suffered a terrible loss. I know how hard you've fought to work through the grief. It's only natural to want to protect yourself, to be afraid of moving out of the safe place you've created for yourself out of that grief."

"Terrified," she admitted.

His heart ached for her and the struggle he had forced on her. He wanted to reach for her hands but didn't trust himself to touch her right now. "I can tell you this, Faith. You have too much love inside you to spend the rest of your life hiding inside that safe haven while the world moves on without you."

Her gaze narrowed. "That's easy for you to say. You never lost someone you loved with all your heart."

He wanted to tell her he *had*, only in a different way. He had lost her over and over again—though could a guy really lose what he'd never had?

"You're right. I can only imagine," he lied.

As tempting as it was to tell her everything in his heart—that he had loved her since that afternoon he took her shopping for Aunt Mary—he didn't dare. Not yet. Something told him that would send her running away even faster.

She would have to be the one to make the decision about whether she was ready to open her heart again.

The storm rattled the window again, fierce and demanding, and she shivered suddenly, though he couldn't tell if it was from the cold or from the emotional winds battering them. Either way, he didn't want her to suffer.

"Let's get you back to the house. Mary will be wondering where we are."

She nodded. After one more check of the puppies, she tugged her gloves back on and headed out into the night.

Faith was fiercely aware of him as they walked from the barn to the ranch house with the wind and snow howling around them.

She felt as if all the progress she had made toward rebuilding her world had been tossed out into this storm. She had been so proud of herself these last few months. The kids were doing well, the ranch was prospering, she had finally developed a new routine and had begun to be more confident in what she was doing.

While she wouldn't say she had been particularly happy, at least she had found some kind of acceptance with her new role as a widow. She was more comfortable in her own skin.

Now she felt as if everything had changed again. Once more she was confused, off balance, not sure how to put one more step in front of the other and forge a new path.

She didn't like it.

Even in the midst of her turmoil, she couldn't miss the way he placed his body in the path of the wind to protect her from the worst of it. That was so much like Chase, always looking out for her. It warmed her heart, even as it made her ache.

"You still need your groceries," she said when they reached the house. "Come in and I'll grab them."

He looked as if he had something more to say but he finally nodded and followed her inside.

Though she could hear the television playing down the hall in the den, the kitchen was dark and empty.

A clean, vacant kitchen on Sunday night after the big family party always left her feeling a little bereft, for some strange reason.

She flipped on the light and discovered a brown paper bag on the counter with his name on it. She couldn't resist peeking inside and discovered it contained a half dozen of the dinner rolls. Knowing Aunt Mary and her habits, she pulled open the refrigerator and found another bag with his name on it.

"It looks like Mary saved some leftovers for you."

"Excellent. It will be nice not having to worry about dinner tomorrow."

She knew he rarely cooked when Addie was with her mother, subsisting on frozen meals, sandwiches and the occasional steaks he grilled in a batch. Mary knew it, too, which might be another reason she invited him over so often.

Faith headed to the walk-in pantry where she had left the things she bought at the store for him.

"Here you go. Dishwashing detergent, dish soap and paper towels."

"That should do it. Thanks for picking them up for me."

"It was no trouble at all."

"I'll check in with you first thing in the morning to see if you had any storm damage."

If she were stronger, she would tell him thank you but it wasn't necessary. At some point in a woman's life, she had to figure out how to clean up her own messes. Instead, she did her best to muster a smile. "Be careful driving home."

He nodded. Still looking as if he had something more to say, he headed for the door. He put a hand on the knob but before he could turn it, he whirled back around, stalked over to her and kissed her hard with a ferocity and intensity that made her knees so weak she had to clutch at his coat to keep from falling.

She could only be grateful none of her family members came into the kitchen just then and stumbled over them.

When he pulled away, a muscle in his jaw worked but he only looked at her out of solemn, intense eyes.

"Good night," he said.

She didn't have the breath to speak, even if she trusted herself to say anything, so she only nodded.

The moment he left, she pulled her ranch coat off with slow, painstaking effort, hung it in the mudroom, then sank down into a kitchen chair, fighting the urge to bury her face in her hands and weep.

She felt like the world's biggest idiot.

She knew she relied on him, that he had become her rock and the core of her support system since Travis died. He made her laugh and think, he challenged her, he praised her when things went well and held her when they didn't.

All this time, when she considered him her dearest friend, some part of her already knew the feelings she had for him ran deeper than that.

She felt so stupid that it had taken her this long to figure it out. She had always known she loved him, just as she had told him earlier.

She had just never realized she was also *in love* with him.

How had it happened? How could she have *let* it happen?

She should have known something had shifted over

the last few months when she started anticipating the times she knew she would see him with a new sort of intensity, when she became more aware of the way other women looked at him when they were together, as she started noticing a ripple of muscle, the solid strength of him as he did some ordinary task in the barn.

She should have realized, but it all just seemed so... natural.

She was still sitting there trying to come to terms with the shock when Mary came into the kitchen wearing her favorite flannel nightgown over long underwear and thick socks.

"Did Chase take off? I had leftovers for him."

She summoned a smile that felt a little wobbly at the edges. "He took them. Don't worry."

"Oh, you know me. Worrying is what I do best." Mary looked out the window where the snow lashed in hard pellets. "I'll tell you, I don't like him driving into the teeth of that nasty wind. All it would take would be one tree limb to fall on his pickup truck."

Her heart clutched at the unbearable thought.

This. This was why she couldn't let herself love him. She would not survive losing a man she loved a second time.

She pushed the grim fear away, choosing instead to focus on something positive.

"Rosie had her puppies. Five of them."

"Is that right?" Mary looked pleased.

"They're adorable. I'm sure the kids will want to see them first thing."

"I made them take their showers for the night. Barrett isn't very happy with me right now but I'm sure he'll get over it. They're both in their rooms, reading."

She would go read to them in a moment. It was her favorite part of the day, those quiet moments when she could cuddle her children and explore literary worlds with them. "Thank you," she said to her aunt. "I don't tell you enough how much I appreciate your help."

Mary sat down across from her at the table. "Are you okay? You seem upset."

For a moment, she desperately wanted to confide in her beloved great-aunt, who was just about the wisest person she knew. The words wouldn't come, though. Mary wouldn't be an unbiased observer in this particular case as Mary adored Chase and always had.

"I'm just feeling a little down tonight."

Mary took Faith's hands in her own wrinkled, age-spotted ones. "I get that way sometimes. The holidays sure make me feel alone."

A hard nugget of guilt lodged in her chest. She wasn't the only one in the world who had ever suffered heartache. Uncle Claude had died five years earlier and they all still missed him desperately.

"You're not alone," she told her aunt. "You've got us, as long as you want us."

"I know that, my dear, and I can't tell you how grateful I am for that." Mary squeezed her fingers. "It's not quite the same. I miss my Claude."

She thought of her big, burly, white-haired great-uncle, who had adored Christmas so much that he had started The Christmas Ranch with one small herd of reindeer to share his love of the holiday with the community.

"I'm thinking about dating again," Mary announced. "What do you think?"

She blinked at that completely unexpected piece of information. "Really?"

"Why not? Your uncle's been gone for years and I'm not getting any younger."

"I… No. You're not. I think it's great. Really great."

Her aunt made a face. "I don't know about *great*. More like a necessary evil. I'd like to get married again, have a companion in my old age, and unfortunately you usually have to go through the motions and go on a few dates first in order to get there."

Her seventy-year-old great-aunt was braver than she was. It was another humbling realization. "Do you have someone in mind?"

Her aunt shrugged. "A couple of widowers at the senior citizens center have asked me out. They're nice enough, but I was thinking about asking Pat Walters out to dinner."

She tried not to visibly react to yet another stunner. For years, Pat had been one of the men who played Santa Claus at The Christmas Ranch. His wife had died just a few months after Uncle Claude.

She digested the information and the odd *rightness* of the idea.

"You absolutely should," she finally said. "He's a great guy."

"He is. Truth is, we went out a few times three years ago when I was living in town and we had a lot of fun together. I didn't tell you girls because it was early days yet and there was nothing much to tell."

She shrugged her ample shoulders. "But then Travis died and I moved back in here to help you with the kids. I just didn't feel like the time was right to complicate things so Pat and I put things on the back burner for a while."

Oh, the guilt. The nugget turned into a full-on boulder. Had she really been so wrapped up in her own pain that she hadn't noticed a romance simmering right under her nose?

What else had she missed?

"I wish you had told me," she said. "I hate that you put your life on hold for me. I would have been okay. Celeste was here to help me out in the evenings and I could have hired someone to help me with Lou and Barrett when I was busy on the ranch and couldn't take them with me."

Mary frowned. "I didn't tell you about Pat to make you feel guilty. You didn't force me to move in after Travis died. You didn't even *ask* me. I did it because I needed to, because that's what family does for each other."

Mary and Claude had been helping her and her sisters for eighteen years, since they had been three traumatized, frightened, grieving girls.

Her aunt, with her quiet strength, support and wisdom, had been a lifesaver to her after her parents died and even more of one after Travis died.

"I can never repay you for everything you've done," she said, her throat tight and the hot burn of tears behind her eyes.

Mary sat back in her chair and skewered her with a stern look. "Is that what you think I want? For you to repay me?"

"Of course! I wish I could."

"Well, you're right. I do."

She blinked. "Okay."

"You can do that by showing me I taught you a thing or two over the years about surviving and thriving, even when the going is tough."

She stared at her aunt, wondering where this was coming from. "I... What do you mean?"

"Life isn't meant to be lived in fear, honey," Mary said.

It was so similar to her recent conversation with Chase that she had to swallow. "I know."

"Do you?" Mary pressed. "I'm just saying. Chase won't wait around for you forever, you know."

Faith pulled her hands from her aunt's and curled them into fists on her lap. "I don't know what you mean."

Mary snorted. "Of the three of you, you were always the worst liar. You know exactly what I mean. That boy is in love with you and has been forever."

She felt hot and then ice-cold. First Celeste, now Aunt Mary. What had they seen that she had missed all this time?

She wanted to protest but even in her head, any counterargument she tried to formulate sounded stupid and trite. Was it true? Had he been in love with her and had she been so preoccupied with life that she hadn't realized?

Or worse, much worse, had she realized it on some subconscious level and simply taken it for granted all this time?

"Chase is my best friend, Mary. He's been like a father to the kids since Travis died. And you and I both know we would have had to sell the ranch if he hadn't helped me pull it back from the brink."

Her aunt gave her a hard look. "Seems to me there

are worse things to base a relationship on. Not to mention, he's one good-looking son of a gun."

She couldn't deny that. And he kissed like a dream.

"I'm so scared," she whispered.

Mary made that snorting noise again. "Who isn't, honey? If you're not scared sometimes, you're just plain stupid. The trick is to decide how much of your life you're willing to sacrifice for those fears."

Before she could come up with an answer, her aunt rose. "I'm going to turn in and you've got kids waiting for you to read to them."

She rose, as well. "Thank you, Mary."

She didn't know if she was thanking her for the advice or the last eighteen years of wisdom. She supposed it didn't really matter.

Her aunt hugged her. "Don't worry. You'll figure it out. Good night, honey. Sleep well."

She would have laughed if she thought she could pull it off without sounding hysterical.

Something told her more than the wind would be keeping her up that night.

She didn't see Chase at all the next week. Maybe he was only giving her space, as she had asked, or maybe he was as busy at his place as she was at the Star N, trying to finish up random jobs before the holidays.

Or maybe he was finally fed up with her cowardice and indecision.

Though she didn't see him, she did talk to him on the phone twice.

He called her once on Monday morning, the day after the storm and that stunning kiss in the barn, to make sure her ranch hadn't sustained significant damage from the winds and snows.

On Thursday afternoon, he called to tell her he was driving to Boise to pick up Addie a day earlier than planned and asked if she needed him to bring anything back from Boise for the kids' stockings.

He had sounded distant and frazzled. She knew how tough it was for him to be separated from Addie over the holidays, which made his thoughtfulness in worrying about Louisa and Barrett even more touching.

Again, she wanted to smack Cindy for her selfishness in booking a cruise over the holidays without consulting him.

He could have withheld permission and the court would have sided with him. After Cindy sprang the news on him, though, he had told Faith he hadn't wanted to drag Addie into a war between her parents.

As a result, he was planning their own Christmas celebration a few days before the actual holiday, complete with Christmas Eve dinner, presents and all.

"I think we're covered," she told him, her heart aching. "Be careful driving back. Oh, and let Addie know she's still on to sing with Louisa and Olivia. Ella is planning on it."

"I'll tell her. She'll be thrilled. Thanks."

She wanted to tell him so many other things. That she hadn't stopped thinking about him. That their kisses seemed to play through her head on an endless loop. That she just needed a little more time. She couldn't find the courage to say any of it so he ended up telling her goodbye rather abruptly and severing the connection.

There had been times when they stayed on the phone

the entire time he drove to Boise to pick up his daughter, never running out of things to talk about.

Were those days gone forever?

She sighed now and headed toward Saint Nicholas Lodge with a couple of letters that had been delivered to the main house by accident, probably because the post office had temporary help handling the holiday mail volume.

Though she waved at the longtime clerk at the gift store, she didn't stop to chat, heading straight for the office instead, where she found Hope sitting behind her desk.

"Mail delivery," Faith announced, setting the letters on the desk. "It looks like a bill for reindeer food and one for candy canes. I might have a tough time convincing my accountant those are legitimate expenses for a cattle ranch."

When Hope didn't reply, Faith's gaze sharpened on her sister. Fear suddenly clutched her when she registered her sister's pale features, her pinched mouth, the haunted eyes. "What is it, honey? What's wrong?"

"Oh, Faith. I… I was just about to call you."

Her sister's last word ended in a sob that she tried to hide but Faith wasn't fooled. She also suddenly realized her sister's arms were crossed protectively across her abdomen.

"What's wrong? Is it the baby?"

Hope nodded, tears dripping down the corners of her eyes. "I've been having crampy aches all day and I… I just don't feel good. I was just in the bathroom and…had some spotting. Oh, Faith. I'm afraid I'm losing the baby."

She burst into tears and Faith instantly went to her

side and wrapped her arms around her. Her younger sister was normally so controlled in any crisis. Even when they had been kidnapped, Hope had been calm and cool.

Seeing her lose it like this broke Faith's heart in two.

"What do you need me to do? I can call Rafe. I can run you into the doctor's. Whatever you need."

"I just called Rafe." Hope wiped at her eyes, though she continued to weep. "He's on his way and we're running into Jake Dalton's office. It might be nothing. I might be overreacting. I hope so."

"I do, too." She whispered a prayer that her sister could endure whatever outcome.

She wouldn't let herself focus on the worst, thinking instead about what a wonderful mother Hope would be. She was made for it. She loved children and had spent much of her adult life following their parents' examples and trying to help those in need around the world in her own way.

Really, coming home and running The Christmas Ranch had been one more way Hope wanted to help people, by giving them a little bit of holiday spirit in a frazzled word.

"It's the worst possible time," Hope said, her eyes distressed. "Within the hour, I've got forty kids showing up to practice for the play."

"That is absolutely the least of your concerns," Faith said, going into big sister mode. "I forbid you to worry about a single thing at The Christmas Ranch. You've got an excellent staff, not to mention a family ready to step in and cover whatever else you might need. Focus on yourself and on the baby. That's an order."

Hope managed a wobbly smile that did nothing to conceal the fear beneath it. "You're always so bossy."

"That's right." She squeezed her sister's fingers. "And right now I'm ordering you to lie down and wait for your husband, this instant."

Hope went to the low sofa in the office and complied. While she rested, Faith found her sister's coat and her voluminous tote bag and carried them both to her, then sat holding her hand for a few more moments, until Rafe arrived.

He looked as pale as his wife and hugged her tightly, green eyes murky with worry. "Whatever happens, we'll be okay," he assured her.

It took all her strength not to sob at the gentleness of the big, tough former navy SEAL as he all but carried Hope out to his SUV and settled her into the passenger side. Faith handed her the tote bag she had carried along.

"Call me the minute you know anything," she ordered.

"I will. I promise. Faith, can you stay during rehearsals to make sure Ella has everything she needs?"

"Of course."

"Don't tell Barrett and Lou yet. I don't want them to worry."

"Nothing to tell," she said. "Because you and that baby are going to be absolutely fine."

If she kept saying that, perhaps she could make it true.

She watched them drive away, shivering a little until she realized she had left her own coat in Hope's office. Before she could go inside for it, she spotted Chase's familiar pickup truck.

How did he always know when she needed him? she wondered, then realized he must be dropping Addie off for rehearsal.

She didn't care why he had come. Only that he was there.

She moved across the parking lot without even thinking it through. Desperate for the strength and comfort of his embrace, she barely gave him time to climb out of his vehicle before she was at his side, wrapping her arms tightly around him.

She saw shock and concern flash in his eyes for just an instant before he held her tight against him. "What's going on? What's wrong?" he asked, his voice urgent.

Addie was with him, Faith realized with some dismay. She couldn't burst into tears, not without the girl wondering about it and then telling Lou and Barrett, contrary to Hope's wishes.

"It's Hope," she whispered in his ear. "She's threatening a miscarriage."

He growled a curse that made Addie blink.

"It's too early to know for sure yet," Faith said quietly. "Rafe just took her to the doctor."

"What can I do?"

It was so like him to want to fix everything. The thought would have made her smile if she weren't so very worried. "I don't think we can do anything yet. Just hope and pray she and the baby will both be okay."

"Will she need extra help here at The Christmas Ranch? I can cover you at the Star N if you need to step in here until the New Year."

Oh, the dear man. He was already doing extra work for their neighbor and now he wanted to add Faith's workload to his pile, as well.

"I hope I don't have to take you up on that but it's too early to say right now."

"Keep me posted."

"I will. I… Thank you, Chase."

"You're welcome."

She would have said more but other children started to arrive and the moment was gone.

Chapter 11

Chase ended up staying to watch the rehearsal, figuring he could help corral kids if need be.

He had plenty of other things he should be doing but nothing else seemed as important as being here if Faith or her family needed him.

A few minutes after the rehearsal started, Celeste showed up. She went immediately to the office, where Faith was staring into space. The two of them embraced, both wiping tears. Not long after, Mary showed up, too, and the three of them sat together, not saying much.

He wanted to go in there but didn't quite feel it was his place so he stayed where he was and watched the children sing about Silver Bells and Holly Jolly Christmases and Silent Nights.

About an hour into rehearsal—when he felt more antsy than he ever remembered—Faith took a call on her cell phone. The anxiety and fear on her features cut through him and he couldn't resist rising to his feet and going to the doorway.

"Are they sure? Yes. Yes. I understand." Her features softened and she gave a tremulous smile. "That's the best news, Rafe. The absolute best. Thank you for calling. I'll tell them. Yes. Give her all our love and tell her to take care of herself and not to worry about a thing. That's an order. Same goes for you. We love you, too, you know."

She hung up, her smile incandescent, then she gave a little cry that ended on a sob. "Dr. Dalton says for now everything seems okay with the baby. The heartbeat is strong and all indications are good for a healthy pregnancy."

"Oh, thank the Lord," Mary exclaimed.

She nodded and they all spent a silent moment doing just that.

"Jake wants to put her on strict bed rest for the next few weeks to be safe," Faith said after a moment. "That means the rest of us will have to step up here."

"I'm available for whatever you need," Chase offered once more.

She gave him a distracted smile. "I know but, again, you have plenty to do at your own place. We can handle it."

"I want to help." He tried to tamp down his annoyance that she was immediately pushing aside his help.

"We actually could use him tomorrow," Celeste said thoughtfully.

Faith didn't look convinced. "We'll just have to cancel that part of the party, under the circumstances. The kids will have to understand."

"They're kids," her sister pointed out. "They won't understand anything but disappointment."

"I'll just do it, then," Faith said.

"How, when you're supposed to be helping me with everything else?"

He looked from one to the other without the first idea what they were talking about. "What do you need me to do?"

"I've been running a holiday reading contest at the library for the last two months and the children who have read enough pages earned a special party tomorrow at the ranch," Celeste said. "Sparkle is supposed to make an appearance and we also promised the children wagon rides around the ranch. Our regular driver will be busy taking the regular customers to see the lights so Rafe has been practicing with our backup team so he could help out at the party. Obviously, he needs to be with Hope now. Flynn is coming back tomorrow but he won't be here in time to help, even if he learns overnight how to drive a team of draft horses."

Why hadn't they just asked him in the first place? Was it because things with him and Faith had become so damn complicated?

"I can do it, no problem—as long as you don't mind if Addie comes along."

Celeste gave him a grateful smile. "Oh, thank you! And Addie would be more than welcome. She's such a reader she probably would have earned the party anyway. Olivia, Lou and Faith are my volunteer helpers and I'm sure they would love Addie's help."

"Great. I'll plan on it, then. Just let me know what time."

They worked out a few more details, all while he was aware of Faith's stiff expression.

At least he would get to see her the next day, even if she clearly didn't want him there.

She lived in the most beautiful place on earth.

Faith lifted her face to the sky, pale lavender with the deepening twilight. As she drove the backup team of draft horses around the Star N barn so she could take them down to the lodge late Sunday afternoon, the moon was a slender crescent above the jagged Teton mountain range to the east and the entire landscape looked still and peaceful.

Sometimes she had to pinch herself to believe she really lived here.

When she was a girl, she had desperately wanted a place to call her own.

She had spent her entire childhood moving around the world while her parents tried to make a difference. She had loved and respected her parents and understood, even then, that they genuinely wanted to help people as they moved around to impoverished villages setting up medical clinics and providing the training to run them after they left.

She wasn't sure *they* understood the toll their self-ordained missionary efforts were taking on their daughters, even before the terrifying events shortly before their deaths.

Faith hadn't known anything other than their transitory lifestyle. She hadn't blinked an eye at the primitive conditions, the language barriers, making friends only to have to tearfully leave them a few months later.

Still, some part of her had yearned for *this*, though

she never had a specific spot in mind. All she had really wanted was a place to call her own, anywhere. A loft in the city, a split-level house in the suburbs, a double-wide mobile home somewhere. She hadn't cared what. She just wanted roots somewhere.

For nearly sixteen years, that had been her secret dream, the one she hadn't dared share with her parents. That dream had become reality only after a series of traumas and tragedies. The kidnapping. The unspeakable ordeal of their month spent in the rebel camp. Her father's shocking death during the rescue attempt, then her mother's cancer diagnosis immediately afterward.

She had been shell-shocked, grieving, frightened out of her mind but trying to put on a brave front for her younger sisters as they traveled to their new home in Idaho to live with relatives they barely knew.

When Claude picked them up at the airport in Boise and drove them here, everything had seemed so strange and new, like they had been thrust into an alien landscape.

Until they drove onto the Star N, anyway.

Faith still remembered the moment they arrived at the ranch and the instant, fierce sense of belonging she had felt.

In the years since, it had never left her. She felt the same way every time she returned to the ranch after spending any amount of time away from it. This was home, each beautiful inch of it. She loved ranching more than she could have dreamed. Whoever would have guessed that she would one day become so comfortable at this life that she could not only hitch up a team of draft horses but drive them, too?

The bells on the horses jingled a festive song as she

guided the team toward the shortcut to the Saint Nicholas Lodge. Before she could go twenty feet, she spotted a big, gorgeous man in a black Stetson blocking their way.

"I thought I was the hired driver for the night," Chase called out.

She pulled the horses to a stop and fought down the butterflies suddenly swarming through her on fragile wings.

"I figured I could get them down there for you. Anyway, we just bought new sleigh bells for the backup sleigh and I wanted to try them out."

"They sound good to me."

"I think they'll do. Where's Addie?"

"Down at the lodge, helping Olivia and Lou set things up for the party. We stopped there first and Celeste sent me up here to see if you needed help with the team."

Faith fought a frown. She had a feeling her sister sent him out here as yet another matchmaking ploy. Her family was going to drive her crazy. "I've got things under control," she lied. She was only recently coming to see it wasn't true, in any aspect of her life.

"That's good," he said as he greeted the horses, who were old friends of his. "How's Hope?"

"I checked on her a few hours ago and she is feeling fine. She had a good night and has had no further symptoms today. Looks like the crisis has passed."

In the fading light, she saw stark relief on his chiseled features. "I'm so glad. I've been worried all day. And how is your other little mama?"

It took her a moment to realize he meant Rosie. "All the pups are great. They opened their eyes yesterday.

The kids have had so much fun watching them. You'll have to bring Addie over."

"I'll try to do that before she leaves on Wednesday but our schedule's pretty packed between now and then. I don't think we'll even have time for Sunday dinner tomorrow."

"Oh. That's too bad," she said, as he moved away from the horses toward the driver's seat of the sleigh. "The family will miss you."

"What about you?" he asked, his voice low and his expression intense.

She swallowed, not knowing what to say. "Yes," she finally said. "Good thing we're not having steak or we wouldn't know how to light the grill."

"Good thing." He tipped his hat back. "Is there room for me up there or are you going to make me walk back to the lodge?"

She slid over and he jumped up and took the reins she handed him.

Though there was plenty of space on the bench, she immediately felt crowded, fiercely aware of the heat of him beside her.

Maybe *she* ought to walk back to the lodge.

The thought hardly had time to register before he whistled to the horses and they obediently took off down the drive toward the lodge, bells jingling.

After a moment, she forced herself to relax and enjoy the evening. She could think of worse ways to spend an evening than driving across her beautiful land in the company of her best friend, who just happened to be a gorgeous cowboy.

"Wow, what a beautiful night," he said after a few

moments. "Hard to believe that less than a week ago we were gearing up for that nasty storm."

"We're not supposed to have any more snow until Christmas Eve."

"With what we already have on the ground, I don't think there's any question that we'll have a white Christmas."

"Who knows? It's Idaho. We could have a heat wave between now and then."

"Don't break out your swimming suit yet," he advised. "Unless you want to take a dip in Carson and Jenna McRaven's pool at their annual party this week."

"Not me. I'm content watching the kids have fun in the pool."

The McRavens' holiday party, which would be the night *after* the show for the senior citizens, had become legendary around these parts, yet another tradition she cherished.

"I don't think I'll be able to make it to that one this year," he said. "It's my last day with Addie."

"You're still doing Christmas Eve the night of the show?"

"That's the plan."

It made her heart ache to think of him getting everything ready for his daughter on his own, hanging out stockings and scattering her presents under the tree.

"You're a wonderful father, Chase," she said softly.

He frowned as the sleigh's movement jostled her against him. "Not really. If I were, I might have tried harder to stay married to her mother. Instead, I've given my daughter a childhood where she feels constantly torn between the both of us."

"You did your best to make things work."

"Did I?"

"It looked that way from the outside."

"I should never have married her. If she hadn't been pregnant with Addie, I wouldn't have."

He was so rarely open about his marriage and divorce that she was momentarily shocked. The cheery jingle bells seemed discordant and wrong, given his serious tone.

"It was a mistake," he went on. "We both knew it. I just hate that Addie is the one who has suffered the most."

"She has a mother and stepfather who love her and a father who adores her. She's a sweet, kind, good-hearted girl. You're doing okay. Better than okay. You're a wonderful father and I won't let you beat yourself up."

He looked touched and amused at the same time as he pulled the sleigh to a stop in front of the lodge. "I've been warned, I guess."

"You have," she said firmly. "Addie is lucky to have you for a father. Any child would be."

His expression warmed and he gazed down at her long enough that she started wondering if he might kiss her again. Instead, he climbed down from the sleigh, then held a hand up to help her out.

She hesitated, thinking she would probably be wise to make her way down by herself on the complete opposite side of the sleigh from him. But for the last ten minutes, they had been interacting with none of the recent awkwardness and she didn't want to destroy this fragile peace.

She took his hand and stepped gingerly over the side of the sleigh.

"Careful. It's icy right there," he said.

The words were no sooner out of his mouth when her boot slipped out from under her. She reached for the closest handhold, which just happened to be the shearling coat covering the muscled chest of a six-foot-two-inch male. At the same moment, he reacted instinctively, grabbing her close to keep her on her feet.

She froze, aware of his mouth just inches from hers. It would be easy, so easy, to step on tiptoe for more of those delicious kisses.

His gaze locked with hers and she saw a raw hunger there that stirred answering heat inside her.

The moment stretched between them, thick and rich like Aunt Mary's hot cocoa and just as sweet.

Why was she fighting this, again? In this moment, as desire fluttered through her, she couldn't have given a single reason.

She was in love with him and according to two of her relatives, he might feel the same. It seemed stupid to deny both of them what they ached to find together.

"Chase," she murmured.

He inched closer, his breath warm on her skin. Just before she gathered her muscles to stand on tiptoe and meet him, one of the horses stamped in the cold, sending a cascade of jingles through the air.

Oh. What was she doing? This wasn't the time or the place to indulge herself, when a lodge full of young readers would descend on them at any moment.

With great effort, she stepped away. "Hang out here and I'll go check with Celeste to see when she'll be ready for the kids to go on the sleigh."

He tipped his hat back but not before she saw frustration on his features that completely matched her own.

Chapter 12

"Wow," Chase said as his daughter rushed down the stairs so they could leave for the Saint Nicholas Lodge. "Who is this strange young lady in my house who suddenly looks all grown-up?"

Addie grinned and swirled around in the fancy red-and-gold velvet dress she was wearing to perform her musical selection with Olivia and Louisa. "Thanks, Dad," she said. "I love this dress *so much*! I wish I could keep it but I have to give it back after the show tonight so maybe someone else can wear it for next year's Christmas show."

"Those are the breaks in show business, I guess," he said. "You've got clothes to change into, right?"

She held up a bag.

"Good. Are you're sure you don't need me to braid your hair or something?"

He was awful with hair but had forced himself to learn how to braid, since it was the easiest way to tame Addie's curls.

"No. Faith said she would help me fix it like Louisa and Olivia have theirs. That's why I have to hurry."

"Yes, my lady. Your carriage awaits." He gave an exaggerated bow and held out her coat, which earned him some of Addie's giggles.

"You're so weird," she said, with nothing but affection in her voice.

"That's what I hear. Merry Christmas, by the way."

She beamed. "I'm so glad we're having our pretend Christmas Eve on the same night as the show. It's perfect."

He buttoned up her coat, humbled by the way she always tried to find a silver lining. "Even though we can't spend the whole evening playing games and opening presents, like we usually do?"

"You only let me open one present on Christmas Eve," she reminded him. "We can still do that after the show, and then tomorrow we'll open the rest of them on our fake Christmas morning."

"True enough."

"Presents are fun and everything. I love them. Who doesn't?"

"I can't think of anyone," he replied, amused by her serious expression.

"But that's not what Christmas is really about. Christmas is about making other people happy—and our show will make a lot of lonely older people very happy. That's what Faith said, anyway."

His heart gave a sharp little jolt at her name, as it always did. "Faith is right," he answered.

About the show, anyway. She wasn't right about him, about them, about the fear that was holding her back from giving him a chance. He couldn't share that with his child so he merely smiled and held open the door for her.

"Let's go make some people happy," he said.

Her smile made her look wiser than her eleven years, then she hurried out into the December evening.

Three hours later, he stood and clapped with the delighted audience as the children walked out onto the small stage at the Saint Nicholas Lodge to take their final bow.

"That was amazing, wasn't it?" Next to him, Flynn beamed at his own daughter, Olivia, whose red-and-gold dress was a perfect match to those worn by Louisa and Addie.

"Even better than last year, which I didn't think was possible," Chase said.

"Those kids have truly outdone themselves this year," Flynn said, gazing out at the smiles on all the wrinkled and weathered faces in the audience as they applauded energetically. "Like it or not, I have a feeling this show for the senior citizens of Pine Gulch has now officially entered into the realm of annual traditions."

Chase had to agree. He had suspected as much after seeing the show the previous year. Though far from an elaborate production—the cast only started rehearsing the week before, after all—the performance was sweet and heartfelt, the music and dancing and dramatic performances a perfect mix of traditional and new favorites.

Of course the community would love it. How could they do otherwise?

"I'm a little biased, but our girls were the best," Flynn said.

Again, Chase couldn't disagree. Olivia had a pure, beautiful voice that never failed to give him chills, while Lou and Addie had done a more than adequate job of backing her up on a stirring rendition of "Angels We Have Heard on High" that had brought the audience to its feet.

"I overheard more than one person saying that was the highlight of the show," Chase said.

He knew Flynn had become more used to his daughter onstage over the last year as she came out of her shell a little more after witnessing the tragedy of her mother's death. While Flynn would probably never love it, he appeared to be resigned to the fact that Olivia, like her mother and grandmother before her, loved performing and making people happy.

Almost without conscious intention, his gaze strayed to Faith, who was hugging the children as they came offstage. She wore a silky red blouse that caught the light and she had her hair up again in a soft, romantic style that made him want to pull out every single pin.

She must have felt his attention. She looked up from laughing at something cute little Jolie Wheeler said and her gaze connected with his. Heat instantly sparked between them and he watched her smile slip away and her color rise.

They gazed at each other for a long moment. Neither of them seemed in a hurry to look away.

He missed her.

He hadn't really spoken with her since that sleigh

ride the other night. She had seemed to avoid him for the rest of that evening, and he and Addie hadn't made it to Sunday dinner that week.

When he dropped Addie off earlier in the evening, he had greeted Faith, of course, but she had seemed frazzled and distracted as she hurried around helping the children with hair and makeup.

He hadn't had time to linger then anyway, as Rafe had sent him out to pick up some of the senior citizen guests who didn't feel comfortable driving at night amid icy conditions.

Now Jolie asked her a question and Faith was forced to look down to answer the girl, severing the connection between them and leaving him with the hollow ache that had become entirely too familiar over the last few weeks.

More than anything, he wished he knew what was in her head.

Addie came offstage and waved at him with an energy and enthusiasm that made Flynn laugh.

"I think someone is trying to get your attention," his friend said to Chase in a broad understatement.

"You think?" With a smile, Chase headed toward his daughter.

"Did you see me, Dad?" she exclaimed.

"It was my very favorite part of the show," he told her honestly.

"Lots of other people have told us that, too. We *were* good, but everyone else was, too. I'm so glad I got to do it, even though I missed the first rehearsals."

"So am I."

She hugged him and he felt a rush of love for his sweet-natured daughter.

"What now?" he asked.

"I need to change out of the dress and give it back, I guess," she said, her voice forlorn.

"You sound so sad about that," Faith said from behind him.

He hadn't seen her approach and the sound of her voice so near rippled down his spine as if she had kissed the back of his neck.

Addie sighed. "I just love this dress. I wish I could keep it. But I understand. They need to keep it nice for someone else to wear next year."

Faith hugged her. "Sorry, honey. I took a thousand pictures of you three girls, though. You did such a great job."

Addie grinned. "Thanks, Faith. I *love* my hair. Thank you for doing it. I wish it could be like this every day."

"You are so welcome, my dear," she said with a smile that sent a lump rising in his throat. These were the two females he loved most in the world, with Louisa, Mary and Faith's sisters filling in the other slots, and he loved seeing them interact.

"I guess I should be wishing you a Merry Christmas Eve," Faith said.

"It's the best Christmas Eve on December 20 I ever had," Addie said with a grin, which made Faith laugh.

The sound tightened the vise around his chest. She hadn't laughed nearly enough over the last three years.

What would everyone in the Saint Nicholas Lodge do if he suddenly tugged her to him and kissed her firmly on the mouth for all to see?

"What's for Christmas Eve dinner?" Faith asked him before he could think about acting on the impulse.

He managed to wrench his mind away from impossible fantasies. "You know what a genius I am in the kitchen. I bought a couple of takeout dinners from the café in town. We *are* having a big breakfast tomorrow, though. I can handle waffles and bacon."

"Why don't you eat your Christmas Eve dinner here? We have so much food left over. I think Jenna always overestimates the crowd. Once the crowd clears, we're going to pull some of it out. Everyone is starving, since we were all too busy for dinner before the show to take time for food. You're more than welcome to stay—though I completely understand if you have plans at home for your Christmas Eve celebration."

"Can we, Dad?" Addie begged. "I won't see my friends for three weeks after this."

She wouldn't see *him* for that amount of time either—a miserable thought.

He shrugged, already missing her. "We don't have any plans that are set in stone. I think the only other thing we talked about, besides the show, was playing a couple of games."

"And reading the Christmas story," she pointed out.

"Right. We can't forget that," he answered. "I don't mind if we stay, as long as you promise to go straight to bed when we're done. Santa can't come if you're not asleep."

She rolled her eyes but grinned at the same time. At eleven, she was too old for Santa but that didn't stop either of them from carrying on the pretense a little longer.

"I'm going to go change and tell Lou and Livvie that we're having dinner here," she announced.

She hurried away, leaving him alone with Faith—or

as alone as they could be in a vast holiday-themed lodge still filled with about twenty other people.

"It really was a wonderful show," he said.

"I can't take any of the credit."

He had to smile, remembering how busy she had been before and during the show. The previous year had been the same. She claimed she wanted nothing to do with the holiday show, then pitched in and did whatever was necessary to pull it off.

His smile slid away when he realized she was gazing at his mouth again.

Yeah. He decided he didn't much care what people would think if he kissed her again right now.

She swallowed and looked away. "I need to, um, probably take Sparkle back to the barn for the night."

Besides the musical number with Addie and her friends, the other highlight of the show had been when Celeste, under duress, read from her famous story "Sparkle and the Magic Snowball" to the captivated audience while the *real* Sparkle stood next to her, looking for all the world as if he were reading the story over her shoulder.

"I'll help," he offered.

Both of them knew she didn't need his help but after a moment, she shrugged and headed toward the front door and the enclosure where Sparkle hung out when he made appearances at the lodge.

Faith paused long enough to grab her coat off the rack by the door and toss his to him, then the two of them walked outside into the night.

The reindeer wandered over to greet them like old friends, the bells on his harness jingling merrily.

"Hey, Sparkle. How are you, pal?"

The reindeer lipped at his outstretched hand, making Chase wish he'd brought along an apple or something.

"I really don't need your help," Faith said. "He's so easygoing this is a one-person job—if that. I could probably tell him to go to bed and he would wander over to the barn, flip the latch and head straight for his stall. He might even turn off the lights on his way."

He had to smile at the whimsical image. "I'm here. Let's do this so we can eat, too."

With a sigh, she reached to unlatch the gate. Before she could, Ella Baker came out of the lodge, bundled against the cold and carrying an armload of sheet music.

"You're not staying for dinner?" Faith asked after they exchanged greetings.

"I can't. My dad is having a rough time right now so I need to take off. But thank you again for asking me to do this. I had so much fun. If you do it again next year and I'm still in town, I would love to help out."

"That's terrific!" Faith exclaimed. "I'll let Hope know. I can guarantee she'll be thrilled to hear this. Thank you!"

"I'm so sorry your sister couldn't be here to see it," Ella said. "I hope the live video worked so she could watch it at home."

Hope was still taking it easy, Chase knew, though she'd had no other problems since that frightening day the week before.

"She saw it," Faith assured her. "I talked to her right afterward and she absolutely loved it, just like everyone else did."

"Oh, I'm so glad." Ella smiled, then turned to him. "Chase, it's really good to see you again. I didn't have the chance to tell you this the other night but I had such a great time dancing with you. I'd love to do it again sometime."

It was clearly an invitation and for a moment, he didn't know what to say. Any other single guy in Pine Gulch would probably think he'd just won the lottery. Ella was lovely and seemed very nice. A relationship with her would probably be easy and uncomplicated— unlike certain other women he could mention.

The only trouble was, that particular woman in question had him so wrapped up in knots, he couldn't untangle even a tiny thread of interest in Ella.

"I'm afraid opportunities to dance are few and far between around here," he said, in what he hoped was a polite but clear message.

"You two could always go to the Renegade," Faith suggested blithely. "They have a live band with dancing just about every Saturday night."

For a moment, he could only stare at her. Seriously? She was pimping him out to take another woman dancing?

"That would be fun," Ella said, obviously taking Faith's suggestion as encouragement. "Maybe we could go after the holidays."

Chase didn't want to hurt her but he was not about to take her up on the invitation to go out dancing while he was standing in front of the woman he loved.

Even if it had been Faith's suggestion in the first place.

"I don't know," he said, in what he hoped was a noncommittal but clear voice. "I have my daughter a couple weekends a month and it's tough for me to get away."

Understanding flashed in her eyes along with a shadow of pained rejection. He hated that he had planted it there—and hated more that Faith had put him in the position in the first place.

"No problem," she said, some of the animation leaving her features. "Let me know if you have a free night. I've got to run. Good night. And Merry Christmas in advance."

She gave a smile that was only a degree or two shy of genuine and headed out into the parking lot toward her car.

He wasn't sure how, exactly, but Chase managed to hold on to the slippery, fraying ends of his temper as they led the reindeer the short distance across the snowy landscape to The Christmas Ranch barn.

It coiled through him as they worked together to take off Sparkle's harness and bells, gave him a good brushing, then made sure he had food and water.

He should just let it go, he told himself after they stepped out of the stall and closed the gate.

The evening had been wonderful and he didn't want to ruin it by fighting with her.

He almost had himself convinced of that but somehow as he looked at her, his anger slipped free and the words rolled out anyway.

"Why the hell would you do that?"

Chapter 13

Faith stared at him, stunned by the anger that seemed to seethe around them like storm-tossed sea waves.

"Do…what?"

"You know. You just tried to set me up with Ella Baker again."

Her face flamed even as she shivered at his hard tone. Oh. That.

"All I did was mention that the Renegade has dancing on Saturday nights. I only thought it would be fun for the two of you."

His jaw worked as he continued to stare down at her. "Is that right?"

"Ella is really great," she said. She might as well double down on her own stupidity. "I've seen her with the kids this week and she's amazing—so patient and kind and talented. You heard her sing. Any single guy would have to be crazy not to want to go out with her."

"Really, Faith. *Really?*" The words came at her like a whip snapping through the cold air.

He was furious, she realized. More angry than she had ever seen him. She could see it in every rigid line of his body, from his flexed jaw to his clenched fists.

"After everything that's happened between us these last few weeks, you seriously want to stand there and pretend you think I might have the slightest interest in someone else?"

She let out a breath, ashamed of herself for dragging an innocent—and very nice—woman into this. She didn't even know why she had. The words had just sort of come out. She certainly didn't *want* Chase dating Ella Baker but maybe on some level she was still hanging on to the hope that they could somehow return to the easy friendship of a few weeks ago and forget the rest of this.

"I can't help it if I want you to be happy," she said, her voice low. "You're my dearest friend."

"I don't want to be your friend." He growled an oath that had her blinking. "After everything, can you really not understand that? Fine. You want me to be clear, I'll be clear. I don't want to be your buddy and I don't want to date Ella Baker. She is very nice but I don't have the slightest flicker of interest in her."

"Okay," she whispered. She shouldn't be relieved about that but she couldn't seem to help it.

He gazed down at her, features hard and implacable. "There is only one woman I want in my life and it's you, Faith. You have to know that. I'm in love with you. It's you. It has *always* been you."

She caught her breath at his words as joy burst through her like someone had switched on a thousand Christmas trees. She wanted to savor it, to simply close her eyes and soak it in.

I love you, too. So, so much.

The words crowded in her throat, jostling with each other to get out.

Over the last few weeks, she had come to accept that unalterable truth. She was in love with him and had been for a long time.

Perhaps some little part of her had loved him since that day he drove her into town when she was a frightened girl of fifteen.

What might have happened between them if his father hadn't been dying, if Travis hadn't come back to the Star N and she hadn't been overwhelmed by the sweet, kind safety he offered, the anchor she had so desperately needed?

She didn't know. She only knew that Chase had always been so very important in her world—more than she could ever have imagined after Travis died so suddenly.

The reminder slammed into her and she reached out for the rough planks of Sparkle's enclosure for support.

Travis.

The images of that awful moment when she had found him lying under his overturned ATV—covered in blood, so terribly still—seemed to flash through her mind in a grim, horrible slide show. She hadn't been able to save him, no matter how desperately she had tried as she begged him not to leave her like her father, her mother.

She had barely survived losing Travis. How could

she find the strength to let herself be vulnerable to that sort of raw, all-consuming, soul-destroying pain again?

She couldn't. She had been a coward so many years ago as a helpless girl caught up in events beyond her control and she was still a coward.

Faith opened her mouth to speak but the words wouldn't come.

The silence dragged between them. She was afraid to meet his gaze but when she forced herself to do it, she found his eyes murky with sadness and what she thought might be disappointment.

"You don't have to say anything." All the anger seemed to have seeped out of him, leaving his features as bleak as the snow-covered mountains above the tree line. "I get it."

How could he, when *she* didn't understand? She had the chance for indescribable happiness here with the man she loved. Why couldn't she just take that step, find enough strength inside herself to try again?

"It doesn't matter how much time I give you. You've made up your mind not to let yourself see me as anything more than your *dearest friend* and nothing I do can change that."

She wanted to tell him that wasn't true. She saw him for exactly what he was. The strong, decent, wonderful man she loved with all her heart.

Fear held both her heart and her words in a tight, icy grip. "Chase, I—" she managed, but he shook his head.

"Don't," he said. "I pushed you too hard. I thought you might be ready to move forward but I can see now I only complicated things between us and wasted both of our time. It was a mistake and I'm sorry."

"I'm the one who's sorry," she said softly, but he had

turned around and headed for the door and she wasn't sure he heard her.

The moment he left, she pressed a hand to her chest and the sharp, cold ache there, as if someone had pierced her skin with an icicle.

She wanted so badly to go after him but told herself maybe it was better this way.

Wasn't it better to lose a friendship than to risk having her heart cut out of her body?

Chase didn't know how he made it through the next few days.

The hardest thing had been walking back inside the Saint Nicholas Lodge and trying to pretend everything was fine, with his emotions a raw, tangled mess.

He was pretty sure he fooled nobody. Celeste and Mary seemed especially watchful and alert as he and Addie dined with the family. As for Faith, she had come in about fifteen minutes after he did with her eyes red and her features subdued. She sat on the exact opposite side of the room from him and picked at her food, her features tight and set.

He was aware of a small, selfish hope that perhaps she was suffering a tiny portion of the vast pain that seemed to have taken over every thought.

She had left early, ostensibly with the excuse of taking some of the leftovers to Rafe and Hope, though he was fairly certain it was another effort to avoid him.

He did his best to put his pain on the back burner, focusing instead on making his remaining few hours with his daughter until after the New Year memorable for her.

Their premature Christmas Eve went off without a

hitch. When they returned home, she changed into her pajamas and they played games and watched a favorite holiday movie, then she opened the one early present he allowed her—a carved ornament he had made from a pretty aspen burl on a downed tree he found in the mountains. In the morning she opened the rest of her presents from him and he fixed her breakfast, then she helped him take care of a few chores.

Too soon, her mother showed up after visiting her parents at the care center where Cindy's mother was still recovering from her stroke.

Chase tried to put on a smile for Cindy, sorry all over again for the mess he had made of his marriage.

He had tried so hard to love her. Those early days had been happy, getting ready for the baby and then their early days with Addie, but their shared love of their daughter hadn't provided strong enough glue to keep them together.

It hadn't been Cindy's fault that his heart hadn't been completely free. Despite his best efforts, she somehow had sensed it all along and he regretted that now.

He understood why disappointment and hurt turned her bitter and cold toward him and he resolved to do his best to be kinder.

Addie had decided to leave some of the gifts he had given her at the ranch so she could enjoy them during her time with him there, but she still had several she wanted to take home. After he loaded them into her mom's SUV, he hugged his daughter and kissed the top of her head. "Have a fun cruise, Addie-bug, and at Disney World. I want to hear every detail when you get back."

"Okay," she said, her arms tight around his neck.

"You won't be by yourself on Christmas, will you, Dad? You'll go open presents at the Star N with Louisa and Barrett, right?"

His heart seemed to give a sharp little spasm. That's what he had done for several years, even before Travis died, but that was looking unlikely this year.

"I'm not sure," he lied. "I'll be fine, whatever I do. Merry Christmas, kiddo."

As they drove away, he caught sight of the lights of the Star N and The Christmas Ranch below the Brannon Ridge.

How was he going to make it through the remainder of his life without her—and without Lou and Barrett and the rest of her family he loved so much?

He didn't have the first idea.

"Why isn't Chase coming for dinner tonight?" Louisa asked as she and Barrett decorated Christmas cookie angels on the kitchen island.

"Yeah. He always comes over on Christmas Eve," Barrett said.

"And on Christmas morning when we open presents," Louisa added.

Faith had no idea how to answer her children. It made her chest ache all over again, just thinking about it.

That morning she had gathered her nerve and called to invite him for dinner and to make arrangements for transferring Louisa's Christmas present from Brannon Ridge to the Star N. She had been so anxious about talking to him again after four days of deafening silence, but the call went straight to voice mail.

He was avoiding her.

That was fairly obvious, especially when he texted

just moments later declining her invitation but telling her that he already had a plan to take care of the other matter and she didn't need to worry about it.

The terse note after days of no contact hurt more than she could have imagined, even though she knew it was her own fault. She wanted so much to jump in her truck and drive to his ranch, to tell him she was sorry for all the pain she had put them both through.

"I guess he must have made other plans this year," she said now in answer to her daughter.

Mary made a harrumphing sort of noise from her side of the island but said nothing else in front of the children, much to Faith's relief.

Though her aunt didn't know what had transpired between Faith and Chase, Mary knew *something* had. She blamed Faith for it and had made no secret that she wasn't happy about it.

"Addie texted me a while ago. She's worried he'll be all by himself for the holidays," Louisa said. Her daughter made it sound like that was the worst possible fate anyone could endure and the guilty knot under Faith's rib cage seemed to expand.

Her children loved Chase—and vice versa. She hated being the cause of a rift between them.

"We should take him some of our cookies," Barrett suggested.

"That's a great idea," Mary said, with a pointed look at her. "Faith, why don't you take him some cookies? You could be there and back before everybody shows up for dinner."

He didn't want cookies from her. He didn't want *any-thing*—except the one thing she wasn't sure she had the strength to give.

"Maybe we can all take them over later," she said.

The three looked as if they wanted to argue but she made an impromptu excuse, desperate to escape the guilt and uncertainty. "I need to go. I've got a few things I need to do out in the barn before tonight."

"Now?" Mary asked doubtfully.

"If I finish the chores now, I won't have to go out to take care of them in the middle of our Christmas Eve party with Hope and Celeste," she said.

It was a flimsy excuse but not unreasonable. She did have chores—and she had plans to hang a big red ribbon she had already hidden away in the barn across the stall where she planned to put Lou's new horse. She could do that now, since Louisa had no reason to go out to the barn between now and Christmas morning.

She grabbed her coat and hurried out before any of them could argue with her.

Outside, a cold wind blew down off Brannon Ridge and she shivered at the same time she yawned.

She hadn't been sleeping much the last few weeks, which was probably why her head ached and her eyes felt as if they were coated with gritty sandpaper.

Maybe she could just go to bed and wake up when Christmas was over.

She sighed. However tempting, that was completely impossible. She had hours to go before she could sleep. It was not yet sunset on Christmas Eve—she still had to make it through dinner with her sisters and their families. Both of them were coming, since Hope had been cleared to return to her normal activities.

They would want to know where Chase was and she didn't know how to answer them.

Not only that but her kids would likely be awake for

hours yet, jacked up on excitement and anticipation—not to mention copious amounts of sugar from the treats they had been making and sampling all day.

She should take sugar cookies to Chase. He loved them and probably hadn't made any for himself.

How could she possibly face him after their last encounter?

Tears burned behind her eyes. She wanted to tell herself it was from the wind and the lack of sleep but she knew better. This was the season of hope, joy, yet she felt as if all the color and light had been sucked away, leaving only uniform, lifeless gray.

She was in love with him and she didn't know what to do about it.

The worst part was knowing that even if she could find the strength and courage to admit she loved him, she was afraid it was too late.

He had looked so bleak the last time she saw him, so distant. Remembering the finality in that scene, the tears she had been fighting for days slipped past her defenses.

She looked out at the beautiful landscape—the snow-covered mountains and the orange and yellows of the sunset—and gave in to the torment of her emotions here, where no one could see her.

After a few moments, she forced herself to stop, wiping at the tears with her leather gloves. None of this maudlin stuff was helping her take care of her chores and now she would have to finish quickly so she could hurry back to the house to fix her makeup before her sisters saw evidence of her tears and pressed her about what was wrong.

How could she tell them what a mess she had made of things?

With another sigh, she forced herself to focus on the job at hand. She walked through the snow to the barn and pushed the door open but only made it a few steps before she faltered, her gaze searching the interior.

Something was wrong.

Over the past two and a half years, she had come to know the inside of this barn as well as she did her own bedroom. She knew it in all seasons, all weather, all moods.

She knew the scents and the sounds and the shifting light—and right now she could tell something was different.

Someone was here.

She moved quietly into the barn, reaching for the pitchfork that was usually there. It was missing but she found a shovel instead and decided that would have to do.

No one else should be here.

She had two part-time ranch hands but neither was scheduled to be here on Christmas Eve. She had given both time off for the holidays and didn't expect to see them until the twenty-seventh. Anyway, if it had been Bill or Jose, wouldn't she have seen their vehicles parked out front?

With the shovel in hand, she headed farther into the interior of the big barn, eyes scanning the dim interior. Seconds later she spotted it—a beautiful paint mare in one of the stalls near the far end of the barn.

At almost that exact moment, she heard a noise coming from above her. She whirled toward the hayloft that took up one half of the barn and spotted him there, his back to her, along with the missing pitchfork.

"Chase!" she exclaimed. "What are you doing here?"

He swiveled around, and for an arrested moment, he looked at her with so much love and longing, she almost wept again.

Too quickly, he veiled his features. "Feeding Lou's new horse. While I was at it, I figured I could take care of the rest of your stock in the barn so you wouldn't have to worry about it tonight. I was hoping to get out of here before you came down from the house but obviously I'm not fast enough."

He had done that for her, even though he was furious with her. She wanted to cry all over again.

Happiness seemed to bloom through her like springtime and the old barn had never looked so beautiful.

She swallowed, focusing on the least important thought running through her head. "How did you get the new horse down here? I never saw your trailer."

"I didn't want Lou to see it and wonder what was going on so I came in the back way, down the hill. I rode Tor and tied the mare's lead line to his saddle."

"You came down through all that snow?" she exclaimed. "How on earth did you manage that?" There were drifts at least four feet deep in places on that ridgeline.

"It was slow going but Tor is tough and so's the new little mare. She's going to be a great horse for Lou."

She felt completely overwhelmed suddenly, humbled and astonished that he would go to such lengths for her daughter.

And for her, she realized.

This was only one of a million other acts over the last

few years that provided all the evidence anyone could need that he loved her.

"I can't believe you would do that."

"Don't make a big deal out of it," he said, his tone distant.

"It is a big deal to me. It's huge. Oh, Chase."

The tears from earlier broke free again and a small sob escaped before she could cover her mouth with her fingers.

"Cut it out. Right now."

She almost laughed at the alarm in his voice, despite the tears that continued to trickle down her cheeks.

"I can't. I'm sorry. When the man I love shows me all over again how wonderful he is, I tend to get emotional. You're just going to have to deal with that."

Her words seemed to hang in the air of the barn like dust motes floating in the last pale shafts of Christmas Eve sunlight. He stared at her for a second, then lurched toward the ladder. Before he reached it, his boot heel caught on something. He staggered for just a moment and tried to regain his balance but he didn't have anything to hold on to.

He fell in what felt like slow motion, landing with a hard thud that sounded almost as loud as her instinctive scream.

He couldn't breathe—and not because her words had stunned him. No. He literally couldn't breathe.

For a good five seconds, his lungs were frozen, the wind knocked hard out of him. He was aware on some level of her running toward him to kneel next to him, of her panicked, tearstained features and her hands on his face and her cries of "breathe, breathe, *breathe*."

He wasn't sure if the advice was for him or herself but then, just as abruptly, the spasm in his diaphragm eased and he could inhale again, a small breath and then increasingly deeper until he dared talk again.

"I'm...okay."

She was reaching for her phone when he spoke. At his voice, she gasped, dropping it to the concrete floor of the barn and throwing herself across him with an impact that made him grunt.

She immediately eased away. "Where does it hurt? I need to call an ambulance. It will probably take them a while to get here so it might be faster for me to just drive you."

The panic in her voice seeped through his discomfort and he reached out a hand to cover hers.

"I don't...need an ambulance. The breath...was knocked out of me...but I'm okay."

The alfalfa he had been forking down for the animals had cushioned most of the impact and he knew there was no serious damage, even though everything still ached. He might have a broken rib in there, but he wasn't about to tell her that.

"Are you sure? That was a hard fall."

"I'm sure."

Her hand fluttered in his and he suddenly remembered what she had said and his complete shock that had made him lose his footing.

He sat up and wiped at her tears.

"Faith. What were you saying just before I fell?"

She looked down, her cheeks turning pink. "I... Nothing."

It was the exact antithesis of *nothing*. "You said you loved me," he murmured.

She rubbed her cheek on her shoulder as if trying to hide evidence of the tears trickling down. "That was a pretty hard fall," she said again. "Are you sure you didn't bump your head, too?"

"Positive. I know what I heard. Why do you think I fell? You shocked me so much I forgot I was ten feet up in the air. Say it again."

Her hand fluttered in his again but he held it tight. He wasn't going to let her wriggle away this time. After a moment, she stopped and everything about her seemed to sigh.

"I love you," she whispered. "I've known it for a while now. I just… I've been so afraid."

"I know. I'm sorry."

He hadn't wanted to make her suffer more than she already had. But maybe they both had to pass through this tough time to know they could make it through to the other side.

He pulled her toward him and his breath seemed to catch all over again—and not at all from the pain—when she wrapped her arms around his waist and rested her cheek against his chest.

Joy began to stir inside him, tentative at first and then stronger.

She belonged exactly here. Surely she had to know that by now.

"After Travis died, I never wanted to fall in love again. Ever," she said, her voice low. "I guess it's a good thing I didn't."

He frowned in confusion, nearly groaning at the possibility of more mixed signals from her.

And then she kissed him. Just like that. She lifted her head, found his mouth and kissed him with a fierce emotion that sent joy rushing through him like the Cold Creek swollen with runoff.

"I didn't need to fall in love," she said, her beautiful eyes bright with more tears and a tenderness that made *him* want to weep. "I was already there, in love with my best friend. That love surrounded me every moment of every day. I just had to find the strength to open my heart to it."

"And have you?"

She kissed him again in answer and he decided he wanted to spend every Christmas Eve right here with her in her barn, surrounded by animals and hay and possibilities.

He had no idea how all his Christmas wishes had come true but he wasn't about to question it.

"I love you, Chase Brannon," she murmured against his mouth.

He didn't want to ask but he had to know. "What changed?"

"Why am I not afraid to admit I love you?" She smiled a little. "Who said I'm not? But I have been thinking about something my dad told us over and over when we were held prisoner in Colombia. *Remember, girls*, he would say in that firm voice. *Faith is always stronger than fear.* He was talking about faith in the abstract, not me in particular, but I have decided to listen to his words and apply them to me. I can't let my fear control me. I *am* stronger than this—and during the times when I'm not, I've got your strength to lean on."

He kissed her, humbled and overwhelmed and incredibly grateful for this amazing woman in his arms, who had been through incredible pain but came through with grace, dignity and a beautiful courage.

He wiped a tear away with his thumb, grateful beyond words that such a woman was willing to face her completely justifiable fears for *him*.

"I thought I was going to have a heart attack just now when you fell. For an instant, it was like Travis all over again—but it also confirmed something I had already been thinking."

"Oh?"

She pressed her cheek against his hand. "I've been worried that I'm not strong enough to open my heart to you. The real question is whether I'm strong enough to live without you. When I saw you fall, in those horrible few seconds when you weren't breathing, I realized the answer to that is an unequivocal, emphatic no. I can't bear the idea of not being with you."

He couldn't promise nothing would ever happen to him—but he could promise he would love her fiercely every single day of his life.

"I love you, Chase. I love you, my kids love you, my entire family loves you. I need you. You are my oldest and dearest friend—and my oldest and dearest love."

He framed her face in his hands and kissed her with all the pent-up need from all these years of standing on the sidelines, waiting for their moment to be right. He almost couldn't believe this was real. Maybe he was simply hallucinating after having the wind knocked out of him. But his senses seemed even more acute than usual, alive and invigorated, and the joy expanding in his chest was too bright and wild and beautiful to be imaginary.

People said Christmas was a time for miracles.

He would never doubt that again.

Epilogue

Christmas Eve, one year later

"Okay, help me out, Mary. Where do you keep the salad tongs since you and Pat have renovated the kitchen?"

With whitewashed cabinets and new stainless steel appliances, the new Star N kitchen was beautiful, Faith had to admit—almost as pretty as the renovated kitchen at the Brannon Ridge that had been her wedding present from Chase. But after two months, she still couldn't seem to figure out how to find things here now.

Mary headed to a large drawer on the island. "It made more sense to keep all the utensils in the biggest drawer here where they can all fit instead of scattered throughout the kitchen. I don't know why it took me fifty years to figure that out. Is this what you're looking for?"

"Yes! Thank you."

She added the dressing to the rest of the ingredients in her favorite walnut cranberry salad and tossed it with the tongs. "There. That should do it. Everything looks great, Mary."

"Thanks." Her aunt beamed and Faith thought, not for the first time, that Mary seemed years younger since her marriage to Pat.

"Thank you for hosting the party here at the Star N."

"Christmas is about home and this old house is home to you girls," Mary said simply. "It seemed right, even though all of you have bigger places now. Your kitchen up at Brannon Ridge is twice the size as this one."

As they were discussing how they would merge their lives after they were married, she and Chase had looked at both houses and decided to run both ranches from Brannon Ridge. The house was bigger for all three of their kids and assorted horses, dogs and barn cats.

It had been a good decision, confirmed just a few months after Faith and Chase's wedding, when Mary announced she and her beau were getting married and wanted to renovate the Star N—a process now in the final phases.

"Anything else I can carry out to the dining room?" she asked.

"I made a fruit salad, too. It's in the refrigerator," Mary said.

Faith grabbed it and, with one bowl under each arm, headed for the two long tables that had been set up in the great room to hold the growing family.

She was arranging the bowls when Hope wandered

over. "Hey, do you have any idea where I can find tape? I've still got one present to wrap."

"Let me get this straight. You run the most famous Christmas attraction in the Intermountain West *and* you've illustrated a holiday book that was turned into a movie currently ranked number one at the box office for the fourth consecutive week. Yet here it is five p.m. on Christmas Eve and you're still not finished wrapping your presents?"

"Oh, give me a break. I've had a little bit on my plate. You would not *believe* how much of my day this little creature takes up."

Faith smiled. "I think I would. I've had two of my own, remember? Here. Give."

Her sister held up the wriggling adorableness that was her six-month-old son, Samuel, born healthy and full-term, with no complications whatsoever from that early scare more than a year ago.

"You can have him if you tell me where I can find tape."

"The desk drawer in the office." She grinned and admitted the truth. "That's where I put it a half hour ago, anyway, when I finished wrapping my last present."

Hope snorted but fulfilled her part of the deal by handing over the boy.

After she left, Faith nuzzled his neck. Oh, he smelled delicious. Her heart seemed to burst with happiness. "Hey, Sammy. How's my favorite guy?"

"Wow. I guess that puts us in our place, right, Barrett?"

She looked up to find Chase and her son in the doorway, stomping snow off their boots after coming in from shoveling the driveway.

He was smiling but she didn't miss the light in his gaze as he watched her cuddle Hope's cute little boy.

How was it possible that, even after a year, she loved Chase more every single time she saw him?

"My favorite *little* guy," she amended. "You two are my favorite bigger guys. How's the snow out there?"

"Still coming down," Chase said. "Mary said she thinks we'll get another six or seven inches out of the storm. Perfect for cuddling in by the fire and hanging out with the family on Christmas morning."

"I hope Celeste and Flynn make it."

"They pulled in right as we were finishing the drive-way," he assured her.

"That's good," Mary said from the kitchen. "Every-thing's ready and I'm *starving*."

"Sorry we're late," Celeste said as she, Flynn and Olivia came in with their arms loaded down with gifts.

"We still had to wrap a couple of presents," Olivia explained.

Hope paused in the act of setting her hastily wrapped final present under the big tree in the window. "Seri-ously, CeCe? On Christmas Eve? Maybe next year you should plan ahead a little better," she said virtuously.

Faith had to laugh, which ended up startling Sammy. "Sorry, kiddo."

"Here, I'll take him back."

She didn't want to surrender the soft little bundle but Mary came in just then. "Great. Everybody's here. Find your places."

After handing Sammy back to his mother, she found a place beside Chase. Addie and Louisa sat at her other side while Barrett sat on Chase's other side.

When they were all settled, Celeste looked around at their family.

"I have an announcement to make. *We* do, actually."

Olivia, Faith noticed, was just about jumping out of her chair in excitement.

"Is this about *Sparkle and the Magic Snowball* being number one again at the box office?" Addie asked.

"Everybody knows that already," Olivia said.

"Is it about the new Sparkle book that's coming out next summer or the movie sequel they're already making?" Louisa asked.

"No," Flynn said. "Though that's all very exciting."

He reached for Celeste's hand and Faith held her breath, sensing what was coming next before her sister even said it.

"We're having a baby."

The table erupted into squeals of excitement and hearty congratulations.

"Another baby. What wonderful news—and the perfect time to find out, on Christmas Eve," Mary exclaimed, her features soft with delight. "When are you due?"

"June. Right around the book launch, which isn't the greatest of timing, I know."

"We'll figure it out," Hope said. "This is so great! Maybe you'll have a boy, too, and he and Sammy can be best friends!"

Faith felt a big, strong hand reach out and grip hers. She glanced at her husband and saw a secret little smile there, the same one exploding in her heart. The two new cousins would soon become three, but she and Chase were the only ones at the table who knew that, for now.

They wouldn't share their news yet. Faith was only

eight weeks along and they had decided to wait until after the New Year to tell anyone. Even Barrett, Lou and Addie didn't know yet.

It was tough to keep the news under wraps but there would be time enough to let the family know even more joy would soon be on the way.

For now, she would celebrate her sister's happiness.

Her heart seemed filled to overflowing and tears welled up as she looked around the table at her family, these people she loved so much.

Pregnancy hormones were making her *crazy*. She cried at everything these days. This, the chance to spend Christmas Eve with all the people she loved most in the world, was worth a few tears, she decided.

Chase's strong, callused fingers threaded through hers and more tears leaked out. He nudged her shoulder with his, and then her oldest and dearest friend—and the man she loved with all her heart—handed her his napkin so she could dry her tears.

"What's wrong? Why are you crying, Mom?" Louisa asked, concern in her eyes that could look so fierce and determined when she and the horse she adored galloped through a barrel course.

Faith sniffled a little more. "I'm happy. That's all."

"Cut it out or you'll set me off," Celeste said.

"And me," Hope said. "Since I had Sammy, I cry if the wind blows at me from the wrong direction."

Faith gave her sisters a watery smile. Their father's words certainly held true for his daughters. Each of them had proved that faith *was* stronger than fear, that they could move past the tough experiences in their past and let love help them heal.

She tightened her fingers around Chase's, the joy

in her heart blazing as brightly as the lights on Aunt Mary's big Christmas tree that sent out warmth and color and hope across the snowy night.

* * * * *

A COLD CREEK NOEL

To Tennis and Kjersten Watkins, with love. We can't wait to see what life has in store for the two of you!

Chapter 1

"Come on, Luke. Come on, buddy. Hang in there."

Her wipers beat back the sleet and snow as Caidy Bowman drove through the streets of Pine Gulch, Idaho, on a stormy December afternoon. Only a few inches had fallen but the roads were still dangerous, slick as spit. For only a moment, she risked lifting one hand off the steering wheel of her truck and patting the furry shape whimpering on the seat beside her.

"We're almost there. We'll get you fixed up, I swear it. Just hang on, bud. A few more minutes. That's all."

The young border collie looked at her with a trust she didn't deserve in his black eyes and she frowned, her guilt as bitter and salty as the solution the snowplows had put down on the roads.

Luke's injuries were *her* fault. She should have been watching him. She knew the half-grown pup had a curious streak a mile wide—and a tendency not to listen to her when he had an itch to investigate something.

She was working on that obedience issue and they had made good strides the past few weeks, but one moment of inattention could be disastrous, as the past hour had amply demonstrated. She didn't know if it was arrogance on her part, thinking her training of him was enough, or just irresponsibility. Either way, she should have kept him far away from Festus's pen. The bull was ornery as a rattlesnake on a hot skillet and didn't take kindly to curious young border collies nosing around his turf.

Alerted by Luke's barking and then the bull's angry snort, she had raced to old Festus's pen just in time to watch Luke jig the wrong way and the bull stomp down hard on his haunches with a sickening crunch of bone.

Her hands tightened on the steering wheel and she cursed under her breath as the last light before the vet's office turned yellow when she was still too far away to gun through it. She was almost tempted to keep going. Even if she were nabbed for running a red light by Pine Gulch's finest, she could probably talk her way out of a ticket, considering her brother was the police chief and would certainly understand this was an emergency. If she were pulled over, though, it would mean an inevitable delay and she just didn't have time for that.

The light finally changed and she took off fast, the back tires fishtailing on the icy road. She would just have to trust the salt bags she carried for traction in the bed of the pickup would do the job. Even the four-wheel drive of the truck was useless against black ice.

Finally, she reached the small square building that held the Pine Gulch Veterinary Clinic and pulled the pickup to the side doors where she knew it was only a short transfer inside to the treatment area.

She briefly considered carrying him in by herself, but it had taken the careful efforts of both her and her brother Ridge to slide a blanket under Luke and lift him into the seat of her pickup. They could bring out the stretcher and cart, she decided.

She rubbed Luke's white neck. "I'm going to go get some help, okay? You just hold tight."

He made a small whimper of pain and she bit down hard on her lip as her insides clenched with fear. She loved the little guy, even if he was nosy as a crow and even smarter, which was probably why his stubbornness was such a frustration.

He trusted her to take care of him and she refused to let him die.

She hurried to the front door, barely noticing the wind-driven sleet that gouged at her even under her Stetson.

Warm air washed over her when she opened the door, familiar with the scent of animals and antiseptic mixed in a stomach-churning sort of way with new paint.

"Hey, Caidy." A woman in green scrubs rushed to the door. "You made good time from the River Bow."

"Hi, Joni. I may have broken a few traffic laws, but this is an emergency."

"After you called, I warned Ben you were on your way and what the situation was. He's been getting ready for you. I'll let him know you've arrived."

Caidy waited, feeling the weight of each second ticking away. The new vet had only been in town a few weeks and already he had made changes to the clinic. Maybe she was just being contrary, but she had liked things better when Doc Harris ran the place. The whole reception area looked different. The cheerful yellow walls had been painted over with a boring white and the weathered, comfortable, old eighties-era couch and chairs were gone, replaced by modern benches covered in a slate vinyl that probably deflected anything a veterinarian's patients could leak on it. A display of Christmas gifts appropriate for pets, including a massive stocking filled to the top with toys and a giant rawhide bone that looked as if it came from a dinosaur, hung in one corner.

Most significant, the reception area used to sit out in the open but it was now stuck behind a solid half wall topped with a glass partition.

It made sense to modernize from an efficiency point of view, but she had found the comfortably worn look of the office before more appealing.

Not that she cared about any of that right now, with Luke lying out in her truck, cold and hurt and probably afraid.

She shifted impatiently. Where was the man? Trimming his blasted nails? Only a few moments had passed but every second delay was too much. Just when she was about call out to Joni to see what was taking so long, the door into the treatment area opened and the new vet appeared.

"Where's the dog?" he asked abruptly, and she had only a vague impression of a frowning dark-haired man in blue scrubs.

"Still out in my truck."

He narrowed his gaze. "Why? I can't treat him out there."

She wanted to take that giant rawhide bone out of

that stocking and bean him with it. "Yes, I'm aware of that," she said, fighting down her frustration. "I didn't want to move him. I'm afraid something might be broken."

"I thought he was gored."

She wasn't sure what, exactly, she had said in that frantic call to let Joni know she was on her way.

"He did end up on the business end of a bull at some point. I'm not sure if that was before or after that bull stepped on him."

His mouth tightened. "A young dog has no business running wild in the same vicinity as a dangerous bull."

His criticism stung far too close to her own guilt for comfort. "We're a working ranch at the River Bow, Dr. Caldwell. Accidents like this can happen."

"They shouldn't," he snapped before turning around and heading back through the treatment area. She followed him, heartily wishing for Doc Harris right now. The grizzled old vet had taken care of every dog she had ever owned, from her very first border collie and best friend, Sadie, whom she still had.

Doc Harris was her friend and mentor. If he had been here, he would have wrapped her in a warm hug that smelled of liniment and cherry Life Savers and promised her everything would be all right.

Dr. Ben Caldwell was nothing like Dr. Harris. He was abrasive and arrogant and she already heartily disliked him.

His eyes narrowed with surprise and displeasure when he saw she had followed him from the waiting room to the clinic area.

"This way is quicker," she explained. "I'm parked by

the side door. I thought it would be easier to transport him on the stretcher from there."

He didn't say anything, only charged through the side door she indicated. She trotted after him, wondering how the Pine Gulch animal kingdom would get along without the kindness and compassion Dr. Harris had been renowned for.

Without waiting for her, he opened the door of the truck. As she watched, it was as if a different man had suddenly taken over. His harsh, set features seemed to ease and even the stiff set of his shoulders relaxed.

"Hello there," he crooned from the open vehicle door to the dog. "You've got yourself into a mess, haven't you?"

Even through his pain, Luke responded to the gentle-sounding stranger by trying hard to wag his tail. There was no room for both of them on the passenger side, so she went around to the driver's side and opened that door, intent on helping to lift the dog from there. By the time she made it that short distance, Dr. Caldwell had already slipped a transfer sheet under the dog and was gripping the edges.

His hands were big, she noticed, with a little light area of skin where a wedding ring once had been.

She knew a little about him from the gossip around town. It was hard to miss it when he was currently staying at the Cold Creek Inn—owned and operated by her sister-in-law Laura, married to Caidy's brother Taft.

Though Laura usually didn't gossip about her guests, over dinner last week her other brother, Trace—who made it his business as police chief to find out about everyone moving into Pine Gulch—had interrogated her so skillfully, Laura probably didn't realize what she had revealed.

From that conversation, Caidy had learned Ben Caldwell had two children, a girl and a boy, ages nine and five, respectively, and he had been a widower for two years.

Why on earth he had suddenly pulled up stakes to settle in a quiet town like Pine Gulch was a mystery to everyone. In her experience, people who came to this little corner of Idaho in the shadow of the Tetons were either looking for something or running away.

None of that was her business, she reminded herself. The only thing she cared about was the way he treated her dogs. Judging by how carefully he moved his hands over Luke's injuries, he appeared competent and even kind, at least to animals—something she generally considered a far more important character indicator than how a man treated other people.

"Okay, Luke. Just lie still, there's a good boy." He spoke in a low, calm voice. "We're going to move you now. Easy. Easy."

He handed the stretcher across the cab to her and then reached for the transfer sheet. "I'm going to lift him slightly and then you can slide the board under him. Slowly. Yes. That's it."

She had plenty of experience transferring injured animals. Years of experience. It bothered her to be treated as if she didn't know the first thing about this kind of emergency care, but now didn't seem the time to correct him.

Together they carried the stretcher into the emergency treatment room and set the dog gingerly down on the exam table.

She didn't like the pain in Luke's eyes. It reminded her a lot of how Lucky, her brother Taft's little beagle cross, had looked right after the car accident that had nearly killed him.

Now Lucky was happy as a pig in clover, she reminded herself. He lived with Taft and Laura and their two children at Taft's house near the mouth of Cold Creek Canyon and thought he ruled the universe. If Lucky could survive his brush with death, she couldn't see any reason for Luke to do otherwise.

"That's a nasty puncture wound. At least an inch or two deep. I'm surprised it's not deeper."

That could be because she had managed to pull Luke to safety before Festus could finish taking his bad mood out on a helpless dog.

"What about the leg? Can you save it?"

"I'm going to have to x-ray before I can answer that. How far are you prepared to go for his care?"

It took her a moment to realize what he was asking in his blunt way. A difficult part of life as a vet was the knowledge that, although a vet might have the power to treat an animal successfully, sometimes the owner's ability—or willingness, for that matter—to pay was the ultimate decision maker.

"Whatever is necessary," she answered stiffly. "I don't care about the cost. Just do what you have to do."

He nodded, his attention still on her dog, and she wanted to think his hard expression thawed slightly, like a tiny crackle of ice on the edge of a much deeper lake.

"Regardless of what the X-ray shows, his treatment is going to take a few hours. You can go. Leave your number with Joni and I'll have her call you when I know more."

"No. I'll wait."

That surprise in his blue eyes annoyed the heck out of her. Did he think she would just abandon her dog here with a stranger for a couple of hours while she went off to have her hair done?

"Your choice."

"I can help you back here. I've...had some training and I often helped Doc Harris. I actually worked here when I was a teenager."

If her life had gone a little more according to plan, *she* might have been the one taking over Doc Harris's clinic, though she hoped she wouldn't be as surly and unlikable as this new veterinarian.

"That won't be necessary." Dr. Caldwell dismissed all her hopes and dreams and volunteer work at the clinic as if they meant nothing. "Joni and I can handle it. If you insist on waiting, you can go ahead and have a seat in the waiting room."

What a jerk. She could push the matter. She *was* paying for the treatment here, after all. If she wanted to stay with her dog, there was nothing Dr. Ben No-Bedside-Manner Caldwell could do about it. But she didn't want to waste time and possibly jeopardize Luke's treatment.

"Fine," she muttered. She turned and pushed through the doors into the waiting room, seething with frustration.

After quickly sending a message to Ridge updating him on the situation and reminding her brother he would have to pick his daughter, Destry, up from the bus stop, she plopped onto one of the uncomfortable gray benches and grabbed a magazine off the side table.

She was leafing through it, barely even registering the headlines in her worry over her dog, when the bells on the door chimed and a little boy of about five burst through, followed a little more slowly by an older girl.

"Daaad! We're here!"

"Hush." A round, cheerful-looking woman who looked to be in her early sixties followed more slowly. "You know better than that, young man. Your father might be in the middle of a procedure."

"Can I go back and find him?" the girl asked.

"Because Joni isn't out here either, they must both be busy. He won't want to be bothered. You two sit down here and I'll go back to let him know we're here."

"I could go," the girl said a little sulkily, but she plopped onto the bench across from Caidy. Like father, like daughter, she thought. This was obviously the new vet's family, and his daughter, at least, seemed to share more than blue eyes with her father.

"Sit down," the girl ordered her brother. The boy didn't quite stick his tongue out at his sister, but it was a close one. Instead, he ignored her—probably a much worse insult, if Caidy remembered her own childhood with three pesky brothers—and wandered over to stand directly in front of Caidy.

The little boy had a widow's peak in his brown hair and huge dark-lashed blue eyes. A Caldwell trait, apparently.

"Hi." He beamed at her. "I'm Jack Caldwell. My sister's name is Ava. Who are you?"

"My name is Caidy," she answered.

"My dad's a dog doctor."

"Not just dogs," the girl corrected. "He's also a cat doctor. And sometimes even horses and cows."

"I know," Caidy answered. "That's why I'm here."

"Is your dog sick?" Jack asked her.

"In a way. He was hurt on our ranch. Your dad is working on him now."

"He's really good," the girl said with obvious pride. "I bet your dog will be just fine."

"I hope so."

"Our dog was hit by a car once and my dad fixed him and now he's all better," Jack said. "Well, except he only has three legs. His name is Tri. My dad says it's 'cause he always tries hard, even though he only has three legs."

Despite her worry, she managed a smile, more than a little charmed by the boy—and by the idea of the taciturn veterinarian showing any hint of sweetness.

"Tri means three," Ava informed her in a haughty sort of tone. "You know, like a *tri*cycle has three wheels."

"Good to know."

Before the children could say anything else, the older woman came back through the door leading out of the treatment room, her features set in a rueful smile.

"Looks like we're on our own for dinner, kids. Your dad is busy fixing an injured dog and he's going to be a while. We'll just go catch some dinner and then head back to the hotel for homework and bed."

"You're staying at the Cold Creek Inn, aren't you?" Caidy asked.

The other woman looked a bit wary as she nodded. "I'm sorry. Have we met?"

"I'm Caidy Bowman. My sister-in-law Laura runs the inn."

"You're Chief Bowman's sister?" There was a definite warmth in the woman's voice now, Caidy noticed wryly. Her charmer of a brother often had that effect on those of the female persuasion, no matter their age.

"I am. Both Chief Bowmans." With one brother who was the police chief and the other who headed up the fire department, not much exciting happened in town without someone in her family being in the thick of it.

"How nice to meet you. I'm Anne Michaels. I'm Dr. Caldwell's housekeeper. Or I will be when he finally gets into his house. With the maids at the inn cleaning our rooms for us, there's not much for me to do in that department. Right now I'm just the nanny, I suppose."

"Oh?"

The woman apparently didn't need any more encouragement than that simple syllable. "Dr. Caldwell is building a house on Cold Creek Road. He was supposed to close on it last week, but the contractor ran into some problems and here we are, still staying at the inn. Which is lovely, don't get me wrong, but it's still a hotel. After three weeks, all of us are a little tired of it. And now it looks like we'll be there until after the New Year. Christmas in a hotel. Can you imagine such a thing?"

Maybe that explained the man's grouchiness. She felt a little pang of sympathy, then she remembered how he had basically shoved her out of the treatment area. No, he was probably born with that temperament. He and Festus would get along just fine.

"It must be very frustrating for all of you."

"You don't know the half of it. Two children in a hotel, even a couple of rooms, for all those weeks is just too much. They need space to run. All children do. Why, in San Jose, the children had a huge backyard, complete with a pool and a swing set that rivaled the equipment at the nearest park."

"Is that where you're from, then? California?"

Anne Michaels nodded and Caidy thought she saw a note of wistfulness in the woman's eyes that didn't bode well for the chances of Dr. Caldwell's housekeeper-slash-nanny sticking around in Pine Gulch.

Anne watched the children, who were paying them no heed as they played a game on an electronic device Ava had pulled out of her backpack.

"Yes. I'm from California, born and bred. Not Dr. Caldwell. He's from back East. Chicago way. But he left everything without a backward look to head west for veterinary school at UC-Davis and that's where he met the late Mrs. Caldwell. They hired me to help out around the house when she was pregnant with little Jack there and I've been with them ever since. Those poor children needed me more than ever after their mother died. Dr. Caldwell too. That was a terrible time, I tell you."

"I'm sure."

"When he decided to move here to Idaho, he gave me the option of leaving his employment with a glowing recommendation, but I just couldn't do it. I love those children, you know?"

Caidy could relate. She loved her niece Destry as fiercely as if the girl were her own. Stepping in to help raise her after her mother walked out on Ridge and their daughter had created a powerful bond between them as unshakable as the Tetons.

"I'm sure you do."

Anne Michaels gave a rueful shake of her head. "Look at me, going on to a perfect stranger. Staying at that hotel all these weeks is making me batty!"

"Perhaps you could find a temporary rental situation until the house is finished," she suggested.

"That's what I wanted to do but Ben doesn't think we can find anyone willing to rent us a place for only a few weeks, especially over the holidays."

Caidy thought of the foreman's cottage, empty for the past six months since the young married couple Ridge had hired to help around the ranch had moved on to take a job at a Texas ranch.

It was furnished with three bedrooms and would probably fit the Caldwells' needs perfectly, but she was hesitant to mention it. She didn't like the man. Why on earth would she want him living only a quarter mile away?

"I could ask around for you if you'd like. We have a few vacation rentals in town that might be available. At least it might give you a little breathing space over the holidays until the house is finished."

"How kind you are!" Mrs. Michaels exclaimed.

A fine guilt pinched at her. If she were truly kind, she would immediately offer the foreman's cottage.

"Everyone here in Pine Gulch has been so nice and welcoming to us," the woman went on.

"I hope you feel at home here."

Again that wistfulness drifted across the woman's features like an autumn leaf tossed by the breeze, but she blinked it away. "I'm guessing the dog Dr. Caldwell is working on back there is yours, then."

Caidy nodded. "He had a run-in with a bull. When you pit a forty-pound dog against a ton of beef, the bull usually wins."

She should be back there with him. Darn it. If she were better at handling confrontations, she would have told Dr. Arrogant that she wasn't going anywhere. Instead, she was sitting out here fretting.

"He's a wonderful veterinarian, my dear. I'm sure your pet will be better before you know it."

The border collies at the River Bow Ranch weren't exactly pets—they were a vital part of the workload. Except for Sadie, anyway, who was too old to work the cattle anymore. She didn't bother to correct the woman, nor did she express any of her own doubts about the new veterinarian's competence.

"I'm hungry, Mrs. Michaels. When are we going to eat?" Bored with the game apparently, Jack had wandered back to them.

"I think your father is going to be busy for a while yet. Why don't you and Ava and I go find something? Perhaps dinner at the café tonight would be fun and we can pick something up for your father for later."

"Can I have one of the sweet rolls?" he asked, his eyes lighting up as if it were already Christmas morning.

The housekeeper laughed. "We'll have to see about that. I'd say the café's business in sweet rolls has tripled since we came to town, thanks to you alone."

"They are delish," Caidy agreed, smiling at the very cute boy.

Mrs. Michaels rose to her feet with a creak and a pop of some joint. "It was lovely to meet you, Caidy Bowman."

"I'm happy to meet you too. And I'll keep my eye out for a suitable vacation rental."

"You'll need to take that up with Dr. Caldwell, but thank you."

The woman seemed to be efficient, Caidy thought as she watched her herd the children out the door.

The reception room seemed even more bleak and colorless after the trio left. Though it was just past six, the night was already dark on this, one of the shortest days of the year. Caidy fidgeted, leafing aimlessly through her magazine for a few moments longer, then finally closed it with a rustle of pages and tossed it back onto the pile.

Darn it. That was her dog back there. She couldn't sit out here doing nothing. At the very least she deserved to know what was going on. She gathered her courage, took a deep breath and pushed through the door.

Chapter 2

Ben made the last stitch to close the incision on the puncture wound, his head throbbing and his shoulders tight from the long day that had started with an emergency call to treat an ailing horse at four in the morning.

He would have loved a nice evening with his kids and then a few hours of zone-out time watching basketball on the hotel television set. Even if he had to turn the sound low so he didn't wake up Jack, the idea sounded heavenly.

The past week had been a rough one, busy and demanding. This was what he wanted, he reminded himself. Even though the workload was heavy, he finally had the chance to build his own practice, to forge new relationships and become part of a community.

"There. That should do it for now."

"What a mess. After seeing how close that puncture

wound was to the liver, I can't believe he survived," Joni said.

He didn't want to admit to his assistant—who, after three weeks, still seemed to approve of the job he was doing—that the dog's condition was still touch and go.

"I think he's going to make it," she went on, ever the optimist. "Unlike that poor Newfoundland earlier."

All his frustration of earlier in the afternoon came surging back as he began dressing the wound. A tragedy, that was. The beautiful dog had jumped out of the back of a moving pickup truck and been hit by the car driving behind it.

That dog hadn't been as lucky as Luke here. Her injuries were just too severe and she had died on this very treatment table.

What had really pissed him off had been the attitude of the owner, more concerned at the loss of all the money he had invested in the animal than in the loss of life.

"Neither accident would have happened if not for irresponsible owners."

Joni, busy cleaning up the inevitable mess he always left behind during a surgery, looked a little surprised at his vehemence.

"I agree when it comes to Artie Palmer. He's an idiot who should have his privileges to own any animals revoked. But not Caidy Bowman. She's the last one I would call an irresponsible owner. She trains dogs and horses at the River Bow. Nobody around here does a better job."

"She didn't train this one very well, did she, if he was running wild and tangled with a bull?"

"Apparently not."

He turned at the new voice and found the dog's owner standing in the doorway from the reception area, her lovely features taut. He swore under his breath. He meant what he said, but he supposed it didn't need to be said to *her*.

"I thought I suggested you wait in the other room."

"A suggestion? Is that what you city vets call that?" She shrugged. "I'm not particularly good at doing as I'm told, Dr. Caldwell."

Sometime during the process of caring for her dog, Ben had come to the uncomfortable realization that he had acted like a jerk to her. He never insisted owners wait outside the treatment room unless he thought they might have weak stomachs. So why had he changed policy for Caidy Bowman?

Something about her made him a little nervous. He couldn't quite put a finger on it, but it might have something to do with those impossibly green eyes and the sweet little tilt to her mouth.

"We just finished. I was about to call you back."

"I'm glad I finally disregarded your strongly worded *suggestion,* then. May I?"

He gestured agreement and she approached the table, where the dog was still working off the effects of the anesthesia.

"There's my brave boy. Oh, Luke." She smoothed a hand over the dog's head. The dog's eyes opened slightly then closed again and his breathing slowed, as if he could rest comfortably now, knowing she was near.

"It will probably take another half hour or so for the rest of the anesthesia to wear off and then we'll have to keep him here, at least overnight."

"Will someone stay with him?"

At his practice in San Jose, he and a technician would alternate stopping in every few hours through the night when they had very ill dogs staying at the clinic, but he hadn't had time yet to get fully staffed.

He nodded, watching his plans for a nice steak dinner and a basketball game in the hotel room go up in smoke. He had become pretty used to the cot in his office lately. Whatever would he do without Mrs. Michaels?

"Someone will be here with him. Don't worry about that."

A look of surprise flickered in her eyes. He couldn't figure out why for a moment, until he realized she was reacting to his soft tone. He really must have been a jackass to her.

"I'm sorry about…earlier." Apologies didn't come easily. He could probably thank his stiff, humorless grandfather for that, but this one seemed necessary. "About not letting you come in during the treatment, I mean. I should have. And about what I said just now. I'm usually not so…harsh. It's been a particularly hard day and I'm afraid I may have been taking it out on you."

She blinked a little but concealed her emotions behind an impassive look. For some reason, that made him feel even more like an idiot, a sensation he didn't like at all.

"You were able to save his leg. I thought for sure you would have to amputate."

"He wouldn't be much use as a ranch dog, then, would he?"

Her look was as cool as the December night. "Probably not. Isn't it a good thing that's not the only thing that matters to me?"

So she wasn't like his previous client, who hadn't cared about his injured dog—only dollars and cents.

"I was able to pin the leg for now, but there's no guarantee it will heal properly. We still might have to take it. He was lucky, if you want the truth. Insanely lucky. I don't know how he made it through a run-in with a bull in one piece. His injuries could have been much worse."

"What about where he was gored?"

"The bull missed all vital organs. The puncture wound is only a couple inches deep. I guess the bull wasn't that serious."

"You would think otherwise if you had been there. He definitely was seeing red. After I pulled the dog out, he rammed the fence so hard he knocked one of the poles out of its foundation."

She pulled the dog out? Crazy woman, to mess with a bull on a rampage. What was she thinking?

"Looks like he's coming around," he said, not about to enter that particular fray.

The dog whimpered and Caidy Bowman leaned down, her dark hair almost a match to the dog's coat. "Hey there. You're in a fix now, aren't you, Luke-my-boy. You'll be all right. I know it hurts now and you're confused and scared but Dr. Caldwell fixed you up and before you know it you'll be running around the ranch with King and Sadie and all the others."

Though he had paperwork to complete, he couldn't seem to wrench himself away. He stood watching her interact with the dog and winced to himself at how quickly he had misjudged her. By the gentleness of her tone and the comforting way she smoothed a hand over his fur, it was obvious the woman cared about her animal and was not inexperienced with injuries.

Next time maybe he wouldn't be quick to make surly comments when he was having a miserable day.

She smelled delicious, like vanilla splashed on wild-flowers. The scent of her drifted to him, a bright counterpoint to the sometimes unpleasant smells of a busy veterinary clinic.

It was an unsettling discovery. He didn't want to notice anything about her. Not the sweet way she smelled or the elegant curve of her neck or how, when she tucked her hair behind her ear, she unveiled a tiny beauty mark just below the lobe…

He caught the direction of his thoughts and shut them down, appalled at himself. He forced himself to move away and block the sound of her low voice crooning to the dog.

He had almost forgotten about his technician until she came out of the employee changing room, shoving her arms through the sleeves of her parka. "Do you mind if I go? I'm sorry. It's just past six-thirty and I'm supposed to be at my Bible study Christmas party in half an hour and I still have to run home and pick up my cookies for the swap."

"No. Get out of here. I'm sorry I kept you late."

"Wasn't your fault."

"Blame my curious dog," Caidy said with an apologetic smile that didn't mask the concern in her eyes.

Joni shrugged. "Accidents happen, especially on a ranch."

Ben felt another twist of guilt. She was right. Even the most careful pet owner couldn't prevent everything.

"Thanks, Ben. You both have a good night," Joni said.

"I'll walk you out," he said.

She rolled her eyes—this was an argument they had been having since he arrived. His clinic in San Jose hadn't been in the best part of the city and he would always make sure the women who worked for him made it safely to their cars in the parking lot.

It was probably an old-fashioned habit, but when he had been in vet school, a fellow student and friend had been assaulted on the way to her car after a late-night class and had ended up dropping out of school.

The cold air outside the clinic blew a little bit of energy into him. The snow of earlier had slowed to just a few flurries. The few houses around his clinic blinked their cheerful holiday lights and he regretted again that he hadn't strung a few strands in the window of the clinic.

Joni's SUV was covered in snow and he helped her brush it off.

"Thank you, Dr. Caldwell," Joni said with a smile. "You're the only employer I've ever had who scrapes my windows."

"I don't know what I'd do without you right now," he said truthfully. "I just don't want you getting into an accident on the way home."

"Thanks. Have a good night. Call me if you need me to spell you during the night."

He nodded and waved her off, then returned to the office invigorated from the cold air. He pulled open the door and caught the incongruous notes of a soft melody.

Caidy was humming, he realized. He paused to listen and it took just a moment for him to recognize the tune as "Greensleeves." He was afraid to move, not wanting to intrude on the moment. The notes seemed to seep through him, sweet and pure and somehow peaceful amid the harsh lights and complicated equipment of the clinic.

Judging by her humming, he would guess Caidy Bowman had a lovely voice.

He didn't think he had made a sound, but she somehow sensed him anyway. She looked up and a delicate pink flush washed over her cheeks. "Sorry. You must think I'm ridiculous, humming to a dog. He started to get agitated and…it seemed to calm him."

No surprise there. The melody had done the same to *him*. "Looks like he's sleeping again. I can take things from here if you need to go."

She looked uncertain. "I could stay. My brother and niece can handle chores tonight for the rest of my animals."

"We've got this covered. Don't worry. He'll be well taken care of, Ms. Bowman."

"Just Caidy. Please. No one calls me Ms. anything."

"Caidy, then."

"Is someone coming to relieve you?"

"I'm not fully staffed yet and Joni has her party tonight and then her husband and kids to get back to. No big deal. I have a cot in my office. I should be fine. When we have overnight emergency cases, I make do there."

He had again succeeded in surprising her, he saw.

"What about your children?" she asked.

"They'll be fine with Mrs. Michaels. It's only for a night."

"I… Thank you."

"You'll have a hefty bill for overnight care," he warned.

"I expected it. I worked here a decade ago and know

how much things used to cost—and I've seen those charges go up in the years since." She paused. "I hate to leave him."

"He'll be fine. Don't worry. Come on. I'll walk you out."

"Is that a service you provide for every female who comes through your office?"

Close enough. "I need to lock up anyway."

She gathered her coat and shrugged into it, and then he led her back the way he had just come. The moon was filtering through the clouds, painting lovely patterns of pale light on the new snow.

Caidy Bowman drove a well-used late-model pickup truck with a king cab that was covered in mud. Bales of hay were stacked two high in the back.

"Be careful. The roads are likely to be slick after the snows of earlier."

"I've been driving these roads since before I turned sixteen. I can handle a little snow."

"I'm sure you can. I just don't want you to be the next one in need of stitching."

"Not much chance of that, but thank you for your concern. And for all you've done today. I'm sorry you won't see much of your children."

"The clinic is closed tomorrow. I can spend the whole day with them. I suppose we'll have to go look for a temporary furnished house somewhere or I'm going to have a mutiny on my hands from Mrs. Michaels, which would be a nightmare."

She opened her mouth, then closed it again, and he had the distinct impression she was waging some internal debate. Her gaze shifted to the door they had just exited through and back to him, then she drew in a breath.

"We have an empty foreman's cottage on the River Bow where you could stay."

The words spilled out of her, almost as if she had been trying to hold them back. He barely noticed, stunned by the offer.

"It's nothing fancy but it's fully furnished," she went on quickly. "It does only have three bedrooms, but if you took one and Mrs. Michaels took the other, the children could share."

"Whoa. Hold on. How do you know Mrs. Michaels? And who told you we might be looking for a place?"

"We met in the waiting room earlier. I knew you were staying at the inn because my sister-in-law Laura runs it."

If not for that moment of sweetness when he had found her humming a soothing song to her dog, he would have had a tough time believing the warm and welcoming innkeeper could be any relation to this prickly woman.

"Anyway, your housekeeper mentioned you might be looking for a place. I, uh, immediately thought of the foreman's cottage on our ranch. Nobody's using it right now, though I do try to stop in once a week or so to keep the dust down. Like I said, it's not much."

"We could manage. Are you certain?"

"I'll have to ask my brother first. Though all four of us share ownership of the ranch, Ridge is really the one in charge. I don't think he'll say no, though. Why would he?"

He didn't understand this woman. He had been extraordinarily rude to her, yet she was offering to help solve all his domestic problems in one fell swoop.

"I'm astonished, Ms. Bowman. Er, Caidy. Why would you make such an offer to a complete stranger?"

"You saved my dog," she said simply. "Besides that, I liked Mrs. Michaels and I gather she's had enough of hotel living. And how will St. Nick find your children in a hotel, as lovely as the Cold Creek Inn might be these days? They should have a proper house for the holidays, where they can play."

"I agree. That was the plan all along, but circumstances haven't exactly cooperated."

He had planned to spend the entire next day looking around for somewhere that better met their needs. He never expected the answer would fall right in his lap. A less cynical man might even call it a Christmas miracle.

"I still have to talk to Ridge. I can let you know his answer in the morning when I come to check on Luke."

"Thank you."

She gave him a hesitant smile just as the moonlight shifted. The light combined with her smile managed to transform her features from pretty to extraordinarily beautiful.

"Good night. Thank you again for your hard work."

"You're welcome."

He watched her drive away, her headlights cutting through the darkness. When he had agreed to buy James Harris's practice, he had been seeking a quiet, easy community to raise his family, a place where they could settle in and become part of things.

Pine Gulch had already provided a few more surprises than he expected—and he suddenly suspected Caidy Bowman might be one more.

Chapter 3

"You say the new vet only needs a place to stay for a few weeks?"

Caidy nodded at her oldest brother, who stood at the sink loading his and Destry's supper dishes into the dishwasher. "That's my understanding. He's building a new house on Cold Creek Road. I'm guessing it's in that new development near Taft's place. Apparently, it was supposed to be finished before he took the job, but it's behind schedule. Now it won't be ready until after Christmas."

"That's a nice area. Heck of a view. I imagine his house is probably a good sight better than our foreman's cottage."

"They're at the inn now. I got the impression the children and the housekeeper might be going a little stir-crazy there."

Ridge straightened and gave her a look she recognized well. It was his patented *What were you thinking?* look. He was ten years older than she was and she loved him dearly. He had stepped in after their parents died and had raised her for the last few years of high school and she would never be able to repay him for being her rock, even when his own marriage was faltering. He was tough and hard on the outside and sweet as could be underneath all the layers.

He still drove her crazy sometimes.

"You ever stop to think that Laura might not be too thrilled if you go around finding other lodging arrangements for her paying guests?"

"I called her already and she was cool with it. I know it's lost business, but all I had to do was paint the mental picture of Alex and Maya cooped up in a couple of hotel rooms for weeks on end—including through Christmas—and she had complete sympathy for Dr. Caldwell and his housekeeper. She thought it was a great idea."

She didn't bother telling her brother that Taft's wife had also dropped a couple of matchmaking hints a mile wide about how gorgeous the new vet was. He was kind to animals and he loved his kids. What more did she need? Laura had implied.

Ridge didn't need to know that. Much as she loved both of her sisters-in-law and considered Laura and Becca perfect for each respective twin, she didn't need her brothers joining in and trying to look around for prospective partners for her. The very idea of what they might come up with gave her chills.

After one of his long, thoughtful pauses, Ridge finally nodded. "Can't see any harm in Dr. Caldwell and his family moving in for a few weeks. The house is only sitting there empty. I can run the tractor down the lane to make sure it's cleared up for them. It might need the cobwebs swept and a little airing out."

"I'll take care of everything tomorrow after I check on Luke."

So it was settled, then. She had to fight the urge to give a giant, cartoon-style gulp. What had she just gotten herself into? She didn't want the man here.

Okay, he had been a little less like a jackass toward the end of her visit to the clinic with Luke, but that didn't mean she was obligated to invite him to move in down the road, for Pete's sake.

She still wasn't quite sure what had motivated her offer. Maybe that little spark of compassion in his blue eyes when he had tended to Luke with that surprising gentleness. Or maybe it was simply that she couldn't resist his cute son's charm.

Whatever the reason, they would only be there a few weeks. She likely wouldn't even see the man, especially as it appeared he spent most of his time at the veterinary clinic. And she could be comfortable knowing she had done her good deed for the day. Wasn't Christmas the perfect time for a little welcoming generosity?

"What did you think of his doctoring?" Ridge asked.

She thought of Luke and his carefully bandaged injuries. "He's not Doc Harris but I suppose he'll do."

Ridge chuckled. "You'll never think anybody is as good as Doc Harris. The two of you have taken care of a lot of animals together."

She had loved working at the vet clinic when she was in high school. It was just about the only thing that had kept her going after her parents died, those quiet moments when she would be holding a sick or injured animal and feeling some measure of peace.

"He's a good man. Dr. Caldwell has some pretty big boots to fill," she answered.

"From rumors I've been hearing around town, he's doing a good job of it so far."

She didn't want to talk about the veterinarian anymore. It was bad enough she couldn't seem to think about anything else since she had left the clinic.

"What were you saying to Destry after I started clearing the dishes? I heard something about the wagon," Caidy said.

He glanced through the open doorway into the dining room, where Destry was bent over the table working on a homework assignment about holiday traditions in Europe.

"Des asked me if she could invite Gabi and a couple of their other friends over for a wagon ride Sunday night. She suggested caroling to the neighbors."

She never should have shared with Destry her memories of doing that very thing with their parents when she and the boys were young. "What did you tell her?"

He didn't answer, but he didn't need to. She could tell by his expression that he had given in. Ridge might be a hard man when it came to their cattle and the ranch, but when it came to his daughter he was soft as new taffy.

"You're a good father, Ridge."

"She loves Christmas," he finally said. "What can I do?"

The rest of them weren't quite as fond of the holidays as Des but they put on a good show for her sake. Since their parents' murders just a few days before Christmas eleven years ago, the holidays seemed to dredge up difficult emotions.

Becca and Laura had worked some kind of sparkly holiday magic over Trace and Taft. This year the twins seemed to be more into the spirit of Christmas than she'd ever seen them. They had both volunteered to cut trees for everyone. They had even gone a little overboard, cutting a few extras for neighbors and friends.

She and Ridge didn't share their enthusiasm, though they both went through the motions every year. Caidy even had all her Christmas presents wrapped and the actual holiday was still more than a week away. No more last-minute panics for her this year.

"What time are they coming?"

"I told her to make arrangements for about seven. I figured we would be done with Sunday dinner by then."

Though Taft and Trace both lived closer to town, her brothers usually brought their families out to the ranch every week. With the hectic pace of their lives protecting and serving the good people of Pine Gulch, it was sometimes the only chance she had to see them all week.

"I'll throw some cookies in just before they get here so they can have something warm in their little bellies before they go. And I'll make hot chocolate for the ride, of course."

"Thanks. Destry will appreciate that, I'm sure." He finished wiping down the countertop and set the cloth on the sink's edge. "You won't consider coming with us?"

By his solemn expression, she knew he was aware just what he asked of her. "I don't think so."

"You would really send me off on my own with five or six giggly girls?"

"You can take one of the dogs with you," she offered with a grin.

He made a face but quickly grew serious again. "It's been eleven years, Caidy. Taft and Trace have moved on and both have families. Of all of us, you deserve to do the same. I wish you could find a little Christmas joy again."

"I find plenty of joy the rest of the year. Just not so much in December."

His mouth tightened, his eyes darkening with familiar sadness. Each of them had struggled in different ways after their parents' deaths. Ridge had become more stoic and controlled, Taft had gone a little crazy dating all the wild women at the tavern in town and Trace had become a dedicated lawman.

And she was still hiding away here at the River Bow.

"You need to move on," her brother said. "Maybe it's time you think about trying school again."

"Maybe." She gave a noncommittal answer, too tired to fight with him right now after the ordeal of Luke's injury and the hours spent in the waiting room of the veterinary clinic. "Hey, thanks again for letting the vet stay in the foreman's cottage. It shouldn't be longer than a few weeks."

Ridge wasn't fooled for a moment. He knew she was trying to change the subject. For once he didn't try to call her on it.

"Just think. For a few weeks anyway we'll have our own veterinarian-in-residence. With your menagerie, that should come in pretty handy."

She made a face. Given her unwilling reaction to the

man, she would rather not have need of his professional services again anytime soon.

A good four inches of snow fell during the night. It clung to the trees and bowed down the branches, turning the town into an enchanting winter wonderland, especially with the craggy mountains looming in the distance.

Added to the few inches that had fallen the previous evening, that should be plenty for Destry to have a great time with her friends on the sleigh ride the next night, Caidy thought as she drove through the quiet stillness of the unplowed roads on her way to the clinic the next morning.

It wasn't yet seven. She hadn't slept well, her dreams a troubled, tangled mess. With worry for Luke uppermost in her mind, she had risen early and finished her chores. Ridge could take care of breakfast for him and Destry when he finished his own chores. Saturday morning pancakes were his specialty.

Even with her restless sleep, she could appreciate the beauty of the morning. Colorful Christmas trees gleamed in the windows of a few houses, and she liked to imagine the children there rushing to plug in the lights the moment they woke up so they could enjoy the display before the sun was fully up.

When she reached Dr. Caldwell's office, she wasn't particularly surprised to see the parking lot hadn't been plowed yet. Like many of the small businesses in Pine Gulch, he probably paid a service to take care of that for him and the plows hadn't made it here yet.

With four-wheel drive and high clearance, her truck had no problem navigating through the snow. Mindful of helping the plow work around her vehicle, she parked at the edge of the lot, next to a snow-covered Range Rover she assumed must belong to Ben.

As she headed for the building, she worried she might be waking him after a long night of watching over Luke. The sidewalks had been cleared, though. Unless he paid someone else to take care of that chore, she guessed Ben had taken care of the shoveling himself.

She wasn't surprised to find the front door locked. When Doc Harris was here, she never had to bother with the front door; she could use the side entrance she had used the night before.

Likely that's where she would find Ben Caldwell. She trudged through the snow, enjoying the brisk cold and the scent of snowy pine. A couple hard raps on the door elicited no response. She checked the door and the knob turned easily in her hand.

After a quick internal debate, she turned the knob and stepped inside. She opened her mouth to call out a greeting but the words vanished somewhere in the vicinity of her tongue—along with any remaining air in her lungs—at the sight of the new veterinarian coming out of the locker room wearing only jeans and toweling off his wet hair.

That dramatic cartoon gulp sounded in her head again. Wow. Double wow. With ice cream on top.

His chest was broad and well-defined with solid muscle and a little line of hair arrowed down to disappear in the waistband of his Levi's, where he hadn't yet fastened the top button.

Awareness bloomed inside her, as bright and vivid as the always unexpected crocuses that popped up through the snow along the fenceline of the River Bow every spring.

Her toes tingled and her heartbeat kicked up a notch and she wanted to stand here for the next few years and just stare.

He continued toweling his hair, oblivious to her, biceps flexing with the motion, and she completely forgot about the reason she had come. Suddenly he dropped the towel and saw her standing there.

His pupils widened and for a long moment, he returned her stare. Tension seethed between them, writhing and alive. Her insides trembled and every thought in her head seemed scrambled and incoherent.

Finally he cleared his throat. "Oh. Hi. I didn't hear you come in."

"Sorry." Her voice sounded raspy and she quickly cleared it, mortified that he had caught her gaping at him like Destry and her friends at a Justin Bieber concert. "I knocked and was just checking the door and it opened and…there you were."

Could she sound any more stupid? Good grief. She wanted to slink away through the door and bury her face in a pile of snow somewhere. Anybody might think she'd never seen a gorgeous, half-naked man before.

"I just… I can go and come back, uh, later."

"Why?" He grabbed a clean scrub top and she couldn't seem to look away as he pulled it over that delicious chest, her gaze fixed on the disappearance of that little strip of hair trailing down his abdomen.

Despite his towel job, his hair was still wet and sticking up in spikes. He made an effort to smooth it down but only ended up making it look more tousled and sexy.

She wanted to gulp again, feeling very much like some ridiculous maiden aunt.

Which she was.

"I shouldn't have come so early. I was just...concerned about how you made it through the night."

He shrugged, though she thought she noticed a little spark of *something* in the depths of his blue eyes. "Not too badly. Luke slept most of the night. I imagine he's going to be ready for a walk around the yard soon."

That must have been why he had cleared away the snow around the sidewalk. She had wondered why that had been a priority, especially because he had told her the clinic would be closed that day.

She fought the little burst of warmth in her chest. *Get a grip,* she told herself. She wasn't interested in some prickly veterinarian who jumped to conclusions and made snap judgments about people before he knew the facts.

Even if he did have a flat stomach she wanted to trail her fingers along...

She blushed and looked away. Her dog. That's why she was here—to check on Luke. Not to engage in completely inappropriate fantasies about a man who would be living just a stone's throw away from her.

"I can take him out if you're sure he's up to it."

"We made one trip out in the night. He seemed to handle it okay. Let's try again."

She headed to the crate where Luke lay. As if sensing her presence, his eyes opened and he tried to wag his tail, which just about broke her heart. "Shhh. Easy. Easy. There's my boy. How's my favorite guy?"

The dog's black tail flapped again on the soft blankets inside the crate. He tried to scramble up, then subsided again with a whimper.

"He's due for pain meds again. I was planning to try to slip a pill in some peanut butter."

She unlatched the door of the crate and reached in to rub his chin. "I hope you didn't keep Dr. Caldwell up all night."

"Not too bad." Ben hadn't shaved yet and the dark shadow along his jawline gave him a rugged, rather disreputable air. He probably wouldn't appreciate her pointing that out—and he *definitely* wouldn't be interested in knowing about her unwilling attraction to him.

"We had a few rough moments." He paused, giving her a careful look. "To tell the truth, I wasn't completely convinced he would make it through the night. He's a tough little guy."

"It helps to have a good vet," she said. Even Doc Harris wouldn't have stayed all night. It was a hard admission, but honesty compelled her to face it. As much as she loved the old veterinarian, she had noticed he sometimes had a bit of a cavalier attitude about the seriousness of some cases.

Apparently that wasn't the case with Dr. Caldwell.

"Sometimes all the veterinarian skills in the world aren't enough. I guess you would know that, as an animal lover."

That was her big worry right now with Sadie. Her old border collie, the very first dog who had been only hers, was thirteen. In border collie terms, that was ancient. As much as she loved her, Caidy knew she wouldn't be around forever.

"Luke seems alert now. That's a good sign, isn't it?"

He joined her in petting the dog. Their fingers accidentally touched and she didn't miss the way he quickly lifted his hands. "You can call him Lucky Luke."

"My brother and his family already have a dog named Lucky Lou," she said with a smile. "He survived being hit by a car."

"Your brother?"

She rolled her eyes. "No, but there was a time plenty of the scorned women of Pine Gulch would have gladly tried to run him down. No, Lou. He was a stray, a little corgi-beagle mix who used to wander around our ranch. I was trying to lure him in so I could find his owner, but he was pretty skittish. Then one afternoon he didn't move fast enough and some speeder hit him. He's doing great now and is extremely spoiled by Taft's kids."

Stepchildren, actually, but Maya and Alex had quickly been absorbed into the Bowman clan.

"Well, you can add this one to your collection of lucky pups."

"When can I take him home?"

"Maybe later today, as long as he remains stable."

"That would be great. Thank you for everything."

He shrugged. "It's my job."

She owed him now. It was an uncomfortable realization—she didn't like being beholden to anyone, especially not very attractive veterinarians.

In this case, she could even the playing field a little bit. "I talked to Ridge last night. He says you and your family are more than welcome to move into the foreman's cottage until your house is finished."

"Did he?" he asked, his expression pleased and more than a little relieved. "That would make the holidays much more comfortable all the way around."

"You may want to come out to the ranch and take a

look at the place before you agree. We've kept it up well, but it could probably use a remodel one of these days."

"Three bedrooms, you said?"

"Yes. And Ridge suggested we work something out with rent in trade for vet services, if you're agreeable. I'll still probably owe you my firstborn but maybe not my second."

He smiled—not a huge smile but a genuine one. Her stomach flip-flopped again and she remembered that moment when she had walked into the clinic and found him half-dressed.

What in heaven's name had come over her? She did *not* react to men this way. She just didn't. Oh, she dated once in a while. She wasn't a complete hermit, contrary to what her brothers teased her about. She enjoyed the occasional dinner or movie out, but she usually worked hard to keep things casual and fun. The few times a guy had tried to push for more, she had felt panicky and pressured and had done her best to discourage him.

She couldn't remember having such an instant and powerful reaction to a man, this immediate curl of desire. She certainly wasn't used to this jittery, off-balance feeling, as if she were teetering in the loft door of the barn, gearing up to jump into the big pile of hay below.

Ridiculous. She wasn't even sure she *liked* Ben Caldwell yet. She certainly wasn't ready to jump into any pile of hay with him, literally or figuratively.

"I'm sure it's fine," he answered. "If it has three bedrooms and a halfway decent kitchen for Mrs. Michaels, I don't care about much else."

She drew in a breath and subtly shifted to ease her shoulder away from his. "For all you know, it might be a hovel. You would be surprised at the living conditions some ranchers force on their workers."

"I would like to think you wouldn't have suggested it if you didn't think it would work for my family."

"That's trusting of you. You don't know anything about me. For all you know, maybe I make it a habit of bilking unsuspecting newcomers out of their rent money."

"Since we're talking about trading veterinary services for rent, that's not an issue, is it? But if you insist, I guess I could stop by your ranch later this morning after Joni comes in to relieve me. She's coming in around ten."

"That should work. I should have just enough time to rush back there and hide all the mousetraps and roach motels."

This time he laughed outright, as she had intended. It was a full, rich sound that shimmied down her spine as if he'd pressed his lips there.

This was a gigantic mistake. Why had she ever opened her big, stupid mouth about the foreman's cottage in the first place? The last thing she needed on the ranch right now was a gorgeous man with a sexy chest and a delicious laugh.

"Should I help you take Luke outside before I go?"

He seemed to know she was doing her best to change the subject. "No. I can handle it."

She nodded. "I'll see you in a bit, okay?" she said, rubbing the dog's head again. "You need to stay here just a little longer and then you can come home."

Luke whined as if he knew she were going to leave. It was tough but she shut the crate door again.

"You know he'll probably never be a working dog

now. I set the bones as well as I could, but he'll never be fast enough or strong enough to do what he used to."

"We're not so cruel that we'll make him sing for his supper, Dr. Caldwell. We'll still find a place for him on the River Bow, whether he can work the cattle or not. We have plenty of other animals who live on in comfortable retirement."

"I'm glad to hear that," he answered.

She firmly ignored his disreputable smile and the jumping nerves it set off in her stomach.

"Thanks again for everything. I guess I'll see you later."

She headed to the door, but to her dismay, he beat her to it and held it open, leaving her no choice but to brush past him on her way out. She ignored the little shiver of awareness, just as she had ignored all the others.

She could do this, she told herself. It would only be for a few weeks and she likely would see far more of his housekeeper and children than she would Ben, especially if he consistently maintained these sorts of hours.

Chapter 4

"But I *like* staying at the hotel. We have Alex and Maya to play with there and someone makes breakfast for us every day. It's kind of like Eloise at the Plaza."

Ben swallowed a laugh, certain his bristly nine-year-old daughter wouldn't appreciate it. If there was one thing Ava hated worse than eating her brussels sprouts, it was being the object of someone else's amusement.

Still, as lovely as the twenty-four room Cold Creek Inn was, the place was nothing like the grand hotel in New York City portrayed in the series of books Ava adored.

"It has been fun," he conceded, "but wouldn't you like to have a little more room to play?"

"In the middle of nowhere with a bunch of cows and horses? No. Not really."

He sighed, not unfamiliar with Ava's condescending

attitude. He knew just where it came from—her maternal grandparents.

Ava wasn't thrilled to be separated from his late wife's parents. She loved the Marshalls and tried to spend as much time as she could with them. For the past two years, since Brooke's death, Robert and Janet had filled Ava's head with subtle digs and sly innuendo in an ongoing campaign to undermine her relationship with her father.

The Marshalls wanted nothing more than to take over guardianship of the children any way they could.

He blamed himself for the most part. Right after Brooke's death, he had been too lost and grief-stricken to see the fissures they were carving in his relationship with his children. The first time he figured it out had been about six months ago. After an overnight stay, Jack had refused to give him a hug.

It had taken several days and much prodding on his part, but the boy had finally tearfully confessed that Grandmother Marshall told him he killed dogs and cats nobody wanted—a completely unfair accusation because he was working at a no-kill shelter at the time.

He had done his best to keep distance between them after that, but the Marshalls were insidious in their efforts to drive a wedge between them and had even gone to court seeking regular visitation with their grandchildren.

He knew he couldn't keep them away forever, but he had decided his first priority must be strengthening the bond between him and his children, and eventually he had decided his only option was to resettle elsewhere to make the interactions between them more difficult.

"It's only for a few weeks, until our house is finished," he said now to Ava. "Haven't you missed Mrs. Michaels's delicious dinners?"

"I have," Jack opined from his booster seat next to his sister. "I looove the way she makes mac and cheese."

Ben's mouth watered as he thought of the caramelized onions she scattered across her gooey macaroni and cheese.

"If we move into this new place, that will be the first thing I ask her to make," he promised Jack and was rewarded with a huge grin.

"It hasn't been bad going for dinner at the diner or having stuff from the microwave in the hotel room," Ava insisted. "I haven't minded one single bit."

He sighed. Her constant contrariness was beginning to grate on every nerve.

"What about Christmas? Do you really want to spend Christmas Eve in the hotel, where we don't even have our own tree in our rooms?"

She didn't immediately answer and he could see her trying to come up with something to combat that. Before she could, he pursued his advantage. "Let's just check it out. If we all hate it, we can stay at the hotel through the holidays. With any luck, our new house will be done by early January."

"Will I have to ride the bus to school for the last week of school before Christmas vacation?"

He hadn't thought that far ahead. He supposed he should have considered the logistics before considering this option. "You can if you want to. Or we can try to arrange our schedules so I can take you to school on my way to the clinic."

"I wouldn't want to ride a bus. It's probably totally gross."

That was another lovely gift from his late wife's parents, thank you very little. Janet Marshall had done her best to turn his daughter into a paranoid germaphobe.

"You can always use hand sanitizer." This had become his common refrain, used to combat her objections for everything from eating in a public restaurant to sitting on Santa's lap at the mall.

She sniffed but didn't have a response for that. Much to his relief, she let the subject go and subsided into one of her aggrieved silences. He had a feeling Ava was going to drive him crazy before she made it to the other side of puberty.

A few moments later, he pulled into a side road with a log arch over it that said River Bow Ranch. Pines and aspens lined the drive. Though it was well plowed, he was still grateful for his four-wheel drive as he headed up a slight hill toward the main log ranch house he could see sprawling in the distance.

Not far from the house, the drive forked. About a city block down it, he saw a smaller clapboard home with two small eaves above a wide front porch.

He couldn't help thinking it looked like something off of one of the Christmas cards the clinic had received, a charming little house nestled in the snow-topped pines, with split rail fencing on the pastures that lined the road leading up to it.

"Can we ride the horses while we're here?" Jack asked, gazing with excitement at a group of about six or seven that stood in the snow eating a few bales of alfalfa that looked as though they had recently been dropped into the pasture.

"Probably not. We're only renting a house, not the whole ranch."

Ava looked out the window at the horses too, and he didn't miss the sudden light in her eyes. She loved horses, just like most nine-year-old girls.

But even the presence of some beautiful horseflesh wasn't enough. "You said we were only looking at it and if we didn't like it, we didn't have to stay," she said in an accusatory tone.

Oh, she made him tired sometimes.

"Yes. That's what I said."

"I like it," Jack offered with his unassailable kindergarten logic. "They have dogs and horses and cows."

A couple of collies that looked very much like the one currently resting in his clinic watched them from the front porch of the main house as he pulled into the circular drive in front.

Before he could figure out what to do next, the door opened and Caidy Bowman trotted down the porch steps, pulling on a parka. She must have been watching for them, he thought. The long driveway would certainly give advance notice of anybody approaching.

She wore her dark hair in a braid down her back, topped with a tan Stetson. She looked rather sweet and uncomplicated, but somehow he knew the reality of Caidy Bowman was more tangled than her deceptively simple appearance would indicate.

He opened his door and climbed out as she approached his vehicle.

"The house is just there." She gestured toward the small farmhouse in the trees. "Why don't you drive closer so you don't have to walk through the snow? Ridge plowed it out with the tractor this morning so you shouldn't have any trouble. I'll just meet you there."

"Why?" He went around the vehicle and opened the passenger door. "Get in. We can ride together."

For some reason she looked reluctant at that idea, but after a weird little pause, she finally came to where he was standing and jumped up into the vehicle. He closed the door behind her before she could change her mind.

The first thing he noticed after he was once more behind the wheel was the scent of her filling the interior. Though it was a cold and overcast December day, his car suddenly smelled of vanilla and rain-washed wildflowers on a mountain meadow somewhere.

He was aware of a completely inappropriate desire to inhale that scent deep inside him, to sit here in his car with his children in the backseat and just savor the sweetness.

Get a grip, Caldwell, he told himself. So she smelled good. He could walk into any perfume counter in town and probably get the same little kick in his gut.

Still, he was suddenly fiercely glad his house would be finished in only a few weeks. Much longer than that and he was afraid he would develop a serious thing for this prickly woman who smelled like a wild garden.

"Welcome to the River Bow Ranch."

He almost thanked her before he realized she was looking in the backseat and talking to his children. She wore a genuine smile, probably the first one he had seen on her, and she looked like a bright, beautiful ray of sunshine on an overcast day.

"Can I ride one of your horses sometime?"

"Jack," Ben chided, but Caidy only laughed.

"I think that can probably be arranged. We've got several that are very gentle for children. My favorite is Old Pete. He's about the nicest horse you could ever meet."

Jack beamed at her, his sunny, adorable self. "I bet I can ride a horse good. I have boots and everything."

"You're such a dork. Just because you have boots doesn't make you a cowboy," Ava said with an impatient snort.

"What about you, Ava? Do you like horses?"

In the rearview mirror, he didn't miss his daughter's eagerness but she quickly concealed it. He wondered sometimes if she was afraid to hope for things she wanted anymore because none of their prayers and wishes had been enough to keep Brooke alive.

"I guess," she said, picking at the sleeve of her parka.

"You've come to the right place, then. I bet my niece Destry would love to take you out for a ride."

Ava's eyes widened. "Destry from my school? She's your niece?"

Caidy smiled. "I guess so. There aren't too many Destrys in this neck of the woods. You've met her?"

Ava nodded. "She's a couple years older than me but on my very first day, Mrs. Dalton, the principal, had her show me around. She was supernice to me and she still says hi to me and stuff when she sees me at school."

"I'm very glad to hear that. She better be nice. If she's not, you let me know and I'll give her a talking-to until her ears fall off."

Jack laughed at the image. Ava looked as if she wanted to join him but she had become very good at hiding her amusement these days. Instead, she looked out the window again.

"Here we are," Caidy said when he pulled up front of the house. "I turned up the heat earlier when I came down to clean a little. It should be nice and cozy for you."

How much work had she done for them? He hoped it wasn't much, even as he wondered why she was making this effort for them when he wasn't at all sure she really wanted them there.

"So all the rattraps are gone?" he asked.

"Rats?" Ava asked in a horrified voice.

"There are no rats," Caidy assured her quickly. "We have too many cats here at the River Bow. Your father was making a joke. Weren't you?"

Was he? It had been quite a while since he had found much to joke about. Somehow Caidy Bowman brought out a long-forgotten side of him. "Yes, Ava. I was teasing."

Judging by his daughter's expression, she seemed to find that notion just as unsettling as the idea of giant rodents in her bed.

"Shall we go inside so you can see for yourself?" Caidy said.

"I want to see the rats!" Jack said.

"There are no rats," Ben assured everybody again as Caidy pushed open the front door. It wasn't locked, he noticed—something very different from his security-conscious world in California.

The scent of pine washed over them the moment they stepped inside.

"Look!" Jack exclaimed. "A Christmas tree! A real live one of our very own!"

Sure enough, in the corner was a rather scraggly pine tree as tall as he was, covered in multicolored Christmas lights.

He gazed at it, stunned at the sight and quite certain the tree hadn't been there a few hours earlier. She had said the house was empty, so somehow in the past few hours Caidy Bowman must have dragged this tree in, set it in the stand and strung the Christmas lights.

She had done this for them. He didn't know what to say. Somewhere inside him another little chunk of ice seemed to fall away.

"You didn't need to do that," he said, a little more gruffly than he intended.

"It was no big deal," she answered. In the warmth of the room he thought he saw a tinge of color on her cheeks. "My brothers went a little crazy in the Christmas tree department. We cut our own in the mountains above the ranch after Thanksgiving, and this year they cut a few extras to give to people who might need them. This one was leftover."

"What about the lights?"

"We had some extras lying around. I'm afraid this one is a little on the scrawny side, but paper garland and some ornaments will fix that right up. I bet your dad and Mrs. Michaels can help you make some," she told Ava and Jack. As he might have expected, Jack looked excited about the idea but Ava merely shrugged.

He wouldn't know the first thing about making ornaments for a Christmas tree. Brooke had always taken care of the holiday decorating and his housekeeper had stepped in after her death.

"Come on. I'll give you the grand tour. It's not much, as you can see. Just this room, the kitchen and dining room and the bedrooms upstairs."

She was too modest. This room alone was already half again as big as one of the hotel rooms. The living room was comfortably furnished with a burgundy plaid sofa and a couple of leather recliners, and the television set was an older model but quite large.

One side wall was dominated by a small river rock fireplace with a mantel made of rough-hewn lumber. The fireplace was empty but someone—probably Caidy—had stacked several armloads of wood in a bin next to it. He could easily imagine how cozy the place would be with a fire in the hearth, the lights flickering on the tree and a basketball game on the television set. He wouldn't even have to worry about turning the volume down so he didn't wake Jack. It was an appealing thought.

"Through here is the kitchen and dining area," she said.

The appliances looked a little out-of-date but perfectly adequate. The refrigerator even had an ice maker, something he had missed in the hotel. Ice from a bucket wasn't quite the same for some reason.

"There's a half bath and a laundry room through those doors. It's pretty basic. Do you want to see the upstairs?"

He nodded and followed her up, trying not to notice the way her jeans hugged her curves. "We've got a king bed in one room, a queen in the second bedroom and bunk beds in that one on the left. The children won't mind sharing, will they?"

"I want to see!" Jack exclaimed and raced into the room she indicated. Ava followed more slowly, but even she looked curious about the accommodations, he saw.

The whole place smelled like vanilla and pine, fresh and clean, and he didn't miss the vacuum tracks in the carpet. She really must have hurried over to make it ready for them.

"There's a small bathroom off the master and another one in the hall between the other bedrooms. That's it. Not much to it. Do you think it will work?"

"I like it!" Jack declared. "But only if I get the top bunk."

"What do you think, Ava?"

She shrugged. "It's okay. I still like the hotel better but it would be fun to live by Destry and ride the bus with her and stuff. And *I* get the top bunk. I'm older."

"We can work that out," Ben said. "I guess it's more or less unanimous. It should be great. Comfortable and spacious and not that far from the clinic. I appreciate the offer."

She smiled but he thought it looked a little strained. "Great. You can move in anytime. Today if you want. All you need are your suitcases."

The idea of a little breathing space was vastly appealing. "In that case, we can go back to the inn and pack our things and be back later this afternoon. Mrs. Michaels will be thrilled."

"That should work."

"Can we decorate the tree tonight?" Jack asked eagerly.

He tousled his son's hair, deeply grateful for this cheerful child who gave his love unconditionally. "Yeah. We can probably do that. We'll pick up some art supplies while we're in town too."

Even Ava looked mildly excited about that as they headed back outside.

"Oh, for goodness' sake," Caidy said suddenly. "What are you doing all the way down here, you crazy dog? Just want to make a few new friends, do you?"

She spoke to an ancient-looking collie, with a gray

muzzle and tired eyes, that was sitting at the bottom of the porch steps. Caidy knelt down, heedless of the snow, and petted the dog. "This is Sadie. She's just about my best friend in the world."

Ava smiled at the dog. "Hi, Sadie."

Jack, however, hovered behind Ben. His son was nervous about any dog bigger than a Pekingese.

"She's really old. Thirteen. I got her when I was just a teenager. We've been through a lot, Sadie and me."

"Sadie and Caidy. That rhymes," Ava said unexpectedly, earning a giggle from Jack.

"I know, right? My brothers used to call the dog and I would think they wanted me. Or they would call me and Sadie would come running. It was all very confusing but we're used to it now after all these years. I didn't name her, though—the rancher my parents got her from had already given her a name. By then she was already used to it so we decided not to change it."

He saw a hint of sadness in her eyes and wondered at the source of it as she hugged the dog. "Do you know, she was a Christmas present the year I turned fourteen? That's not much older than you, Ava."

His daughter looked thrilled that someone would think she was anywhere close to the advanced age of fourteen instead of nine and he suddenly knew Caidy had said it on purpose.

"For months I'd been begging and begging for a dog of my own," she went on. "We always had ranch dogs but my brothers took over working with them. I wanted one I could train myself. I was so excited that morning when I found her under the tree. She was so adorable with a big red bow around her neck."

He pictured it clearly, a teenage Caidy and a cute

little border collie puppy with curious ears and a wagging tail. He could certainly relate to the story. When he had been a boy, he had begged for a dog every year from about the time he turned eight. Every year, he had hoped and prayed he would find a puppy under the tree and every year had been another disappointment.

He held the door open. "Ava, you can sit in the middle next to Jack so we can make room for Sadie."

"Oh, no. That's not necessary. She's probably wet and stinky. We can walk. It's not that far."

"If there's one thing we don't mind in this family, it's wet stinky dogs, isn't that right? Just wait until we bring Tri out here to romp in the snowdrifts."

Both children giggled, even Ava, which filled him with a great sense of accomplishment.

He turned his attention away from his children to find Caidy watching him, her hand still on her dog's scruff and an arrested expression in her eyes. He felt a return of that tensile connection of earlier, when he had walked out of the shower room to find her standing in the hallway.

The moment stretched between them and he couldn't seem to look away, vaguely aware of Jack and Ava climbing into the SUV with their usual bickering.

Finally she cleared her throat. "Thanks anyway, but I'm not quite ready to go. I just need to dust out the two spare bedrooms."

This wasn't going to work. He didn't want this sudden attraction. He didn't want to feel this heat in his gut again, the sizzle of his blood.

He thought about telling her he had changed his mind, but how ridiculous would that sound? *I can't stay here because I'm afraid I'll do something stupid if I'm in the same general vicinity of you.*

Anyway, now that he had seen the charming little house, he really didn't want to go back to the cramped quarters of the inn. He would just have to work hard to stay out of her way. How tough could that be?

"The place looked fine. We can dust," he said. "You don't have to do that."

"We Bowmans are a proud lot. Though we might not be in the landlord business as a regular thing, I'm not about to let you stay in a dirty place."

He decided not to argue. "I'll check on Luke while we're in town. If I feel like he is stable enough to be here, I'll pick him up and bring him out with us when we come back."

She smiled her gratitude and he felt that inexorable tug toward her again. "Thank you! We would love that, wouldn't we, Sadie?"

The dog nudged her hand and seemed to smile in agreement.

"Luke is her great-grandson," she explained to the children. "So I guess I'll see you all later. I'm glad the house will work for you."

Space-wise, the house was perfect. Neighbor-wise, he wasn't so sure.

After he loaded up the kids and started down the gravel drive, he glanced in the rearview mirror. Caidy Bowman was lifting her face to the pale winter sun peeking between clouds, one hand on the dog's grizzled head.

For some ridiculous reason, a lump rose in his throat at the sight and he had a hard time looking away.

Chapter 5

For the next few hours, Caidy couldn't shake a tangled mix of dread and anticipation. Offering Ben and his family a place to stay over the holidays had been a friendly, neighborly gesture. She was grateful those cute kids would be able to have the fun of sneaking downstairs Christmas morning to see their presents under their very own tree and that Mrs. Michaels could cook a proper dinner for them instead of something out of the microwave.

Even so, she had the strangest feeling that life on the ranch was about to change, maybe irrevocably.

It was only for a few weeks, she told herself as she finished mucking out the stalls with Destry while Sadie plopped on her belly in the warm straw and watched them. She could handle anything for a few weeks. Still, the strange, restless mood dogged her heels like the collies in a thunderstorm as she went through her Saturday chores.

"You ladies need a hand in here?"

Destry beamed at her father, thrilled when he called her a lady. She was, Caidy thought. Her little girl was growing up—nearly eleven now and going to middle school the next year. She didn't know what she would do then.

"Since we've got your muscles here, why don't you bring us a couple new straw bales? I'd like to put some fresh down for the foaling mares."

"Will do. Des, come give your old man a hand."

The two of them took off, laughing together about something Destry said in answer, and Caidy again felt that unaccountable depression seep over her.

Her brother didn't really need her help anymore with Destry. She had been happy to offer it when the girl was young and Ridge had been alone and struggling. *More* than happy, really. Relieved, more like, to have something useful to do with her time, something she thought she could handle.

Destry was almost a young woman now and Ridge was an excellent father who could probably handle things here just fine by himself.

She leaned her cheek on the handle of the shovel and watched Sadie snoring away. They didn't need her. Nobody did. She sighed heavily just as Ridge came back alone with a bale on each shoulder.

"That sounds serious. What's wrong? Having second thoughts about the new vet and his family moving in?"

And third and fourth. She shrugged, picked up a pitchfork and started spreading the straw around. "What's to have second thoughts about? He needed a place to stay for a few weeks and we have an empty, furnished house just sitting there."

"Destry will enjoy having other children around the ranch, especially for Christmas."

"Where is she?"

He grabbed the other pitchfork to help her. "She got distracted by the new barn kittens. She's up in the loft giving them a little attention."

Her niece loved animals every bit as much as Caidy had at her age. Maybe she would be a veterinarian someday. "I'm afraid we're not very good company for her this time of year, are we? Things will be better in January."

Ridge gave her a long look. "You remember how much Mom loved Christmas. She would hate thinking you would let her and Dad's deaths ruin the holidays forever."

"I know." It wasn't a new argument between them and right now she wasn't in the mood, not with this melancholy sidling through her. "Don't make it sound like I'm the only one. You hate Christmas too."

"Yeah, well, I think it's time we both moved forward with our lives. Taft and Trace both have."

You weren't there, she wanted to cry out. None of her brothers were. She had been the one hiding under that shelf in the pantry, listening to her mother's dying gasps and knowing there wasn't a damn thing she could do about it.

You weren't there and you weren't responsible.

She couldn't say the words to him. She never could. Instead she spread a little more straw in an area that already had plenty.

"I think it's time you went back to school."

She didn't need this again, today, of all days, when she felt so oddly as if she were teetering on the brink of some major life shift.

"I'm twenty-seven years old, Ridge. I think my school days are past me."

Her brother's handsome features twisted into a scowl. "They don't have to be. Plenty of people finish college when they're a little older than the traditional student. Sometimes it takes a person a few years to figure out what they want out of life."

"Have I figured that out yet?" she muttered.

"You won't while you're stuck here. I should never have let you come home after your first year of college. I should have made you stick it out. Believe me, I've regretted it bitterly, more than I can say. The truth is, after Melinda walked out, I needed you here to help me with Destry. I was lost and floundering, trying to run the ranch and take care of her too."

He pulled his gloves off and shoved them in his back pocket, then tugged at an earlobe. These words weren't easy for him, she knew. Of all her brothers, Ridge was the most stoic, hiding his emotions and his thoughts behind the hard steel it took to run a ranch like the River Bow.

"The truth is, I chose the easy path instead of the right one," he said, regret in his eyes.

"You didn't choose anything. I did. I wanted to come home. I would have dropped out regardless of whether you needed me here."

"Not if I hadn't made it so easy for you to find a soft place to land back home."

She wasn't sure if her brothers blamed her for the

murders of her parents. She had always been afraid to ask and none of them had ever talked about it.

How could they not blame her on some level? Neither she nor her parents were even supposed to have been home that night. That was the reason an art burglary had turned into a surprise home invasion robbery and then a double murder when her father had tried to stop the thieves.

Caidy would have died with them if her mother hadn't shoved her into the pantry and ordered her to hide.

Sometimes she felt as if she had been hiding ever since.

"*You* should be the new veterinarian in town, not some new guy from the coast," Ridge went on, his voice fierce. "It's been eating at me ever since this Caldwell showed up. Becoming a vet was all you ever wanted. I know Doc Harris had once hoped you would follow in his footsteps. I can't help thinking how, if things had gone differently, you could have taken over his practice when he retired."

He managed to hit exactly on the reason for her restlessness. The straw rustled under her feet as she shifted her boots, releasing its earthy scent. Ben Caldwell was living her dream now. It was hard to admit, especially when she knew she had absolutely no right to be upset.

"I made my choices, Ridge. I don't regret them. Not for a moment."

"You need a life of your own. A home, a family. You never even date."

"Maybe I'll just run off with the new veterinarian. Then where would you be?"

As soon as the words escaped, she heartily wished

she had kept her big mouth shut. Again. What could possibly have possessed her to say such a thing? Ridge lifted an eyebrow and gave her a long, searching look, and she had to hope the heat she could feel in her cheeks wasn't as bright red as it felt.

"I would be happy for you as long as he's a good man who treats you well," Ridge said quietly. For some unaccountable reason, her heart ached sharply. Before she could come up with a response, Destry clambered down the loft ladder. "They're here! I just saw a couple of cars driving up."

The heat in her cheeks spread down her neck and over her shoulders. "Great," she managed to say, trying for a cheerful voice.

"Do you think they'll have Luke with them?"

"I guess we'll find out."

The three of them walked out of the barn into the cold, overcast afternoon just as one SUV pulled up, followed closely by another one. Neither vehicle took the fork in the driveway that led to the foreman's house. They headed toward the main house, pulling into the circular driveway.

Ben climbed out as she, Ridge and Destry approached the vehicles. Her stomach did that ridiculous little jumpy thing again. She had forgotten in the past few hours just how gorgeous the man was. The memory she had been trying without success to forget flooded back into her head in excruciating detail—of walking into the clinic that morning and finding him wet and hard-muscled as he came out of the shower.

She thought of what she had said to her brother. *Maybe I'll just run off with the new veterinarian, and then where would you be?*

The bigger question was, where would *she* be? She could easily see herself making a fool over this man and she had to do her very best to make sure that didn't happen, especially when she couldn't logically find a way to avoid him, when she trained dogs for a living and he was the town's only veterinarian.

He waved at them all and held a hand out to Ridge. "Hi. You must be Caidy's brother."

"Right. I'm Ridge Bowman. This is my daughter, Destry. I guess you know our Caidy. Nice to meet you. Welcome to the River Bow."

"Thank you."

The two of them shook hands and then, much to the girl's astonished delight, Ben shook hands with Destry too. She grinned at him, braids flying under her cowboy hat as she turned the handshake into a vigorous exercise.

Ben gave Caidy a friendly sort of smile—much warmer than any he'd given her so far. Her cheeks flamed and she didn't miss Ridge's careful look at the two of them. Drat her big mouth. She should never have said what she did earlier in the barn. Knowing her brother, now he was never going to let her forget it.

"I really appreciate you opening the house for us like this."

Ridge shrugged. "Why not? It's empty. With apologies to my sister-in-law, children ought to be in a house at Christmastime if they can."

"A little breathing room will certainly make the holidays more comfortable for all of us," he answered. "I've got someone else back here who's anxious to be on the River Bow."

He headed to the back of the SUV and reached to open the hatch.

"You really think Luke is ready to be home?" she asked.

"He should be. He was moving on his own and seemed far more comfortable this afternoon than earlier. He's a fighter, this one. You'll still have to keep a sharp eye on him, but there's no reason he can't be home for that. It'll save you a little on the clinic bill."

All of them converged on the rear of the vehicle. Sure enough, Luke was resting in a travel crate. When he saw her, he whimpered and whined. Ben unlatched the door and the dog's nails scrabbled on the plastic floor of the crate as he tried to stand.

"Easy," Ben said, and his calm voice did the trick. Luke subsided again.

"Hey, Lukey. Hey, buddy." Destry rubbed her cheek against the dog's and scratched under his ears. "You poor thing. Look at that big bandage."

"Hi, Destry. I'm sorry your dog got hurt."

Destry smiled into the backseat, where both Ava and Jack were watching the proceedings with interest.

"Me too. But he's not really my dog. He's one of my aunt Caidy's. I like cats most of all."

"I like cats too," Ava said.

"Not me," Jack answered cheerfully. "I like dogs. This is our dog. His name is Tri."

The dog yipped in answer to his name and Caidy had to smile at the adorable little thing, some kind of chihuahua.

"Can he walk?" Ridge was asking as he studied the injured dog in the crate.

Ben nodded. "He can, but it won't be comfortable for him for a while now. Probably better if we let him take it easy. Do you mind helping me carry him inside?"

"No problem," Ridge said. The two of them carried the crate with Luke inside. Caidy wondered if she should stay with the children or take them inside. Before she could make a decision, Mrs. Michaels joined them from the other vehicle. "You probably want to go help settle your dog, don't you?"

"Yes," she said quickly. "Why don't you all come inside?"

"I think we'll be better off staying put. I'm sure Dr. Caldwell won't be long and the children are anxious to start settling into the house."

She followed the low murmur of men's voices and found them in the kitchen, setting the crate down in the small area she had arranged earlier, in hopes for this very moment.

"Caidy likes to keep her patients right here in the kitchen," Ridge was saying. "This way her bedroom, right down the hall, is close enough to keep an eye on them."

"It's close to the back door for easy trips outside. That's the important thing," she said.

"This works. I like the enclosure," he said. Years ago, she had purchased a small baby play yard that worked well when she was treating an animal whose physical activity needed to be limited.

"Come on out," Ben coaxed the dog. Luke didn't seem to want to move but with their encouragement and Dr. Caldwell helping him along, he rose slowly and hobbled out of the crate, then headed immediately for the soft bed of old blankets she had fashioned in the enclosure.

"What sort of special instructions do I need?"

"Our biggest fear right now is infection. We need to

keep the injuries as clean as possible, especially that puncture wound from the bull."

"You don't have to worry about anything," Ridge said. "Caidy's an expert. She used to work at the clinic with Dr. Harris."

"So I hear."

"She should have become a veterinarian," Ridge went on. "It's all she ever wanted to do."

Apparently blabbermouth syndrome ran in the family.

"Is that right?" Ben said, giving her a curious look. She could tell he was wondering why she hadn't pursued her dreams. What was so wrong about a person's life changing direction?

"Yes. I also wanted to be a ballerina when I was eight. And a famous movie star when I was eleven."

And a singer. She decided not to mention she had once wanted to sing professionally. That was another dream she had pushed aside.

"I suppose you're anxious to move into the house. The key is inside on the kitchen table. All the information, like the phone number to the house and the address, are on a paper I've also left for you there."

"Thanks."

One thing she had never anticipated doing with her life was being a landlord to an entirely too sexy veterinarian. Yet here she was. "Call if you have any problems or can't figure out any of the appliances."

"I'm sure we'll be fine. Make sure you let me know if you have any problems with Luke. Here. Let me leave my cell number."

He pulled a business card out of the inside pocket of his coat and left it on the kitchen counter. "If he starts to run a fever or has any other unusual symptoms that concern you, I want you to call me. Day or night."

She doubted she ever would. Even after all her years of working with Doc Harris, she hadn't felt comfortable calling the old veterinarian in the middle of the night.

"Thank you," she answered.

"I'd better head out. The kids are anxious to start decorating their tree."

"Oh. That reminds me. Destry and I dug through our old Christmas things earlier and found a few things we're not using. You're welcome to them."

She picked up the box off the kitchen table and handed it to him. He looked a little disconcerted but then smiled.

"Thank you. I'm sure Mrs. Michaels and the children will find great use for them."

"Not you?"

"I'm sure I'll be roped into helping, like it or not." He looked more resigned than truly reluctant.

"If you'd like, I can carry it out for you while you two get the crate."

"That would be great. Thanks." He smiled at her and she felt those ridiculous flutters again.

"He seems nice," Ridge said after they had loaded the crate and the ornaments and stood on the porch watching the two SUVs head back down the driveway toward the foreman's house.

She thought of how abrupt and harsh he had been the evening before at the clinic. *Nice* wouldn't have been the word she used to describe Ben Caldwell then, but now she was beginning to wonder.

"I guess," she answered in what she hoped was a noncommittal voice.

Ridge gave her a sidelong look. "You might want to think about showing a little more enthusiasm if you plan to run off with the man. At least to him. Occasionally a guy needs a little encouragement."

She rolled her eyes but quickly hurried into the house before Ridge could notice the blush she felt heating her cheeks. She suddenly had a very strong feeling she would have to work hard at being casual and uninterested in order to keep Ridge—and probably the rest of the Bowmans—from trying to do a little matchmaking for Christmas.

A woman's body was a mysterious thing, full of secret hollows and soft, delectable curves.

He was in heaven, warm, sweetly scented heaven. Ben trailed his fingers over the woman in his arms, his hands exploring all those hidden delights. He wanted to stay here forever with his face buried in skin that smelled sweetly of vanilla and rain-washed wildflowers and his hands finding new and exciting terrain to discover.

His body was rock-hard and he pressed against her heat, tangling his fingers in acres of dark, silky hair. She smiled at him out of that sinfully delicious mouth that sent his imagination into overdrive, and her green eyes were bright as springtime. He groaned, his hunger at fever pitch, and kissed her.

Her mouth was as warm and welcoming as the rest of her and when she danced her tongue along his, he groaned and gripped her hands, kissing her with all the pent-up need aching inside him.

"Yes. Kiss me," she murmured in that lilting, musical voice. "Just like that, Ben. Don't stop. Please, don't stop."

All he could think about was burying himself inside. He shifted and prepared to do just that, his body taut and ready, when a phone trilled close to his ear.

He froze…and woke up from the first sexy dream he'd had in ages.

He could still see Caidy Bowman, tangled around him, her body soft and warm, but when he blinked she disappeared.

The phone trilled again and a quick glance at the alarm read 3:00 a.m. Nobody called at this hour unless it was an emergency. He grabbed for it, ignoring the lingering arousal of his body that had no chance in hell of being satisfied by an actual female right now.

"Hello?" he growled.

"I shouldn't have called. I'm sorry." Hearing Caidy Bowman's voice in his ear after he had just heard her in his dreams, pleading with him for more, was so disorienting that for a moment he couldn't process the shift.

"Hello? Are you there?" she asked. The urgency and, yes, fright in her voice pushed away the last clinging tendrils of his sultry dream.

"I'm here. Sorry." He swung his legs over the side of the bed and reached for the jeans he'd left there the night before. "What's wrong? Luke?"

"Yes. He's not… Something's wrong. I wouldn't have called you, except… I don't think it's good. He's struggling to breathe. I thought it might be an infection, but I haven't seen any signs of a fever or anything. I lifted both dressings and they looked clean."

He growled and flipped on the bedside light, then

scrubbed at his face to rub the last tendrils of that blasted dream away.

"Give me five minutes."

"Is there something I can do so you don't have to come up here?"

"Probably not. Five minutes."

As he threw on a T-shirt and his jacket, a hundred possibilities raced through his head, very few of them leading to a good outcome. He quickly scribbled a note for Mrs. Michaels and stuck it on her door, though by now she was used to him dashing out in the middle of the night.

Snow lightly gleamed in his headlights as he drove up to the ranch house. He saw lights in the kitchen and pulled as close as he could to the side door on the circular driveway, then hurried up the snow-covered walkway, his emergency kit in his hand.

He didn't even have to rap softly on the door before she yanked it open, her hair tangled around her face and her eyes huge with worry.

"Thank you for coming so quickly. I didn't want to call you but I didn't know what else to do."

He had a strong feeling that wasn't an easy admission for her to make. She struck him as a woman who didn't like relying on others.

Yes. Kiss me. Just like that, Ben. Don't stop. Please, don't stop.

He pushed away the memory of that completely inappropriate dream and did his best not to notice her faded T-shirt or the yoga pants she wore that stretched over every curve, to focus instead on the issue at hand.

"It's fine. I'm here now. Let's see what we have going on."

The dog was clearly in distress, his respiratory rate fast and his breathing labored. His gums and lips were blue and Ben quickly pulled out his emergency oxygen mask and fit it over the dog's mouth and nose.

"It's gotten worse, just in the few minutes since I called you. I don't know what to do."

He ran his hand over the dog's chest and knew instantly what the problem was. He could hear the rattle of air inside the chest cavity with each ragged breath. He bit out an oath.

"What is it?"

"Traumatic pneumothorax. He has air trapped in his chest cavity. We're going to have to get it out. I have a couple of options here. I can take him into the clinic and do an X-ray first, or I can go with my instincts. I can feel the problem. I can try to extract the air with a needle and syringe, which will help his breathing. It's your choice."

She paused for just a moment, then nodded. "I trust you. If you think you can do it here, go ahead."

Her faith in him was humbling, especially given the cold way he had treated her the day before. He fished in his bag for the supplies he would need, then knelt down beside the dog again.

"What can I do?" she asked.

"Try to calm him as best you can and keep him still."

The next few moments were a blur. He was aware of her speaking softly, of her strong, capable hands at his side as she held the dog as firmly as possible. For the most part, he entered that peculiar zone he found whenever he was in the middle of a complicated procedure. He listened with his stethoscope until he could isolate the pneumothorax. The rest was quick and efficient:

cleaning the area, inserting the needle in just the right spot, extracting the air with a gurgle, then listening again with the stethoscope to the dog's breath sounds.

This was one of those treatments that was almost instantly effective. Miraculous, even. One moment the dog was frantically struggling to breathe, the next his airway was free and clear and his respiratory rate slowed, his wild trembling with it.

In just moments, he was moving air just as he should through his lungs and had calmed considerably. Satisfied, Ben took the emergency oxygen mask off Luke and returned the syringe to its packaging to be discarded back at the clinic.

"That's it?" Caidy's eyes looked stunned.

"Should be. We're still going to want to watch him closely. If you'd like, I can take him back for another night at the clinic just to be safe."

"No. I… That was *amazing!*"

She was gazing at him as if he had just hung the moon and stars and Jupiter too. He had a funny little ache in his chest, and another inappropriate bit of that crazy dream flashed through his head.

"Thank you. Thank you so much. I was worried sick."

"I'm glad I was close enough to help."

"I'm sorry I had to wake you, though."

So was he. Or he told himself he was anyway. If she hadn't, he probably would have a great deal more of his unruly subconscious to be embarrassed about. "No problem. It was worth it."

"Is there anything else I need to be concerned about?"

"I don't think so. We cleared his lungs. If he has any

more breathing trouble, we're going to want to x-ray to see if something else is going on. If you don't mind, I'd like to stick around a little longer to make sure he remains stable."

"Can I get you something? Coffee probably isn't a good idea at three-thirty in the morning if you want to catch a few hours of sleep when we're done here, but we have tea or hot cocoa."

"Cocoa would be good."

He didn't want to think about how comfortable, almost intimate, it was to sit here in this quiet kitchen while the snow fluttered softly against the window and the big log house creaked and settled around them. Only a few moments later, she returned with a couple of mugs of hot chocolate.

"It's from a mix. I thought that would be faster."

"Mix is fine," he answered. "It's all I'm used to anyway."

He took a sip and almost sighed with delight at the rich mix of chocolate and raspberry. "That's not any old mix."

She smiled. "No. I buy from a gourmet food store in Jackson Hole. It's imported from France."

He sipped again, letting the sensuous flavors mix on his tongue. Worth an interrupted night's sleep, just for a little of that divine hot chocolate.

She sat across the table from him and he couldn't help noticing how the loose neckline of her shirt gaped a little with each breath.

"So how is the house working out?"

"Fine, so far. But then, I haven't even had one full night's sleep in it." And what little sleep he *had* enjoyed had been tormented by futile dreams of something he couldn't have.

"I'm sorry again about that, especially considering you had to stay the night with Luke last night."

He shrugged. "Don't be sorry. I didn't mean that. It's just part of my life, something I'm very used to. I often get emergency calls."

Even without the work-related sleep disruptions, his sleep was frequently restless. "The house works well. The kids are happy to have a little more room and Mrs. Michaels is over the moon to have a kitchen again. She made her famous macaroni and cheese for dinner. You'll have to try it sometime. It's as much a gourmet treat as your hot chocolate. I have to admit, I've missed her cooking."

"You must feel very lucky that she was willing to come with you from California."

"Lucky doesn't begin to describe the half of it. I would be completely lost without her. Since Brooke— my wife—died, Anne has kept us all going."

"Of all the places you could have bought a practice, why did you pick Pine Gulch?" She seemed genuinely interested and he leaned back in his chair, sipping at his drink, enjoying the quiet conversation more than he probably should.

"Doc Harris and I have known each other since before I graduated from veterinary school. We met at a conference and had kept up an email correspondence. When he told me he was retiring and wanted to sell his practice, it seemed the perfect opportunity. I had…reasons for wanting to leave California."

She didn't press him, though he could see the curiosity in her eyes. He wanted to tell her. He wasn't sure why—perhaps the quiet peace of the kitchen or the way she had looked at him with such admiration after the thoracentesis. Or maybe just because he hadn't talked about it with anyone, not even Mrs. Michaels.

"My wife has been gone for two years now and I think the kids and I both needed a new start, you know? Away from all the old patterns and relationships. The familiar can sometimes carry its own burdens."

"I can understand that. I've had plenty of moments when I just want to pick up and start over."

What would she want to run from? he wondered. He had a feeling there was far more beneath the surface of Caidy Bowman than a beautiful cowgirl who loved animals and her family.

"So you just packed everybody up and headed to the mountains of Idaho?"

"Something like that."

She sipped at her hot cocoa and they lapsed into silence broken only by the dog's breathing, comfortable and easy now, he was gratified to see. She had a little dab of chocolate on her upper lip and he wondered what she would do if he reached across the table and licked it off.

"Is it rude and intrusive for me to ask about your wife?"

That was one way to squelch his inappropriate desire. He shifted in a chair that suddenly felt as hard and unforgiving as a cold block of cement.

"She…died in a car accident after slipping into a diabetes-related coma while she was behind the wheel."

He didn't add the rest, about the unborn child he hadn't wanted who had died along with her, about how angry he had been with her for the weeks leading up to her death, furious that she would put him in such an untenable position after they had both decided to stop once Jack was born, when doctors warned of the grave risks of a third pregnancy.

He hated himself for the way he had reacted. The temper he had inherited from his grandfather, the one he worked constantly to overcome, had slipped its leash and he had been hateful and mean and had even taken to sleeping in the guest room after she told him she was pregnant, just days after they had decided he would have a vasectomy.

Caidy gave him a sympathetic look, which he definitely did not deserve. "Diabetes. How tragic. She must have been young."

"Thirty."

Her mouth twisted. "I'm sorry. Really sorry."

Yes. Tragic. Something that never should have happened. He blamed himself—and so did Brooke's parents, which was the reason they were trying to poison Ava and Jack against him.

"You must miss her terribly. I can understand why you wanted to make a new start away from the memories."

He did miss her. He had adored her when they first married, until the rather willful, spoiled part of her he had overlooked as part of her charm when they were dating began to show itself in difficult ways.

Brooke had selfishly believed she was stronger than her diabetes. She didn't deserve to have it, thus she shouldn't have to worry about taking care of herself. She was cavalier to the point of recklessness about checking her levels and taking her insulin.

She had been a loving mother, he would never say

otherwise, even if he sometimes wondered how a loving mother could risk her own health when she already had so much simply because she wanted more.

"What about you?" he asked to change the subject. "Ever been married?"

She was in midsip with her hot cocoa and coughed a little. "Me? No. I date here and there but...nothing serious. The dating pool around Pine Gulch is a little shallow. I've known most of the unmarried men around here my whole life."

You haven't known me.

The dangerous thought whispered through his mind and seemed to move right in. No. He definitely didn't want to go there. She was a beautiful woman and he was very attracted to her—he only needed to remember that dream if he needed proof—but he would never do anything about that attraction but sneak those tantalizing glimpses at her and wonder.

He had his children to consider and a new practice he was trying to build. He could see no room for a complicated woman like Caidy Bowman in that picture anywhere.

Why did she hide herself away here in a small town like Pine Gulch? Why hadn't she become a veterinarian? He had the same strange thought of earlier in the day when he had seen her standing on the River Bow porch with her brother and her niece. She was lonely. He had no idea why he thought so, but he was suddenly certain of it.

"So why not dip your feet in other waters? It's a big world. You could always try internet dating."

"Wow. You're a veterinarian *and* a relationship

coach. Who would have guessed? It seems an odd combination, but, okay."

He laughed gruffly, only because that was absolutely *not* his usual modus operandi. Usually he was completely oblivious to the interpersonal dramas and entanglements of other people, except when it came to their relationships with their pets.

"That's me. I'll fix up your dog and your broken heart, all for one low fee. And I offer monthly installment plans."

She smiled, the right side of her mouth just a bit higher than the left to create a sweetly pleasing imbalance. The quiet, companionable silence wrapped around them like the trailing tendrils of a woolen scarf.

He wanted to kiss her.

The hunger for a taste—just one little sampling—of chocolate and raspberry and soft, warm woman was intense and bewitching. He needed to get out of there. Now, before he did something completely insane like try to turn his midnight fantasies into reality and received a well-earned slap for it.

The dog snuffled softly and that was the excuse he needed to leave her side and return to the cozy little warren she had created for Luke.

Unfortunately, she followed right behind as he crouched down to check the dog's breathing with his stethoscope.

"How does he sound?"

"Good. Breathing is normal now. I think we solved the problem."

"Thank you again, for everything. I'm not sure Doc Harris could have done the job as well."

Her words seeped inside him. He was inordinately pleased by the compliment. "You're very welcome."

"I hope I don't need to call you in the middle of the night again."

"Please don't hesitate. I'm just down the lane now."

She smiled. "Ridge said it would be like having our own veterinarian-in-residence. Just to put your mind at ease, I promise not to take advantage."

Please. Take advantage all you want. He cleared his throat. "For what it's worth, I think the guys around here are crazy. Even if you did grow up with them."

He wasn't quite sure why he said the words. He was no more a player than he was a relationship coach, for heaven's sake. She flashed him a startled look, her eyes wide and her mouth slightly parted.

He might have left things at that, safe and uncomplicated, except her eyes suddenly shifted to his mouth and he didn't miss the flare of heat in her gaze.

He swore under his breath, already regretting what he seemed to have no power to resist, and then he reached for her.

Chapter 6

As his mouth settled over hers, warm and firm and tasting of cocoa, Caidy couldn't quite believe this was happening.

She was being kissed by the sexy new veterinarian just a day after thinking him rude and abrasive. For a long moment, she was shocked into immobility, then heat began to seep through her frozen stupor. Oh. Oh, yes!

How long had it been since she had enjoyed a kiss and wanted more? She was astounded to realize she couldn't remember. As his lips played over hers, she shifted her neck slightly for a better angle.

She splayed her fingers against his chest—that strong, muscled chest she had seen firsthand just that morning—and his heat soaked into her skin, even through the cotton of his shirt.

Her insides seemed to give a collective shiver. Mmm. This was exactly what two people ought to be doing at 3:00 a.m. on a snowy December day.

He made a low sound in his throat that danced down her spine and she felt the hard strength of his arms slide around her, pulling her closer. In this moment, nothing else seemed to matter but Ben Caldwell and the wondrous sensations fluttering through her.

This was crazy. Some tiny voice of self-preservation seemed to whisper through her. What was she doing? She had no business kissing someone she barely knew and wasn't even sure if she liked yet. If she kept this up, he was going to think she kissed every guy who happened to smile at her.

Though it took every last ounce of strength, she managed to slide away from all that delicious heat and moved a few inches away from him, trying desperately to catch her breath.

The distance she created between them seemed to drag Ben back to his senses. He stared at her, his eyes as dazed as she felt. "That was wrong. I don't know what I was thinking. Your dog is a patient and… I shouldn't have…."

She might have been offended by the dismay in his voice if not for the arousal in his eyes and the way he couldn't seem to catch his breath. Because she was having the same sort of reaction—dismay mixed with lingering arousal and a sudden deep yearning—she couldn't very well complain.

His hair was a little rumpled and he had the evening shadow of a beard and all she could think was *yum*.

She cleared her throat, compelled to say something in the strained moment. "Relax, Dr. Caldwell. You didn't do anything wrong, as far as I can see. I didn't exactly push you out the door, did I?"

He ran a hand through his hair. "No. No, I guess you didn't."

"It's late and we're both tired and not quite thinking straight. I'm sure that's all this was."

A muscle flexed in his jaw. He looked as if he would like to argue with her, but after a moment he only nodded. "I'm sure you're right."

"No harm done. We'll both just forget the past five minutes ever happened and go back to our regularly scheduled lives."

"Great idea."

His ready agreement sent a hard kernel of regret to lodge somewhere in her sternum. For a moment, she had felt almost normal, just like any other woman. Someone who could flirt and smile and attract the interest of a sexy male.

He wanted to forget it ever happened, whereas she was quite certain she would never be able to erase these few moments from her memory.

"I should, uh, go."

"Yes." *Or you could stay and kiss me for a few more hours.*

"Call me if anything changes with the dog."

She drew in a breath. "I hope we're past the worst of it. But I will."

That last was a lie. She had absolutely no intention of calling him again in the middle of the night. She would drive Luke to the vet in Idaho Falls before she would drag Ben Caldwell out here again anytime soon.

"Good night."

She nodded, not trusting herself to reply, just wishing he would go already. He gave her a long, searching look before he shrugged back into his ranch coat and left through the side door.

A blast of cold air curled into the room from that brief moment he had opened the door. Chilled by more than just the winter night, she shivered as it sidled under her T-shirt.

What in heaven's name just happened here?

She wrapped her arms around herself. She had *known* he would be trouble. Somehow she had known. She never should have suggested he move into the foreman's house. If she had only used her brain, she might have predicted she would do something stupid around him, like develop a very awkward and embarrassing crush.

She spent most of her days here on the ranch, surrounded by her brothers and his few ranchhands, most of whom were either fresh-faced kids just out of high school or grizzled veterans who either were already married or held absolutely no appeal to her.

The ranch was safe. It had always been her haven from the hardness of the world. Now she had messed that up by inviting a tempting man to set up temporary residence smack in the middle of her comfort zone.

The man certainly knew how to kiss. She couldn't deny that. She pressed a hand to her stomach, which still seemed to be jumping with nerves. The last time she had been kissed so thoroughly and deliciously had been...well, never.

She sighed. It wouldn't happen again. Neither of them wanted this. She had only to remember the stunned dismay in Ben's eyes in that moment when he had come to his senses. He was likely still grieving for his wife, taken from him far too soon. And she…well, she had told herself she wasn't interested in a relationship, that she was content here helping Ridge with Destry and training her dogs and the occasional horse.

For the first time in a long time, she was beginning to wonder what else might be out in the big, scary world, waiting for her.

"I think he's feeling better, don't you?"

Caidy glanced up from the dough she was kneading to see her niece sitting cross-legged beside Luke's blanket. The dog's head was in her lap and he was gazing up at the girl with adoration.

"Yes. I think so. He seems much happier than he was even a few hours ago."

"I'm glad. I really thought he was a goner when I saw old Festus go after him."

Guilt socked her in the gut again. If she had kept a closer eye on Luke, he wouldn't be lying there with those bandages and she wouldn't be so beholden to Ben Caldwell.

"I hope that's a good reminder to you about how dangerous the bulls can be. That could just as easily have been you. I don't ever want you to take a chance with Festus or any of the bulls. They're usually placid guys most of the time, even Festus, but you never know."

"I know. I know. You and Dad have told me that like a thousand times. I'm not a little kid anymore, Aunt Caidy. I'm smart enough to know to keep my distance."

"Good. The ranch can be a dangerous place. You can't ever let your guard down. Even one of the cows could trample you if you lost your footing."

"It's a miracle I ever survived to be eleven years old, isn't it?"

Caidy made a face. "Smarty. You can't blame your dad and me for worrying about you. We just want you to be safe."

And happy, she added silently. She wanted to think her presence here at the ranch had contributed in that department. If Ridge had been left on his own after Melinda left, forced to employ a string of nannies and babysitters, she wasn't sure Destry would have come through childhood with the same cheerful personality.

"What's going to happen to Luke? You can't train him to be a real cow dog now, can you?"

Even without his injuries, she suspected Luke would always be nervous around the cattle. How could she blame him, especially when she could relate, in a sense? Not to fearing cattle. She had no problem with the big animals. Her fears were a little closer to home. This time of year, her heartbeat always kicked up a bit when the doorbell rang, even when they were expecting company.

The memory of that fateful night was as much a part of her as the sprinkle of freckles on her nose and the tiny scar she had at the outside edge of her left eyebrow from an unfortunate encounter with the business end of a pitchfork when she was eight.

"I'm not really sure yet about Luke," she finally answered Destry as she formed a small ball of dough and set it into the prepared pan. "I'm guessing from this point on, he'll just be a pet."

"Here at the River Bow?"

"Sure. Why not?" They had plenty of dogs and didn't really need another one that was just a pet. Sadie, too old to work, sort of filled that role, but she supposed they would make room for one more.

"Good," Destry said, cuddling the dog close. "It's not his fault he got hurt. Not really. He was only being curious. It doesn't seem fair to get rid of him for an accident."

Destry was a sweet girl, compassionate and loving. Maybe too compassionate sometimes. Caidy smiled, remembering the previous Christmas when she had claimed she didn't want any presents that year. Instead she only wanted cash.

They all learned later she and some of her schoolmates were being scammed out of money and belongings…by none other than Gabi, the youngest sister of Trace's new wife.

She hadn't been part of their family then, of course. She had only been a troubled, lost young girl abandoned by her heartless witch of a mother and trying to find her way.

Trace had given both Becca and Gabi the loving family they all deserved—and Gabi and Destry had moved on and become best friends. That wasn't always a good thing. Trouble seemed to find the two of them like a pack of bloodhounds on the scent.

With the dog sleeping soundly now, Destry carefully set his head back down on the blankets, then rose and wandered over to the work island. "Need help rolling out the dough?"

"Sure. I'm doing cloverleaf rolls for dinner this afternoon. You remember, you roll three small balls and stick them together. Wash your hands first."

Destry complied quickly and the two of them worked together in mostly silence for a few moments. Caidy savored these small moments with her niece, who was growing up far too quickly.

She loved making dinner for her family on Sundays, when everyone gathered together to laugh and talk and catch up. Having all these new children—Alex, Maya, Gabi—only made family time together more fun.

She would never be a gourmet chef, but she enjoyed creating meals her family enjoyed. Warm rolls slathered in her homemade jam were her specialty. She still used the recipe her mother had taught her in this very kitchen when she was about Destry's age.

Her life was pretty darn good, she thought as she worked the elastic dough in a kitchen that was warm and comfortable and already smelled delicious from the roast beef that was cooking. She had family and friends, a couple of jobs she enjoyed, a home she loved, a dog who was on the mend.

She didn't need Ben Caldwell blowing into her world, bringing that sweet, rare smile and those stunning kisses, making her feel as if something vital was missing.

"Can I turn on the radio?" Destry asked after a few more minutes.

"Sure. Something we can dance to," she said, pushing away thoughts of Ben with a smile. A moment later, the kitchen filled with music—upbeat Christmas songs. Not really what she had in mind, but what could she do?

Destry was singing "Winter Wonderland" at the top of her lungs and jigging from side to side when the door opened and Ridge came in, stomping snow off his boots.

"It's coming down pretty hard out there. You might be in for a chilly sleigh ride, kiddo."

Destry grinned. "Snow is perfect. What could be

more fun? Aunt Caidy already said she would make some of her good hot cocoa and we're going to mix up dough for oatmeal raisin cookies so we can put them in the oven right before we go. That way they'll still be hot on the wagon."

"Sounds like you've got it all figured out."

"It's going to be *great!* Thanks so much for agreeing to take us. You're awesome, Dad."

"You're welcome, kid."

He smiled at his daughter for a moment then turned to Caidy. She noticed with no small degree of apprehension the deceptively casual expression on her brother's rugged features. "Hey, how would you feel if we added a few more at dinner?"

It wasn't a completely unusual request. Ridge had a habit of inviting in strays. She took care of the four-legged kind, and he often focused on the human variety.

"Shouldn't be a problem. It's a big roast and I can always throw in a few more potatoes and add more carrots. Who did you invite?"

He shrugged. "Just the new vet and his kids."

Just the new vet? The man she happened to have tangled lips with in this very kitchen twelve hours earlier? The very man she was trying to shove out of her brain. She opened her mouth to answer but nothing came out except an embarrassing sort of squeak.

"He was out shoveling when I cleared the drive with the tractor and we started chatting. I mentioned dinner and then the sleigh ride after and asked if they would like to join us."

She suddenly wanted to take the ball of dough in her hand and fling it at her brother. How could he do this to her? She had warned him not to get any ideas in his head about matchmaking, yet here he was doing exactly that.

She supposed she shouldn't be so surprised. All three of her brothers seemed to think their mission in life was to set her up with some big, gorgeous cowboy. Ben wasn't exactly a cowboy, but he had the big and gorgeous parts down.

How was she supposed to sit across the dinner table from the man when all she could remember was the silky slide of his tongue against hers, the hardness of those muscles against her, his sexy, ragged breathing as he tasted her mouth?

"You don't mind, do you?"

She would have laughed if she suddenly wasn't feeling queasy.

"No. Why should I mind?" she muttered, while in her head she went through about a dozen reasons. Starting and ending with that kiss.

"That's what I figured. You and Becca and Laura are always making way too much food. Inviting the vet and his family for dinner seemed like a nice way to welcome them to the ranch. And I figured his kids might get a charge out of going with us on the sleigh ride later."

Of all her three brothers, Ridge was the most taciturn. His failed marriage and the burden of responsibility that came with running the family ranch while the twins pursued other interests made him seem hard sometimes, but he also showed these flashes of kindness that tugged at her heart.

"I'm sure they will. It's bound to be something new and exciting for a couple of kids from California. They probably don't have much snow where they're from."

"Awesome!" Destry exclaimed. "I hope they're good singers."

Right. Singing and Ben Caldwell. Two things she should avoid at all costs thrown right in her face. This should prove to be a very interesting evening.

Chapter 7

"Do you think Alex and Maya will be there?"

"It's a good bet, kid," Ben told his son as the three of them walked down the plowed lane through the gentle snowfall toward the ranch house. The snow muted all sounds, even the low gurgle of the creek, on the other side of the trees that formed an oxbow around the ranch.

The cold air smelled of hay and pine and woodsmoke. He breathed deeply, thinking it had been far too long since he had taken time to just savor his surroundings. The River Bow was unexpectedly serene, with the mix of aspens and pine and the mountains soaring to the east.

"I hope Gabi is there," Ava said, looking more enthusiastic about the outing than she had about anything in a long time. "She's superfunny."

"I'm sure she will be. Ridge said their whole family was coming for dinner and she's part of the family."

He and his kids, however, were *not*. They were only temporary guests and he probably had no business dragging his children to their family dinner, especially after the events of the night before.

He should have said no. Ridge Bowman took him by surprise with the invitation while they were out clearing snow and he had been so caught off guard, he hadn't known quite how to reply.

The kids would enjoy it. He had known that from the get-go. He was fairly sure he wouldn't. He didn't mind socializing. Brooke had loved to throw parties and some part of him had missed that since her death. But this party was obviously a family thing and he hated to impose.

If that wasn't enough, he also wasn't ready to face a certain woman yet—Caidy Bowman, of the soft curves and the silky hair and the warm mouth that tasted like cocoa and heaven.

That kiss, coming on the heels of his vivid, sexy dream about her, left him aching and restless. He hadn't slept at all after he left her house. He had tossed and turned and punched his pillow until he had finally gotten up at 6:00 a.m., before the children, and started shoveling snow to burn away some of this edgy hunger. Mother Nature had dumped quite a bit of snow throughout the day, so he had plenty of chances to work it off.

That kiss. He had wanted to drown in it, just yank her against him and tease and taste and explore until they were both shaking with need. Somehow he knew she would respond just as he had dreamed, with soft, eager enthusiasm.

How did a guy engage in casual chitchat with a woman after he had kissed her like that without wanting to do it all over again?

Despite the December chill, he unzipped his coat. He probably couldn't do much about his overheated imagination, but the rest of him didn't need to simmer.

A couple of dogs came up to greet them as they approached the house and Jack eased behind him. Though his son saw plenty of strange dogs at the clinic, he was often apprehensive around animals he didn't know. A large, untrained mastiff had cornered him once at the clinic a few years earlier, intent only on friendliness, but Jack had been justifiably frightened by the encounter and wary ever since.

"They won't hurt you, Jack. See, both of their tails are wagging. They just want to say hi."

"I don't want to," Jack said, hiding even further behind him.

"You don't have to, then. Ava, can you carry the bag with Mrs. Michaels's salad and toffee while I give your brother a lift?"

She grabbed the bag away from him and hurried ahead while he scooped up his son and set him on his shoulders for the last hundred yards of the walk, much to Jack's delight. It wouldn't be long before the boy grew too large for this but for now they both enjoyed it, even with his son's snowy boots hitting his chest.

In the gathering dusk, the log ranch house was lit up with icicle lights that dripped from the eaves and around the porch. People on the coast would pay serious money for the chance to spend Christmas here at a picturesque cattle ranch in the oxbow of a world-class fly-fishing creek.

Several unfamiliar vehicles were parked in the circular driveway in front of the ranch house and that awkwardness returned. If not for his children's anticipation, he probably would have turned on his heels and headed back to the cottage.

Ava reached the porch before they did and skipped up the stairs to ring the doorbell. As Ben and Jack reached the steps a woman he didn't know with dark hair and a winsome smile answered. "You must be the new veterinarian. Ridge mentioned you and your family were joining us. Hi. I'm Becca Bowman, married to Trace. Come in out of the snow."

He walked inside and went to work divesting the children of their abundance of outerwear: coats, gloves, hats, scarves and boots. Becca gathered them all up and set them inside a large closet under the curving log staircase.

"Are you Gabi's mom?" Ava asked, sitting on the bottom step to slip out of her boots.

"I'm her big sister actually. It's a long story. But I guess in every way that matters, I'm her mother."

An intriguing story. He wondered at the details but decided they weren't important. Becca had obviously stepped up to raise her sister and he couldn't help but find that admirable.

"Where is Gabi?" Ava asked eagerly.

"She and Destry are around somewhere. They'll be so excited to see you. They've been waiting impatiently for you to get here for the past hour."

Ava beamed with an enthusiasm that had been missing for far too long. Maybe staying here at the ranch near a friend for a few weeks would be good for her. Maybe it would finally help her resign herself to their move to Idaho, to the distance now between her and her grandparents.

"Last I saw them, they were playing a video game in the den. Straight down that hall and to the left."

Ava took off, with Jack close on her heels. He thought about calling them back but decided to let them figure things out. Kids usually did a much better job of that than adults.

"I think dinner is nearly ready," Becca said to him. "Come on into the great room and I'm sure one of the boys can hook you up with something to drink."

She led him into a huge room dominated by a massive angled wall of windows and the big Christmas tree he had seen glimmering from outside as they approached. Where was Caidy? he wondered, then was embarrassed at himself for looking for her straight away.

Her brother Ridge headed over immediately with a cold beer. "Hey, Doc Caldwell. Glad you could make it."

At least one of them was. "Thanks."

"Have you met my brothers?" Ridge asked.

"I know Chief Bowman. Fire Chief Bowman," he corrected. He could only imagine how confusing that must be for the town, to have a fire chief and police chief who were not only brothers but identical twins.

"You've deserted us at the inn, I understand," Taft Bowman said.

He winced. The only thing that bothered him worse than being obligated to Caidy was knowing he had checked out prematurely from the Cold Creek Inn. "Sorry. We were bursting at the seams there."

"Oh, no worries about that. Laura's already booked your rooms through the holiday. She had to turn away several guests in the past few weeks and ended up contacting some of them who wanted to be on standby. They were thrilled at the last-minute cancellation."

He had expected the immensely popular inn would do just fine without his business. "That's a relief."

"She's been saying for a week how she thought your kids needed to be in a real house for the holidays. She was thrilled when Caidy talked to her about having you stay here. As soon as she hung up the phone, she said she couldn't believe she'd never thought of the foreman's cottage out here."

"I'm already missing those delicious breakfasts at the inn," he said. That was true enough, though Mrs. Michaels was also an excellent cook and had taken great delight just that morning in preparing pancakes from scratch and her famous fluffy scrambled eggs.

In his three weeks of staying at the Cold Creek Inn, Laura Bowman had struck him as an extraordinarily kind woman. The whole family, really, had welcomed him and his children to town with warm generosity.

"The guy over there on his cell phone is my husband, Trace," Becca said. "He's the police chief and is lucky enough to be off duty tonight, though his deputies often forget that."

The man in question waved and smiled a greeting but continued on the phone. Ben suddenly remembered the toffee and pulled out the tin. "Where would you like me to put this?"

"You didn't have to fix anything," Becca scolded.

"I didn't have anything to do with it," he admitted. "My housekeeper did all the heavy lifting. She sends her apologies, by the way. She would have come but she needed to take a call from her daughter. She's expecting her first grandchild and the separation has been difficult."

He felt more than a little guilty about that. Anne had come with them to Idaho willingly enough but he knew she missed her daughter, especially during this exciting, nerve-racking time of impending birth. They communicated via videoconferencing often, but it wasn't the same as face-to-face interaction.

"Let's just set it on the table here. Wow. I've got to taste some first. I love toffee."

"Ooh, send some this way," Taft said, so Becca passed the tin of candy around to all the brothers.

"She also made a salad. Greek pasta."

"That sounds delicious too. I'll take it in to see where Caidy wants it."

"I can do that." His words—and anticipation to see her again—came out of nowhere. "I should probably check in on my patient while I'm here anyway."

"Okay. Sure. Just through the hall and around the corner."

He remembered. He had a feeling every detail of the Bowman kitchen would be etched in his memory for a very long time.

When he entered, his gaze immediately went to Caidy, and the restlessness that had dogged him all day seemed to ease. She stood at the stove with her hair tucked into a loose ponytail, wearing an apron over jeans and a crisp white shirt.

She looked pretty and fresh, and something soft and warm seemed to unfurl inside him.

She must have sensed his presence, though it was obvious she was spinning a dozen different plates. She glanced around and he saw her cheeks turn pink, though he wasn't certain if it was from the heat of the stove or the memory of the kiss they had shared in this very room.

"Oh. Hi. You're here."

"Yes. I've brought a salad. Greek pasta. My housekeeper made it, actually. And toffee. I brought toffee too."

Good grief. Could he sound any more like an idiot?

"That's great. Thank you. The salad can go on the buffet in the dining room. I don't imagine the toffee will last long with my brothers around."

"They were already working on it," he said.

"Oh, man. I love toffee. They know it, too, but do you think they're going to save me any? Highly doubtful. It's going to be gone before I get a taste."

"I'll have Mrs. Michaels make more for you," he offered, his voice gruff.

She smiled. "That's sweet of you. Or I could just arm wrestle my brothers for the last piece."

"Right." He cleared his throat. "Uh, I'll just take this into the dining room."

This was stupid. Why couldn't he talk to her? Yes, she was a beautiful, desirable woman who had moaned in his arms just a few hours earlier, but that didn't mean he couldn't carry on a semi-intelligent conversation with her.

Determined to do just that, after he had taken the salad into the dining room he returned to the kitchen instead of seeking the safety of the great room with the rest of the Bowmans.

Caidy looked surprised to see him again so soon.

"I wanted to check on Luke," he explained.

"He seems to be feeling better. I moved him into my

room so he has a chance to rest during all the commotion of dinner."

"You mind if I take a look at him?"

She glanced up, surprise in her eyes. "Really? You don't have to do that. Ridge didn't invite you to dinner to get free vet care out of the deal."

Why *had* Ridge invited him? He had been wondering that all afternoon. "I'm here. I might as well see how he's progressing."

"Can I take over stirring the gravy so you can show Ben to your room?"

For the first time, he noticed Laura Bowman, who had been standing on the other side of the kitchen slicing olives.

"Thank you. It should be done in just a few minutes."

Caidy washed her hands, then tucked a loose strand of hair behind her ear, nibbling her lip between her teeth just enough to remind him of how that lip had tasted between his own teeth and sent blood pooling in his groin.

She led the way down the hall to a door just off the kitchen and he heard a little bark from inside the room just before she pushed open the door.

He had a vague impression of, not so much fussiness, as feminine softness. A lavender-and-brown quilt and a flurry of pillows covered a queen-size bed, and lace curtains spilled from the windows. His gaze was drawn to a lovely oil painting of horses grazing in a flower-strewn field that looked as if it could be somewhere on the River Bow. It hung on the wall at the foot of the bed, the first thing she must see upon awakening and drifting off to sleep.

He shouldn't be so interested in where she slept— or what she might dream about—he ordered himself, and he quickly shifted attention to the dog. The border collie was lying beside the bed near the window, in the same enclosure he had rested in while in the kitchen.

When he saw Caidy, Luke wagged his tail and tried to get up but she bent over and rested a comforting hand on his head. He immediately subsided as if she had tranquilized him.

"Look who's here. It's our friend Dr. Caldwell. Aren't you glad to see him?"

Because he had spent two hours operating on the dog and shoved a needle into his lungs a few hours earlier, Ben highly doubted he ranked very high on the animal's list of favorite humans, but he wasn't going to argue with her.

"No more breathing trouble?"

"No. He slept like a rock the rest of the night and has been sleeping most of the day."

"That's the best thing for him."

"That's what I figured. I've been keeping his pain medication on a consistent schedule. Ridge has been helping me carry him outside for his business."

He stepped over the enclosure and knelt inside so he could run his hand over the dog. Though he focused on his patient, some part of him was aware the whole time of her watching him intently.

Did she feel the tug and pull between them, or was it completely one-sided?

He didn't think so. She had definitely kissed him back. He vividly relived the sweetness of her mouth softening under his, the little catch in her breathing, the way her pulse had raced beneath his fingers. His gut ached at the memory, especially at the knowledge that a memory and those wild dreams were all he was likely to have from her.

"I think he's healing very nicely. I would think in a day or two you can let him have full mobility again. Bring him into the office around the middle of the week and I can check the stitches. I'm happy to see he's doing so well."

"You didn't think he would survive, did you?"

"No," he said honestly. "I'm always happy when I'm proved wrong."

"You've really gone above and beyond in caring for him. Coming out in the middle of the night and everything. I...want you to know I appreciate it. Very much."

He shrugged. "It's my job. I wouldn't be very good at it if I didn't care about my patients, would I?"

She opened her mouth as if to say something else but then closed it again. Awkwardness sagged between them, heavy and clumsy, and he suddenly knew she was remembering the kiss too.

He sighed. "Look, I need to apologize about last night. It was...unprofessional and should never have happened."

She gazed at him out of those impossibly green eyes without blinking and he wondered what the hell she might be thinking.

"I don't want you to think I'm in the habit of that."

"Of what?"

He felt stupid for bringing it up but didn't know how else to move past this morning-after sort of discomfort. Better to face it head-on, he figured. "You know what. I came over to help you with your dog. I shouldn't have kissed you. It was unprofessional and shouldn't have happened."

Unexpectedly, she gave a strained-sounding laugh. "Maybe you ought to think about adding that to your list of services, Dr. Caldwell. Believe me, if word got out what a good kisser you are, every woman in Pine Gulch who even *thought* about owning a cat or dog would be lining up at the adoption day at the animal shelter just for the perk of being able to lock lips with the sexy new veterinarian."

He could feel himself flush. She was making fun of him, but he supposed he deserved it. "I was only trying to tell you there's no reason to worry it will happen again. It was late and I was tired and not really myself. I never would have even *thought* about kissing you otherwise."

"Oh, well. That explains it perfectly, then."

He had the vague feeling he had hurt her feelings somehow, which absolutely hadn't been his intention. He suddenly remembered how much he had hated the dating scene, trying to wade through all those nuances and layers of meaning.

"Good to know your weaknesses," she went on. "Next time I need veterinary care in the middle of the night for one of my animals, I'll be sure to call the vet over in Idaho Falls. We certainly wouldn't want a repeat of that hideous experience."

"I think we can both agree it wasn't hideous. Far from it." He muttered the last bit under his breath but she caught it anyway. Her pupils flared and her gaze dipped to his mouth again. His abdominal muscles contracted and he felt that awareness seethe and curl between them again, like the currents of Cold Creek.

"Just unfortunate," she murmured.

"Give me a break here, Caidy. What do you want me to say?"

"Nothing. We both agreed to forget it happened."

"That's a little easier said than done," he admitted.

"Isn't everything?"

"True enough."

"It's no big deal, Ben. We kissed. So what? I enjoyed it, and you enjoyed it. We both agree it shouldn't happen again. Let's just move on, okay?"

As easy as that? Somehow he didn't think so, but he wasn't about to argue.

"I should get back to the kitchen. Thank you for taking the time to check on Luke."

"No problem," he said. He followed her out of the room, wishing more than anything that circumstances could be different, that he could be the sort of man a woman like Caidy Bowman needed.

Chapter 8

Insufferable man!

When they left her bedroom, Ben headed into the great room with the others while Caidy, unsettled and annoyed, returned to the kitchen to finish the preparations for dinner.

How could he reduce what had been one of the single most exhilarating moments of her life to a terrible mistake teeming with awkwardness?

Yes, the kiss shouldn't have happened. They both accepted it. He didn't have to act as if the two of them had committed some horrible crime and should beat themselves up with guilt about it for the rest of their lives.

It was late and I was tired and not really myself. I never would have even thought *about kissing you otherwise.*

That removed any doubt in her mind that he was attracted to her. He had kissed her because he was tired and because she was there. The humiliation of that was almost more than she could bear, especially given the enthusiastic way she had responded to him and the silly fantasies she had been spinning all day.

"Is something wrong? Are you ready for us to start taking dishes out to the dining room?" Becca asked.

With a jolt, Caidy realized she had been staring without moving at the roast she had taken out of the oven. She frowned, frustrated at herself and at Ben, and did her best to drag her attention away from her pout.

"Yes. That would be great, thank you. Everything should be just about ready to go. I ought to let the roast sit for another few minutes, but by the time we get everything else on the table, it will be ready to carve."

Becca and Laura picked up covered bowls and took them out to the table, chattering as they went about their respective plans for Christmas Eve. Caidy smiled as she listened to them. She loved both of her sisters-in-law deeply. Having sisters had turned out to be far more wonderful than she ever imagined. The best part about them was that each was perfect for her respective Bowman brother.

Becca, with that hidden vulnerability and her flashes of clever humor, brought out the very best in Trace. Since she and Gabi had come into his life the previous Christmas, Caidy had seen a soft gentleness in Trace that had been missing since their parents were murdered.

Laura Pendleton was exactly the woman Caidy had always wanted for Taft to soothe the wildness in him. Taft and Laura had once been deeply in love until their engagement abruptly and mysteriously ended just days before their wedding.

Seeing them together, reunited after all these years, filled her with delight. She especially loved seeing Taft shed his carefree player image and step up to be a caring father to Laura's two children, energetic Alex and the adorable Maya.

She wasn't jealous of the joy her brothers had found—she was happy for them all. Maybe she grew a little wistful when she watched those sweet little moments between two people who loved each other deeply, but she did her best not to think about them.

Still chattering, both Laura and Becca came back into the kitchen to grab the salads they had each prepared out of the refrigerator. At least the Sunday dinners had become much easier since her brothers married. She used to fix the whole shebang on her own, but now the two women and often Gabi pitched in and contributed their own salads or desserts.

She didn't know how much longer this Sunday dinner tradition could continue. She wouldn't blame Taft and Trace for wanting to spend their free time with their own nuclear families. For now, everyone seemed content to continue gathering each week when they could.

"So the new veterinarian is gorgeous. Why didn't anybody tell me?" Becca said, putting the rolls Caidy had removed from the second oven into a basket.

"I don't know," Laura answered. "Maybe we figured since you're married to Trace Bowman, who is only second in all-around gorgeousness to his twin brother, you really didn't need to know about the cute new vet."

Caidy felt another of those little pangs of envy at Becca's sudden cat-who-ate-the-canary smile.

"True," she answered. "But you should have warned me before I opened the door to find this yummy man on the doorstep—and added to the yum factor, the very adorable little boy on his shoulders."

Caidy didn't say anything as she carved the roast beef. This was usually Ridge's job, for some reason, but she didn't want to call him in from entertaining said veterinarian out in the other room.

"What about you, Caidy?" Becca said. "You're the only available one here. Don't you think he's gorgeous? Something about those big blue eyes and those long, long lashes…"

She had a sudden vivid memory of those eyes closing as he kissed her the night before, of his mouth teasing and licking at hers, of the heat and strength of his arms around her and how she had wanted to lean into that broad chest and stay right there.

Her knees suddenly felt a little on the weak side and she narrowly avoided slicing off her thumb.

"Sure," she said. "Too bad he's got the personality of a honey badger."

She didn't miss the surprised looks both women gave her. Laura's mouth opened and Becca's eyebrows just about crept up to her hairline, probably because Caidy rarely spoke poorly about anyone. Every time she started to vent about someone when they weren't present, her mother's injunction about not saying something behind a person's back you wouldn't say to his face would ring in her ears.

She wouldn't have said anything if she wasn't burning with humiliation about that kiss he obviously regretted.

Laura was the first to speak. "That's odd you would

say that. I found him very nice while he was staying at the inn. Half of my front desk staff was head over heels in love with him from the start."

After that kiss, she was very much afraid it wouldn't take more than a slight jostle for her to join them. She couldn't remember ever being this drawn to a man—the fact that she was so attracted to a man who basically found her a nuisance was just too humiliating.

"I'm not surprised," she finally said, hoping they would attribute the color she could feel soaking her cheeks to the overwarm kitchen and her exertions fixing the meal. "Do you want to know what I think about Ben Caldwell? I think he's a rude, arrogant, opinionated jerk. Some women are drawn to that kind of man. Don't ask me why."

"Don't forget, he's also often inconveniently in the wrong place at the wrong time."

At the sudden deep voice, she and both of her sisters-in-law gave a collective gasp and turned to the doorway. Every single molecule inside her wanted to cringe at the sight of Ben standing there, watching the three of them, his face void of expression.

"My son spilled a glass of water," he explained. "I came in looking for a towel to clean it up. Unless you think that's too rude of a request."

Becca reached almost blindly into the drawer where Caidy kept the dish towels, pulled one out and handed it to him.

"Thanks," he answered, then left without another word. Caidy wanted to bury her face in the gravy.

"Wow. I guess the two of you haven't exactly hit it off," Becca said.

Caidy thought of that sizzling kiss, apparently mostly one-sided. "You could say that," she answered.

Her mother would have yanked her earlobe and sent her to her bedroom for being so unconscionably rude to a guest in their home. She couldn't face him again. How could she sit at the table beside him after what he had heard her say? The worst of it was, none of it was true. She was just being petty and small, embarrassed that she was so fiercely attracted to a man who regretted ever touching her.

How could she figure out a way to stay here in the kitchen all evening?

She let out a heavy breath. She was going to have to find a way to apologize to him, but how on earth could she manage that without giving him some kind of explanation? She couldn't tell him the truth. That would only add another layer of mortification onto her humiliation.

"Um, I think I'll just take these rolls out," Becca said into the sudden painful silence.

After she hurried out of the kitchen, Laura placed a hand on Caidy's arm. "Okay, what was that about? Did something happen between the two of you?"

Her dear friend had known her for many years—long before her parents were killed, when everything in her world changed. She didn't want to tell her. She didn't want to talk to *anyone*—she just wanted to hide out in her room with Luke. He, at least, was one male she didn't feel awkward and stupid around.

She sighed. "I called him to come over last night. One of those frantic, middle-of-the-night emergencies. Luke was having trouble breathing and I was upset and didn't know what else to do. He... Before he left, he... We kissed. It was...great. Really great. But today he told me what a mistake it was. He acted like it was this horrible experience that we should both pretend never happened. I guess I was more hurt than I realized by his reaction. I lashed out, which wasn't fair. I don't believe any of those things. Well, I did at first. He was quite rude to me after Luke's accident and treated me like it was my fault. I guess it was, in some ways, but he really twisted the knife. He's been... We've been fine since then, except just now in my room."

Laura was silent for a moment, apparently digesting that barrage of information. Finally she spoke with that calm common sense Caidy loved about her.

"I've had the chance over the past few weeks while he's been staying at the inn to talk with Mrs. Michaels," she said. "She's told me a few things about Ben's situation. More than she probably should have, probably. Take it easy on the man, okay? He's been through a rough few years. His wife's death was horrible apparently."

"He told me she died of complications from diabetes."

"Did he also tell you she was pregnant at the time?"

"No. Oh, no."

Laura nodded. "Apparently she went into a diabetic coma while she was driving and crashed into a tree. Their baby died along with her. It was a miracle Ava and Jack weren't in the car too. They were with their grandparents."

Those poor children. And poor Ben. If she felt bad before about what she had said, now she felt about a zillion times worse.

"According to Mrs. Michaels, his late wife's parents blame him for their daughter and grandchild's death and have done all they can to drive Ava and Jack away from him. That's the main reason he came here, I believe. To put some distance between them and try salvaging his family."

She paused and squeezed Caidy's arm. "I think he could really use a friend."

She had never considered herself a petty person before but she was beginning to discover otherwise. So what if the man regretted kissing her? So her pride was bruised. She tried to be a good person most of the time. Couldn't she look past that and be that friend Laura was talking about?

"Thanks for telling me. I'll…figure out a way to apologize. But not right now, okay? Right now I have a dozen people to feed."

Laura hugged her. "I know you will. Apologize, I mean. You're a good person, Caidy. Someone I'm pleased to call my sister. I just have one more question and it's an important one. I want you to think long and hard before you answer me."

She felt more than a little trepidation. "What's that?"

"Besides being arrogant and rude, how is our Dr. Caldwell in the kissing department?"

Despite everything, she gave a strained laugh. "Let me put it this way. Luke wasn't the only one having trouble breathing last night."

Laura grinned at her, which gave her a little burst of courage. Enough, at least, that she could draw in a deep breath, pick up the platter with the roast beef slices and head out into the other room with squared shoulders to face what just might be the most embarrassing meal of her life.

* * *

Dinner wasn't quite the ordeal she had feared.

By the time she reached the table, the only seat left was at the opposite end of the table from Ben, between Ridge at the head and Destry. Good. She needed a little space from Ben while she tried to figure out how she could possibly face the man after making a complete idiot of herself over him, again and again.

He was deep in conversation with her brothers and Becca when she sat down, and he didn't look in her direction, much to her relief. After Ridge said grace, blessing the food and welcoming their guests to the ranch, various conversations flowed around her. Caidy moved her food around in silence, for the most part, until Destry, Gabi and Ava enlisted her opinion about how old she was when she started wearing makeup.

She didn't wear much now unless she was dressing up for something. "I think I was about thirteen or fourteen before I wore anything but lip gloss. You've got a few years to go, girls."

"I'm ready now," Gabi declared.

"Me too," Destry chimed in.

"My grandma let me keep some eye makeup and lip stuff at her house when we lived in California," Ava said. "I could only put it on while I was there or when we went shopping or out to lunch. I had to wash it off before I left so my dad didn't freak, which was totally stupid."

Destry looked slightly appalled at the idea of keeping makeup—or anything else—from her father. "I could never do that!"

"My grandma said it was okay."

In the mode of adults sticking together, Caidy gave

the three girls a mild look. "Here's a pretty good rule—if you can't wear it, taste it or say it in front of your dad, you probably shouldn't wear it, taste it or say it when he's not there."

"Agreed." Ridge interjected into the conversation. "You hear that, Des?"

The three girls giggled and started talking about something from school, leaving Caidy's mind to follow the conversation between the twins and Ben at the other end of the table.

"So, Dr. Caldwell, how are you finding Pine Gulch?" Trace was asking.

"Ben. Please, call me Ben. We're enjoying living here so far. The town seems to be filled with very kind people. For the most part anyway."

He didn't look in her direction when he spoke but she cringed anyway, certain his pointed barb was aimed at her.

"It's the *least part* you have to worry about," Taft said with a wink. "I could name a few people in town whose bad side you want to stay far clear of. I'm sure Trace knows a few more on the law enforcement side. We've got our share of bad customers."

"I'm sure you do," Ben murmured. "Rude, arrogant jerks."

"You better believe it," Taft said.

Becca quickly cleared her throat. "Uh, can you pass the potatoes?" she asked Ben.

"Sure, if there are any left." He picked up the bowl Caidy always served the mashed potatoes in, the flower-lined earthenware that had always been one of her mother's favorites.

For the first time since she sat down, he looked in

her direction, though his gaze was focused somewhere above her head. "Everything is really delicious," he said. "Isn't that right, Ava? Jack?"

"Supergood," Jack said. He had a smudge of gravy on his cheek and looked absolutely adorable. "Can I have another roll? Ooh, with jam! I *love* strawberries."

Ben grabbed one of her cloverleaf rolls and spread some of her jam on it. When he handed it to his son, Jack gobbled it in three bites, smearing red along with the gravy. Ben shook his head, picked up his napkin and dabbed at the mess on Jack's face. She watched out of the corner of her gaze as those big hands that had held her close attended to his child, and something soft and warm unfurled inside her chest.

He looked up at just that moment and caught her watching. Their gazes held for one long, charged moment while the conversation flowed around them. Then Ridge asked him another question and he looked away, breaking the connection.

He and his children fit in well with the family. Taft's stepson, Alex, and Jack seemed like two peas in a proverbial pod, with Maya attending closely to their every word, and Gabi and Des had been quick to absorb Ava into their circle.

This was only temporary, she reminded herself. After the holidays, he would take his cute kids and his friendly housekeeper and move into the big house he was building. In a matter of days, he would be just a peripheral figure in her world. He wouldn't even be that if she didn't need to take one of the dogs for the occasional visit to the veterinarian.

She should be relieved about that, she told herself. Not glum.

"I love that painting over the fireplace," Ben said into a temporary lull of the conversation. "I see the artist's last name is Bowman. Any relation?"

The rest of the table fell silent—even the children. Nobody seemed willing to jump in to answer him except Ridge.

"Yes," her oldest brother finally said. "She is a relation. She was our mother."

Ben glanced around the table, obviously picking up on the sudden shift in mood.

"I'll admit, I don't know much about art, but I find that piece striking. I don't know if it's the horses in the foreground or the mountains or the fluttery curtains in the window of the old cabin but every time I look away for a few moments, something draws me back. That's real talent."

Her heart warmed a little at his praise of their mother's talent. "She was brilliant," Caidy murmured.

He looked at her and she saw an unexpected compassion in his eyes. Seeing it made her feel even more guilty. She didn't deserve compassion from him, not after her mean words.

"Several of her paintings were stolen eleven years ago," Trace said. "Since then, we've done our best to recover what we can. We've had investigators tracking some of them down. This one was located about three years ago in a gallery in the Sonoma area of California."

"It was always Caidy's favorite," Ridge put in. "Finding it again was something of a miracle."

This shifted all attention to her again and she squirmed. Did anybody besides Laura and Becca pick up the tension in the room? She doubted it. Her brothers usually were oblivious to social currents and the kids were too busy eating and talking and having fun. Just as they should be.

To her relief, Laura—sweet, wonderful Laura— stepped up to deflect attention. "So, Dr. Caldwell, you and your children are coming along on the sleigh ride after dinner, aren't you?"

"Sleigh ride!" Jack exclaimed and he and Alex, best buddies now, did a cute little high-five maneuver.

Ben watched them ruefully. "I don't know. I kind of feel like we've intruded enough on your family."

"Oh, you have to come," Destry exclaimed.

"Yes!" Gabi joined her. "It's going to be awesome! We're going to sing Christmas carols and have hot chocolate and everything. Oh, please, come with us!"

If things weren't so funky between them right now, she would have told him he was fighting a losing battle. One man simply couldn't fight the combined efforts of the Bowmans and their progeny, adopted or otherwise.

"We're not going far," Ridge promised. "Only a couple miles up the canyon. Probably shouldn't take more than an hour."

"Resistance is futile," Taft said with a grin. "You might as well give in gracefully."

Ben laughed. "In that case, sure. Okay."

The kids shrieked with excitement. Caidy wished she could share even a tiny smidgen of their enthusiasm. The only bright spot for her in the whole thing was that Ben's presence probably eliminated the need for her to go along. Ridge couldn't claim they didn't have enough adults now. She would just offer an excuse to stay at the house and let the rest of them have all the Christmas fun.

She was still going to have to figure out a way to apologize to the man, but at this point she would take any reprieve she could find, however temporary.

Chapter 9

After dinner had been cleared, the girls' other friends began arriving. Caidy threw in the trays of cookies she and Destry had readied, her brothers headed out to hitch up the big draft horses to the hay wagon and everyone else began donning winter gear. After the cookies came out, Caidy walked through the house gathering all the blankets she could find.

As she headed down the stairs with an armload of blankets, she saw through the big windows that the snow had eased and was only falling now in slow, puffy flakes. Moonlight had peeked behind the storm clouds, turning everything a pearlescent midnight-blue.

It was stunning enough from here. She could only imagine how beautiful it would be to ride through the night on the wagon, with the cold air in her face and the sound of children's laughter swirling through the night.

She was almost sorry she wasn't going with them. Almost.

She continued down the stairs, doing her best to avoid making eye contact with Ben, who was helping Jack into his boots.

"Sleigh ride. Sleigh ride. Sleigh ride," Maya chanted, wiggling her hips that were bundled up along with the rest of her in a very cute pink snowsuit with splashy orange flowers.

Caidy couldn't help laughing. "You're going to have a wonderful time, little bug," she said, kissing Maya's nose. She loved all of the children in her family but sweet, vulnerable Maya held a special place in her heart.

"You come," Maya said, reaching for her hand.

"Oh, honey. I'm not going. I'll be here when you get back."

"What do you mean, you're not going? You have to come," Ridge said sternly. "Where's your coat?"

"In the closet. Where it's staying. I figured somebody needs to stay here. Keep the home fire burning and all that."

"Don't worry about that," Becca said from underneath Trace's arm. "I've got that covered."

For the first time, Caidy realized her sister-in-law wasn't wearing a coat either.

"Why aren't *you* going?" Ridge asked, looking even more disgruntled.

"I'm planning to sit this one out. I have court tomorrow and some work to do before then. And, to be honest, I'm not sure being bounced around on a hay wagon right now would be the best thing for, well, for the baby."

For a moment everyone stared at her. Even the girls

who had come for Gabi's little sleigh ride party stopped their giggly chatter.

"Baby? You're having a baby?" Laura exclaimed.

Becca nodded and Trace hugged her more tightly, then kissed the top of her head, clearly a proud papa.

"When?" Caidy asked, thrilled for both of them.

"June," Gabi declared proudly. "I've been *dying* to tell everyone! I kept my mouth shut, see, Trace? You said I couldn't. Ha!"

Her brother laughed and grabbed his wife's sister with his free arm, pulling her into their shared embrace. "You did good, kid. We were going to tell everyone at dinner but the right moment never quite came."

"There's never a *wrong* moment for that kind of great news," Ridge said. "Congratulations. Another Bowman. Just what the world needs."

The next few moments were spent with hugs and kisses and good wishes all the way around. Even Ben shook both of their hands and kissed Becca's cheek, though he had just met her that afternoon.

She suddenly remembered with a pang that he had lost a child when his wife died. Was this spontaneous celebration of impending parenthood difficult for him? If it was, he didn't show it by his manner.

Now Maya's chant changed to "baby, baby, baby," but she didn't lose the hip wiggle. Caidy hugged her too. "It's wonderful news, isn't it? You'll have a new cousin."

"I like cousins," Maya said.

"Me too, bug."

When Caidy finally worked her way around the crowd, she hugged Becca. "I can't wait to be an aunt again. I'm thrilled for both of you."

Becca hugged her back. "Thank you, my dear."

"All the more reason I should stay here and keep you company, just in case you need anything."

Becca gave her a knowing look. "You're the soul of helpfulness, Caidy. Either that, or you're trying to avoid a certain rude, arrogant veterinarian."

She cringed at the reminder. "Well, there is that."

"Sorry, hon. I'd like to help you out but I think Ridge probably needs your help corralling all those kids. Besides that, I don't think it's a good idea to keep avoiding him."

"Am I that obvious?" she asked ruefully.

"A little bit. Probably Laura and I were the only ones who picked up on it. And maybe Ben."

Caidy blew out a breath. Drat. Becca was right. Ridge probably *did* need her help. "I hate being a coward," she murmured.

"It's only a sleigh ride. An hour out of your life. You can handle that. You've been through much worse."

"I don't want to leave you."

"I could use a little quiet, if you want the truth. Go, Caidy."

"As exciting as this news is, we need to get this show on the road," Ridge declared, as if on cue. "Let's load up."

The girls squealed loudly. Maya covered her ears with her mittened hands, wearing a look of alarm.

Caidy gave her a reassuring smile. "Don't worry about those silly girls. They just want to go have fun."

"Me too. You come."

She sighed, resigned to her fate. "Yes, Queen Maya."

The girl gave her sweet giggle as Caidy grabbed her coat out of the closet and quickly found mittens and a quite fancy chapeau handmade by Emery Kendall Cavazos that she had won in the gift exchange a few weeks earlier at the Friends of the Library Christmas party.

"Hurry up, Caid," Taft said. "We don't have all night. The sooner we go, the sooner we can get it over with and come back to watch the basketball game. Come on, Maya."

"I stay with Auntie," the girl said and Caidy's heart melted, as it frequently did around her.

"I've got her," she told her brother.

"Are you sure?"

"Yes. We're coming. I'm almost ready."

Taft left and she quickly finished shoving on boots, grabbed Maya's hand and hurried out to the hay wagon.

The horses stamped and blew in the cold air, which smelled of woodsmoke and snow. What a beautiful night. Perfect for a sleigh ride. Well, not officially a sleigh ride because the wagon had wheels, not runners, but she didn't think any of them would quibble.

Ridge had lined the wagon with straw bales. To her dismay, everyone else was settling as they approached the wagon and the only free space left for her and Maya was near the back of the wagon—right next to Ben. Had her brothers colluded to arrange that? She wouldn't put it past them.

Right now, Ben was more likely to throw her over the side than cooperate with any Bowman matchmaking efforts, but her brothers had no way of knowing that—unless Laura or Becca had spilled to their husbands.

"Auntie, up," Maya said.

How was she going to manage this? Maya wasn't heavy but Caidy didn't think she could climb the ladder with her in her arms and she wasn't sure Maya could negotiate them on her own. "If you want to lift her up, I can help her the rest of the way," Ben said, obviously noticing her predicament.

Caidy scooped Maya into her arms and held her up for him. Their arms brushed as he easily tugged the girl the rest of the way. Did he feel the sparks between them, or was it just her imagination? Caidy climbed the ladder and stood for a moment, wishing she could squeeze up front with Ridge. Unfortunately, he already had Alex and Jack riding shotgun.

"Sit down, Caidy, or you're going to fall over when Ridge takes off," Taft ordered. Heaven save her from brothers who didn't think she had a brain in her head.

Left with no choice, she sat on the same bale as Ben—who looked rugged and masculine in a fleece-lined heavy ranch coat the color of dust. At least Maya sat between them, providing some buffer.

Ridge turned around to make sure all his passengers were settled and then clicked to the big horses. They took off down the driveway, accompanied by the jangle of bells on the harnesses.

"Go, horsies! Jingle bells, jingle bells!" Maya exclaimed and Caidy smiled at her. When she lifted her gaze, she found Ben smiling down at the girl too. Her heart stuttered a little at the gentleness on his expression. She had called him rude and arrogant, yet here he was treating Maya, with her beautiful smile and Down syndrome features, with breathtaking sweetness.

She had to say something. Now was the perfect time. She clenched her fingers into her palms inside her mittens and turned to him. "Look, I… I'm sorry about earlier. What I said. It wasn't true. Not any of it. I was just being stupid."

"What?" he yelled, leaning down to hear over the rushing wind and the eight laughing girls.

"I said I'm sorry." She spoke more loudly but at that moment all the girls started actually singing "Jingle Bells" in time with the chiming bells from the horses.

"What?" He leaned his head closer to hers, over Maya's head, and she didn't know what else to do but lean in and speak in his ear, though she felt completely ridiculous. She wanted to tell him to just forget the whole thing. She had come this far, though. She might as well finish the thing.

Up close, he smelled delicious. She couldn't help noticing that outdoorsy soap she had noticed when they were kissing....

She dragged her mind away from that and focused on the apology she should be making. "I said I was sorry," she said in his ear. "For what I said in the kitchen to my sisters-in-law, I mean. They were teasing me, uh, about you...and I was being completely stupid. I'm sorry you overheard. I didn't mean it."

He turned his head until his face was only inches from hers. "Any of it?"

"Well, you are pretty arrogant," she answered tartly.

To her surprise, he laughed at that and the low, sexy timbre of it shivered down her spine and spread out her shoulders to her fingertips.

"I can be," he answered.

"Sing!" Maya commanded as the girls broke into "Rudolph the Red-Nosed Reindeer."

She laughed and picked the girl onto her lap, grateful for her small, warm weight and the distraction she provided from this very inconvenient attraction she didn't know what to do about to a man who was sending her more mixed signals than a broken traffic light.

She was taken further off guard when Ben began to sing along with Maya and the girls in a very pleasing tenor. He even sang all the extra lines about lightbulbs and reindeers playing Monopoly.

She had to turn away, focusing instead on the homes they passed, their holiday lights glittering in the pale moonlight.

This wasn't such a bad way to spend an evening, she decided. Even with the caroling, she was surrounded by family she loved, by beautiful scenery, by the serenity of a winter night. She was happy she had come, she realized with some shock.

The girls broke into "Silent Night" after that, changing up the lighthearted mood a little, and she hummed softly under her breath while Maya mangled the words but did her best to follow along. In the middle of the first "Sleep in heavenly peace" injunction, Ben leaned down once more.

"Why aren't you singing?" His low voice tickled her ear and gave her chills underneath the layers of wool.

She shrugged, unable to answer him. She wasn't sure she could tell him at all and she certainly couldn't tell him on a jangly, noisy sleigh ride surrounded by family and Destry's friends.

"Seriously," he pressed, leaning away when the song ended and they could converse a little more easily. "Do you have some ideological or religious objection to Christmas songs I should know about?"

She shook her head. "No. I just…don't sing."

"Don't listen to her," Taft said. She must have spoken

louder than she intended if her brother could overhear from the row of hay bales ahead of them.

"Caidy has a beautiful voice," he went on. "She used to sing solos in the school and church choir. Once she even sang the national anthem by herself at a high school football game."

Goodness. She barely remembered that. How did Taft? He had been a wildlands firefighter when she was in high school, traveling across the West with an elite smoke-jumper squad, but she now recalled he had been home visiting Laura and had come to hear her sing at that football game.

He was the only one of her brothers who had been able to make it. Ridge had still been feuding with their father and had been living on a ranch in Montana and Trace had been deployed in the Middle East.

She suddenly remembered how freaked she had been as she walked out to take the microphone and had seen the huge hometown crowd gathered there, just about everybody she knew. Despite all her hours of practice with her voice teacher and the choir director, panic had spurted through her and she completely forgot the opening words—until she looked up in the stands and saw her mother and father beaming at her and Taft and Laura giving her an encouraging wave. A steady calm had washed over her like water from the irrigation canals, washing away all the panic, and she had sung beautifully. Probably the best performance of her life.

Just a few months later, her parents were dead because of her and all the songs inside her had died with them.

"I don't sing *anymore,*" she said, hoping that would be the end of it. She didn't want to answer the question. It was nobody's business but her own—certainly not Ben Caldwell's.

He gave her a long look. The wagon jolted over a rut in the road and his shoulder bumped hers. She could have eased far enough away that they wouldn't touch but she didn't. Instead, she rested her cheek on Maya's hair, humming along with "O Little Town of Bethlehem" and gazing up at the few stars revealed through the wispy clouds as she waited for the ride to be over.

He sensed a story here.

Something was up with the Bowmans when it came to Christmas. He noticed that while Laura and the children were singing merrily away, Caidy's brothers seemed as reluctant as she to join in. The police chief and fire chief would occasionally sing a few lines and Caidy hummed here and there, but none of them could be called enthusiastic participants in this little sing-along.

At random moments over the evening he had picked up a pensive, almost sad mood threading through their family.

He thought of that beautiful work of art in the dining room, the vibrant colors and the intense passion behind it, and then the way all the Bowmans shut down as if somebody had yanked a window screen closed when he had asked about the artist.

Their mother. What happened to her? And the father was obviously gone too. He was intensely curious but didn't know how to ask.

The three-quarter moon peeked behind a cloud, and in the pale moonlight she was almost breathtakingly lovely, with those delicate features and that soft, very kissable mouth.

That kiss hadn't been far from his mind all day, probably because he still didn't quite understand what had happened. He wasn't the kind of man to steal a kiss from a beautiful woman, especially not at the spur of the moment like that. But he hadn't been able to resist her. She had looked so sweet and lovely there in her kitchen, worry for her ailing dog still a shadow in her eyes.

Holding her in his arms, he had desired her, of course, but had also been aware of something else tangled with the hunger, a completely unexpected tenderness. He sensed she used her prickly edges as a defense against the world, keeping away potential threats before they could get too close.

He remembered her cutting words to her brothers' wives and that awkward moment when he had walked into the kitchen just in time to hear her call him arrogant and rude.

Why hadn't he just slipped out of the kitchen again without any of the women suspecting he might have overheard? He should have. It would have been the polite thing to do, but some demon had prompted him to push her, to let her know he wasn't about to be dismissed so easily.

She had apologized for it, said she hadn't meant any of her words. So why had she said them?

He made her nervous. He had observed at dinner that she was warm and friendly to everyone else, but she basically ignored him and had been abrupt in their few interactions. It was an odd position in which to find himself and he wasn't sure how he felt about it—just as he didn't know how to deal with his own conflicted reaction to her.

One moment he wanted to retreat into his safe world as a widower and single father. The next, she forcibly reminded him that underneath those roles, he was still a man.

Brooke had been gone for two years. He would always grieve for his wife, for the good times they had shared and the children she had loved and raised so well. He had become, if not complacent in his grief, at least comfortable with it. This move to Idaho seemed to have shaken everything. When he agreed to take the job, he intended to create a new life for the children, away from influences he considered harmful. He never expected to find himself so drawn to a lovely woman with secrets and sadness in her eyes.

Through the rest of the sleigh ride, though he tried to focus on the scenery and the enjoyment his children were having, he couldn't seem to stop watching Caidy. She was amazing, actually, keeping her attention focused on entertaining the very cute niece on her lap and making sure none of the gaggle of preadolescent girls suddenly fell out of the wagon. She managed all of those tasks with deft skill.

She obviously loved children and she was very good with them. Why didn't she have a husband and a wagonload of children herself?

None of his business, he reminded himself. Her dog was his patient and he was currently a temporary tenant at her ranch, but that was the extent of their relationship. He would be foolish to go looking for more. That didn't stop him from being intensely aware of her as the wagon jostled his shoulder against hers every time Ridge hit a rut.

"Brrr. I'm cold," Maya said, snuggling deeper into Caidy's lap.

"So am I," she answered. "But look. Ridge is taking us home now."

Ben looked around. Sure enough, her brother had perfect timing. Just as the enthusiasm began to wane and the children started to complain of the cold, Ben realized the big, beautiful draft horses were trudging under the sign announcing the entrance to the River Bow Ranch.

"No more horsies?" Maya asked.

"Not today, little bug." Taft held his arms out and his stepdaughter lunged into them. "We'll come back and go for another ride sometime soon, though, I promise."

"She's a huge fan of our horses," Caidy said with a fond smile for the girl. "Especially the big ones for some odd reason."

Instead of heading toward the ranch house, Caidy's brother turned the horses down the little lane that led to the house he was renting. The wagon pulled up in front.

"Look at that. Curb service for you," Caidy said. She finally met his gaze with a tentative smile. He was aware of an unsettling urge to stand here in the cold, staring into those striking green eyes for an hour or two. He managed a brief smile in return, then turned his attention to climbing out of the wagon and gathering his kids.

"Let's go. Jack, Ava."

"I don't want to get off! Why does everyone else get to keep riding?" Jack had that tremor in his voice that signaled an impending five-year-old tantrum.

"Only for another minute or two," Ridge promised. "We're just heading back to the house and then the ride will be done. The horses are tired and need their beds."

"So do you, kiddo," Ben said. "Come on."

To Ben's relief, Jack complied, jumping down into his arms. Ava clearly wanted to stay with the other girls but she finally waved to them all. "See you tomorrow on the bus," she said to Destry.

"Great. I'll bring that book we were talking about."

"Okay. Don't forget."

Ava waved again and jumped down without his help.

"Thanks for letting us tag along," he said to the wagon in general, though he meant his words for Caidy. "Ava and Jack had a blast."

"What about you?" she asked.

He didn't know her well enough yet to interpret her moods. All he knew was that she looked remarkably pretty in the moonlight, with her eyes sparkling and her cheeks—and the very tip of her nose—rosy.

"I enjoyed it," he answered. He was a little surprised to realize it was true. He hadn't found all that many things enjoyable since his wife died. Who would have expected he would enjoy a hayride with a bunch of giggly girls and Caidy and her forbidding brothers, who would probably have thrown him off the wagon if they had known about that late-night kiss—and about how very much he wanted to repeat the experience?

"I especially enjoyed the peppermint hot cocoa."

She looked pleased. "I'm glad. Peppermint is my favorite too."

"Good night."

He waved and carried Jack into the foreman's cottage, wondering what the hell he was going to do about

Caidy Bowman. She was an intriguing mystery, a jumble full of prickles and sweetness, vinegar and sugar, and he was far more fascinated by her than he had any right to be.

Chapter 10

After the sleigh ride, Caidy made it a point for the next few days to stay as far as possible from the foreman's house. She had no reason to visit. Why would she? Ben and the children and Mrs. Michaels were perfectly settled and didn't need help with anything.

If she stood at her bedroom window, looking out at the night and the sparkling lights nestled among the trees, well, that was her own business. She told herself she was only enjoying the peace and serenity of these quiet December nights, but that didn't completely explain away the restlessness that seemed to ache inside her.

It certainly had nothing to do with a certain dark-haired man and the jittery butterflies he sent dancing around inside her.

She couldn't hope to avoid him forever, though. On

Wednesday, less than a week before Christmas, she woke from tangled dreams with an odd sense of trepidation.

The vague sense of unease dogged her heels like a blurred shadow as she headed out to the barn with a still-sleepy Destry to feed and water the horses and take care of the rest of their chores.

She couldn't figure it out until they finished in the barn and headed back to the welcoming warmth of the house for breakfast before the school bus came. When they walked into the kitchen, they were greeted by a happy bark from the crate she had returned to the corner and she suddenly remembered.

This was the day she had to take Luke back to the veterinarian to have his wound checked and his stitches removed. She stopped stock-still in the kitchen, trepidation pressing down on her. Drat. She couldn't avoid the man forever, she supposed. A few more days would be nice, though. Was it too late to make an appointment with the vet in Idaho Falls?

"What's wrong?" Destry asked. "Your face looks funny. Did you see a mouse?"

She raised an eyebrow. "In my kitchen? Are you kidding me? I better not. No. I just remembered something…unpleasant."

"Reverend Johnson said in Sunday school that the best way to get rid of bad thoughts is to replace them by thinking about something good."

The girl measured dry oatmeal into her bowl and reached for the teakettle Caidy always turned on before they headed out to the barn. "I've been trying to do that whenever I think about my mom," she said casually.

Thoughts of Ben flew out the window as she stared

at her niece. Destry *never* talked about her mother. In recent memory, Caidy could only recall a handful of times when Melinda's name even came up. Destry was so sweet and even-tempered, and Ridge was such an attentive father, she had just assumed the girl had adjusted to losing her mother, but she supposed no child ever completely recovered from that loss, whether she was three at the time or sixteen.

"Does that happen often?" she asked carefully. She didn't want to cut off the line of dialogue if Destry wanted to open up. "Thinking about your mother, I mean?"

Destry shrugged and added an extra spoonful of brown sugar to her oatmeal. Caidy decided to let it slide for once. "Not really. I can hardly remember her, you know? But I still wonder about her, especially at Christmas. I don't even know if she's dead or alive. Gabi at least knows her mom is alive—she's just being a big jerk."

Jerk was a kind word for the mother of both Gabi and Becca. She was a first-class bitch, selfish and irresponsible, who had given both of her daughters childhoods filled with uncertainty and turmoil.

"Have you asked your dad about...your mother?"

"No. He doesn't like to talk about her much." Destry paused, a spoonful of steaming oatmeal halfway between the bowl and her mouth. "I really don't remember much about her. I was so little when she left. She wasn't very nice, was she?"

Another kind phrase. Melinda showed up in a thesaurus as the antonym to nice. She had fooled them all in the beginning, especially Ridge. She had seemed sweet and rather needy and hopelessly in love with him, but time—or perhaps her own natural temperament—had showed a different side of her. By the time she finally left River Bow, just about all of them had been relieved to see her go.

"She was…troubled." Caidy picked through her words with caution. "I don't think she had a very happy life when she was your age. Sometimes those bad things in the past can make it tough for a person to see all the good things they have now. I'm afraid that was your mother's problem."

Destry appeared to ponder that as she took another spoonful of oatmeal. "It stinks, doesn't it?" she said quietly after a long moment. "I don't think I could ever leave my kid, no matter what."

Her heart ached for this girl and for inexplicable truths. "Neither could I. And yes, you're right. It does stink. She made some poor choices. Unfortunately, you've had to suffer for those. But you need to look at the good things you have. Your dad didn't go anywhere. He loves you more than anything and he's been here the whole time showing you that. I'm here and the twins and now their families. You have lots and lots of people who love you, Des. If your mom couldn't see how wonderful you are, that's her problem—not yours. Don't ever forget that."

"I know. I remember. Most of the time anyway."

Caidy leaned over and hugged her niece. Des rested her head on her shoulder for just a moment before she returned to her breakfast with her usual equanimity.

Caidy wasn't the girl's mother, but she thought she was doing a pretty good job as a surrogate. Worlds better than Melinda would have done, if Caidy did say so herself.

After Destry finished breakfast and helped her clean up the dishes, Caidy had just enough time to spare to run her the quarter mile from the house to the bus stop.

"Ava and Jack aren't here," her niece fretted. "Do you think they forgot what time the bus comes? Maybe we should have picked them up."

"I'm sure Mrs. Michaels knows what time the bus comes," she answered. "They've been here the past few days in plenty of time, haven't they? Maybe they just caught a ride with their father today."

"Maybe," Destry said, though she still looked worried.

Caidy could have given Des a ride into town this morning on her way to the vet, she realized. She hadn't even thought about that until right now—just as the school bus lumbered over the hill and stopped in front of them with a screech of air brakes.

After Destry climbed on the bus and Caidy waved her off, she hurried back to the house and carried the dog crate out to the ranch's Suburban, then returned for the dog, who was moving around much more comfortably these days.

"Luke, buddy, you're not making things easy on me. If not for you, I could pretend the man doesn't exist."

The dog tilted his head and gazed at her with an expression that looked almost apologetic. She laughed a little and hooked up his leash before leading him carefully out to the Suburban, where she lifted him carefully into the crate.

Maybe Ridge could take him into the vet for her.

The fleeting thought was far too tempting. As much as she wanted to ask him for the favor, she knew she couldn't. This was all part of her ongoing effort to prove to herself she wasn't a complete coward.

For a brief instant as she slid behind the wheel, a random image flitted through her memory—cowering under that shelf in the pantry, gazing at the ribbon of light streaming in under the door and listening to the squelchy sounds of her mother's breathing.

She pushed away the memories.

Oh, how she loathed Christmas.

She was in a lousy mood when she pulled up in front of the vet clinic, a combination of her worry over Destry missing her mother and missing her *own* mother, not to mention her reluctance to walk inside that building and face Ben again after all the awkwardness between them.

This was ridiculous. She frowned at herself. She was tough enough to go on roundup every year to get their cattle from the high mountain grazing allotment. She helped Ridge with branding and with breaking new horses and even with castrating steers.

Surely she was tough enough to endure a fifteen-minute checkup with the veterinarian, no matter how sexy the dratted man was.

With that resolve firmly in mind, she moved around to the back of the Suburban with Luke's leash. Border collies were ferociously smart, though, and he clearly was even more reluctant than she to go inside the building. He fought the leash, wriggling his head this way and that and trying to scramble as far back as he could into the crate.

She imagined this building represented discomfort and fear to him. She could completely understand that, but that didn't change the fact that he would have to suck it up and go inside anyway.

If she did, he did.

"Come on, Luke. Easy now. There's a boy. Come on."

"Problem?"

Her heart kicked up a beat at the familiar voice. She turned with an air of trepidation and there he was in all his gorgeousness. A flood of heat washed over her, seeping into all the cold corners.

"You've got a reluctant patient here." *And his reluctant person.*

"A common problem in my line of work. I saw you from the window and thought it might be something like that."

"I didn't want to yank him out for fear of hurting something."

He gestured to the crate. "May I?"

"Of course."

She moved out of the way and he stepped forward, leaning down to the opening of the crate. She tried not to notice the way the morning sunshine gleamed in his dark hair or the breadth of those shoulders under his blue scrubs.

She was beginning to find it extremely unfair that the only man to rev her engine in, well, ever, was somebody who was obviously not interested in a relationship. At least with her.

"Hey there, Luke. How's my bud?" He spoke in a low, calm voice that sent shivers down her spine. If he ever turned that voice on *her,* she would turn into a quivery mass of hormones.

"You want to come inside? There's a good boy. Come on. Yeah. Nothing to worry about here."

As she watched, Luke surrendered to the spell of that gentle voice and stood docile while Ben hooked on the leash and carefully lifted the dog down to the snowy ground.

"He's moving well. That's a good sign."

Luke promptly lifted a leg against the tire of the Suburban, just in case any other creatures around wondered to whom it might belong. Ben didn't seem fazed. No doubt that also was a natural occurrence in his line of work.

After Luke finished, Ben led them to the side door she had used so many times when she worked for Doc Harris. "Let's just head straight to the exam room. I had a break between patients this morning and I'm all ready for you. We can take care of the paperwork afterward."

He closed the door and she immediately wondered how such an ordinary act could completely deplete all available oxygen. Being alone with him in this enclosed space left her breathless, off balance and painfully aware of him.

She sank into a chair while he started his exam of the dog. The whole time she tried to ignore that low, calming voice and his easy, comfortable manner with the animal, focusing instead on her mental to-do list before Christmas Eve, which was in less than a week.

"Everything looks good," Ben finally said. "He's progressing much more quickly than I expected."

"Great news. Thank you."

"If it's all right with you, I'd like to leave the stitches in for a few more days. I'll try to stop by over the holidays to remove them."

"I don't want you to go to so much trouble. I can probably remove them. I've done it before."

He raised an eyebrow. "You *have* had experience at this."

She shrugged. "Most everybody who grows up on a ranch gets basic veterinary experience. It's part of the life. I took it a little further when I worked with Doc Harris, that's all."

"If you ever want another job, I could use an experienced tech."

Oh, wouldn't that be a disaster? She couldn't think straight around the man. She could only imagine what sort of mess she could create trying to help him in a professional capacity.

"I'll keep that in mind."

"Actually, I do need a favor. Advice, really. You know just about everybody in town, don't you?"

"Most of them. We've had some new people move in lately but I'm sure I'll get around to meeting them."

"Do you know any after-school babysitters?"

"Is something wrong with Mrs. Michaels?" she asked, concerned all over again about the children not making it to the bus stop that morning.

His sigh was heavy. "No. Not with her, but she has a married daughter in California who just had a baby."

"Oh, that's great. I remember you mentioned her daughter was expecting."

"She wasn't due for another month, but apparently she went into premature labor yesterday and had the baby this morning. The baby is in the newborn ICU. Anne wants to be there, which I completely get. She's trying to make arrangements to fly out today so she can be there when her daughter comes home from the hospital, and then she plans to stay through the holidays."

"Understandable."

"I know. I do understand, believe me. It just makes *my* life a little more complicated right now, at least temporarily. The children can always come here after school. I don't mind having them. But according to Ava, hanging out at the clinic is 'totally boring.' Plus Jack can usually find trouble wherever he goes, a skill that sometimes can be a little inconvenient at a clinic filled with ailing animals."

"I can see where that might pose a problem."

"I need to find someone for this Saturday at least. We have clinic appointments all day because of our shortened holiday hours next week and I don't feel right about sticking them here for ten hours."

Against her will, she felt a pang of sympathy for the man. It couldn't have been easy, moving to Pine Gulch where he didn't know anyone. He and his children had left behind any kind of support network, all trace of the familiar. Starting over in a new community would be tough on anyone, especially a single father also trying to keep a demanding business operating.

"This is easily fixed, Ben," she said impulsively. "Ava and Jack can come to the ranch house after school and hang out with me and Destry. It will be great fun."

He looked faintly embarrassed. "That wasn't a hint, I swear. I honestly never even thought about asking you. Because you know everyone in town and all, I thought you might be aware of someone who might be willing to help out this time of year."

"I do know a few people who do childcare. I can certainly give you some names, if that's your preference. But I promise, having them come to the ranch after school would be no big deal. Destry would love the company and I might even put them to work with chores. They can ride the bus home with Destry the rest of the week, just like they would if Mrs. Michaels were there. Saturday's no problem either. Des and I are making Christmas cookies and can always use a couple more hands."

He shifted. "I don't want to bother you. I'm sure you're busy with Christmas."

"Who isn't? Don't worry about it, Ben. If I thought it would be too much of a bother, I wouldn't have offered."

"I don't know."

He was plainly reluctant to accept the help. Stubborn man. Did he think she was going to attach strings to her offer? One kiss per hour of childcare?

Tempting. Definitely tempting…

"I was only trying to help. I thought it would be a convenient solution to your problem with the side benefit of helping me keep Destry entertained in the big crazy lead-up to Christmas Eve, but it won't hurt my feelings if you prefer to make other arrangements. You can think about it and let me know."

"I don't need to think about it. You're right. It is the perfect solution." He was quiet, his hands petting Luke's fur. Lucky dog.

"It's tough for me to accept help," he finally said, surprising her with his raw honesty. "Tougher, probably, to accept help from *you,* with things so…complicated between us."

"Complicated. Is that what you call it?" Apparently she wasn't the only one in tumult over this attraction that simmered between them.

"What word would you use?"

Tense. Sparkly. Exhilarating. She couldn't use any of those words, despite the truth of them.

"Complicated works, I guess. But this, at least, is relatively easy when you think about it. I like your kids,

Ben. I don't mind having them around. Jack has a hilarious sense of humor and I'm sure he'll talk my ear off with knock-knock jokes. Ava is a little tougher nut to crack, I'll admit, but I'm looking forward to the challenge."

"She's struggling right now. I guess that's obvious."

"The move?"

"She's angry about that. About everything. My former in-laws did a number on her. They blame me for Brooke's death and have spent the past two years trying to shove a wedge between Ava and me. Both kids, really, but Jack is still too young to pay them much attention."

"Do they have any real reason to blame you?" she asked.

"They think they do. Brooke had type 1 diabetes and nearly died having Jack. The doctors told us not to try again. She was determined to have a third child despite the danger. She could be like that. If she wanted something, she couldn't see any reason why she couldn't have it. I wasn't about to risk a pregnancy. We took double precautions—or at least I thought I did. I intended to make things permanent, but the day I was scheduled for the big snip, she told me she was pregnant."

"Oh, no."

He raked a hand through his hair with a grimace. "Why am I compelled to spill all this to you?"

She chose her words with Ben as carefully as she had with Destry earlier, sensing if she said the wrong thing to him this fragile connection between them would fray. "I would like to think we can be friends, even if things between us are…complicated."

He gave a rough laugh. "Friends. All right. I guess I don't have enough of those around."

She sensed that wasn't an admission he was comfortable with either. "You will. Give it time. You just moved in. It takes time to build that kind of trust."

"Even with my friends back in California, I never felt right about talking about this. It sounds terrible of me. Disloyal or something. I loved my wife but…some part of me is so damn angry at her. She got pregnant on purpose. I guess that's obvious. She stopped taking birth control pills and sabotaged the condoms. She thought she knew better than the doctors and me."

What kind of mother risked her life, her future with a husband who loved her and children who needed her, simply because she wanted something she didn't have? Caidy couldn't conceive of it.

"I loved her but she could be stubborn and spoiled when she wanted her way. She wouldn't consider terminating the pregnancy despite the dangers," Ben went on. Now that he had started with the story, she sensed he wanted to tell her all of it. "For several months, things were going well. We thought anyway. Then when she was six months along, her glucose levels started jumping all over the place. As best we can figure out, it must have spiked that afternoon and she passed out."

His hands curled in Luke's fur. "She was behind the wheel at the time and drove off an overpass. She and the baby both died instantly."

"Oh, Ben. I'm so sorry." She wanted to touch him, offer some sort of comfort, but she was afraid to move. What would he do if she wrapped her fingers around his? Friends did that sort of thing, right? Even complicated friends?

"Her parents never forgave me." He spoke before she could move. "They thought it was all my fault she got pregnant in the first place. If only I'd stayed away from her, et cetera, et cetera. I can't really blame them."

She stared. "I can. That's completely ridiculous. Are they nuts? You were married, for heaven's sake. What were you supposed to do? It's not like you were two teenagers having a quickie in the backseat of your car."

He gave a rough, surprised-sounding laugh, and she was aware of a tiny bubble of happiness inside her that she could make him laugh despite the grim story.

"You're right. They are a little nuts." He laughed again and some of the tension in his shoulders started to ease. "No, a *lot* nuts. That's the real reason I moved here. Ava was becoming just like my mother-in-law. A little carbon copy, right down to the tight-mouthed expressions and the censorious comments. I won't let that happen. I'm her father and I'm not about to let them feed her lies and distortions until she hates me."

"Is the move working the way you hoped?"

"I think it's too soon to tell. She's still pretty upset at moving away from them. They can give her things I can't. That's a tough thing for a father to stomach."

This time she acted on the impulse to touch him and rested a hand on his bare forearm, just below the short sleeve of the scrub shirt. His skin was warm, the muscle hard beneath her fingers.

"They can't give either Ava or Jack the most important thing. Your love. That's what they're going to remember the rest of their lives. When they see how much you have loved them and sacrificed for them, it won't matter what lies their grandparents try to feed them."

"Thank you for that." He smiled at her, his eyes crinkling a little at the corners, and she wanted to stand in this little office basking in the glow forever.

Why, again, hadn't she wanted to bring Luke to the vet? She couldn't imagine anywhere she would rather be right now.

"I mean it about the kids, Ben." Though it took a great deal of effort, she managed to slide her hand away. "Destry and I would love to have the children hang out with us for a few days. And if you need help between Christmas and New Year's, we'll be happy to keep an eye on them."

The conviction in her voice seemed to assuage the last of his concerns. "If you're sure, that would be great. Thank you. You've lifted a huge weight off my mind."

"No problem." She smiled to seal the deal. His gaze flickered to her mouth and stayed there as if he couldn't look away. He was thinking of their kiss. She was certain of it. Awareness fluttered through her, low and enticing. When his gaze lifted to hers, she knew she wasn't imagining the sudden hunger there.

She swallowed, her face suddenly hot. She wanted him to kiss her again, just wrap his arms around her and press her back against the wall for the next hour or two.

Not the time or the place. He was working and had other patients he needed to see. Besides that, though he might be forging this tentative friendship with her, she had a feeling the rest of it was just too tangled for either of them right now.

"I'll, um, see you later," she mumbled. "Thanks for... everything."

"You're very welcome." His low voice thrummed over her nerves. She did her best to ignore it as she grabbed the end of Luke's leash and escaped.

Chapter 11

Two nights later, Ben pulled off the main road onto the drive into the River Bow, wishing he could hang a left at the junction, climb into his bed at the cottage and sleep for the next two or three days.

His shoulders were tight with exhaustion, his eyes gritty and aching. When he finally found time to sleep, just past midnight, he had only been under for a few minutes when he received an emergency call to help a dog that had been hit by a car on one of the ranch roads. He had ended up packing his sleepy kids—poor things—into the backseat of the SUV and taking them inside his office to sleep while he attended to the dog.

He really needed Mrs. Michaels—or someone like her. At least the kids had fallen quickly back to sleep. He considered that a great blessing. Even after he packed them back to the ranch and into their beds, they had again fallen asleep easily.

He had envied them that as he tossed and turned, energized by the case and the successful outcome. Before he knew it, the alarm was going off and he had stumbled out of bed to face a packed schedule of people rushing to take their animals into the vet before the clinic went on its brief holiday hiatus.

So far, he hadn't seen any slowdown in business after taking over from Dr. Harris. Another blessing there. Although he was grateful for the business and glad that the people of Pine Gulch had decided to continue bringing their animals to him, right now he was too tired to savor his relief.

As he pulled up to the River Bow ranch house, Christmas lights gleamed against the winter night and the darker silhouettes of the mountains in the distance and the pines and aspens of the foreground. Warm light spilled out the windows into the snow and that big Christmas tree twinkled with color.

The place offered a cheery welcome against the chilly night. He couldn't help thinking about his grandparents' home in Lake Forest. In sheer square footage, Caldwell House was probably three times as big as the River Bow, but instead of warmth and hominess, he remembered his childhood home as being sterile and unfriendly to a young boy, all sharp angles, dark wood and uncomfortable furniture.

His grandparents hadn't wanted him. He had known that from the beginning when their daughter, his mother, had dropped him and his sister off before running off with her latest hard-living boyfriend.

She hadn't come back, of course. Even at age eight,

he had somehow known she wouldn't. Now he knew she had died of a drug overdose just months after dropping him and Susie with her parents, but for years he had watched and waited for a mother who would never return.

Oh, his grandparents had done their duty. They had given him and Susie a roof over their head, nutritious meals, an excellent education. But he and his sister had never been allowed to forget they came from a selfish, irresponsible woman who had chosen drugs over her own children.

He had his own family now. Children he loved more than anything. He would never treat them as unwanted burdens.

Eager to pick them up now, he pulled up in front of the River Bow. The night was clear and cold, with a brilliant spill of stars gleaming above the mountains. Inside the door, he could hear laughter and a television show, along with a couple of well-mannered barks.

The door opened just seconds after he rang the bell. His stomach rumbled instantly as the spicy, doughy smells wafting outside immediately transported him to his favorite pizzeria in college.

"Hi, Dad!" Jack let go of the doorknob just an instant before launching himself toward Ben. With a laugh, he held his arms out and Jack did his traditional move of spider-walking up his legs before Ben flipped him upside down, then scooped him up into his arms.

He always found it one of life's tiny miracles that his exhaustion could seep away for a while when he was reunited with his kids at the end of the day, even if Ava was in a cranky mood.

"How was your day, bud?"

"Great! I got to help feed the horses and play with some kittens. And guess what? I don't have to go back to school until next year."

"That's right. Last day of school and now it's Christmas vacation."

"And Santa Claus comes in *three days!*"

He had so dang much to do before then, Ben didn't even want to think about it. "I can't wait," he lied.

As he spoke, Ben became aware of what Jack would have called a disturbance in the Force. Some kind of shift in air currents or spinning and whirling of the ions in the air or something, he wasn't sure, but he sensed Caidy's approach even before she came into view.

"Hi! I thought I heard a doorbell."

She was wearing a white apron and had a bit of flour on her cheek, just a little dusting against her heat-flushed skin.

"Sorry I'm a little later than I told you I would be on the phone," he answered, fighting the urge to step forward and blow away the flour.

"No problem. We've been having fun, haven't we, Jack?"

"Yep. We're making pizza and I got to put some cheese on."

His stomach growled again and he realized he hadn't had time for lunch. "It smells great. Really great."

Jack grabbed one of his hands in both of his. "Can we stay and have some? Please, Dad!"

He glanced at Caidy, embarrassed that his son would offer invitations to someone else's meal. "I don't think so. I'm sure we've bothered the Bowmans long enough. We'll find something back at our place."

Exactly what, he wasn't quite sure. Maybe they

would run into town to grab fast food, though right now loading up into the vehicle again and heading to the business district was the last thing he felt like doing. Maybe there was a pizza restaurant he hadn't discovered yet—because that smell was enticing.

"Of course you'll stay!" Caidy exclaimed. "I was planning on it."

"You're doing us enough favors by letting the kids come hang out with you. I don't expect you to feed us too."

She narrowed her gaze at him. "I just spent an hour making enough pizza dough to feed the whole town of Pine Gulch. You can stay a few minutes and eat a slice or two, can't you?"

He should make an excuse and leave. This house was just too appealing—and Caidy was even more so. But he didn't have plans for dinner. If they ate here, that was one less decision he would have to make. Besides, pizza on a cold winter night seemed perfect.

They could stay for a while, just long enough to eat, he decided. Then he and his children would head for home. "If you're sure, that would be great. It really does smell delicious."

"I'm going to be a lousy hostess and ask you to hang your own coat up because my hands are covered in flour, then come on back to the kitchen."

Without waiting for an answer, she turned around and walked back down the hall, Jack scampering after her. After a pause, Ben shrugged out of his ranch coat and hung it alongside Jack's and Ava's coats on the rack in the corner.

He expected to see a crowd of children when he walked into the kitchen but Caidy was alone. She tucked a strand of hair behind her ear, leaving another little smudge of flour, and gave him a bright smile that seemed to push off another shackle of his fatigue.

"The kids are just getting ready to watch a Christmas show in the other room. You're more than welcome to join them while I finish throwing things together in here."

He should. A wise man would take the escape she was handing him, but he didn't feel right about leaving her alone to do all the work. "Is there anything I can help you do in here?"

Surprise flickered in her eyes, then she smiled again. "You're a brave man, Ben Caldwell. Sure. I've got a cheese pizza cooking now to satisfy the restless natives. Give me a minute to toss out another pie and then you can put the toppings on."

He washed his hands, listening to the familiar opening strands of a holiday television special he had watched when *he* was a kid in the big rec room of Caldwell House. He found something rather comforting about the continuity of it, his own children enjoying the same things that had once given him pleasure.

"Would you like a drink or something? We don't keep much in the house but I can probably rustle up a beer."

"What are you having?"

"I like root beer with my pizza. It's always been kind of a family tradition and I apparently haven't grown out of it. Silly, isn't it?"

"I think it's nice. Root beer sounds good, but I can wait until the pizza is done."

She smiled as her hands expertly continued tossing

the dough into shape. "What about you? Any traditions in the Caldwell family kitchen?"

"Other than thoroughly enjoying whatever Mrs. Michaels fixes us, no. Not really."

"What about when you were a kid?"

Traditions? No, not unless she might count formal family dinners with little conversation and a serious dearth of kindness. "Not really. I didn't come from a particularly close family."

"No brothers or sisters?"

"A sister. She's several years younger than I am. We've lost touch over the years."

Susan had rebelled against their grandparents by following in their mother's footsteps, burying her misery in drugs and alcohol. Last he heard, she was in her third stint at rehab to avoid a prison sentence.

"I can't imagine losing touch with my brothers." Sympathy turned Caidy's eyes an intense green. "They're my best friends. Laura and Becca are like sisters to me now too."

"You Bowmans seem a united front against the world."

"I guess so. It hasn't always been that way, but it's the now that counts, right?"

"Yes. You're very lucky."

She opened her mouth to speak, then appeared to think better of it. "I think this should be ready now."

With a twist of her wrist, she deftly tossed the dough onto a pizza peel sprinkled with cornmeal and crimped the edges before handing the whole peel to him with a flourish.

"Here you go. All yours."

"Uh." He stared helplessly at the naked pizza dough, not quite sure what she expected of him.

"You haven't done this before, have you?"

He gave a rough laugh. "No. But I can tell you by heart the phone number of about half a dozen great pizza places in California."

She shook her head and stepped closer to him, stirring the air with the scent of wildflowers, and suddenly he forgot all about being hungry for pizza. Now he was just hungry for her.

"Okay, I'll walk you through it this time. Next time you come over for Friday night pizza, though, you're on your own."

Next time. Whoever would have guessed those two words could hold so much promise? He knew darn well he shouldn't feel this little kick of anticipation for something so nebulous and uncertain as a next time.

Better to just enjoy *this* moment. As she said, it was *now* that mattered. In a few weeks, he and his children would be moving away and Caidy Bowman and this wild attraction to her would be conveniently distant from him.

For now, she was here beside him, her skin unbelievably soft-looking and her hair teasing him with the scent of flowers and springtime.

"Okay, first thing you do is spoon a little sauce on. I like to use the bowl of the big spoon to spread it to the edge of the dough. That's it. Good."

He supposed it was fairly ridiculous to feel the same sense of pride in spreading sauce on a pizza dough as he had the first time he helped deliver a difficult foal.

"Now sprinkle as much cheese as you usually like. Perfect. I see you like it gooey."

She smiled at him and he suddenly wanted to toss the unfinished pizza to the floor, press her up against that counter and kiss her until they were both breathing hard.

"Okay, now put your toppings on. I was planning a pepperoni and olive for the next one but you can be creative. Whatever you think the kids might like."

"Pepperoni and olive sounds good." He cleared away the ragged edge to his voice. "My kids always like that."

She didn't appear to notice. "The third one can be a little more sophisticated. By then, Destry and her friends—and Ridge, when he's home—have had their fill."

Who made three homemade pizzas on a Friday night? Caidy Bowman apparently.

She was a woman of more layers than a supreme pizza and he was enjoying the process of uncovering each one.

"Now your toppings. Don't skimp on the olives."

He picked up a stack of pepperoni and dealt them like cards on poker night, then tossed handfuls of olives to the edge of the crust. This was going to be the best damn Friday night pizza she had ever had, he vowed.

"Okay, now another layer of cheese and then a bit of fresh Parmesan on the top. Oh, that looks delicious."

"Thank you."

"If the vet thing ever gets old, you can always get a job at the pizza place in town."

He laughed. "A backup plan is always helpful. Good to know I can still feed my kids."

She smiled back at him and he knew he didn't imagine it when her gaze flickered to his mouth and stayed there long enough to send heat pulsing through him.

The moment stretched between them, heady and intoxicating, and he again wanted to kiss her, but she stepped away before he could act on the urge.

"I guess this one is ready."

"Now what?"

"Now I take the cheese pizza out, then we call in the locusts and watch it disappear."

He watched while she did just that, shoving a second pizza peel under the cooked pizza on a stone in the oven and deftly working the dough onto the peel before pulling the whole thing back out.

The cheese bubbled exactly the way he loved and the crust was golden perfection.

"Des!" she called. "The first pizza's ready. Can you pause the show and bring everybody in here?"

The herd of children galloped in a moment later, a few more than he expected. Ava was deep in conversation with Destry and Gabi while Jack was chattering away with Caidy's nephew, Alex, and niece Maya.

"Hi." Maya grinned at him in her adorable way and he couldn't help smiling back.

"Hi there."

"Did I mention I was babysitting Maya and Alex for a few hours tonight? Taft and Laura had some last-minute Christmas things to take care of. Laura's mom usually helps them out but she had a party tonight so I offered. I figured, what's a few more? And when Gabi heard Ava was coming over, of course she had to come too."

Now he understood why she was making so many pizzas.

Six kids. How did she handle it? He was overwhelmed most of the time with his own two, but Caidy seemed to juggle everything with ease. After transferring the other pizza from the peel to the stone in the oven, she poured drinks for the younger children, handed plates to the older girls and passed out napkins to everyone.

"Better grab a slice fast or it's going to be gone," she advised him. He snagged one of the few remaining pieces and a glass of frothy root beer and took a place at the kitchen table next to Jack.

All the children seemed ramped up for the holidays but Caidy managed to keep them distracted by asking about the show they were watching, about their school parties that day, about what they wanted Santa to bring them.

He was too busy savoring the pizza to contribute much to the conversation but after the first blissful moments, he decided he had to try. "This is really delicious. I grew up in Chicago so I know pizza. The sauce is perfect."

"Thank you." She probably meant her pleased smile to be friendly and warm but he was completely seduced by it, by her, by this warm kitchen that seemed such a haven against the harsh, cold world outside.

"What about the third one? What's your pleasure?"

He could come up with several answers to that, none of them appropriate to voice with six children gathered around the table. "I don't really care. What's your favorite?"

"I like barbecue chicken. The kids generally tolerate it in moderation, so that only leaves more for me."

"I didn't realize you were such a devious woman, Caidy Bowman."

"I have my moments."

She smiled at him and he was struck by how lovely she was, with her dark hair escaping the ponytail and her cheeks flushed from the warmth of the stove.

He was in deep trouble here, he thought. He didn't know what to do about this attraction to her. He was hanging on with both hands to keep from falling hard for her, and each time he spent time with her, he slid down a few more inches.

"Do you know my dog?" Maya asked him earnestly. "His name is Lucky."

Grateful for the diversion, he shifted his gaze from Caidy to her very adorable stepniece. "I don't think I've met Lucky yet. That's a very nice name for a dog."

"He *is* nice," Maya declared. "He licks my nose. It tickles."

"We have a dog named Tri," Jack announced.

"My dog's name is Grunt," Gabi said. "Trace says he's ugly but I think he's the most beautiful dog in the world."

"Lucky's beautiful too," Alex said. "He has super-long ears."

"Tri only has three legs," Jack said, as if that little fact trumped everything else.

"Cool!" Gabi said. "How does he get around?"

"He hops," Ava, who usually only barely tolerated the dog, piped in. "It's really kind of cute. He walks on his front two and then hops on the one back leg he's got. It takes *forever* to go on a walk with him, but I don't mind. Maya, you drank all your root beer. Do you want some more?"

Maya nodded and Ben smiled at his daughter as she poured a small amount of soda for the girl. All the children treated Maya with sweet consideration and it touched him, especially coming from Ava. Though she could be self-absorbed sometimes, like most children, she had these moments of kindness that heartened him.

"Here's pizza number two!" Caidy sang out to cheers from the children. While they had been talking about dogs, he had missed her pulling his pepperoni-and-olive creation out of the oven. Now she set it on the middle of the table and expertly sliced it. As before, the children each grabbed a slice. He nabbed a small one but noticed Caidy didn't take one.

"Want me to save you a piece? You'd better move fast."

She sat down on the one remaining chair at the table, which happened to be on his other side. "I'm saving my appetite for the barbecue chicken."

"It's all delicious. Especially this one, if I do say so myself." He gave a modest shrug.

"You're a pro." She smiled and he felt that connection between them tug a little harder.

"I love pizza. It's my favorite," Maya declared.

"Me too!" Alex said. "I could eat pizza every single day."

"It's my triple favorite," Jack, not to be outdone, announced. "I could eat it every day and every night."

Ava rolled her eyes. "You're such a dork."

The kids appeared to be done after finishing most of the second pizza.

"Can we go finish the show now?" Destry asked.

Caidy glanced at him. "As long as Dr. Caldwell doesn't mind sticking around a little longer."

He should leave. This kitchen—and the soft, beautiful woman in it—were just too appealing. A little fuel had helped push away some of the exhaustion, but he still worried his defenses were slipping around Caidy.

However, that barbecue chicken pizza currently baking was filling the kitchen with delicious, smoky smells. She had gone to all the effort to make it. He might as well stay to taste it.

"How much time is left on the show?" he asked.

"I don't know. Not that much, I'm sure," Destry said, rather artfully, he thought.

Caidy looked doubtful but she didn't argue with her niece.

"We can stay awhile more," he finally said. "If it goes on too much longer, we might have to leave before the show ends."

Despite the warning, his ruling was met with cheers from all the children.

"Thanks, Dad," Ava said, gifting him with one of her rare smiles. "We're having too much fun to go yet."

"I love this show," Jack said. "It's *hilarious*."

A new word in kindergarten apparently. He smiled, feeling rather heroic to give his children something they wanted. As soon as all the kids hurried out to start the show again, he realized his mistake. He was alone again with Caidy, surrounded by delicious smells and this dangerous connection shivering between them.

She rose quickly, ostensibly to check on the pizza, but he sensed she was also aware of it. As she slid the third pizza onto the peel and then out of the oven, he racked his brain to come up with a topic of polite conversation.

He could only come up with one. "What happened to your parents?"

The words came out more bluntly than he intended.

Apparently, they startled her too. She nearly dropped the paddle, pizza and all, but recovered enough to carry it with both hands to the table, where she set it down between them.

"Wow. That was out of the blue."

He was an idiot who had no business being let out around anything with less than four feet. Or three, in Tri's case.

"It's none of my business. You don't have to tell me. I've been wondering, that's all. Sorry."

She sighed as she picked up the pizza slicer and jerked it across the pie. "What have you heard?"

"Nothing. Only what you've said, which isn't much. I've gathered it was something tragic. A car accident?"

She didn't answer for a moment, busy with slicing the pizza and lifting a piece to a plate for him and then for herself. He was very sorry he had said anything, especially when it obviously caused her so much sadness.

"It wasn't a car accident," she finally said. "Sometimes I wish it were something as straightforward as that. It might have been easier."

He took a bite of his pizza. The robust flavors melted on his tongue but he hardly noticed them as he waited for her to continue.

She took a small bite of hers and then a sip of the root beer before she spoke again. "It wasn't any kind of accident," she said. "They were murdered."

He hadn't expected that one, not here in quiet Pine Gulch. He stared at the tightness of her mouth that could be so lush and delicious. "Murdered? Seriously?"

She nodded. "I know. It still doesn't seem real to me either. It's been eleven years now and I don't know if any of us has ever really gotten over it."

"You must have been just a girl."

"Sixteen." She spoke the word softly and he felt a pang of regret for a girl who had lost her father and mother at such a tender age.

"Was it someone they knew?"

"We don't know who killed them. That's one of the toughest aspects of the whole thing. It's still unsolved. We do know it was two men. One dark-haired, one blond, in their late twenties."

Her mouth tightened more and she sipped at her root beer. He wanted to kick himself for bringing up this obviously painful topic.

"They were both strangers to Pine Gulch," she went on. "That much we know. But they didn't leave any fingerprints or other clues. Only, uh, one shaky eyewitness identification."

"What was the motive?"

"Oh, robbery. The whole thing was motivated by greed. My parents had an extensive art collection. I know you saw the painting in the dining room the other day and probably figured out our mother was a brilliant artist. She also had many close friends in the art community who gave her gifts of their work or sold them to her at a steep discount."

A brazen art theft here in quiet Pine Gulch. Of all the things he might have guessed, that was just about last on the list.

"It was a few days before Christmas. Eleven years ago tomorrow, actually. None of the boys lived at home then, only me. Ridge was working up in Montana, Trace was in the military and Taft had an apartment in town. No one was supposed to be here that night. I had a

Christmas concert that night at the high school but I...
I was ill. Or said I was anyway."

"You weren't?"

She set her fork down next to her mostly uneaten
pizza and he felt guilty again for interrupting her meal
with this tragic topic. He wanted to tell her not to finish, that he didn't need to know, but he was afraid that
sounded even more stupid—and besides that, he sensed
some part of her needed to tell him.

"It's so stupid. I was a stupid, selfish, silly sixteen-
year-old girl. My boyfriend, Cody Spencer—the asshole—had just broken up with me that morning in
homeroom. He wanted to go out with my best friend, if
you can believe that cliché. And Sarah Beth had wanted
him ever since we started going out and decided dating the captain of the football team and president of the
performance choir was more important than friendship.
I was quite certain, as only a sixteen-year-old girl can
be, that my heart had broken in a million little pieces."

He tried to picture her at sixteen and couldn't form
a good picture. Was it because that pivotal event had
changed her so drastically?

"The worst part was, Cody and I were supposed
to sing a duet together at the choir concert—'Merry
Christmas, Darling.' I couldn't go through with it. I
just...couldn't. So I told my parents I thought I must
have food poisoning. I don't think they believed me for
a minute, but what else could they do when I told them I
would throw up if I had to go onstage that night? They
agreed to stay home with me. None of us knew it would
be a fatal mistake."

"You couldn't have known."

"I know that intellectually, but it's still easy to blame myself."

"Easy, maybe, but not fair to a sixteen-year-old girl with a broken heart."

She gave him a surprised look, as if she hadn't expected him to demonstrate any sort of understanding. Did she think him as much an asshole as Cody Spencer?

"I know. It wasn't my fault. It just…feels that way sometimes. It happened right here, you know. In the kitchen. They disarmed the security system and broke in through the back door over there. My mom and I were in here when we heard them outside. I caught a quick glimpse of their faces through the window before my mother shoved me into the pantry and ordered me to stay put. I thought she was coming in after me so I hid under the bottom shelf to make room for her, but…she went back out again, calling for my father."

She was silent and he didn't know what to say, what to do, to ease the torment in her eyes. Finally, he settled for resting a hand over hers on the table. She gave him another of those surprised looks, then turned her hand over so they were palm against palm and twisted her fingers in his.

"The men ordered her to the ground and… I could hear them arguing. With her, with themselves. One wanted to leave but the other one said it was too late, she had seen them. And then my father came in. He must have had one of his hunting rifles trained on them. I couldn't see from inside the pantry, but the next thing I knew, two shots rang out. The police said my dad and one of the men must have fired at each other at the same moment. The other guy was hit and injured. My dad… died instantly."

"Oh, Caidy."

"After that, it was crazy. My mom was screaming at them. She grabbed a knife out of the kitchen and went after them and the…the bastard shot her too. She…took a while to die. I could hear her breathing while the men hurried through the house taking the art they wanted. They must have made about four or five trips outside before they finally left. And I stayed inside that pantry, doing nothing. I tried to help my mother once but she made me go back inside. I didn't know what else to do."

Outside the kitchen he could hear laughter from the children at something on the show they were watching. Caidy's fingers trembled slightly, her skin cool now, and he tightened his hand around hers.

"I should have helped her. Maybe I could have done something."

"You would have been shot if they'd known you were here."

"Maybe."

"No 'maybe' about it. Do you think they would have hesitated for a moment?" He couldn't bear thinking about the horrific possibility.

"I don't know. I… When I finally heard them drive away, I waited several more minutes to make sure they weren't coming back, then went out to call nine-one-one. By then, it was too late for my mother. She was barely hanging on when Taft and the rest of the paramedics arrived. Maybe if I had called earlier, she wouldn't have lost so much blood."

Everything made so much sense now. The close bond between the siblings masked a deep pain. He had sensed it and now he knew the root of it.

Did that explain why she was still here at the River

Bow all these years later, why she hadn't finished veterinary school? Did guilt keep her here, still figuratively hiding in the pantry?

Was this the reason she didn't sing anymore?

He curled her fingers in his, wishing he had some other way to ease her burden. "It wasn't your fault. What a horrible thing to happen to anyone, let alone a young girl."

"I guess you understand now why I don't like Christmas much. I try, for Destry's sake. She wasn't even born then. It doesn't seem fair to make her miss out on all the holiday fun because of grief for people she doesn't know."

"I can see that."

Much to his disappointment, she slid her hand out from underneath his and rose to take her plate to the sink. Though he sensed she was trying to create distance between them again, he cleared his own dishes and carried them to the sink after her.

She looked surprised. "Oh, thanks. You didn't have to do that. You're a guest."

"A guest who owes you far more the few moments it takes to bus a few dishes," he countered before returning to the table to clean up the mess of plates and napkins and glasses the children had left behind.

She smiled her thanks when he carried the things to the sink and he wanted to think some of the grimness had left her expression. She still hadn't eaten much pizza but he decided it wasn't his place to nag her about that.

He grabbed a dish towel and started to dry the few dishes in the drainer by the sink. Though she looked as if she wanted to argue, she said nothing and for a few moments they worked in companionable silence.

"My mom really loved the holidays," she said when the last few dishes were nearly finished. "Both of my parents did, really. I think that's what makes it harder. Mom would decorate the house even before Thanksgiving and she would spend the whole month baking. I think Dad was more excited than us kids. He used to sing Christmas songs at the top of his lungs. All through December—after we were done with chores and dinner and homework—he would gather us around the big grand piano in the other room to sing with him. Whatever musical talent I had came from him."

"I'd like to hear you sing," he said.

She gave him a sidelong look and shook her head. "I told you, I don't sing anymore."

"You think your parents would approve of that particular stance?"

She sighed and hung the dish towel on the handle of the big six-burner stove. "I know. I tell myself that every year. My dad, in particular, would be very disappointed in me. He would look at me underneath those bushy eyebrows of his and tell me music is the medicine of a broken heart. That was one of his favorite sayings. Or he would quote Nietzsche: 'without music, life is a mistake.' I know that intellectually, but sometimes what we know in our head doesn't always translate very well to our heart."

"Tell me about it," he muttered.

She gave him a curious look, leaning a hip against the work island.

He knew he should keep his mouth shut but somehow the words spilled out, like a song he didn't realize he knew. "My head is telling me it's a completely ridiculous idea to kiss you again."

She gazed at him for a long, silent moment, her eyes huge and her lips slightly parted. He saw her give a long, slow inhale. "And does your heart have other ideas? I hope so."

"The kids—" he said, rather ridiculously.

"—are busy watching a show and paying absolutely no mind to us in here," she finished.

He took a step forward, almost against his will. "This thing between us is crazy."

"Completely insane," she agreed.

"I don't know what's wrong with me."

"Probably the same thing that's wrong with me," she murmured, her voice husky and low. She also took a step forward, until she was only a breath away, until he was intoxicated by the scent of her, fresh and clean and lovely.

He had to kiss her. It seemed as inevitable as the sunrise over the mountains. He covered the space between them and brushed his mouth against hers once, twice, a third time. He might have found the willpower to stop there but she sighed his name and gripped the front of his shirt with both hands, leaning in for more, and he was lost.

She tasted of root beer—vanilla and mint. Delicious. He couldn't seem to get enough. He forgot everything when she was in his arms—his exhaustion, the music she didn't sing, the children in the other room.

All he could think about was Caidy, sweet and warm and lovely.

There was something intensely *right* about being here with her. He couldn't have explained it, other than he felt as if with every passing moment, some dark, empty corner inside him was being filled with soothing light.

She thought their first kiss that night at the clinic had been fantastic. This surpassed that one. The physical reaction was the same, instant heat and hunger, this wild surge of desire for more and more.

But she had barely known him that first time. Now she wasn't only kissing the very sexy veterinarian who had saved Luke's life. She was kissing the man who treated sweet Maya with such kindness, who looked adorably out of his depth making pizza but who trudged gamely on, who listened to her talk about her past without judgment or scorn but with compassion for the frightened young girl she had been.

She was kissing Ben, the man she was falling in love with.

She wrapped her arms around him, wanting to soak up every moment of the kiss. They kissed for several moments more, until his hand had slipped beneath the edge of her shirt to trace delicious patterns on her bare skin at her waist.

They might have continued kissing there in the quiet kitchen for a long time but the children suddenly laughed hard at something in the other room and Ben stiffened as if someone had dropped snow down his back.

He slid his mouth away from hers. "We've got to stop doing this." His voice sounded ragged and his chest moved against her with each rapid breath.

"We...do?" She couldn't seem to make her brain work.

"Yes. This… I'm not being fair to you, Caidy."

Something in his tone finally penetrated the haze of desire around her and she took a deep breath and stepped away, willing herself to return to sensible thought.

"In what way?" She managed to make her voice sound cool and controlled, at odds with the tangled chaos of her thoughts.

He raked a hand through his hair, finishing the job of messing it that her own hands had started. "As much as I obviously…want you, I can't have a relationship right now. I'm not ready, the kids aren't ready. I've thrown too many changes at them in a very short time. A new town, a new school, a new job. Eventually a new house. I can't add another woman into the mix."

His words doused the last embers of heat between them. She shivered a little and pulled her shirt down while she struggled to chase after the tattered ends of her composure.

What could she say to that? He was right. His children had survived a great deal of tumult in a short time. The last thing she wanted to do was hurt Ava and Jack. They were great kids and she already cared for them. Just that afternoon, she felt as if she'd had a breakthrough with Ava when she had helped her ride around the practice ring on one of their more gentle horses.

Ben was the children's father. If he felt as though a relationship between him and Caidy would be harmful to his children, how could she argue?

He had obligations bigger than his own wants and needs. She had to accept that, no matter how painful.

Much to her horror, she could feel the heavy burn of tears. She never cried! She certainly couldn't remember ever crying over a *man*. Not since that idiot Cody Spencer when she was sixteen.

She took a deep breath and then another, concentrating hard on pushing the tears back. She didn't dare speak until she could trust her voice wouldn't wobble.

"I'm really glad we're on the same page here," she said, pretending a casual, breezy tone. "I'm not looking for a relationship right now. This attraction between us is…inconvenient, yes, but we're both adults. We can certainly ignore it for the short time you'll be living on the River Bow. After that, it shouldn't be a problem. I mean, how often do I need to take one of the dogs to the vet? We'll hardly ever see each other after you move into your new house."

Instead of reassuring him as to her insouciance, her words seemed to trouble him further. His brow furrowed and he gave her a searching look.

"Caidy—" he began, but Des came into the kitchen before he could complete the thought.

"You're still in here making pizza? This kitchen is so hot!"

Isn't that the truth? Caidy thought.

"You didn't even come in and watch the show with us and now it's almost over."

She seized on the diversion. "You really left the movie before the end?"

"Jack wanted more root beer. I told him I'd take care of it."

Ben made a face. "Jack has probably had all the root beer one kid needs for a night. How about we switch his beverage of choice to water? If he complains, you can tell him his mean old dad said no."

Destry grinned. "Right, Dr. Caldwell. Like anybody would believe you're mean. Or old."

"You'd be surprised," he muttered.

"Why don't you watch the end of the show with the kids?" she suggested.

"What about you?"

"I have a few things to take care of in here. After that, I'll be right in."

After a moment's hesitation, he nodded. "I can take Jack's water, if you'd like," he said to Destry, who handed over the cup and led the way to the television room.

When he was gone, taking all his heat and vitality and these seething emotions between them, Caidy slumped into a chair at the kitchen table and just barely refrained from burying her head in her hands.

She was becoming an idiot over Ben. All he needed to do was give her that rare, charming smile and her insides caught fire and she wanted to jump into his arms.

Worse than that, she was developing genuine feelings for him. How could she not? She remembered him at dinner with Maya and her heart seemed to melt.

She had to stop this or she would be in for serious heartbreak. He wasn't interested in a relationship. He had made that plain twice now. He didn't want anything she had to offer and she would be a fool if she allowed herself to forget that, even for a moment.

Okay, she could do this. A few more weeks and he would be gone from her life, for the most part. She would just have to work hard these remaining weeks while he was still on the River Bow to guard her emotions. Ben and his children could easily slip right past her defenses and into her heart. She was just going to have to do everything she could to keep that from happening, no matter how hard it might be.

Chapter 12

Three more days.

She could smile and make conversation and pretend to be excited about Christmas for three more days.

Less than three days actually. Two and a half, really. This was Sunday evening, the day before Christmas Eve. She had tonight, Christmas Eve and then Christmas Day to survive, and then she could toss another holiday into her personal history book.

Okay, that didn't count the week leading up to New Year's, but she wasn't going to think about that. Once Christmas itself was over, she usually could relax and enjoy the remaining days of the holidays and the time it gave her with her family.

For now, she had to survive this particular evening. Caidy stepped out of her bedroom wearing her best black slacks and a dressy white silk blouse she had worn only once before, to the annual cattleman's harvest dinner a few years earlier. With it, she wore a triple strand of colorful glass beads she had picked up at a craft fair that summer.

This was about as dressed up as she could manage. Was it too much? Not enough? She hated trying to figure out proper attire for parties, especially this one.

She fervently wished that she could stay home, pop a big batch of buttery popcorn and find something on TV that wasn't a sappy holiday special.

She had an excuse just about every year to avoid going to the big party Carson and Jenna McRaven had been hosting the past few years at Carson's huge house up Cold Creek Canyon, but Destry had begged and pleaded this year with both Ridge and Caidy.

Destry had trotted out a dozen reasons why they should make an exception and attend this year: all her friends were going. It was going to be *a blast*. Attending was the neighborly thing to do. The McRavens would think the Bowmans didn't like them if they continued to decline the invitation every year.

Finally, she pulled the "you just don't want me to have any fun" card and Ridge had reluctantly accepted his fate and agreed to go. Though she knew it was ridiculous, Caidy had felt obligated to accompany them both.

She wasn't looking forward to any aspect of the party except the food. Jenna was a fantastic cook and catered events all over the county. Her friend, though, tended to go a little overboard when it came to Christmas. Her very gorgeous husband did too. Raven's Nest was always decorated to the hilt for the holidays and the McRavens loved hosting holiday gatherings for family and friends.

She could get through it, she told herself. Less than seventy-two hours, right? With that little pep talk firmly in mind, she headed for the kitchen for the two Dutch apple pies she had baked that morning and found both Destry and Ridge there.

"Oh, you look beautiful, Aunt Caidy!" Destry exclaimed.

Ridge gave one of his rare smiles. "It's true, sis. You do. Much too fancy to be saddled with the likes of us."

Her oldest brother looked handsome and commanding, as usual, in a Western-cut shirt and one of his favorite bolo ties while Destry wore her best pair of jeans and the cute wintry sweater they had bought in Jackson the last time they went shopping together.

At the neckline, Caidy could see the flowered straps of her swimming suit peeking through.

"You're all set to swim?"

The McRavens had the only private indoor pool in town and it was a big hit among the area kids. The stuff of legend.

Destry lifted a mesh bag off the table. "I've got everything here. I can't wait. I've heard it's a superawesome pool. That's what Tallie and Claire told me. I just hope Kip Wheeler isn't too much of a tease. He can be *such* a pest."

Kip was Jenna's son from her first marriage, which had ended in the tragic death of her husband several years ago. He and his two older brothers and younger sister had been adopted by Carson McRaven after he married Jenna. They now had a busy toddler of their own, who kept all of them hopping.

"Everybody ready?"

"I am!" Destry jumped up and threw on her coat.

"As I'll ever be," Caidy muttered. Ridge gave her a sympathetic look as he lifted one of the pies and carried it out to the Suburban.

A light snow speckled the windshield, reflecting the colorful holiday light displays they passed on their way to the McRavens' house. They approached the house through a long line of parked cars on either side of the curving driveway. It looked as if half the town was inside the big house. She recognized Trace's SUV and Taft's extended-cab pickup. Apparently, even when they canceled the regular Sunday night Bowman dinner for a special occasion, the family couldn't manage to stay apart.

"I'll let you two off near the door, then find a place to park," Ridge said.

She wanted to tell him to forget it, but because she was wearing her completely impractical high-heeled black boots, she didn't argue.

"Want me to take a pie inside?" Destry asked.

"You've got your swim stuff. I can manage," she answered.

As she expected, the entrance to the McRavens' house was beautifully decorated with grapevine garlands entwined with evergreens and twinkling lights. A trio of small live trees was also adorned with lights.

The door opened before they could even knock and Jenna McRaven answered. She smiled, pretty and blonde and deceptively fragile-looking. "Oh, Caidy. You made it! I thought the day would never come when we could convince you to come to our Christmas party."

Carson joined her at the door and gave all of them a wide, charming smile. He was vastly different from the cold man she remembered coming to town five years ago.

"Caidy, great to see you." He kissed Caidy's cheek before slipping an arm around his wife. The two of them plainly adored each other. Caidy had noticed before that when they were together, scarcely a moment passed when one of them didn't touch the other in some way. A hand on the arm, a brush of fingers.

She told herself she had no right to be envious of their happiness together.

"And you brought food!" Carson exclaimed.

"Where would you like the pies?"

"Besides in my stomach?" Carson asked. "They look fantastic. We can probably find room on the dessert table. What am I saying? There's always room for pie."

"I'll help you," Jenna said, taking one of the pies. "Carson, will you show Destry where she can change into her swimming suit?"

"I've already got it on," Des proclaimed, yanking the neck of her sweater aside to show the swimming suit strap.

"Good thinking." Carson smiled at her. "I'll just show you where you can leave your things, then."

They walked away and Jenna led her into the opposite direction, into the beautiful gourmet kitchen of the home, which currently bustled with about a dozen of her friends.

"Hey, Caidy!" Emery Cavazos greeted her with a smile, looking elegant and composed as always while she transferred something chocolate and rich-looking onto a tray.

"Hi, Em."

Nothing to worry about in here, she thought. She

loved these women and got together with them often at various social functions. She could just pretend this was one of their regular parties.

"You know, Caidy would be perfect for that little matter we were discussing earlier," Maggie Dalton exclaimed.

"What matter?" she asked warily. With the Cold Creek women, one could never be too careful.

"We've all been admiring the new vet—a gorgeous widower with those two adorable kids," Jenna said. "We were trying to figure out someone we could subtly introduce him to."

"We've already met." And locked lips. More than once. She decided to keep that tidbit of information to herself. If she didn't, the whole town would join her brothers in trying to hook her up with Ben, who had made it quite plain they would never be matched.

Caroline Dalton—married to the oldest Dalton brother, Wade—tilted her head and gave Caidy a long, considering look. "You know, Mag, I think you're absolutely right. She's perfect for him."

"I...am?"

"Yes! You both love animals and you're wonderful with children."

"We need to figure out some way to get them together." Emery, the traitor, joined into the scheming.

Had she become such an object of pity that all the women in town felt they had to step in and take drastic action to practically arrange a marriage for her? It was a depressing thought, especially because Ben had made it clear he wasn't even interested in *kissing* her.

"Thank you, but that's not necessary," she said quickly, hoping to cut off this disastrous conniving at the pass. "As I said, Dr. Caldwell and I have met. He treated a dog of mine who was injured a few weeks ago. And in case you didn't know, he's currently living on the foreman's cottage at the River Bow."

"Oh, I hadn't heard he and the children moved out of the inn," exclaimed Jenny Boyer Dalton, principal of the elementary school. "I'm so happy they're not staying there for Christmas. No offense, Laura."

"None taken," Caidy's sister-in-law said. "I agree."

"That was a brilliant idea," Caroline said. "See, you *are* perfect for him!"

She could see this whole situation quickly spiraling out of control, with everybody in town jumping on board to push her and Ben together. What a nightmare that would be. He would hate it, especially when he had clearly brushed her off two nights ago after that stunning kiss.

In desperation, she hurried to try a little damage control. "I think you all need to give Ben a break and let him settle into Pine Gulch before you start picking out china patterns for him. The poor man hasn't even had the chance to move into his own house yet."

He would be going soon, though. The house he was building would be finished after the holidays and he and the children would be moving off the River Bow. The thought of not seeing those lights gleaming in the windows of the foreman's cottage—of not having the chance to listen to Jack's knock-knock jokes or being able to tease a reluctant smile from Ava—filled her with a poignant sense of loss.

The rest of winter stretched out ahead of her, long and empty. Not just the winter. The months and years to come, each day the same as the one before.

She would miss all of them dearly. How would she live in Pine Gulch knowing he was so close but out of her reach?

Maybe the time had come for her to take a different path. She could probably find a job somewhere outside Pine Gulch. Separating from her family would be painful but she wasn't sure which would hurt more—leaving or staying.

"Only friends, huh? That's too bad." Maggie Dalton gave a rueful sigh. "Don't you think if you tried, you could stir up a little interest in more? I mean, the man is *hot.*"

Yes, she was fully aware of that—and was positive none of these women had known the magic of his kiss. The problem wasn't how attractive she found Ben Caldwell. He didn't feel the same way about her and she couldn't figure out a darn thing to do about it.

She wanted to cry, suddenly, right here in front of her dearest friends—each of whom had the great fortune to be married to a wonderful man who loved her deeply. They were all so happily married, they wanted everyone else to know the same joy. Caidy didn't know how to tell them the likelihood of that happening to her was pathetically slim.

Not that she wanted that. She was perfectly happy right now.

"You'd be surprised how often friendship can develop into more," Emery said. "Dr. Caldwell really does seem like a nice guy. We don't get all that many available men in Cold Creek besides the guys who come to snowmobile or fish. Maybe you should think about seeing if he wants to be more than friends."

Those tears burned harder behind her eyelids. Coming to this party was a phenomenally bad idea. If she'd had any idea she would face a gauntlet of matchmakers, she would have hidden in her room and locked the door.

"Don't, okay? Just…don't. Ben and I are friends. That's all. Not everyone is destined to live happily ever after like all of you are. Is it so hard to believe that maybe I like my life the way it is? Maybe Ben does too. Back off, okay?"

Her friends gaped at her and she could tell her vehemence had shocked them. She wasn't usually so firm, she realized. Now they were going to wonder why this was such a hot button for her.

Damn.

And Laura knew she and Ben had kissed. She was going to have to hope her beloved sister-in-law didn't decide to mention that little fact to the rest of the women.

She just couldn't win. Sometimes escaping with the remains of her dignity was the best option.

"I need to take one of my pies out to the dessert table. What about that tray, Emery? Is it ready to go out?"

"Um, sure." Her friend handed the delicious-looking bar cookies to her without another word. Feeling the heat of all their gazes on her back, Caidy escaped from the kitchen.

The party was crowded and noisy. For all its size, having a hundred people, many of them children, crammed into the McRavens' house didn't lend itself to quiet, relaxing conversation. Several neighbors and friends greeted her on her way to the food tables and she tried to smile and talk with them for a few moments but quickly broke away, using the excuse of the treats.

The tables were covered with all manner of culinary delights, as she had expected. Jenna loved to cook and loved coming up with new recipes for her clients and family. Caidy didn't have much appetite but she filled a small plate with a few possibilities—to have something to hold, more than anything.

"Those look good. Any idea what they are?"

At the deep voice at her elbow, she whirled and her heart stuttered. How had she missed Ben's approach? Probably a combination of the crowd and her own distraction.

"I'm not sure. Jenna is famous for her spinach pinwheels, so that's what I'm hoping for. I should tell her to put signs up so we know what we're eating."

He smiled and she wanted to drink in the sight of him, tall and gorgeous and dearly familiar.

"I hadn't realized you were coming to the McRavens' party," she said rather inanely. As always, she felt as if she were operating on half-brain capacity around him. "It's a bit of a legend around here."

"Mrs. McRaven invited us when they brought their dog Frank in to me last week. Apparently he swallowed a Lego, but the trouble, uh, passed. I thought coming to the party might be a good way to get to know some of the neighbors."

He tilted his head and studied her and she could feel herself flush. She had to hope none of her friends decided to come out of the kitchen just now to see her standing flustered and off balance next to Ben Caldwell.

"What about you?" he said. "I didn't expect to see you here. It's kind of hard to escape the holiday spirit in a crowd like this."

Had he *wondered* if she would come? She wasn't sure she wanted to know.

"Destry begged and begged this year. All her cousins and most of her friends were coming."

Before he could respond, someone jostled her from behind. She wobbled a little in her impractical boots and would have fallen if he hadn't reached out and grabbed her. For a charged moment, they stared at each other and she saw heat and hunger leap into his eyes.

The noise of the crowd seemed to fade away as if someone had switched down the volume, and she was aware of nothing but Ben. Of his arms, strong and comforting, of his firm mouth that had tasted so delicious against hers, of his eyes that studied her with desire and something else, something glittery and bright she couldn't identify.

"Oh. I'm so sorry. Are you all right, my dear?"

She recognized Marjorie Montgomery's voice and realized the mayor's wife—and the Dalton boys' mother—must have been the one who bumped into her. Still breathless—and grateful she had just set her plate on the table before she was jostled, so at least she didn't have spinach pinwheel smeared all over both of them—she managed to extricate herself from Ben's arms and turned.

"I'm fine. No problem."

Marjorie smiled innocently at her but she thought she saw a crafty light in the older woman's eyes. Oh, great. She and Ben would have no peace now that her friends had decided they were destined for each other. She wondered if she ought to warn him but decided that would just be too awkward.

"It's crazy in here," Ben said. "I saw some open chairs over by the French doors into the pool if you're looking for a place to sit down."

She didn't miss the delight in Marjorie's eyes. The woman probably thought her transparent ploy was paying off. She ought to politely decline and keep as far away as she could from Ben. The last thing she wanted to do was give anybody else ideas about linking the two of them.

But she was weak when it came to him and she couldn't resist spending whatever time she had with him, even though he had made it quite clear they couldn't have a relationship. Maybe, like her, he knew he should stay away but couldn't quite manage it.

She probably shouldn't find that so heartening.

"Sure." She picked up her plate and a glass of water and headed with him toward the chairs he indicated.

"Where are the kids?"

"Where else? In the pool." He gestured through the glass doors and she saw Jack playing in the shallow end with Laura's son, Alex. Ava was huddled with a group of girls, including Destry and Gabi.

"Taft offered to keep an eye on them for me so I could grab something to eat, since he was watching Alex and Maya anyway. I figured they were pretty safe with the fire chief on lifeguard duty."

They lapsed into silence and she nibbled at a little delicacy that tasted of pumpkin and cinnamon.

"So are you ready for Christmas?" she finally asked when the silence grew awkward. She regretted the words the instant they left her mouth. Good grief, could she sound any more mindless?

"No. Not at all," he answered with a slight note of panic in his voice. "I should be home wrapping presents right now. I don't know the first thing about how to do that. My wife usually took care of those details and then Mrs. Michaels has stepped in since Brooke died. Maybe I'll tell the kids Santa decided not to wrap the presents this year and just jumble them under the tree."

"You can't do that! The mystery and anticipation of unwrapping the gifts is part of the magic!"

He raised an eyebrow. "Says the woman who would like to forget all about the holidays."

"Just because I don't particularly enjoy Christmas doesn't mean I don't know what makes the day a perfect one, especially for children," she protested. "Destry's gifts have been wrapped and hidden away since Thanksgiving."

He was quiet for a long moment and then he shook his head. "You're remarkable, aren't you?"

His words baffled her. Was he making fun of her? "Why do you say that?"

"You hate Christmas but wouldn't think for a moment of short-shrifting your niece in any way. I just find that amazing. You really love her, don't you?"

She watched Destry through the glass, now playing ball with the other girls. "I do. She's the daughter I'll probably never have."

"Why not? You're young. What makes you think you won't have a family of your own someday?"

She wanted to answer that she was very much afraid she was falling in love with a veterinarian who had made it plain he was only interested in friendship, but of course she couldn't. "Some of us are just meant to be favorite aunts, I guess."

Before he could respond to what she suddenly realized sounded rather pathetic, she quickly changed the subject. "Do you want some help with the children's presents? I can sneak over after they're in bed tonight and help you wrap them. How long would it take? An hour, maybe. Tops."

He stared at her for a long moment, then shook his head. "I'm sure that's not necessary. I'll probably fumble my way through. Or just leave things unwrapped. It won't be the end of the world."

Another rejection. She almost sighed. She should be used to it by now. This time she had only been offering to help him but apparently even that was more than he wanted from her.

"No problem. I wouldn't want to impose."

"That's my line. I don't want you to feel obligated to come over at midnight on a pity mission to wrap presents for the inept single father."

"I never even thought of it that way!" she exclaimed. "I only wanted to... I don't know. Ease your burden a little."

He opened his mouth and then closed it again, an odd light in his eyes. "In that case, all right," he said after a long moment. "Everything is so crazy this year, with the rented house and Mrs. Michaels gone. I probably should try to keep the rest of our holiday traditions as consistent as possible. Santa Claus has always wrapped their gifts. I'm sure Jack won't care but Ava will probably consider it another failing of mine if I don't do things the way she's used to."

He paused. "I'm afraid my ledger of debt to you is growing longer and longer."

She managed a smile. "Friends don't keep track of things like that, Ben."

Because that's all they apparently would ever be, at least she could be the best damn friend he'd ever had.

"Thank you."

She couldn't sit here and make polite conversation with him, she decided. Not when she wanted so much more.

"Oh, there's Becca and Trace. I promised Becca I would talk to her about the menu for Christmas dinner. I should go do that. Will you excuse me?"

He rose. "Sure."

"I'm serious about helping you with the presents. Why don't you call me after the kids are asleep and I'll run over?"

He looked rueful. "I should refuse. This is something I should probably be able to handle myself, but the truth is I'm grateful for your help."

She smiled, doing her best to conceal any trace of yearning, and walked away from him.

She was twenty-seven years old and had just discovered she must have a streak of masochism. Why else would she continue to thrust herself into situations that would only bump up her heartache?

Chapter 13

Ben gazed at his phone, at the OK. They're asleep text message he had typed but hadn't sent.

He should delete it right now and tell her he had changed his mind. Caidy Bowman was dangerous to him, especially at ten-thirty at night.

He thought of how beautiful she had looked at the McRavens' party, sweetly lovely, like a spun sugar Christmas angel. The first moment he saw her at the party, standing by the refreshment table, he had been stunned by his desire to whirl her around and into his arms. As ridiculously medieval as it sounded, he had wanted to kiss her soundly and claim her as his for everyone at the party to see.

"I'm crazy, Tri, aren't I?"

The chihuahua cocked his head and appeared to ponder the question.

"Never mind. It was rhetorical. You don't have to answer."

Tri yipped and jumped into his lap with amazing agility for a three-legged dog. Resilient, the little dog, adjusting to whatever challenges life delivered to him. Ben could only wish for a small portion of the dog's courage.

He glanced at his phone again and without taking time to think it through, he hit the send button before he could change his mind.

Her answer came instantly, as if she had been waiting for him: Be right there.

Something in his chest gave a silly little kick and he shook his head, reminding himself of all the very valid reasons he had given her a few nights earlier. He wasn't in a good place for a relationship with her. His kids were struggling enough with this move. He couldn't suddenly throw a woman into the chaos to distract his attention from their needs.

This would be the last time, he told himself. He would accept her help with his presents and then he had to do a better job of maintaining a safe distance from her. He had talked to his contractor at the party and learned the house was on schedule to be finished in about ten days, just after the New Year. Maybe when he moved a few miles away, he could regain a little perspective and be able to spend a few moments of the day without thinking about her, longing for her.

"Yeah, I'm crazy," he said to Tri. He set the dog onto the ground and headed for Mrs. Michaels's room, where all the children's presents were hidden in her locked closet.

Before she left, she had wrapped a few of the presents. He found plenty of wrapping paper, tape and scissors in the closet. *Efficient Anne,* he thought fondly, missing her calming presence in his life. If not for the chaos of living in a hotel and then moving here to the ranch, his housekeeper probably would have finished the job weeks ago.

He carried the wrapping supplies down to the table in the kitchen. After a careful look inside the children's room to make sure they were soundly sleeping, he made a few more quiet trips up and down the stairs to transport the unwrapped gifts to the table.

Just as he finished the last load, he saw a flicker of movement outside and then Caidy approaching from the ranch house, making her way through the lightly falling snow. She had a couple of dogs with her and carried two large reusable shopping bags that piqued his curiosity. As she neared the porch steps, she gestured with one of her hands and gave an order to the dogs. Though he couldn't hear what she said, he guessed she was telling them to go back home. One of the dogs moved with eagerness ahead of the other, which seemed to trudge behind more slowly.

Caidy watched the dog in the moonlight for a moment and when she turned, he thought she looked worried about something but he didn't have time to wonder about it before she climbed the steps and knocked softly on the door.

She was bundled up from head to toe in a heavy wool coat and nubby red scarf and hat. With her cheeks rosy from the cold, she looked delicious.

"Hi," she said, her voice pitched low, probably afraid of waking the children.

"Hello," he murmured and was struck by the quiet

intimacy of the night. With the fire crackling in the living room and the snow falling softly, it would be easy to make the mistake of thinking they were alone here, tucked away against the world.

Tri greeted her with a few eager sniffs of her boots and she smiled at the dog. "Hi there. How are you, little friend?"

The dog seemed to grin at her and Ben wished for a little of that easy charm.

"What's all this?" he asked, gesturing to her shopping bags.

"Christmas dinner. My arms are going to fall off if I don't set it down. Can I put it in the kitchen?"

"Of course. What do you mean, Christmas dinner?"

"It's not much. We had an extra ham and I always keep mashed potatoes in the freezer. You just have to add a little milk when you reheat them in the microwave. And then I always make too much pie so I brought one of those too. Without Mrs. Michaels, I wasn't sure if you would have had much time to think about fixing something nice for you and the kids."

Right now he couldn't think much beyond the next meal he had to fix for the kids. Christmas dinner. She went to all that trouble?

Against his will, warmth seeped through him. Her thoughtfulness astounded him and he didn't quite know what to say.

"Thank you," he finally managed to say. "Wow. Just…thank you."

She smiled and the sweetness of it nearly took his breath away. "You're welcome. Shall I put it in the refrigerator?"

He stirred himself to reach for the bags. "That would be great."

Caidy Bowman astonished him. She had endured unimaginable horror and pain. Despite it, she was a nurturer, doing her best to make the world around her a little brighter.

For the next few moments, he pulled out package after package. It was more than just ham and potatoes. She had sent a jar of homemade strawberry jam, some frozen bread dough with instructions for thawing and baking written on them, even a small cheese ball and a box of crackers.

He was sure he would have muddled through some kind of dinner with the children, but the fact that she had thought far enough ahead to help touched something deep inside him.

I just want to help lift your burden a little, she had said earlier in the evening. He couldn't remember anybody ever spontaneously offering such a thing to him. Mrs. Michaels helped him tremendously but he paid her well for it. This was pure generosity on Caidy's part and he was stunned by it.

"Shall we get started with wrapping?"

He wasn't sure he trusted himself right now to spend five minutes with her, but because she had come all this way—and brought Christmas dinner to boot—he didn't know how to kick her out into the snow.

"I've brought everything down, including all the wrapping paper I could find."

"Perfect."

She took in the pile of presents with a slight smile dancing across that expressive mouth. "Looks like the children will have a great Christmas."

He hurried to disabuse her of the notion that he ought to win any Father of the Year awards. "Mrs. Michaels did a lot of the shopping, though I did buy a few things online. So where do we start?"

"I guess we just dive in. You know, I can handle this, if you have something else to do."

Did she want him to leave? For an instant, he was unbelievably tempted to do just that, escape into another room and leave her to it. But not only would that be rude, it would be cowardly too, especially when she had gone to all this trouble to walk down in the snow—and carrying a sumptuous meal too.

"No. Let's do this. With both of us working together, it shouldn't take long. You might have to babysit me a little."

"Surely you've wrapped a present before."

He racked his brain and vaguely remembered wrapping a gift for his grandparents that first Christmas after they had taken him in, a macaroni-covered pencil holder he had worked hard on in school. His grandfather hadn't even opened it, had made some excuse about saving it for later. Christmas night when he had taken out a bag of discarded wrapping paper, he had seen it out in the trash can, still wrapped.

"I probably did when I was a kid. I doubt my skills have improved since then."

"How can a man reach thirtysomething without learning how to wrap a present?"

"I rely on two really cool inventions. You may have heard of them. Store gift-wrapping and the very handy and ubiquitous gift bag."

She laughed, and the sound of it in the quiet kitchen entranced him. "I'll tell you what. I'll take care of all the oddly shaped gifts and you can handle the easy things. The books and the DVDs and other basic shapes. It's a piece of cake. Let me show you."

For the next few moments, he endured the sheer torture of having her stand at his side, her soft curves just a breath away as she leaned over the table beside him.

"The real trick to a beautifully wrapped present is to make sure you measure the paper correctly. Too big and you've got unsightly extra paper to deal with. Too small and the package underneath shows through."

"Makes sense," he mumbled. He was almost painfully aware of her, but beneath his desire was something deeper, a tenderness that terrified him. He meant his words to her earlier in the evening. She was an amazing person and he didn't know how much longer he could continue to ignore this inexorable bond between them.

"Okay, after you've measured your paper, leaving an extra inch or two on all sides, you bring the sides up, one over the other, and tape the seam. Great. Now fold the top and bottom edges of the end on the diagonal like this—" she demonstrated "—and then tape those down. Small pieces of tape are better. Can you see that?"

Right now, he would agree to anything she said. She smelled delicious and he wanted to pull her onto his lap and just nuzzle her neck for a few hours. "Okay. Sure."

"After that, you can use ribbon to wrap around it or just stick on a bow. Doesn't it look great? Do you think you can do it now on your own?"

He looked down blankly at the present. "Not really," he admitted.

She frowned, so close to him he could see the shimmery gold flecks in her eyes. "What part didn't you get? I thought that was a great demonstration."

He sighed. "It probably was. I only heard about half of it. I was too busy remembering how your mouth tastes like strawberries."

She stared at him for a long charged moment and then she quickly moved to the chair across the table from him.

"Please stop," she said, her voice low and her color high.

"I'd like to. Believe me."

"I'm serious. I can't handle this back-and-forth thing. It's not fair. You flirt with me one minute and then push me away the next. Please. Make up your mind, for heaven's sake. I don't know what you want from me."

"I don't either," he admitted. He was an ass. She was absolutely right. "I think that's the problem. I keep telling myself I can't handle anything but friendship right now. Then you show up and you smell delicious and you're so sweet to bring dinner for us. To top it all off, you're so damned beautiful, all I can think about is kissing you again, holding you in my arms."

She stared at him, her eyes wide. He saw awareness there and something else, something fragile.

He wanted her fiercely. Because she trembled whenever he touched her, he suspected she shared his hunger. He could kiss her—and possibly do more—now, but at what cost?

She was a vulnerable woman. He was no armchair psychologist, but he guessed she was hiding herself away here on this ranch because she saw only weakness and fear in herself. She saw the sixteen-year-old girl who had cowered from her parents' killers. She didn't see herself as the strong, powerful, desirable woman he did.

He could hurt her—and that was the last thing he wanted to do.

"Sorry. Forget I said that. We'd better get these presents wrapped so you can go home and get some sleep."

She stared at him, her eyes wide and impossibly green. Finally she nodded. "Yes. I would hate to be down here wrapping gifts if one of the children woke up and came down for a drink of water or something."

She turned her attention to the task at hand. He fumbled through wrapping a book for Ava and did an okay job but nothing as polished as Caidy's presents. After a few more awkward moments with only the sound of rustling paper and ripping tape, he decided he needed something as a buffer between them.

He rose from the table and headed for Mrs. Michaels's radio/CD player in the corner. When he turned it on, jazzy Christmas music filled the empty spaces. She didn't like holiday songs, he remembered, but she didn't seem to object so he left the station tuned there.

The pile dwindled between them, and at some point she started talking to him again, asking little questions about the gifts he and Mrs. Michaels had purchased, about the children's interests, about their early Christmases.

When he left to look for one more roll of paper in Mrs. Michaels's room, he returned to find her humming softly under her breath to "Angels We Have Heard on High," her voice soft and melodious.

He stood just on the other side of the doorway, wondering what it might take for her to sing again. She stopped abruptly when she sensed his presence and returned to taping up a box containing yet another outfit for Ava's American Girl doll.

"You found more paper. Oh, good. That should help us finish up."

He sat back down and started wrapping a DVD for Jack.

"Tell me about Christmas when you were a kid," she said after a moment.

That question came out of left field and he fumbled for an answer. "Fine. Nothing memorable."

"Everybody has some fond memory of Christmas. Making Christmas cookies, delivering gifts to neighbors. What were your traditions?"

He tried to think back and couldn't come up with much. "We usually had a nice tree. My grandmother's decorator would spend the whole day on it. It was really beautiful." He didn't add that he and Susie weren't allowed to go near it because of the thousands of dollars in glass ornaments adorning the branches.

"Your grandmother?"

Had he said that? "Yeah. My grandparents raised my sister and me from the time I was about eight until I left for college."

"Why?"

He could feel her gaze on him as he tried to come up with the words to answer her. He wanted to ignore it but couldn't figure out a way to do that politely. And suddenly, for a reason he couldn't have explained, he wanted to tell her, just like in his office earlier in the week when he had told her about Brooke.

"My childhood wasn't very happy, I guess, but I feel stupid complaining about it. I don't know who my father is. My mother was a drug addict who dumped my half sister and me on her parents and disappeared without a word. She died of an overdose about three months later."

Her eyes darkened with sympathy. "Oh, no. I'm so sorry. What a blessing that you had your grandparents to help you through it."

He gave a rough laugh. "My grandparents were extremely wealthy and important people in Chicago social circles but they didn't want to be saddled with the obligation of raising the children of an out-of-control daughter they had cut off years earlier. They probably would have chucked us into the foster care system if they weren't afraid of how it would look to their acquaintances. Sometimes I wish they had done just that. They didn't have the patience for two small children."

"Then it's even more wonderful that you work so hard to give your children such a great Christmas," she said promptly. "You've become the father you never had."

Her faith in him was humbling. At her words, he felt this shifting and settling inside his heart.

This wasn't simply attraction. He was in love with her. The realization settled over him like autumn leaves falling to earth, like that snow drifting against the windows.

How had *that* happened?

Perhaps during that sleigh ride, when he had seen her holding her sweet niece Maya on her lap, or when she had come to the door the other night, flour on her cheek from making three pizzas for a houseful of children. Or maybe that first night at the clinic, when she had knelt beside her injured dog and hummed away the animal's anxiety.

Oblivious to his sudden staggering epiphany, she tied an elaborate bow on the gift she was wrapping and snipped the ends. "There. That should be the last one."

Through his dazed shock, he managed to turn his attention to the pile of presents. Somehow he, Mrs. Michaels and Caidy had managed to pull off another Christmas.

She was right. He was a good father—not because he could provide them a pile of gifts but because he loved them, because he was doing his best to provide a safe, friendly place for them to grow, because he treated them with patience and respect instead of cold tolerance.

"Thank you." The words seemed inadequate for all she had done for him this holiday season.

She smiled and rose from the kitchen table. She stretched her arms over her head to work all the kinks out from being huddled over a table for nearly an hour, and it took all his strength not to leap across the table and devour her.

"Just imagining their faces on Christmas morning is enough thanks for me. You've got a couple of really adorable kids there, Ben."

"I do." His voice sounded strangled and she gave him an odd look but shrugged into her coat. He knew he should help her, but right now he didn't trust himself to be that close to her.

"Good night."

As she started for the door, he came to his senses. "I forgot you walked down here. Let me grab my coat and I'll walk you back to your house."

"That's not necessary."

It was to him. In answer, he pulled his coat down from the hook and drew it on while she watched him with a disgruntled expression.

"I've been walking this lane my whole life. I'm fine. You shouldn't leave the children."

"I'll be gone five minutes, with the house in view the whole time."

She sighed. "You're a stubborn man, Dr. Caldwell."

He could be. He supposed it was stubbornness that had kept him from admitting the truth to himself—that he was falling for her. As they walked out into the light snow, Tri hopping along ahead of them, he was struck again by the peace that seemed to enfold him when he was with her.

She smiled at the little dog's valiant efforts to stay in front as leader of the pack, then lifted her face to let snowflakes kiss her cheeks. Tenderness, sweet and healing, seemed to wash through him. He wanted to protect her, to make her smile—to, as she had said earlier, lift her burdens if she would let him.

His marriage hadn't quite been that way. He had loved Brooke but as he walked beside Caidy, he couldn't help thinking that in many ways it had been an immature sort of love. They had met when he had been in veterinary school and she had been doing undergraduate work in public relations.

For some reason he still didn't quite comprehend, she had immediately decided she wanted him, in that determined way she had, and he hadn't done much to change the course she set out for both of them.

He had come to love her, of course, though his love had been intertwined with gratitude that she would take a lonely, solitary man and give him a family and a place to belong.

He thought he would never fall in love again. When Brooke died, he thought his world was over. It had taken all these months and years for him to feel as though he could even think about moving forward with his life.

Here he was, though, crazy in love with Caidy Bowman and it scared the hell out of him. Could he risk his heart, his soul, all over again?

And why was he even thinking about this? Yes, Caidy responded to his kisses, but she had spent her adult life pushing away any relationship beyond her family. She might not even be interested in anything more with him. Why would she be? He didn't have that much to offer in the relationship department. He was surly and impatient, with a couple of energetic kids to boot.

"I wonder if I can ask you a favor," she said after they were nearly to the barn. "If you have time this week, could you take a look at my Sadie? I'm worried about her. She's not been acting like herself."

He pictured her old border collie, thirteen years old and moving with slow, measured movements. "Sure. I can come over tomorrow morning."

"Oh, I don't think it's urgent. After Christmas would probably be fine."

"All right. First thing Wednesday. Or if the kids and I feel like taking a walk after they open presents, maybe I'll stop up at the house to take a look."

"Thank you. You should probably go back. You left a fire in the fireplace, don't forget."

"Yes." He wanted to kiss her, here in the wintry cold. He wanted to tuck her against him and hold her close and keep her safe from any more sorrow.

He didn't have that right, he reminded himself. Not now. Maybe after the holidays, after he and the children moved into the new house and Mrs. Michaels came back, he could ask her to dinner, see where things might progress.

"Thank you again for your help with the gifts."

"You're welcome. If I don't see you again, Merry Christmas."

"Same to you."

She gave that half smile again. Against his better judgment, he stepped forward and brushed a soft kiss on her rosy cheek, then turned around, scooped up his little dog and walked swiftly away through the snow— while he still could.

Chapter 14

"Hang on. Just a few more moments. There's my sweet girl. Hang on."

Icy fear pulsed through Caidy as she drove her truck through the wintry Christmas Eve in a grim repeat of a scene she had already played a few weeks earlier with Luke. She was much more terrified this time than she had been with the younger dog, and the quarter mile to the foreman's cottage seemed to stretch on forever.

Sadie couldn't die. She just couldn't. But from the instant she had walked into the barn just moments earlier and found her beloved dog lying motionless in the straw of one of the stalls, all her vague concerns about the dog's health over the past few days had coalesced into this harsh, grinding terror.

Sadie, her dearest friend, was fading. She knew it in her heart and almost couldn't breathe around the pain.

She couldn't seem to think straight either. Only one thought managed to pierce her panic.

Ben would know what to do.

She had picked up the dog, shoved her into the bed of the nearest vehicle, Ridge's pickup, pulled the spare key out of the tackroom and drove like hell to Ben's place.

Now that she approached the house nestled in the pines, reality returned. It was nearly midnight on Christmas Eve. The children would be sound asleep. She couldn't rush in banging on the door to wake them up, tonight of all nights, when they would never be able to go back to sleep.

Adrenaline still shooting through her, she pulled up to the front door, trying to figure out what to do. The Christmas tree lights still blazed through the window. Maybe Ben was still awake.

Sadie hadn't made a sound this entire short trip, though Caidy could see her ribs still moving with her shallow breathing.

Caidy opened her door and was just trying to figure out which bedroom was his, wondering if she could throw a snowball at it or something in an effort to wake only him, when the porch light flicked on and the front door opened. An instant later, he walked out in stocking feet, squinting into the night.

"Caidy!" he exclaimed when he recognized her. "What is it? What's wrong?"

Relief poured through her, blessed relief. Ben would know what to do.

"It's Sadie," she said on a sob, hurrying to the passenger side of the pickup. "She's… Oh, please, Ben. Help me."

He didn't even stop to throw on shoes—he just raced

down the frozen sidewalk toward her. "Tell me what happened."

"I don't know. I just… After Destry and Ridge went to bed, I was just sitting by the Christmas tree by myself and I… I decided to go out to the barn. It's a…sacred sort of place on Christmas Eve, among the animals. Peaceful. I needed that tonight. But when I got there, I found Sadie lying in the straw. She wouldn't wake up."

She choked back her sob, knowing she needed to retain control if she had any hope of helping her beloved dog.

"Let's get her inside out of the cold and into the light so I can have a look at her."

He scooped the old dog into his arms and carried her back across that snowy walk. Caidy followed. Her heart felt as fragile as her mother's antique Christmas angel. How would she bear it if Sadie died tonight, of all nights?

No. She wasn't going to think about that. Only positive thoughts. Ben would take care of things, she was sure of it.

She thought of that day when she had taken Luke to the clinic, battered and broken. She had thought Ben so cold and uncaring. As she watched him gently lay Sadie on a blanket she had quickly grabbed from the sofa to spread in front of the still-glowing fireplace, she wondered if she had ever so poorly judged a person.

He was kind and compassionate. Wonderful. How could she ever have imagined that first day that he would become so dear to her?

"What's going on, girl?"

At least Sadie opened her eyes at his voice, but she

didn't move as the veterinarian's hands moved over her, seeking answers.

"You said she hasn't been acting like herself. What have you seen?" he asked her.

She tried to think back over the past few days. The truth was, she had been so busy coping with the stress of Christmas, she hadn't paid as much attention to her dog as usual.

"She's been lethargic for three or four days. And it seems like on the nights when she wanted to sleep inside, she was always having to go out to pee. She hasn't eaten much, but she has been more thirsty than usual."

He frowned. "Exactly what I suspected."

"What?"

He looked at her with such gentleness, she wanted to weep. "I'll have to do labwork to be sure but I suspect she's having chronic kidney failure. It's not unusual in older dogs."

She drew in a heavy breath. "Can you...can you fix it?"

"The good news is, I can probably help her feel better tonight. She needs fluids and I always keep a few liters in my emergency kit. I can give her an IV right here."

"The bad news?"

"It's called chronic kidney failure for a reason," he said, his eyes compassionate. "There's no miracle cure, I'm afraid. We can perhaps make her more comfortable for a few months, but that's the best we can do. I'm so sorry, Caidy."

She nodded, those tears threatening again. "She's thirteen. I've known it was only a matter of time. But... even a few more months with her would be the greatest gift you could ever give me."

"I don't know for sure it's kidney failure. It could be something entirely different, but from the symptoms you describe and the exam, I'm ninety-nine percent certain. If you want me to, I can wait to treat her until I run bloodwork."

"No. I trust you. Completely." She paused. "I knew you would be able to help her. When I found her in the barn, all I could think about was bringing her to you."

He appeared startled at that, then gave her an unreadable look. "I'll go grab the supplies for an IV, then."

After he left the room, she knelt down beside the sweet-natured border collie, who had provided her with uncomplicated love and incalculable solace during the darkest moments of her life, when she had been a lost and grieving sixteen-year-old girl.

"Ben will help you," she told the dog, stroking her head softly. "You'll feel better soon. We can't have you missing your Christmas stocking. Here's a secret. Don't tell any of the others but I got you a new can of tennis balls. Your favorite."

Sadie's tail flapped halfheartedly on the carpet. It was a small sign of enthusiasm, yes, but more than Caidy had seen from the dog since she walked into the barn.

What would have happened if she hadn't found Sadie in time? The dog would never have made it. She was certain of that. When she and Destry and Ridge went out for chores on Christmas morning, they would have discovered her cold, lifeless body.

Just the thought of it made her stomach clutch. She *had* found her, though. Something had prompted her to brave the weather so she could find the dog in time and bring her here, to Ben, who knew just what to do.

Why *had* she gone out to the barn? Yes, she had found peace and solitude in the barn a few times before on Christmas Eve over the years, but it wasn't as if she made a habit of it.

She had been standing at the window gazing out at the cottage lights flickering in the trees, ready to collapse in her bed after a long day with her family, when some impulse she still didn't understand had compelled her to slip into her coat and head outside.

Coincidence? Maybe. Somehow she didn't think so. More like inspiration. Perhaps her own little miracle.

The thought raised chills on her arms as she gazed down at her beloved dog. What else could she call it? She had gone to the barn just in time to save a life. Even more miraculous, a wonderful veterinarian who knew just what to do lived just a quarter mile away—and he had the ready supplies necessary to help her dog.

Yes. A miracle.

A sweet sense of peace and love trickled over her, healing and cleansing, washing away the fear and sadness that had become so much a part of Christmas for her.

The clock on the mantel chimed softly. Midnight. It was Christmas. What better time for miracles, for second chances, for hope and light and life?

She leaned down to Sadie and began to hum one of her favorite Christmas songs, "It Came Upon a Midnight Clear." After a few bars, the words seemed to crowd through her heart, bursting to break free.

And for the first time in eleven years, she began to sing.

With the IV bag in his hand, Ben stood outside the room, afraid to move, to breathe, as he listened to the soft strains filling the air. He needed to help her dog quickly but surely he could wait a few more seconds.

Caidy was singing to her dog and her voice was the most beautiful sound he had ever heard, clear and pure and sweet.

"The world in solemn stillness lay, to hear the angels sings."

As she finished the song, he forced himself to move into the room and knelt beside her and the dog. She glanced over, color soaking her cheeks.

"You don't have to stop," he said as he pulled on surgical gloves and went to work finding a spot for the IV. "In fact, I hope you don't. It appeared to comfort her."

She was silent for a moment and then she began to sing "Away in a Manger" in her sweet, lovely soprano. The song seemed to shimmer through the air.

"Your brother is right," he said when she sang the last note of the third verse. "You do have a beautiful voice. I feel blessed I had the chance to hear it."

She smiled a little tremulously. "I can't tell you how strange it feels to sing. Strange and wonderful. All this time, the music has been there, just waiting for me to let it out."

"I didn't know them but I can only imagine your parents would be happy you found your voice again." He knew he was taking a chance reminding her of the sadness that had become so much a part of her holidays.

To his relief, she nodded. "You're right. I know you're right."

Moving forward took tremendous courage. He was consumed with love for her and wanted to tell her so but the moment didn't seem right, when her beloved dog was struggling for life.

"Is there anything I can do right now for Sadie?"

He turned his full attention back to her dog. "I'm giving her a bolus now—a great deal of fluid in a short amount of time—and then we'll slowly drip the other bag over the next hour or so. I've also given her some medication in the IV that will help perk her up. We should see results fairly quickly. I'm afraid I'll have to keep her here for the night. Do you mind?"

"Mind?" She gave a rough laugh. "I don't know what I would have done without you, Ben."

"I guess it was my turn to ease your burden a little for a change."

Though she smiled, the Christmas lights from the tree she had given them reflected in green eyes that swam with tears. One dripped free and slid down her cheek and Ben reached his thumb out and brushed it away from her warm, silky skin. "Please don't cry."

"They're happy tears," she promised him. "Well, maybe a little bittersweet. I know she won't be here forever. But she's here now because of you. That's what matters—she's here. I don't think I could be strong enough to endure losing her on Christmas Eve."

"It's not Christmas Eve anymore. It's past midnight. Merry Christmas."

Her smile took his breath away and she leaned slightly into his hand. "Merry Christmas, Ben."

He caressed her cheek with his thumb, tenderness and love pulsing through him. Unable to resist, he framed her face with his hands and kissed her gently. She sighed softly and her arms slid around him.

The moment was so perfect there in his borrowed living room with the Christmas tree as a backdrop and he didn't want to do anything to break the spell, but he knew she couldn't be comfortable for long on her knees like that. He eased them both back against the armchair and sat there on the floor, pulling her almost onto his lap.

They kissed for a long moment with aching softness and it was more magical than any Christmas morning he had dreamed about when he was a lonely boy. Love poured through him as sweetly as the notes of her song.

He loved this strong, courageous woman and needed her in his life. Jack and Ava did too. All his carefully constructed reasons for taking his time, moving slowly, seemed to fade into insignificance.

Yes, this might present another huge change for all of them, but he knew his children were resilient. They both liked Caidy already. Even Ava had said as much after the pizza night. It wouldn't take long for them to love her.

Finally she slid away, her eyes glimmering. She opened her mouth to speak and then must have decided she didn't want to disturb the peace of the moment. She turned slightly in his arms to check on Sadie. He held her as they both listened to the steady pump of the IV and watched the colored lights of the tree reflected in the window and plump snowflakes begin to fall.

After a few moments, Tri hopped in, probably emerging from his favorite sleeping spot at the foot of Ben's bed to wonder where he was. The little dog wandered over to Sadie, who was lying in front of the fire. Ben was about to call him off but Sadie's tail began to wag and she stirred herself to sniff at the other dog. Tri licked at her muzzle and then settled in next to her.

"Look at her." Caidy's laugh was filled with wonder. "The medication metastasizes in her system fairly quickly. I imagine by the time the kids wake up, she'll have as much energy as they do."

"It's amazing. *You're* amazing."

When she looked at him that way, he felt like the most brilliant veterinarian in the country. She kissed him and though he knew some part of it was motivated by gratitude, he sensed something else in the way her mouth moved across his, the way her arms tightened around his neck.

Finally he knew he couldn't remain quiet any longer. "Do you think it's any kind of conflict of interest for a veterinarian to be in love with his patient's human?"

Caidy stared at him, certain the stress of the past half hour—coupled with her abject relief—must be playing tricks with her hearing. Did he just say…?

Her heart pounded as if that belligerent bull that had started this whole thing had just caught her in his sights and she couldn't seem to catch hold of any coherent thought. "Is that a hypothetical question?" she finally said, her voice low and thready.

Ben—wonderful, strong, brilliant Ben—tightened his arms around her, a soft, tender light in his eyes that made her catch her breath.

"I think you know the answer to that. I've been fighting this like crazy for a hundred different, stupid reasons. But tonight when I listened to you sing, I realized none of them matter. I love you, Caidy. I wasn't looking for it. Especially not now, when my life has so much chaos in it. I told myself I didn't want to take that kind of risk again."

He smiled at her and she felt as bright and sparkly as that angel on the top of the tree. "But here's the thing. Somehow, you calm the chaos. I don't know how you did it, but you burst into my life with your fierce courage and your dogs and your smile and turned everything I thought I wanted spinning into an entirely different direction."

"Ben," she said softly, unbelievably touched that the man she thought so taciturn and hard that first day could be saying these words to her.

"I think I started to fall in love with you that day you came to the clinic, so determined to get the very best care for your dog. I knew for sure when you came here to help me wrap the children's presents the other night, even though you don't like Christmas."

"I don't know. I think my perspective on that is changing a little."

He laughed and kissed her again. When she slid away a few moments later, Sadie was sitting up, gazing around the room alertly while Tri teased at her ear. Caidy didn't know how her heart could contain more joy.

"To answer your question," she said, "I don't believe there is a conflict of interest at all as long as said veterinarian doesn't mind that the human in question is also very much in love with him."

"Is she?"

"Oh, yes. I love you. More than I can say. And Ava and Jack too. I thought I was content with my life here on the ranch helping Ridge, but over the past few weeks, I've come to realize something good and right has been missing. You. All this time, I think I've just been waiting for you."

He gazed at her for a long moment, his eyes fiery and bright, then with aching softness he picked up her hand and kissed her palm. "I'm here now. And I'm not going anywhere."

She couldn't contain the joy bubbling through her. Sadie would be all right, at least for now. It was Christmas morning, the time for miracles and hope, and she had eleven years of Christmases to make up for. What better place to do it than in the arms of the man she loved fiercely?

She wrapped her arms around him and Ben laughed softly, almost as if he couldn't help himself, then kissed her again while the Christmas tree lights gleamed and the two dogs snuggled by the fire and her heart sang.

Epilogue

"I just love Christmas weddings," Laura exclaimed as she adjusted one of the pins keeping Caidy's snowy-white veil in place.

"It's not Christmas," Maya said, with irrefutable logic. In the mirror, Caidy had a clear view of the little girl sitting on a bench in the room reserved for brides at the small church in Pine Gulch, carefully holding Trace and Becca's chubby six-month-old son, who was gumming his fingers.

"Santa doesn't come for five more days," Maya pointed out.

"True," her mother answered with a grin. "I should have said I love Christmas*time* weddings. Is that better?"

"Yes." Maya smiled, looking sweet and adorable in her blue-and-silver flower-girl dress.

"The church looks beautiful," Becca said, hurrying in to scoop little Will out of Maya's lap with unerring instincts, just as both of the children started to get bored with the arrangement. "It looks like a snowy wonderland with all those silvery snowflakes and the blue ribbons. Such a better choice than the traditional red and green. As lovely as it is out there, it doesn't hold a candle to our blushing bride here. You look fantastic. Are you happy, Caidy?"

She smiled at her brothers' wives. She did feel a small pang that her mother wasn't there on her wedding day, but this was a time for joy, not sadness. She might not have her mother with her, and that would always hurt, but she did have these wonderful women who had become so dear to her.

"*Happy* doesn't come close to covering it. I don't think I have room inside me to hold all the joy."

"I don't either," Ava said, looking lovely in the bridesmaid dress she was so very enthralled to be wearing.

"Same here," Destry, in a matching dress, added.

Caidy smiled and squeezed both girls' hands, the daughter of her heart and the daughter she would be gaining officially in a matter of moments.

Sometimes she couldn't take in the changes in her life from last Christmas. Over the years, she had told herself she was happy living at the ranch, helping her brother with Destry, raising her dogs and her horses. Now she could see how much power she had given one horrible, violent event over her life. She had been hiding out there, slowly suffocating in her fears, afraid to take any chances.

Ben had changed that. This past year had been filled

with more happiness than she could ever have imagined. A little sadness too, she had to admit. After her miraculous Christmas recovery, Sadie had made it to springtime. Her last months she had shown more energy than she had in years, but one April morning Caidy had found her under the flowering branches of the crabapple tree beside the house. Ben had helped her bury her friend on a hillside overlooking the ranch and the river and had held her while she wept.

The two of them had taken their time this past year, moving slowly to give the children time to adjust to the idea of her being a regular part of their lives.

Jack, with his sunny nature, had no problem accepting her. As she might have expected, Ava had been a little more resistant. At first, the girl had fought the idea of anyone wanting to replace her mother in their lives. But now, a year after she and Ben started dating, Caidy believed she and Ava had developed a strong, solid relationship.

A December wedding had been his idea, to give her something joyful to remember—instead of pain and fear—during this time of hope and promise.

Waiting all this time to start their lives together had seemed endless. The day was finally here and she couldn't imagine anything more perfect.

"I think you're ready now," Laura said. "Oh, Caidy. I'm so happy for you."

Taft's wife hugged her, though at four months pregnant, she was beginning to bump out a little.

"Same here," Becca said, kissing her cheek and squeezing her hands. "You deserve a wonderful guy like Ben. I'm really glad he turned out not to be a rude, arrogant, opinionated jerk."

Caidy cringed, remembering her stupid words about him so long ago. "None of you will let me forget that, will you?"

"Probably not." Laura smiled.

A knock sounded on the door. When Ava opened it, Ridge poked his head in, looking big and tough and gorgeous in his black Western-cut tuxedo. "Are we ready in here? I know a certain veterinarian who's a little impatient out there."

She drew a breath and adjusted her dress. "I think so."

"Come on, girls. Time to get in your places," Becca said.

Laura gave Caidy's veil one more adjustment, then stood back. "Okay. Perfect."

With a deep breath, Caidy slipped her hand in the crook of her brother's arm.

Ridge reached his other hand over and squeezed her fingers. "You're stunning," he said. "Mom and Dad would have been so proud of the beautiful woman you've become. Inside and out."

"Don't make me cry," she said, her throat thick with emotion.

"It's true. They would have liked Ben too. He's a good man. The highest praise I can give him is that I think he's almost good enough for you. I'm so glad you're happy."

She gave her brother a tremulous smile. "I am. It took me a while to get here but I really am."

"Let's do this, then."

The small but earnest church choir she now joined on Sundays broke into singing Pachelbel's "Canon in D Major" and she drew a deep breath, nerves skittering through her. As she and Ridge started down the aisle behind the bridesmaids, she looked down and saw the gruff, sometimes taciturn veterinarian she loved beyond measure smiling broadly. The best man—Jack—was holding his hand.

Her heart aching with love for him and for his children, Caidy walked down the aisle beside her brother to the beautiful strains of the music toward a future filled with joy and laughter and song.

* * * * *

We hope you enjoyed reading

THE HOLIDAY GIFT AND A COLD CREEK NOEL

by *New York Times* bestselling author

RAEANNE THAYNE

Discover more heartfelt tales of family, friendship and love from the **Harlequin Special Edition** series. Romance is for life, and these stories show that every chapter in a relationship has its challenges and delights and that love can be renewed with each turn of the page!

⊞ HARLEQUIN®

SPECIAL EDITION

Life, Love and Family

When you're with family, you're home!

Look for six *new* romances every month from **Harlequin Special Edition**!

Available wherever books are sold.

www.Harlequin.com

"The dog wasn't the silver lining." He tapped one finger on the top of the box. "You and pie are the silver lining. I hope you have time to have a piece with me." He leaned in. "You know it's bad luck to eat pie alone."

She made a sound that was half laugh and half sigh. "That might explain some of the luck I've had in life. I hate to admit the amount of pie I've eaten on my own."

His heart twisted as a pain she couldn't quite hide flared in those caramel eyes. His well-honed protective streak kicked in, but it was also more than that. He wanted to take up the sword and go to battle against whatever dragons had hurt this lovely, vibrant woman.

It was an idiotic notion, both because Francesca had never given him any indication that she needed assistance slaying dragons and because he didn't have the genetic makeup of a hero. Not with Gerald Robinson as his father.

But he couldn't quite make himself walk away from the chance to give her what he could that might once again put a smile on her beautiful face.

"Then it's time for a dose of good luck." He stepped back and pulled out a chair at the small, scuffed conference table in the center of the office. "I can't think of a better way to begin than with a slice of Pick-Me-Up Pecan Pie. Join me?"

Her gaze darted to the door before settling on him. "Yes, thank you," she murmured and dropped into the seat.

Her scent drifted up to him—vanilla and spice, perfect for the type of woman who would bake a pie from scratch. He'd never considered baking to be a particularly sexy activity, but the thought of Francesca wearing an apron in the kitchen as she mixed ingredients for his pie made sparks dance across his skin.

The mental image changed to Francesca wearing nothing but an apron and—

"I have plates," he shouted and she jerked back in the chair.

"That's helpful," she answered quietly, giving him a curious look. "Do you have forks, too?"

"Yes, forks." He turned toward the small bank of cabinets installed in one corner of the trailer. "And napkins," he called over his shoulder. Damn, he sounded like a complete prat.

Don't miss
A FORTUNE IN WAITING by Michelle Major,
available January 2017 wherever
Harlequin® Special Edition books and ebooks are sold.

HARLEQUIN®

SPECIAL EDITION

Life, Love and Family

Save **$1.00**

on the purchase of ANY
Harlequin® Special Edition book.

Available wherever books are sold, including
most bookstores, supermarkets, drugstores
and discount stores.

Save $1.00

on the purchase of any Harlequin® Special Edition book.

Coupon valid until February 28, 2017.
Redeemable at participating outlets in the U.S. and Canada only.
Not redeemable at Barnes and Noble stores. Limit one coupon per customer.

52614499

5 65373 00076 2   (8100)0 12239

® and ™ are trademarks owned and used by the trademark owner and/or its licensee.

© 2016 Harlequin Enterprises Limited

Celebrate the magic of the season with
New York Times bestselling author

RaeAnne Thayne

There's no place like Haven Point for the holidays, where the snow conspires to bring two wary hearts together for a Christmas to remember!

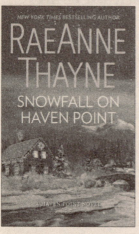

It's been two rough years since Andrea Montgomery lost her husband, and all she wants is for her children to enjoy their first Christmas in Haven Point. But then Andie's friend asks a favor—to keep an eye on her brother, Sheriff Marshall Bailey, who's recovering from a hit-and-run. Andie will do anything for Wyn, even park her own misgivings to check on Wyn's grouchy, wounded bear of a brother.

Marshall hates feeling defenseless and resents the protective impulses that Andie brings out in him. But when a blizzard forces them together for the holidays, something in Marshall begins to thaw. Andie's gentle nature is a salve, and her kids' excitement for the holidays makes him forget why he never wanted a family. If only he and Andie can admit what they really want—each other—their Christmas wishes might come true after all.

Pick up your copy today!

www.RaeAnneThayne.com

www.HQNBooks.com

PHRAT989